E L James

FIFTY SHADES *of* GREY

E L James is a former TV executive, wife, and mother of two based in West London. Since early childhood, she dreamed of writing stories that readers would fall in love with but put those dreams on hold to focus on her family and her career. She finally plucked up the courage to put pen to paper with her first novel, *Fifty Shades of Grey.* She is also the author of *Fifty Shades Darker* and *Fifty Shades Freed.*

BOOKS BY E L JAMES

Fifty Shades of Grey

Fifty Shades Darker

Fifty Shades Freed

FIFTY SHADES *of* GREY

FIFTY SHADES *of* GREY

E L James

Vintage Books
A Division of Random House LLC | New York

FIRST VINTAGE BOOKS EDITION, APRIL 2012

Fifty Shades of Grey is a work of fiction. Names, characters, places, and incidents either are the product of the author's imagination or are used fictitiously. Any resemblance to actual persons, living or dead, events, or locales is entirely coincidental.

The author published an earlier serialized version of this story online with different characters as "Master of the Universe" under the pseudonym Snowqueen's Icedragon.

The Cataloging-in-Publication Data is on file at Library of Congress.

ISBN: 9780345803481
eBook ISBN: 9781612130293
Movie Tie-in ISBN: 9780804172073

Book design by Claudia Martinez

www.vintagebooks.com

Printed in the United States of America
10 9 8 7 6 5 4 3 2 1

For Niall,

the master of my universe

ACKNOWLEDGMENTS

I am indebted to the following people for their help and support:

To my husband, Niall, thank you for tolerating my obsession, being a domestic god, and doing the first edit.

To my boss, Lisa, thank you for putting up with me over the last year or so while I indulged in this madness.

To CCL, I'll never tell, but thank you.

To the original bunker babes, thank you for your friendship and constant support.

To SR, thank you for all the helpful advice from the start and for going first.

To Sue Malone, thanks for sorting me out.

Thank you to Anne Messitte and all at Random House for believing.

FIFTY SHADES *of* GREY

CHAPTER ONE

I scowl with frustration at myself in the mirror. Damn my hair—it just won't behave, and damn Katherine Kavanagh for being ill and subjecting me to this ordeal. I should be studying for my final exams, which are next week, yet here I am trying to brush my hair into submission. *I must not sleep with it wet. I must not sleep with it wet.* Reciting this mantra several times, I attempt, once more, to bring it under control with the brush. I roll my eyes in exasperation and gaze at the pale, brown-haired girl with blue eyes too big for her face staring back at me, and give up. My only option is to restrain my wayward hair in a ponytail and hope that I look semi-presentable.

Kate is my roommate, and she has chosen today of all days to succumb to the flu. Therefore, she cannot attend the interview she'd arranged to do, with some mega-industrialist tycoon I've never heard of, for the student newspaper. So I have been volunteered. I have final exams to cram for and one essay to finish, and I'm supposed to be working this afternoon, but no—today I have to drive 165 miles to downtown Seattle in order to meet the enigmatic CEO of Grey Enterprises Holdings, Inc. As an exceptional entrepreneur and major benefactor of our university, his time is extraordinarily precious—much more precious than mine—but he has granted Kate an interview. A real coup, she tells me. Damn her extracurricular activities.

Kate is huddled on the couch in the living room.

"Ana, I'm sorry. It took me nine months to get this interview. It will take another six to reschedule, and we'll both have graduated by then. As the editor, I can't blow this off. Please," Kate begs me in her rasping, sore throat voice. How does she do it? Even ill she looks gamine and gorgeous, strawberry blond hair in place and green eyes bright, although now red rimmed and runny. I ignore my pang of unwelcome sympathy.

"Of course I'll go, Kate. You should get back to bed. Would you like some NyQuil or Tylenol?"

"NyQuil, please. Here are the questions and my digital recorder. Just press record here. Make notes, I'll transcribe it all."

"I know nothing about him," I murmur, trying and failing to suppress my rising panic.

"The questions will see you through. Go. It's a long drive. I don't want you to be late."

"Okay, I'm going. Get back to bed. I made you some soup to heat up later." I stare at her fondly. *Only for you, Kate, would I do this.*

"I will. Good luck. And thanks, Ana—as usual, you're my lifesaver."

Gathering my backpack, I smile wryly at her, then head out the door to the car. I cannot believe I have let Kate talk me into this. But then Kate can talk anyone into anything. She'll make an exceptional journalist. She's articulate, strong, persuasive, argumentative, beautiful—and she's my dearest, dearest friend.

THE ROADS ARE CLEAR as I set off from Vancouver, Washington, toward Interstate 5. It's early, and I don't have to be in Seattle until two this afternoon. Fortunately, Kate has lent me her sporty Mercedes CLK. I'm not sure Wanda, my old VW Beetle, would make the journey in time. Oh, the Merc is a fun drive, and the miles slip away as I hit the pedal to the metal.

My destination is the headquarters of Mr. Grey's global enterprise. It's a huge twenty-story office building, all curved glass and steel, an architect's utilitarian fantasy, with GREY HOUSE written discreetly in steel over the glass front doors. It's a quarter to two when I arrive, greatly relieved that I'm not late as I walk into the enormous—and frankly intimidating—glass, steel, and white sandstone lobby.

Behind the solid sandstone desk, a very attractive, groomed, blonde young woman smiles pleasantly at me. She's wearing the sharpest charcoal suit jacket and white shirt I have ever seen. She looks immaculate.

"I'm here to see Mr. Grey. Anastasia Steele for Katherine Kavanagh."

"Excuse me one moment, Miss Steele." She arches her eyebrow as I stand self-consciously before her. I'm beginning to wish I'd borrowed one of Kate's formal blazers rather than worn my navy-blue jacket. I have made an effort and worn my one and only skirt, my sensible brown knee-length boots, and a blue sweater. For me, this is smart. I tuck one of the escaped tendrils of my hair behind my ear as I pretend she doesn't intimidate me.

"Miss Kavanagh is expected. Please sign in here, Miss Steele. You'll want the last elevator on the right, press for the twentieth floor." She smiles kindly at me, amused no doubt, as I sign in.

She hands me a security pass that has "visitor" very firmly stamped on the front. I can't help my smirk. Surely it's obvious that I'm just visiting. I don't fit in here at all. *Nothing changes.* I inwardly sigh. Thanking her, I walk over to the bank of elevators and past the two security men who are both far more smartly dressed than I am in their well-cut black suits.

The elevator whisks me at terminal velocity to the twentieth floor. The doors slide open, and I'm in another large lobby—again all glass, steel, and white sandstone. I'm confronted by another desk of sandstone and another young blonde woman, this time dressed impeccably in black and white, who rises to greet me.

"Miss Steele, could you wait here, please?" She points to a seated area of white leather chairs.

Behind the leather chairs is a spacious glass-walled meeting room with an equally spacious dark wood table and at least twenty matching chairs around it. Beyond that, there is a floor-to-ceiling window with a view of the Seattle skyline that looks out through the city toward the Sound. It's a stunning vista, and I'm momentarily paralyzed by the view. *Wow.*

I sit down, fish the questions from my backpack, and go through them, inwardly cursing Kate for not providing me with a brief biography. I know nothing about this man I'm about to interview. He could be ninety or he could be thirty. The uncertainty is galling, and my nerves resurface, making me fidget. I've never been comfortable with one-on-one interviews, preferring the anonymity of a group discussion where I can sit inconspicuously at the back of the room. To be honest, I prefer my own company, reading a classic British novel, curled up in a chair in the campus library. Not sitting twitching nervously in a colossal glass-and-stone edifice.

I roll my eyes at myself. *Get a grip, Steele.* Judging from the building, which is too clinical and modern, I guess Grey is in his forties: fit, tanned, and fair-haired to match the rest of the personnel.

Another elegant, flawlessly dressed blonde comes out of a large door to the right. What is it with all the immaculate blondes? It's like Stepford here. Taking a deep breath, I stand up.

"Miss Steele?" the latest blonde asks.

"Yes," I croak, and clear my throat. "Yes." There, that sounded more confident.

"Mr. Grey will see you in a moment. May I take your jacket?"

"Oh, please." I struggle out of the jacket.

"Have you been offered any refreshment?"

"Um—no." Oh dear, is Blonde Number One in trouble?

Blonde Number Two frowns and eyes the young woman at the desk.

"Would you like tea, coffee, water?" she asks, turning her attention back to me.

"A glass of water. Thank you," I murmur.

"Olivia, please fetch Miss Steele a glass of water." Her voice is stern. Olivia scoots up and scurries to a door on the other side of the foyer.

"My apologies, Miss Steele, Olivia is our new intern. Please be seated. Mr. Grey will be another five minutes."

Olivia returns with a glass of iced water.

"Here you go, Miss Steele."

"Thank you."

Blonde Number Two marches over to the large desk, her heels clicking and echoing on the sandstone floor. She sits down, and they both continue their work.

Perhaps Mr. Grey insists on all his employees being blonde. I'm wondering idly if that's legal, when the office door opens and a tall, elegantly dressed, attractive African American man with short dreads exits. I have definitely worn the wrong clothes.

He turns and says through the door, "Golf this week, Grey?"

I don't hear the reply. He turns, sees me, and smiles, his dark eyes crinkling at the corners. Olivia has jumped up and called the elevator. She seems to excel at jumping from her seat. She's more nervous than me!

"Good afternoon, ladies," he says as he departs through the sliding door.

"Mr. Grey will see you now, Miss Steele. Do go through," Blonde Number Two says. I stand rather shakily, trying to suppress my nerves. Gathering up my backpack, I abandon my glass of water and make my way to the partially open door.

"You don't need to knock—just go in." She smiles kindly.

I push open the door and stumble through, tripping over my own feet and falling headfirst into the office.

Double crap—me and my two left feet! I am on my hands and knees in the doorway to Mr. Grey's office, and gentle hands are around me, helping me to stand. I am so embarrassed, damn my clumsiness. I have to steel myself to glance up. Holy cow—he's so young.

"Miss Kavanagh." He extends a long-fingered hand to me once I'm upright. "I'm Christian Grey. Are you all right? Would you like to sit?"

So young—and attractive, very attractive. He's tall, dressed in a fine gray suit, white shirt, and black tie with unruly dark copper-colored hair and intense, bright gray eyes that regard me shrewdly. It takes a moment for me to find my voice.

"Um. Actually—" I mutter. If this guy is over thirty, then I'm a monkey's uncle. In a daze, I place my hand in his and we shake. As our fingers touch, I feel an odd exhilarating shiver run through me. I withdraw my hand hastily, embarrassed. Must be static. I blink rapidly, my eyelids matching my heart rate.

"Miss Kavanagh is indisposed, so she sent me. I hope you don't mind, Mr. Grey."

"And you are?" His voice is warm, possibly amused, but it's difficult to tell from his impassive expression. He looks mildly interested but, above all, polite.

"Anastasia Steele. I'm studying English literature with Kate, um . . . Katherine . . . um . . . Miss Kavanagh, at WSU Vancouver."

"I see," he says simply. I think I see the ghost of a smile in his expression, but I'm not sure.

"Would you like to sit?" He waves me toward an L-shaped white leather couch.

His office is way too big for just one man. In front of the floor-to-ceiling windows, there's a modern dark wood desk that six people could comfortably eat around. It matches the coffee table by the couch. Everything else is white—ceiling, floors, and walls, except for the wall by the door, where a mosaic of small paintings hang, thirty-six of them arranged in a square. They are exquisite—a series of mundane, forgotten objects painted in such precise detail they look like photographs. Displayed together, they are breathtaking.

"A local artist. Trouton," says Grey when he catches my gaze.

"They're lovely. Raising the ordinary to extraordinary," I murmur, distracted both by him and the paintings. He cocks his head to one side and regards me intently.

"I couldn't agree more, Miss Steele," he replies, his voice soft, and for some inexplicable reason I find myself blushing.

Apart from the paintings, the rest of the office is cold, clean, and clinical. I wonder if it reflects the personality of the Adonis who sinks gracefully into one of the white leather chairs opposite me. I shake my head, disturbed at the direction of my thoughts, and retrieve Kate's questions from my backpack. Next, I set up the digital recorder and am all fingers and thumbs, dropping it twice on the coffee table in front of me. Mr. Grey says nothing, waiting patiently—I hope—as I become increasingly embarrassed and flustered. When I pluck up the courage to look at him, he's watching me, one hand relaxed in his lap and the other cupping his chin and trailing his long index finger across his lips. I think he's trying to suppress a smile.

"S-sorry," I stutter. "I'm not used to this."

"Take all the time you need, Miss Steele," he says.

"Do you mind if I record your answers?"

"After you've taken so much trouble to set up the recorder, you ask me now?"

I flush. He's teasing me? I hope. I blink at him, unsure what to say, and I think he takes pity on me because he relents. "No, I don't mind."

"Did Kate, I mean, Miss Kavanagh, explain what the interview was for?"

"Yes. To appear in the graduation issue of the student newspaper as I shall be conferring the degrees at this year's graduation ceremony."

Oh! This is news to me, and I'm temporarily preoccupied by the thought that someone not much older than me—okay, maybe six years or so, and okay, mega-successful, but still—is going to present me with my degree. I frown, dragging my wayward attention back to the task at hand.

"Good." I swallow nervously. "I have some questions, Mr. Grey." I smooth a stray lock of hair behind my ear.

"I thought you might," he says, deadpan. He's laughing at me. My cheeks heat at the realization, and I sit up and square my shoulders in an attempt to look taller and more intimidating. Pressing the start button on the recorder, I try to look professional.

"You're very young to have amassed such an empire. To what do you owe your success?" I glance up at him. His smile is rueful, but he looks vaguely disappointed.

"Business is all about people, Miss Steele, and I'm very good at judging people. I know how they tick, what makes them flourish, what doesn't, what inspires them, and how to incentivize them. I employ an exceptional team, and I reward them well." He pauses and fixes me with his gray stare. "My belief is to achieve success in any scheme one has to make oneself master of that scheme, know it inside and out, know every detail. I work hard, very hard to do that. I make decisions based on logic and facts. I have a natural gut instinct that can spot and nurture a good solid idea and good people. The bottom line is it's always down to good people."

"Maybe you're just lucky." This isn't on Kate's list—but he's so arrogant. His eyes flare momentarily in surprise.

"I don't subscribe to luck or chance, Miss Steele. The harder I work the more luck I seem to have. It really is all about having the right people on your team and directing their energies accordingly. I think it was Harvey Firestone who said, 'The growth and development of people is the highest calling of leadership.'"

"You sound like a control freak." The words are out of my mouth before I can stop them.

"Oh, I exercise control in all things, Miss Steele," he says without a trace of humor in his smile. I look at him, and he holds my gaze steadily, impassive. My heartbeat quickens, and my face flushes again.

Why does he have such an unnerving effect on me? His overwhelming good looks maybe? The way his eyes blaze at me? The way he strokes his index finger against his lower lip? I wish he'd stop doing that.

"Besides, immense power is acquired by assuring yourself in your secret reveries that you were born to control things," he continues, his voice soft.

"Do you feel that you have immense power?" *Control freak.*

"I employ over forty thousand people, Miss Steele. That gives me a certain sense of responsibility—power, if you will. If I were to decide I was no longer interested in the telecommunications business and sell, twenty thousand people would struggle to make their mortgage payments after a month or so."

My mouth drops open. I am staggered by his lack of humility.

"Don't you have a board to answer to?" I ask, disgusted.

"I own my company. I don't have to answer to a board." He raises an eyebrow at me. Of course, I would know this if I had done some research. But holy crap, he's arrogant. I change tack.

"And do you have any interests outside your work?"

"I have varied interests, Miss Steele." A ghost of a smile touches his lips. "Very varied." And for some reason, I'm confounded and heated by his steady gaze. His eyes are alight with some wicked thought.

"But if you work so hard, what do you do to chill out?"

"Chill out?" He smiles, revealing perfect white teeth. I stop breathing. He really is beautiful. No one should be this good-looking.

"Well, to 'chill out,' as you put it—I sail, I fly, I indulge in various physical pursuits." He shifts in his chair. "I'm a very wealthy man, Miss Steele, and I have expensive and absorbing hobbies."

I glance quickly at Kate's questions, wanting to get off this subject.

"You invest in manufacturing. Why, specifically?" I ask. Why does he make me so uncomfortable?

"I like to build things. I like to know how things work: what makes things tick, how to construct and deconstruct. And I have a love of ships. What can I say?"

"That sounds like your heart talking rather than logic and facts."

His mouth quirks up, and he stares appraisingly at me.

"Possibly. Though there are people who'd say I don't have a heart."

"Why would they say that?"

"Because they know me well." His lip curls in a wry smile.

"Would your friends say you're easy to get to know?" And I regret the question as soon as I say it. It's not on Kate's list.

"I'm a very private person, Miss Steele. I go a long way to protect my privacy. I don't often give interviews . . ."

"Why did you agree to do this one?"

"Because I'm a benefactor of the university, and for all intents and purposes, I couldn't get Miss Kavanagh off my back. She badgered and badgered my PR people, and I admire that kind of tenacity."

I know how tenacious Kate can be. That's why I'm sitting here squirming uncomfortably under his penetrating gaze, when I should be studying for my exams.

"You also invest in farming technologies. Why are you interested in that area?"

"We can't eat money, Miss Steele, and there are too many people on this planet who don't have enough to eat."

"That sounds very philanthropic. Is it something you feel passionately about? Feeding the world's poor?"

He shrugs noncommittally.

"It's shrewd business," he murmurs, though I think he's being disingenuous. It doesn't make sense—feeding the world's poor? I can't see the financial benefit of this, only the virtue of the ideal. I glance at the next question, confused by his attitude.

"Do you have a philosophy? If so, what is it?"

"I don't have a philosophy as such. Maybe a guiding principle—Carnegie's: 'A man who acquires the ability to take full possession of his own mind may take possession of anything else to which he is justly entitled.' I'm very singular, driven. I like control—of myself and those around me."

"So you want to possess things?" *You are a control freak.*

"I want to deserve to possess them, but yes, bottom line, I do."

"You sound like the ultimate consumer."

"I am." He smiles, but the smile doesn't touch his eyes. Again, this is at odds with someone who wants to feed the world, so I can't help thinking that we're talking about something else, but I'm mystified as to what it is. I swallow hard. The temperature in the room is rising, or maybe it's just me. I just want this interview to be over. Surely Kate has enough material now. I glance at the next question.

"You were adopted. How much do you think that's shaped the way you are?" Oh, this is personal. I stare at him, hoping he's not offended. His brow furrows.

"I have no way of knowing."

My interest is piqued. "How old were you when you were adopted?"

"That's a matter of public record, Miss Steele." His tone is stern. *Crap.* Yes, of course—if I'd known I was doing this interview, I would have done some research. Flustered, I move on quickly.

"You've had to sacrifice family life for your work."

"That's not a question." He's terse.

"Sorry." I squirm; he's made me feel like an errant child. I try again. "Have you had to sacrifice family life for your work?"

"I have a family. I have a brother and a sister and two loving parents. I'm not interested in extending my family beyond that."

"Are you gay, Mr. Grey?"

He inhales sharply, and I cringe, mortified. *Crap.* Why didn't I employ some kind of filter before I read this straight out? How can I tell him I'm just reading the questions? Damn Kate and her curiosity!

"No, Anastasia, I'm not." He raises his eyebrows, a cool gleam in his eyes. He does not look pleased.

"I apologize. It's, um . . . written here." It's the first time he's said my name. My heartbeat has accelerated, and my cheeks are heating up again. Nervously, I tuck my loosened hair behind my ear.

He cocks his head to one side.

"These aren't your own questions?"

The blood drains from my head.

"Er . . . no. Kate—Miss Kavanagh—she compiled the questions."

"Are you colleagues on the student paper?" *Oh no.* I have nothing to do with the student paper. It's her extracurricular activity, not mine. My face is aflame.

"No. She's my roommate."

He rubs his chin in quiet deliberation, his gray eyes appraising me.

"Did you volunteer to do this interview?" he asks, his voice deadly quiet.

Hang on, who's supposed to be interviewing whom? His eyes burn into me, and I'm compelled to answer with the truth.

"I was drafted. She's not well." My voice is weak and apologetic.

"That explains a great deal."

There's a knock at the door, and Blonde Number Two enters.

"Mr. Grey, forgive me for interrupting, but your next meeting is in two minutes."

"We're not finished here, Andrea. Please cancel my next meeting."

Andrea hesitates, gaping at him. She appears lost. He turns his head slowly to face her and raises his eyebrows. She flushes bright pink. *Oh, good. It's not just me.*

"Very well, Mr. Grey," she mutters, then exits. He frowns, and turns his attention back to me.

"Where were we, Miss Steele?"

Oh, we're back to "Miss Steele" now.

"Please, don't let me keep you from anything."

"I want to know about you. I think that's only fair." His eyes are alight with curiosity. *Double crap. Where's he going with this?* He places his elbows on the arms of the chair and steeples his fingers in front of his mouth. His mouth is very . . . distracting. I swallow.

"There's not much to know."

"What are your plans after you graduate?"

I shrug, thrown by his interest. *Move to Seattle with Kate, find a job.* I haven't really thought beyond my finals.

"I haven't made any plans, Mr. Grey. I just need to get through my final exams." Which I should be studying for right now, rather than sitting in your palatial, swanky, sterile office, feeling uncomfortable under your penetrating gaze.

"We run an excellent internship program here," he says quietly. I raise my eyebrows in surprise. Is he offering me a job?

"Oh. I'll bear that in mind," I murmur, confounded. "Though I'm not sure I'd fit in here." Oh no. I'm musing out loud again.

"Why do you say that?" He tilts his head to one side, intrigued, a hint of a smile playing on his lips.

"It's obvious, isn't it?" *I'm uncoordinated, scruffy, and I'm not blonde.*

"Not to me." His gaze is intense, all humor gone, and strange muscles deep in my belly clench suddenly. I tear my eyes away from his scrutiny and stare blindly down at my knotted fingers. *What's going on?* I have to go—now. I lean forward to retrieve the recorder.

"Would you like me to show you around?" he asks.

"I'm sure you're far too busy, Mr. Grey, and I do have a long drive."

"You're driving back to Vancouver?" He sounds surprised, anxious even. He glances out of the window. It's begun to rain. "Well, you'd better drive carefully." His tone is stern, authoritative. Why should he care? "Did you get everything you need?" he adds.

"Yes, sir," I reply, packing the recorder into my backpack. His eyes narrow, speculatively.

"Thank you for the interview, Mr. Grey."

"The pleasure's been all mine," he says, polite as ever.

As I rise, he stands and holds out his hand.

"Until we meet again, Miss Steele." And it sounds like a challenge, or a threat, I'm not sure which. I frown. When will we ever meet again? I shake his hand once more, astounded that that odd current between us is still there. It must be my nerves.

"Mr. Grey." I nod at him. Moving with lithe athletic grace to the door, he opens it wide.

"Just ensuring you make it through the door, Miss Steele." He gives me a small smile. Obviously, he's referring to my earlier less-than-elegant entry into his office. I blush.

"That's very considerate, Mr. Grey," I snap, and his smile widens. *I'm glad you find me entertaining,* I glower inwardly, walking into the foyer. I'm surprised when he follows me out. Andrea and Olivia both look up, equally surprised.

"Did you have a coat?" Grey asks.

"A jacket."

Olivia leaps up and retrieves my jacket, which Grey takes from her before she can hand it to me. He holds it up and, feeling ridiculously self-conscious, I shrug it on. Grey places his hands for a moment on my shoulders. I gasp at the contact. If he notices my reaction, he gives nothing away. His long index finger presses the button summoning the elevator, and we stand waiting—awkwardly on my part, coolly self-possessed on his. The doors open, and I hurry in, desperate to escape. *I really need to get out of here.* When I turn to look at him, he's gazing at me and leaning against the doorway beside the elevator with one hand on the wall. He really is very, very good-looking. It's unnerving.

"Anastasia," he says as a farewell.

"Christian," I reply. And mercifully, the doors close.

CHAPTER TWO

My heart is pounding. The elevator arrives on the first floor, and I scramble out as soon as the doors slide open, stumbling once but fortunately not sprawling onto the immaculate sandstone floor. I race for the wide glass doors, and suddenly I'm free in the bracing, cleansing, damp air of Seattle. Raising my face, I welcome the cool, refreshing rain. I close my eyes and take a deep, purifying breath, trying to recover what's left of my equilibrium.

No man has ever affected me the way Christian Grey has, and I cannot fathom why. Is it his looks? His civility? Wealth? Power? I don't understand my irrational reaction. I breathe an enormous sigh of relief. What in heaven's name was that all about? Leaning against one of the steel pillars of the building, I valiantly attempt to calm down and gather my thoughts. I shake my head. What *was* that? My heart steadies to its regular rhythm, and when I can breathe normally again I head for the car.

AS I LEAVE THE city limits behind, I begin to feel foolish and embarrassed as I replay the interview in my mind. Surely I'm overreacting to something that's imaginary. Okay, so he's very attractive, confident, commanding, at ease with himself—but on the flip side, he's arrogant, and for all his impeccable manners, he's autocratic and cold. Well, on the surface. An involuntary shiver runs down my spine. He may be arrogant, but then he has a right to be—he's accomplished so much at such a young age. He doesn't suffer fools gladly, but why should he? Again, I'm irritated that Kate didn't give me a brief biography.

While cruising toward Interstate 5, my mind continues to

wander. I'm truly perplexed as to what makes someone so driven to succeed. Some of his answers were so cryptic—as if he had a hidden agenda. And Kate's questions—ugh! The adoption and asking him if he was gay! I shudder. I can't believe I said that. *Ground, swallow me up now!* Every time I think of that question in the future, I will cringe with embarrassment. Damn Katherine Kavanagh!

I check the speedometer. I'm driving more cautiously than I would on any other occasion. And I know it's the memory of those penetrating gray eyes gazing at me and a stern voice telling me to drive carefully. Shaking my head, I realize that Grey's more like a man twice his age.

Forget it, Ana, I scold myself. I decide that, all in all, it's been a very interesting experience, but I shouldn't dwell on it. *Put it behind you.* I never have to see him again. I'm immediately cheered by the thought. I switch on the stereo and turn the volume up loud, sit back and listen to thumping indie rock music as I press down on the accelerator. As I hit Interstate 5, I realize I can drive as fast as I want.

WE LIVE IN A small community of duplex apartments close to the Vancouver campus of WSU. I'm lucky—Kate's parents bought the place for her, and I pay peanuts for rent. It's been home for four years now. As I pull up outside, I know Kate is going to want a blow-by-blow account, and she is tenacious. Well, at least she has the digital recorder. I hope I won't have to elaborate much beyond what was said during the interview.

"Ana! You're back." Kate sits in our living area, surrounded by books. She's clearly been studying for finals—she's still in her pink flannel pajamas decorated with cute little rabbits, the ones she reserves for the aftermath of breaking up with boyfriends, for assorted illnesses, and for general moody depression. She bounds up to me and hugs me hard.

"I was beginning to worry. I expected you back sooner."

"Oh, I thought I made good time considering the interview ran over." I wave the digital recorder at her.

"Ana, thank you so much for doing this. I owe you, I know. How was it? What was he like?" Oh no—here we go, the Katherine Kavanagh Inquisition.

I struggle to answer her question. What can I say?

"I'm glad it's over and I don't have to see him again. He was rather intimidating, you know." I shrug. "He's very focused, intense even—and young. Really young."

Kate gazes innocently at me. I frown.

"Don't you look so innocent. Why didn't you give me a biography? He made me feel like such an idiot for skimping on basic research."

Kate clamps a hand to her mouth. "Jeez, Ana, I'm sorry—I didn't think."

I huff.

"Mostly he was courteous, formal, slightly stuffy—like he's old before his time. He doesn't talk like a man of twentysomething. How old *is* he, anyway?"

"Twenty-seven. Jeez, Ana, I'm sorry. I should have briefed you, but I was in such a panic. Let me have the recorder and I'll start transcribing the interview."

"You look better. Did you eat your soup?" I ask, keen to change the subject.

"Yes, and it was delicious as usual. I'm feeling much better." She smiles at me in gratitude. I check my watch.

"I have to run. I can still make my shift at Clayton's."

"Ana, you'll be exhausted."

"I'll be fine. I'll see you later."

I'VE WORKED AT CLAYTON'S since I started at WSU. It's the largest independent hardware store in the Portland area, and over the four years I've worked here, I've come to know a little bit about most everything we sell—although ironically, I'm crap at any DIY. I leave all that to my dad.

I'M GLAD I CAN make my shift as it gives me something to focus on that isn't Christian Grey. We're busy—it's the start of the summer season, and folks are redecorating their homes. Mrs. Clayton looks relieved to see me.

"Ana! I thought you weren't going to make it today."

"My appointment didn't take as long as I thought. I can do a couple of hours."

"I'm real pleased to see you."

She sends me to the storeroom to start restocking shelves, and I'm soon absorbed in the task.

WHEN I ARRIVE HOME later, Katherine is wearing headphones and working on her laptop. Her nose is still pink, but she has her teeth into a story, so she's concentrating and typing furiously. I'm thoroughly drained, exhausted by the long drive, by the grueling interview, and by being swamped at Clayton's. I slump on to the couch, thinking about the essay I have to finish and all the studying I haven't done today because I was holed up with . . . *him.*

"You've got some good stuff here, Ana. Well done. I can't believe you didn't take him up on his offer to show you around. He obviously wanted to spend more time with you." She gives me a fleeting quizzical look.

I flush, and my heart rate inexplicably increases. That wasn't the reason, surely. He just wanted to show me around so I could see that he was lord of all he surveyed. I realize I'm biting my lip, and I hope Kate doesn't notice. But she seems absorbed in her transcription.

"I hear what you mean about formal. Did you take any notes?" she asks.

"Um . . . no, I didn't."

"That's fine. I can still make a fine article with this. Shame we don't have some original stills. Good-looking son of a bitch, isn't he?"

"I suppose so." I try hard to sound disinterested, and I think I succeed.

"Oh, come on, Ana—even you can't be immune to his looks." She arches a perfect eyebrow at me.

Crap! I feel my cheeks heating so I distract her with flattery, always a good ploy.

"You probably would have got a lot more out of him."

"I doubt that, Ana. Come on—he practically offered you a job. Given that I foisted this on you at the last minute, you did very well." She glances up at me speculatively. I make a hasty retreat into the kitchen.

"So what did you really think of him?" Damn, she's inquisitive. Why can't she just let this go? *Think of something—quick.*

"He's very driven, controlling, arrogant—scary, but very charismatic. I can understand the fascination," I add truthfully, hoping this will shut her up once and for all.

"You, fascinated by a man? That's a first," she snorts.

I start gathering the makings of a sandwich so she can't see my face.

"Why did you want to know if he was gay? Incidentally, that was the most embarrassing question. I was mortified, and he was pissed to be asked, too." I scowl at the memory.

"Whenever he's in the society pages, he never has a date."

"It was embarrassing. The whole thing was embarrassing. I'm glad I'll never have to lay eyes on him again."

"Oh, Ana, it can't have been that bad. I think he sounds quite taken with you."

Taken with me? Now Kate's being ridiculous.

"Would you like a sandwich?"

"Please."

WE TALK NO MORE of Christian Grey that evening, much to my relief. Once we've eaten, I'm able to sit at the dining table with Kate and, while she works on her article, I work on my essay on *Tess of the d'Urbervilles.* Damn, that woman was in the wrong place at the wrong time in the wrong century. By the time I finish, it's midnight, and Kate has long since gone to bed. I make my way to my room, exhausted, but pleased that I've accomplished so much for a Monday.

I curl up in my white iron bed, wrap my mother's quilt around me, close my eyes, and I'm instantly asleep. That night I dream of dark places, bleak, cold white floors, and gray eyes.

FOR THE REST OF the week, I throw myself into my studies and my job at Clayton's. Kate is busy, too, compiling her last edition of the student newspaper before she has to relinquish it to the new editor while also cramming for her finals. By Wednesday, she's much better, and I no longer have to endure the sight of her pink-flannel-with-too-many-rabbits PJs. I call my mom in Georgia to check on her, but also so she can wish me luck on my final exams. She proceeds to tell me about her latest venture into candlemaking—my mother is all about new business ventures. Fundamentally, she's bored and wants something to occupy her time, but she has the attention span of a goldfish. It'll be something new next week. She worries me. I hope she hasn't mortgaged the house to finance this latest scheme. And I hope Bob—her relatively new but much older husband—is keeping an eye on her now that I'm no longer there. He does seem a lot more grounded than Husband Number Three.

"How are things with you, Ana?"

For a moment, I hesitate, and I have Mom's full attention.

"I'm fine."

"Ana? Have you met someone?" *Wow . . . how does she do that?* The excitement in her voice is palpable.

"No, Mom, it's nothing. You'll be the first to know if I do."

"Ana, you really need to get out more, honey. You worry me."

"Mom, I'm fine. How's Bob?" As ever, distraction is the best policy.

Later that evening, I call Ray, my stepdad, Mom's Husband Number Two, the man I consider my father and the man whose name I bear. It's a brief conversation. In fact, it's not so much a conversation as a one-sided series of grunts in response to my gentle coaxing. Ray is not a talker. But he's still alive, he's still watching soccer on TV (and going bowling or fly-fishing, or making furniture, when he's not). Ray is a skilled carpenter and the reason I know the difference between a hawk and a handsaw. All seems well with him.

FRIDAY NIGHT, KATE AND I are debating what to do with our evening—we want some time off from our studies, from our work, and from student newspapers—when the doorbell rings. Standing on our doorstep is my good friend José clutching a bottle of champagne.

"José! Great to see you!" I give him a quick hug. "Come in."

José is the first person I met when I arrived at WSU, looking as lost and lonely as I did. We recognized a kindred spirit in each other that day, and we've been friends ever since. Not only do we share a sense of humor, but we also discovered that Ray and José Senior were in the same army unit together. As a result, our fathers have become good friends, too.

José is studying engineering and is the first in his family to make it to college. He's pretty damn bright, but his real passion is photography. José has a great eye for a good picture.

"I have news." He grins, his dark eyes twinkling.

"Don't tell me—you've managed not to get kicked out for another week," I tease, and he scowls playfully at me.

"The Portland Place Gallery is going to exhibit my photos next month."

"That's amazing—congratulations!" Delighted for him, I hug him again. Kate beams at him, too.

"Way to go, José! I should put this in the paper. Nothing like last-minute editorial changes on a Friday evening." She feigns annoyance.

"Let's celebrate. I want you to come to the opening." José looks intently at me and I flush. "Both of you, of course," he adds, glancing nervously at Kate.

José and I are good friends, but I know deep down inside he'd like to be more. He's cute and funny, but he's just not for me. He's more like the brother I never had. Katherine often teases me that I'm missing the need-a-boyfriend gene, but the truth is I just haven't met anyone who . . . well, whom I'm attracted to, even though part of me longs for the fabled trembling knees, heart-in-my-mouth, butterflies-in-my-belly moments.

Sometimes I wonder if there's something wrong with me. Perhaps I've spent too long in the company of my literary romantic heroes, and consequently my ideals and expectations are far too high. But in reality, nobody's ever made me feel like that.

Until very recently, the unwelcome, still-small voice of my subconscious whispers. NO! I banish the thought immediately. I am not going there, not after that painful interview. *Are you gay, Mr. Grey?* I wince at the memory. I know I've dreamed about him most nights since then, but that's just to purge the awful experience from my system, surely.

I watch José open the bottle of champagne. He's tall, and in his jeans and T-shirt, he's all shoulders and muscles, tanned skin, dark hair, and burning dark eyes. Yes, José's pretty hot, but I think he's finally getting the message: we're just friends. The cork makes its loud pop, and José looks up and smiles.

SATURDAY AT THE STORE is a nightmare. We are besieged by do-it-yourselfers wanting to spruce up their homes. Mr. and Mrs. Clayton and John and Patrick—the two other part-timers—and I are besieged by customers. But there's a lull around lunchtime, and Mrs. Clayton asks me to check on some orders while I'm sitting behind the counter at the register discreetly eating my bagel. I'm engrossed in the task, checking catalog numbers against the items we need and the items we've ordered, eyes flicking from the order book to the computer screen and back as I make sure the entries match. Then, for some reason, I glance up . . . and find myself locked in the bold gray gaze of Christian Grey, who's standing at the counter, staring at me.

Heart failure.

"Miss Steele. What a pleasant surprise." His gaze is unwavering and intense.

Holy crap. What the hell is *he* doing here, looking all outdoorsy with his tousled hair and in his cream chunky-knit sweater, jeans, and walking boots? I think my mouth has popped open, and I can't locate my brain or my voice.

"Mr. Grey," I whisper, because that's all I can manage. There's a ghost of a smile on his lips and his eyes are alight with humor, as if he's enjoying some private joke.

"I was in the area," he says by way of explanation. "I need to stock up on a few things. It's a pleasure to see you again, Miss Steele." His voice is warm and husky like dark melted chocolate fudge caramel . . . or something.

I shake my head to gather my wits. My heart is pounding at a frantic tempo, and for some reason I'm blushing furiously under his steady scrutiny. I am utterly thrown by the sight of him standing before me. My memories of him did not do him justice. He's not merely good-looking—he's the epitome of male beauty, breathtaking, and he's here. Here in Clayton's Hardware Store. Go figure. Finally my cognitive functions are restored and reconnected with the rest of my body.

"Ana. My name's Ana," I mutter. "What can I help you with, Mr. Grey?"

He smiles, and again it's like he's privy to some big secret. It is so disconcerting. Taking a deep breath, I put on my professional I've-worked-in-this-shop-for-years façade. *I can do this.*

"There are a few items I need. To start with, I'd like some cable ties," he murmurs, his expression both cool and amused.

Cable ties?

"We stock various lengths. Shall I show you?" I mutter, my voice soft and wavering. *Get a grip, Steele.*

A slight frown mars Grey's rather lovely brow. "Please. Lead the way, Miss Steele," he says. I try for nonchalance as I come out from behind the counter, but really I'm concentrating hard on not falling over my own feet—my legs are suddenly the consistency of Jell-O. I'm so glad I decided to wear my best jeans this morning.

"They're with the electrical goods, aisle eight." My voice is a little too bright. I glance up at him and regret it almost immediately. Damn, he's handsome.

"After you," he murmurs, gesturing with his long-fingered, beautifully manicured hand.

With my heart almost strangling me—because it's in my throat trying to escape from my mouth—I head down one of the aisles to the electrical section. *Why is he in Portland? Why is he here at Clayton's?* And from a very tiny, underused part of my brain—probably located at the base of my medulla oblongata near where my subconscious dwells—comes the thought: *He's here to see you.* No way! I dismiss it immediately. Why would this beautiful, powerful, urbane man want to see me? The idea is preposterous, and I kick it out of my head.

"Are you in Portland on business?" I ask, and my voice is too high, like I've got my finger trapped in a door or something. *Damn! Try to be cool, Ana!*

"I was visiting the WSU farming division. It's based in Vancouver. I'm currently funding some research there in crop rotation and soil science," he says matter-of-factly. *See? Not here to find you at all,* my subconscious sneers at me, loud, proud, and pouty. I flush at my foolish, wayward thoughts.

"All part of your feed-the-world plan?" I tease.

"Something like that," he acknowledges, and his lips quirk up in a half smile.

He gazes at the selection of cable ties we stock at Clayton's. What on Earth is he going to do with those? I cannot picture him as a do-it-yourselfer at all. His fingers trail across the various packages displayed, and for some inexplicable reason, I have to look away. He bends and selects a packet.

"These will do," he says with his oh-so-secret smile.

"Is there anything else?"

"I'd like some masking tape."

Masking tape?

"Are you redecorating?" The words are out before I can stop them. Surely he hires laborers or has staff to help him decorate?

"No, not redecorating," he says quickly, then smirks, and I have the uncanny feeling that he's laughing at me.

Am I that funny? Funny looking?

"This way," I murmur, embarrassed. "Masking tape is in the decorating aisle."

I glance behind me as he follows.

"Have you worked here long?" His voice is low, and he's gazing at me, concentrating hard. I blush brightly. Why the hell does he have this effect on me? I feel like I'm fourteen years old—gauche, as always, and out of place. *Eyes front, Steele!*

"Four years," I mutter as we reach our goal. To distract myself, I reach down and select the two widths of masking tape that we stock.

"I'll take that one," Grey says softly, pointing to the wider tape, which I pass to him. Our fingers brush very briefly, and the current is there again, zapping through me like I've touched an exposed wire. I gasp involuntarily as I feel it all the way down to somewhere dark and unexplored, deep in my belly. Desperately, I scrabble around for my equilibrium.

"Anything else?" My voice is husky and breathy. His eyes widen slightly.

"Some rope, I think." His voice mirrors mine, husky.

"This way." I duck my head down to hide my recurring blush and move toward the aisle.

"What sort were you after? We have synthetic and natural filament rope . . . twine . . . cable cord . . ." I halt at his expression, his eyes darkening. *Holy cow.*

"I'll take five yards of the natural filament rope, please."

Quickly, with trembling fingers, I measure out five yards against the fixed ruler, aware that his hot gray gaze is on me. I dare not look at him. Jeez, could I feel any more self-conscious? Taking my Stanley knife from the back pocket of my jeans, I cut it then coil it neatly before tying it in a slipknot. By some miracle, I manage not to remove a finger with my knife.

"Were you a Girl Scout?" he asks, sculptured, sensual lips curled in amusement. *Don't look at his mouth!*

"Organized group activities aren't really my thing, Mr. Grey."

He arches a brow.

"What is your thing, Anastasia?" he asks, his voice soft, and his secret smile is back. I gaze at him, unable to express myself. I'm on shifting tectonic plates. *Try to be cool, Ana,* my tortured subconscious begs on bended knee.

"Books," I whisper, but inside, my subconscious is screaming: *You! You are my thing!* I slap it down instantly, mortified that my psyche is having ideas way out of its league.

"What kind of books?" He cocks his head to one side. *Why is he so interested?*

"Oh, you know. The usual. The classics. British literature, mainly."

He rubs his chin with his long index finger and thumb as he contemplates my answer. Or perhaps he's just very bored and trying to hide it.

"Anything else you need?" I have to get off this subject—those fingers on that face are beguiling.

"I don't know. What else would you recommend?"

What would I recommend? I don't even know what you're doing.

"For a do-it-yourselfer?"

He nods, his eyes alive with wicked humor. I flush, and my gaze strays to his snug jeans.

"Coveralls," I reply, and I know I'm no longer screening what's coming out of my mouth.

He raises an eyebrow, amused yet again.

"You wouldn't want to ruin your clothing." I gesture vaguely in the direction of his jeans.

"I could always take them off." He smirks.

"Um." I feel the color in my cheeks rising again. I must be the color of *The Communist Manifesto. Stop talking. Stop talking NOW.*

"I'll take some coveralls. Heaven forbid I should ruin any clothing," he says dryly.

I try to dismiss the unwelcome image of him without jeans.

"Do you need anything else?" I squeak as I hand him the blue coveralls.

He ignores my inquiry.

"How's the article coming along?"

He's finally asked me an easy question, away from all the innuendo and the confusing double-talk . . . a question I can answer. I grasp it tightly with two hands as if it were a life raft, and I go for honesty.

"I'm not writing it, Katherine is. Miss Kavanagh. My roommate, she's the writer. She's very happy with it. She's the editor of the newspaper, and she was devastated that she couldn't do the interview in person." I feel like I've come up for air—at last, a normal topic of conversation. "Her only concern is that she doesn't have any original photographs of you."

"What sort of photographs does she want?"

Okay. I hadn't factored in this response. I shake my head, because I just don't know.

"Well, I'm around. Tomorrow, perhaps . . ."

"You'd be willing to do a photo shoot?" My voice is squeaky again. Kate will be in seventh heaven if I can pull this off. *And you might see him again tomorrow,* that dark place at the base of my brain whispers seductively at me. I dismiss the thought—of all the silly, ridiculous . . .

"Kate will be delighted—if we can find a photographer." I'm so pleased, I smile at him broadly. His lips part, like he's taking a sharp intake of breath, and he blinks. For a fraction of a second, he looks lost somehow, and the Earth shifts slightly on its axis, the tectonic plates sliding into a new position.

Oh my. Christian Grey's lost look.

"Let me know about tomorrow." Reaching into his back pocket, he pulls out his wallet. "My card. It has my cell number on it. You'll need to call before ten in the morning."

"Okay." I grin up at him. Kate is going to be thrilled.

"*Ana!*"

Paul has materialized at the other end of the aisle. He's Mr. Clayton's youngest brother. I'd heard he was home from Princeton, but I wasn't expecting to see him today.

"Er, excuse me for a moment, Mr. Grey." Grey frowns as I turn away from him.

Paul has always been a buddy, and in this strange moment that I'm having with the rich, powerful, awesomely off-the-charts attractive control freak Grey, it's great to talk to someone who's normal. Paul hugs me hard, taking me by surprise.

"Ana, hi, it's so good to see you!" he gushes.

"Hello, Paul, how are you? You home for your brother's birthday?"

"Yep. You're looking well, Ana, really well." He grins as he examines me at arm's length. Then he releases me but keeps a possessive arm draped over my shoulder. I shuffle from foot to foot, embarrassed. It's good to see Paul, but he's always been overfamiliar.

When I glance up at Christian Grey, he's watching us like a hawk, his eyes hooded and speculative, his mouth a hard, impassive line. He's changed from the weirdly attentive customer to someone else—someone cold and distant.

"Paul, I'm with a customer. Someone you should meet," I say, trying to defuse the antagonism I see in Grey's expression. I drag Paul over to meet him, and they size each other up. The atmosphere is suddenly arctic.

"Er, Paul, this is Christian Grey. Mr. Grey, this is Paul Clayton. His brother owns the place." And for some irrational reason, I feel I have to explain a bit more.

"I've known Paul ever since I've worked here, though we don't see each other that often. He's back from Princeton, where he's studying business administration." I'm babbling . . . *Stop now!*

"Mr. Clayton." Grey holds his hand out, his look unreadable.

"Mr. Grey." Paul returns his handshake. "Wait up—not *the* Christian Grey? Of Grey Enterprises Holdings?" Paul goes from surly to awestruck in less than a nanosecond. Grey gives him a polite smile that doesn't reach his eyes.

"Wow—is there anything I can get you?"

"Anastasia has it covered, Mr. Clayton. She's been very attentive." His expression is impassive, but his words . . . it's like he's saying something else entirely. It's baffling.

"Cool," Paul responds. "Catch you later, Ana."

"Sure, Paul." I watch him disappear toward the stockroom. "Anything else, Mr. Grey?"

"Just these items." His tone is clipped and cool. Damn . . . have I offended him? Taking a deep breath, I turn and head for the register. *What is his problem?*

I ring up the rope, coveralls, masking tape, and cable ties.

"That will be forty-three dollars, please." I glance up at Grey, and I wish I hadn't. He's watching me closely, intently. It's unnerving.

"Would you like a bag?" I ask as I take his credit card.

"Please, Anastasia." His tongue caresses my name, and my heart once again is frantic. I can hardly breathe. Hurriedly, I place his purchases in a plastic bag.

"You'll call me if you want me to do the photo shoot?" He's all business once more. I nod, rendered speechless yet again, and hand back his credit card.

"Good. Until tomorrow, perhaps." He turns to leave, then pauses. "Oh—and Anastasia, I'm glad Miss Kavanagh couldn't do the interview." He smiles, then strides with renewed purpose out of the store, slinging the plastic bag over his shoulder, leaving me a quivering mass of raging female hormones. I spend several minutes staring at the closed door through which he's just left before I return to planet Earth.

Okay—I like him. There, I've admitted it to myself. I cannot hide from my feelings anymore. I've never felt like this before. I find him attractive, very attractive. But it's a lost cause, I know, and I sigh with bittersweet regret. It was just a coincidence, his coming here. But still, I can admire him from afar, surely. No harm can come of that. And if I find a photographer, I can do some serious admiring tomorrow. I bite my lip in anticipation and find myself grinning like a schoolgirl. I need to phone Kate and organize a photo shoot.

CHAPTER THREE

Kate is ecstatic.

"But what was he doing at Clayton's?" Her curiosity oozes through the phone. I'm in the depths of the stockroom, trying to keep my voice casual.

"He was in the area."

"I think that is one huge coincidence, Ana. You don't think he was there to see you?" My heart lurches at the prospect, but it's a short-lived joy. The dull, disappointing reality is that he was here on business.

"He was visiting the farming division of WSU. He's funding some research," I mutter.

"Oh yes. He's given the department a $2.5 million grant."

Wow.

"How do you know this?"

"Ana, I'm a journalist, and I've written a profile on the guy. It's my job to know this."

"Okay, Carla Bernstein, keep your hair on. So do you want these photos?"

"Of course I do. The question is, who's going to do them and where."

"We could ask him where. He says he's staying in the area."

"You can contact him?"

"I have his cell phone number."

Kate gasps.

"The richest, most elusive, most enigmatic bachelor in Washington State just gave you his cell phone number?"

"Er . . . yes."

"Ana! He likes you. No doubt about it." Her tone is emphatic.

"Kate, he's just trying to be nice." But even as I say the words, I know they're not true—Christian Grey doesn't do *nice*. He does polite, maybe. And a small, quiet voice whispers, *Perhaps Kate is right*. My scalp prickles at the idea that maybe, just maybe, he might like me. After all, he did say he was glad Kate didn't do the interview. I hug myself with quiet glee, rocking from side to side, entertaining the possibility that he might like me. Kate brings me back to the now.

"I don't know who we'll get to do the shoot. Levi, our regular photographer, can't. He's home in Idaho Falls for the weekend. He'll be pissed that he blew an opportunity to photograph one of America's leading entrepreneurs."

"Hmm . . . What about José?"

"Great idea! You ask him—he'll do anything for you. Then call Grey and find out where he wants us." Kate is irritatingly cavalier about José.

"I think you should call him."

"Who, José?" Kate scoffs.

"No, Grey."

"Ana, you're the one with the relationship."

"Relationship?" I squeak at her, my voice rising several octaves. "I barely know the guy."

"At least you've met him," she says bitterly. "And it looks like he wants to know you better. Ana, just call him," she snaps and hangs up. She is so bossy sometimes. I frown at my cell, sticking my tongue out at it.

I'm just leaving a message for José when Paul enters the stockroom looking for sandpaper.

"We're kind of busy out there, Ana," he says without acrimony.

"Yeah, um, sorry," I mutter, turning to leave.

"So, how come you know Christian Grey?" Paul's voice is unconvincingly nonchalant.

"I had to interview him for our student newspaper. Kate wasn't well." I shrug, trying to sound casual and doing no better than him.

"Christian Grey in Clayton's. Go figure," Paul snorts, amazed. He shakes his head as if to clear it. "Anyway, want to grab a drink or something this evening?"

Whenever he's home he asks me on a date, and I always say no. It's a ritual. I've never considered it a good idea to date the boss's brother, and besides, Paul is cute in a wholesome all-American boy-next-door kind of way, but he's no literary hero, not by any stretch of the imagination. *Is Grey?* my subconscious asks me, her eyebrow figuratively raised. I slap her down.

"Don't you have a family dinner or something for your brother?"

"That's tomorrow."

"Maybe some other time, Paul. I need to study tonight. I have my finals next week."

"Ana, one of these days you'll say yes." He smiles as I escape to the store floor.

"BUT I DO PLACES, Ana, not people," José groans.

"José, please?" I beg. I pace the living room of our apartment, clutching my cell and staring out the window at the fading evening light.

"Give me that phone." Kate grabs the handset from me, tossing her silken reddish-blond hair over her shoulder.

"Listen here, José Rodriguez, if you want our newspaper to cover the opening of your show, you'll do this shoot for us tomorrow, capiche?" Kate can be awesomely tough. "Good. Ana will call back with the location and the call time. We'll see you tomorrow." She snaps my cell phone off.

"Sorted. All we need to do now is decide where and when. Call him." She holds the phone out to me. My stomach twists. "Call Grey, now!"

I scowl at her and reach into my back pocket for his business card. I take a deep, steadying breath, and with shaking fingers, I dial the number.

He answers on the second ring. His tone is clipped, calm, and cold.

"Grey."

"Er . . . Mr. Grey? It's Anastasia Steele." I don't recognize my own voice, I'm so nervous. There's a brief pause. Inside I'm quaking.

"Miss Steele. How nice to hear from you." His voice has changed. He's surprised, I think, and he sounds so . . . warm—*seductive* even. My breath hitches, and I flush. I'm suddenly conscious that Katherine Kavanagh is staring at me, her mouth open, and I dart into the kitchen to avoid her unwanted scrutiny.

"Um—we'd like to go ahead with the photo shoot for the article." *Breathe, Ana, breathe.* My lungs drag in a hasty breath. "Tomorrow, if that's okay. Where would be convenient for you, sir?"

I can almost hear his sphinxlike smile through the phone.

"I'm staying at the Heathman in Portland. Shall we say nine thirty tomorrow morning?"

"Okay, we'll see you there." I am all gushing and breathy—like a child, not a grown woman who can vote and drink legally in the state of Washington.

"I look forward to it, Miss Steele." I visualize the wicked gleam in his eyes. *How can he make seven little words hold so much tantalizing promise?* I hang up. Kate is in the kitchen, and she's staring at me with a look of complete and utter consternation on her face.

"Anastasia Rose Steele. You like him! I've never seen or heard you so . . . so . . . affected by anyone before. You're actually blushing."

"Oh, Kate, you know I blush all the time. It's an occupational hazard with me. Don't be ridiculous," I snap. She blinks at me with surprise—I very rarely have hissy fits—and I briefly relent. "I just find him . . . intimidating, that's all."

"Heathman, that figures," mutters Kate. "I'll give the manager a call and negotiate a space for the shoot."

"I'll make supper. Then I need to study." I cannot hide my irritation with her as I open one of the cupboards to make supper.

I AM RESTLESS THAT night, tossing and turning, dreaming of smoky gray eyes, coveralls, long legs, long fingers, and dark, dark unexplored places. I wake twice in the night, my heart pounding. *Oh, I'm going to look just great tomorrow with so little sleep,* I scold myself. I punch my pillow and try to settle.

THE HEATHMAN IS NESTLED in the heart of downtown Portland. Its impressive brown stone edifice was completed just in time for the crash of the late 1920s. José, Travis, and I are traveling in my Beetle, and Kate is in her CLK, since we can't all fit in my car. Travis is José's friend and gopher, here to help out with the lighting. Kate has managed to acquire the use of a room at the Heathman free of charge for the morning in exchange for a credit in the article. When she explains at reception that we're here to photograph Christian Grey, CEO, we are instantly upgraded to a suite. Just a regular-sized suite, however, as apparently Mr. Grey is already occupying the largest one in the building. An overkeen marketing executive shows us up to the suite—he's terribly young and very nervous for some reason. I suspect Kate's beauty and commanding manner disarm him, because he's putty in her hands. The rooms are elegant, understated, and opulently furnished.

It's nine. We have half an hour to set up. Kate is in full flow.

"José, I think we'll shoot against that wall, do you agree?" She doesn't wait for his reply. "Travis, clear the chairs. Ana, could you ask housekeeping to bring up some refreshments? And let Grey know where we are."

Yes, mistress. She is so domineering. I roll my eyes but do as I'm told.

Half an hour later, Christian Grey walks into our suite.

Holy crap! He's wearing a white shirt, open at the collar, and gray flannel pants that hang from his hips. His unruly hair is still damp from a shower. My mouth goes dry looking at him . . . he's so freaking *hot.* Grey is followed into the suite by a man in his mid-thirties, all buzz cut and stubble in a sharp dark suit and tie who stands silently in the corner. His hazel eyes watch us impassively.

"Miss Steele, we meet again." Grey extends his hand, and I shake it, blinking rapidly. Oh my . . . he really is quite . . . As I touch his hand, I'm aware of that delicious current running right through me, lighting me up, making me blush, and I'm sure my erratic breathing must be audible.

"Mr. Grey, this is Katherine Kavanagh," I mutter, waving a hand toward Kate, who comes forward, looking him squarely in the eye.

"The tenacious Miss Kavanagh. How do you do?" He gives her a small smile, looking genuinely amused. "I trust you're feeling better? Anastasia said you were unwell last week."

"I'm fine, thank you, Mr. Grey." She shakes his hand firmly without batting an eyelid. I remind myself that Kate has been to the best private schools in Washington. Her family has money, and she's grown up confident and sure of her place in the world. She doesn't take any crap. I am in awe of her.

"Thank you for taking the time to do this." She gives him a polite, professional smile.

"It's a pleasure," he answers, turning his gaze on me, and I flush again. Damn it.

"This is José Rodriguez, our photographer," I say, grinning at José, who smiles with affection back at me. His eyes cool when he looks from me to Grey.

"Mr. Grey." He nods.

"Mr. Rodriguez." Grey's expression changes, too, as he appraises José.

"Where would you like me?" Grey asks him. His tone sounds vaguely threatening. But Katherine is not about to let José run the show.

"Mr. Grey—if you could sit here, please? Be careful of the lighting cables. And then we'll do a few standing, too." She directs him to a chair set up against the wall.

Travis switches on the lights, momentarily blinding Grey, and mutters an apology. Then Travis and I stand back and watch as José proceeds to snap away. He takes several photographs hand-held, asking Grey to turn this way, then that, to move his arm, then put it down again. Moving to the tripod, José takes several more, while Grey sits and poses, patiently and naturally, for about twenty minutes. My wish has come true: I can stand and admire Grey from not so afar. Twice our eyes lock, and I have to tear myself away from his cloudy gaze.

"Enough sitting." Katherine wades in again. "Standing, Mr. Grey?" she asks.

He stands, and Travis scurries in to remove the chair. The shutter on José's Nikon starts clicking again.

"I think we have enough," José announces five minutes later.

"Great," says Kate. "Thank you again, Mr. Grey." She shakes his hand, as does José.

"I look forward to reading the article, Miss Kavanagh," murmurs Grey, and turns to me, standing by the door. "Will you walk with me, Miss Steele?" he asks.

"Sure," I say, completely thrown. I glance anxiously at Kate, who shrugs at me. I notice José scowling behind her.

"Good day to you all," says Grey as he opens the door, standing aside to allow me out first.

Holy hell . . . what's this about? What does he want? I pause in the hotel corridor, fidgeting nervously as Grey emerges from the room followed by Mr. Buzz Cut in his sharp suit.

"I'll call you, Taylor," he murmurs to Buzz Cut. Taylor wanders back down the corridor, and Grey turns his burning gray gaze to me. *Crap . . . have I done something wrong?*

"I wondered if you would join me for coffee this morning."

My heart slams into my mouth. A date? *Christian Grey is asking me on a date.* He's asking if you want a coffee. *Maybe he thinks you haven't woken up yet,* my subconscious whines at me in a sneering mood again. I clear my throat, trying to control my nerves.

"I have to drive everyone home," I murmur apologetically, twisting my hands and fingers in front of me.

"Taylor," he calls, making me jump. Taylor, who had been retreating down the corridor, turns and heads back toward us.

"Are they based at the university?" Grey asks, his voice soft and inquiring. I nod, too stunned to speak.

"Taylor can take them. He's my driver. We have a large 4x4 here, so he'll be able to take the equipment, too."

"Mr. Grey?" Taylor asks when he reaches us, giving nothing away.

"Please, can you drive the photographer, his assistant, and Miss Kavanagh back home?"

"Certainly, sir," Taylor replies.

"There. Now can you join me for coffee?" Grey smiles as if it's a done deal.

I frown.

"Um—Mr. Grey, er—this really . . . look, Taylor doesn't have to drive them home." I flash a brief look at Taylor, who remains stoically impassive. "I'll swap vehicles with Kate, if you give me a moment."

Grey smiles a dazzling, unguarded, natural, all-teeth-showing, glorious smile. *Oh my . . .* He opens the door of the suite so I can go in. I scoot around him to reenter the room, finding Katherine in deep discussion with José.

"Ana, I think he definitely likes you," she says with no preamble whatsoever. José glares at me with disapproval. "But I don't trust him," she adds. I raise my hand up in the hope that she'll stop talking. By some miracle, she does.

"Kate, if you take Wanda, can I take your car?"

"Why?"

"Christian Grey has asked me to go for coffee with him."

Her mouth pops open. Speechless Kate! I savor the moment. She grabs me by my arm and drags me into the bedroom that's off the living area of the suite.

"Ana, there's something about him." Her tone is full of warning. "He's gorgeous, I agree, but I think he's dangerous. Especially for someone like you."

"What do you mean, someone like me?" I demand, affronted.

"An innocent like you, Ana. You know what I mean," she says a little irritated. I flush.

"Kate, it's just coffee. I'm starting my exams this week, and I need to study, so I won't be long."

She purses her lips as if considering my request. Finally, she fishes her car keys out of her pocket and hands them to me. I hand her mine.

"I'll see you later. Don't be long, or I'll send out search and rescue."

"Thanks." I hug her.

I emerge from the suite to find Christian Grey waiting, leaning up against the wall, looking like a male model in a pose for some glossy high-end magazine.

"Okay, let's do coffee," I murmur, flushing a beet red.

He grins.

"After you, Miss Steele." He stands up straight, holding his hand out for me to go first. I make my way down the corridor, my knees shaky, my stomach full of butterflies, and my heart in my mouth thumping a dramatic, uneven beat. *I am going to have coffee with Christian Grey . . . and I hate coffee.*

We walk together down the wide hotel corridor to the elevators. *What should I say to him?* My mind is suddenly paralyzed with apprehension. What are we going to talk about? What on Earth do I have in common with him? His soft, warm voice startles me from my reverie.

"How long have you known Katherine Kavanagh?"

Oh, an easy question for starters.

"Since our freshman year. She's a good friend."

"Hmm," he replies noncommittally. What is he thinking?

At the elevators, he presses the call button, and the bell rings almost immediately. The doors slide open, revealing a young couple in a passionate embrace inside. Surprised and embarrassed, they jump apart, staring guiltily in every direction but ours. Grey and I step into the elevator.

I am struggling to maintain a straight face, so I gaze down at the floor, feeling my cheeks turning pink. When I peek up at Grey through my lashes, he has a hint of a smile on his lips, but it's very hard to tell. The young couple says nothing, and we travel down to the first floor in embarrassed silence. We don't even have bland piped elevator music to distract us.

The doors open and, much to my surprise, Grey takes my hand, clasping it with his long, cool fingers. I feel the current run through me, and my already rapid heartbeat accelerates. As he leads me out of the elevator, we can hear the suppressed giggles of the couple erupting behind us. Grey grins.

"What is it about elevators?" he mutters.

We cross the expansive, bustling lobby of the hotel toward the entrance, but Grey avoids the revolving door, and I wonder if that's because he'd have to let go of my hand.

Outside, it's a mild May Sunday. The sun is shining and the traffic is light. Grey turns left and strolls to the corner, where we wait for the crosswalk to change. He's still holding my hand. *I'm in the street, and Christian Grey is holding my hand.* No one has ever held my hand. I feel giddy, and I tingle all over. I attempt to smother the ridiculous grin that threatens to split my face in two. *Try to be cool, Ana,* my subconscious implores me. The green man appears, and we're off again.

We walk four blocks before we reach the Portland Coffee House, where Grey releases me to hold the door open so I can step inside.

"Why don't you choose a table while I get the drinks? What would you like?" he asks, polite as ever.

"I'll have . . . um—English Breakfast tea, bag out."

He raises his eyebrows.

"No coffee?"

"I'm not keen on coffee."

He smiles.

"Okay, bag out tea. Sugar?"

For a moment, I'm stunned, thinking it's an endearment, but fortunately my subconscious kicks in with pursed lips. *No, stupid—do you take sugar?*

"No thanks." I stare down at my knotted fingers.

"Anything to eat?"

"No thank you." I shake my head, and he heads to the counter.

I surreptitiously gaze at him from beneath my lashes as he stands in line waiting to be served. I could watch him all day . . . he's tall, broad shouldered, and slim, and the way those pants hang from his hips . . . *Oh my.* Once or twice he runs his long, graceful fingers through his now dry but still disorderly hair. *Hmm . . . I'd like to do that.* The thought comes unbidden into my mind, and my face flames. I bite my lip and stare down at my hands again, not liking where my wayward thoughts are headed.

"Penny for your thoughts?" Grey is back, startling me.

I go crimson. *I was just thinking about running my fingers through your hair and wondering if it would feel soft to touch.* I shake my head. He's carrying a tray, which he sets down on the small, round birch-veneer table. He hands me a cup and saucer, a small teapot, and a side plate bearing a lone teabag labeled TWININGS ENGLISH BREAKFAST—my favorite. He has a coffee that bears a wonderful leaf pattern imprinted in the milk. *How do they do that?* I wonder idly. He's also bought himself a blueberry muffin. Putting the tray aside, he sits opposite me and crosses his long legs. He looks so comfortable, so at ease with his body, I envy him. Here's me, all gawky and uncoordinated, barely able to get from A to B without falling flat on my face.

"Your thoughts?" he prompts me.

"This is my favorite tea." My voice is quiet, breathy. I simply can't believe I'm sitting opposite Christian Grey in a coffee shop in Portland. He frowns. He knows I'm hiding something. I pop the teabag into the teapot and almost immediately fish it out again with my teaspoon. As I place the used teabag back on the side plate, he cocks his head, gazing quizzically at me.

"I like my tea black and weak," I mutter as an explanation.

"I see. Is he your boyfriend?"

Whoa . . . What?

"Who?"

"The photographer. José Rodriguez."

I laugh, nervous but curious. What gave him that impression?

"No. José's a good friend of mine, that's all. Why did you think he was my boyfriend?"

"The way you smiled at him, and he at you." His gaze holds mine. He's so unnerving. I want to look away but I'm caught—spellbound.

"He's more like family," I whisper.

Grey nods, seemingly satisfied with my response, and glances down at his blueberry muffin. His long fingers deftly peel back the paper, and I watch, fascinated.

"Do you want some?" he asks, and that amused, secret smile is back.

"No thanks." I frown and stare down at my hands again.

"And the boy I met yesterday, at the store. He's not your boyfriend?"

"No. Paul's just a friend. I told you yesterday." Oh, this is getting silly. "Why do you ask?"

"You seem nervous around men."

Holy crap, that's personal. *I'm just nervous around you, Grey.*

"I find you intimidating." I flush scarlet, but mentally pat myself on the back for my candor, and gaze at my hands again. I hear his sharp intake of breath.

"You should find me intimidating." He nods. "You're very honest. Please don't look down. I like to see your face."

Oh. I glance at him, and he gives me an encouraging but wry smile.

"It gives me some sort of clue what you might be thinking," he breathes. "You're a mystery, Miss Steele."

Mysterious? Me?

"There's nothing mysterious about me."

"I think you're very self-contained," he murmurs.

Am I? *Wow . . . how am I managing that?* This is bewildering. *Me, self-contained? No way.*

"Except when you blush, of course, which is often. I just wish I knew what you were blushing about." He pops a small piece of muffin into his mouth and starts to chew it slowly, not taking his eyes off me. And as if on cue, I blush. *Crap!*

"Do you always make such personal observations?"

"I hadn't realized I was. Have I offended you?" He sounds surprised.

"No," I answer truthfully.

"Good."

"But you're very high-handed."

He raises his eyebrows and, if I'm not mistaken, flushes slightly, too.

"I'm used to getting my own way, Anastasia," he murmurs. "In all things."

"I don't doubt it. Why haven't you asked me to call you by your first name?" I'm surprised by my audacity. Why has this conversation become so serious? This isn't going the way I thought it was going to go. I can't believe I'm feeling so antagonistic toward him. It's like he's trying to warn me off.

"The only people who use my given name are my family and a few close friends. That's the way I like it."

Oh. He still hasn't said, "Call me Christian." He *is* a control freak, there's no other explanation, and part of me is thinking maybe it would have been better if Kate had interviewed him. Two control freaks together. Plus, of course, she's almost blond—well, strawberry blond—like all the women in his office. *And she's beautiful,* my subconscious reminds me. I don't like the idea of Christian and Kate. I take a sip of my tea, and Grey eats another small piece of his muffin.

"Are you an only child?" he asks.

Whoa . . . he keeps changing direction.

"Yes."

"Tell me about your parents."

Why does he want to know this? It's so *dull.*

"My mom lives in Georgia with her new husband, Bob. My stepdad lives in Montesano."

"Your father?"

"My father died when I was a baby."

"I'm sorry," he mutters, and a fleeting, troubled look crosses his face.

"I don't remember him."

"And your mother remarried?"

I snort.

"You could say that."

He frowns at me.

"You're not giving much away, are you?" he says dryly, rubbing his chin as if in deep thought.

"Neither are you."

"You've interviewed me once already, and I can recollect some quite probing questions then." He smirks at me.

Holy shit. He's remembering the "gay" question. Once again, I'm mortified. In years to come, I know I'll need intensive therapy to not feel this embarrassed every time I recall the moment. I start babbling about my mother—anything to block *that* memory.

"My mom is wonderful. She's an incurable romantic. She's currently on her fourth husband."

Christian raises his eyebrows in surprise.

"I miss her," I continue. "She has Bob now. I just hope he can keep an eye on her and pick up the pieces when her harebrained schemes don't go as planned." I smile fondly. I haven't seen my mom for so long. Christian is watching me intently, taking occasional sips of his coffee. I really shouldn't look at his mouth. It's unsettling.

"Do you get along with your stepfather?"

"Of course. I grew up with him. He's the only father I know."

"And what's he like?"

"Ray? He's . . . taciturn."

"That's it?" Grey asks, surprised.

I shrug. What does this man expect? My life story?

"Taciturn like his stepdaughter," Grey prompts.

I refrain from rolling my eyes at him.

"He likes soccer—European soccer especially—and bowling,

and fly-fishing, and making furniture. He's a carpenter. Ex-army." I sigh.

"You lived with him?"

"Yes. My mom met Husband Number Three when I was fifteen. I stayed with Ray."

He frowns as if he doesn't understand.

"You didn't want to live with your mom?" he asks.

This really is none of his business.

"Husband Number Three lived in Texas. My home was in Montesano. And . . . you know, my mom was newly married." I stop. My mom never talks about Husband Number Three. Where is Grey going with this? This *is* none of his business. *Two can play at this game.*

"Tell me about your parents," I ask.

He shrugs.

"My dad's a lawyer, my mom is a pediatrician. They live in Seattle."

Oh . . . he's had an affluent upbringing. And I wonder about a successful couple who adopts three kids, and one of them turns into a beautiful man who takes on the business world and conquers it single-handed. What drove him to be that way? His folks must be proud.

"What do your siblings do?"

"Elliot's in construction, and my little sister is in Paris, studying cookery under some renowned French chef." His eyes cloud with irritation. He doesn't want to talk about his family or himself.

"I hear Paris is lovely," I murmur. Why doesn't he want to talk about his family? Is it because he's adopted?

"It's beautiful. Have you been?" he asks, his irritation forgotten.

"I've never left mainland USA." So now we're back to banalities. What is he hiding?

"Would you like to go?"

"To Paris?" I squeak. This has thrown me—who wouldn't want to go to Paris? "Of course," I concede. "But it's England that I'd really like to visit."

He cocks his head to one side, running his index finger across his lower lip . . . *oh my.*

"Because?"

I blink rapidly. *Concentrate, Steele.*

"It's the home of Shakespeare, Austen, the Brontë sisters, Thomas Hardy. I'd like to see the places that inspired those people to write such wonderful books."

All this talk of literary greats reminds me that I should be studying. I glance at my watch. "I'd better go. I have to study."

"For your exams?"

"Yes. They start Tuesday."

"Where's Miss Kavanagh's car?"

"In the hotel parking lot."

"I'll walk you back."

"Thank you for the tea, Mr. Grey."

He smiles his odd I've-got-a-whopping-big-secret smile.

"You're welcome, Anastasia. It's my pleasure. Come," he commands, and holds his hand out to me. I take it, bemused, and follow him out of the coffee shop.

We stroll back to the hotel, and I'd like to say it's in companionable silence. He at least looks his usual calm, collected self. As for me, I'm desperately trying to gauge how our little coffee morning has gone. I feel like I've been interviewed for a job, but I'm not sure what for.

"Do you always wear jeans?" he asks out of the blue.

"Mostly."

He nods. We're back at the intersection, across the road from the hotel. My mind is reeling. *What an odd question . . .* And I'm aware that our time together is limited. This is it. This was it, and I've completely blown it, I know. Perhaps he has someone.

"Do you have a girlfriend?" I blurt out. Holy crap—*I just said that out loud?*

His lips quirk up in a half smile, and he peers down at me.

"No, Anastasia. I don't do the girlfriend thing," he says softly.

Oh . . . *what does that mean?* He's not gay. Oh, maybe he is! He must have lied to me in his interview. And for a moment, I think he's going to follow up with some explanation, some clue to this cryptic statement—but he doesn't. I have to go. I have to try to reassemble my thoughts. I have to get away from him. I walk forward, and I trip, stumbling headlong into the road.

"Shit, Ana!" Grey cries. He tugs the hand that he's holding so hard that I fall back against him just as a cyclist whips past, narrowly missing me, heading the wrong way up this one-way street.

It all happens so fast—one minute I'm falling, the next I'm in his arms and he's holding me tightly against his chest. I inhale his clean, wholesome scent. He smells of freshly laundered linen and some expensive body wash. It's intoxicating. I inhale deeply.

"Are you okay?" he whispers. He has one arm around me, clasping me to him, while the fingers of his other hand softly trace my face, gently probing, examining me. His thumb brushes my lower lip, and his breath hitches. He's staring into my eyes, and I hold his anxious, burning gaze for a moment, or maybe it's forever . . . but eventually, my attention is drawn to his beautiful mouth. And for the first time in twenty-one years, I want to be kissed. I want to feel his mouth on mine.

CHAPTER FOUR

Kiss me, damn it! I implore him, but I can't move. I'm paralyzed with a strange, unfamiliar need, completely captivated by him. I'm staring at Christian Grey's mouth, mesmerized, and he's looking down at me, his gaze hooded, his eyes darkening. He's breathing harder than usual, and I've stopped breathing altogether. *I'm in your arms. Kiss me, please.* He closes his eyes, takes a deep breath, and gives me a small shake of his head as if in answer to my silent question. When he opens his eyes again, it's with some new purpose, a steely resolve.

"Anastasia, you should steer clear of me. I'm not the man for you," he whispers. *What? Where is this coming from?* Surely I should be the judge of that. I frown, and my head swims with rejection.

"Breathe, Anastasia, breathe. I'm going to stand you up and let you go," he says quietly, and he gently pushes me away.

Adrenaline has spiked through my body, from the near miss with the cyclist or the heady proximity to Christian, leaving me wired and weak. *NO!* my psyche screams as he pulls away, leaving me bereft. He has his hands on my shoulders, holding me at arm's length, carefully watching my reactions. And the only thing I can think is that I wanted to be kissed, made it pretty damned obvious, and he didn't do it. *He doesn't want me.* He really doesn't want me. I have royally screwed up the coffee morning.

"I've got this," I breathe, finding my voice. "Thank you," I mutter, awash with humiliation. How could I have misread the situation between us so utterly? I need to get away from him.

"For what?" He frowns. He hasn't taken his hands off me.

"For saving me," I whisper.

"That idiot was riding the wrong way. I'm glad I was here. I shudder to think what could have happened to you. Do you want to come and sit down in the hotel for a moment?" He releases me, his hands by his sides, and I'm standing in front of him feeling like a fool.

With a shake, I clear my head. I just want to go. All my vague, unarticulated hopes have been dashed. He doesn't want me. *What was I thinking?* I scold myself. *What would Christian Grey want with you?* my subconscious mocks me. I wrap my arms around myself and turn to face the road and note with relief that the green man has appeared. I quickly make my way across, conscious that Grey is behind me. Outside the hotel, I turn briefly to face him but cannot look him in the eye.

"Thanks for the tea and doing the photo shoot," I murmur.

"Anastasia . . . I . . ." He stops, and the anguish in his voice demands my attention, so I peer unwillingly up at him. His gray eyes are bleak as he runs his hand through his hair. He looks torn, frustrated, his expression stark, all his careful control has evaporated.

"What, Christian?" I snap irritably after he says . . . nothing. I just want to go. I need to take my fragile, wounded pride away and somehow nurse it back to health.

"Good luck with your exams," he murmurs.

Huh? This is why he looks so desolate? This is the big send-off? Just to wish me luck in my exams?

"Thanks." I can't disguise the sarcasm in my voice. "Goodbye, Mr. Grey." I turn on my heel, vaguely amazed that I don't trip, and without giving him a second glance, I disappear down the sidewalk toward the underground garage.

Once underneath the dark, cold concrete of the garage with its bleak fluorescent light, I lean against the wall and put my head in my hands. What was I thinking? Unbidden and unwelcome tears pool in my eyes. *Why am I crying?* I sink to the ground, angry at myself for this senseless reaction. Drawing up my knees, I fold in on myself. I want to make myself as small as possible. Perhaps this nonsensical pain will be smaller the smaller I am. Placing my head on my knees, I let the irrational tears fall unrestrained. I am crying over the loss of something I never had. *How ridiculous.* Mourning something that never was—my dashed hopes, my dashed dreams, and my soured expectations.

I have never been on the receiving end of rejection. Okay . . . so I was always one of the last to be picked for basketball or volleyball, but I understood that—running and doing something else at the same time like bouncing or throwing a ball is not my thing. I am a serious liability in any sporting field.

Romantically, though, I've never put myself out there, ever. A lifetime of insecurity—I'm too pale, too skinny, too scruffy, uncoordinated, my long list of faults goes on. So I have always been the one to rebuff any would-be admirers. There was that guy in my chemistry class who liked me, but no one has ever sparked my interest—no one except Christian Damn Grey. Maybe I should be kinder to the likes of Paul Clayton and José Rodriguez, though I'm sure neither of them has been found sobbing alone in dark places. Perhaps I just need a good cry.

Stop! Stop now! my subconscious is metaphorically screaming at me, arms folded, leaning on one leg and tapping her foot in frustration. *Get in the car, go home, do your studying. Forget about him . . . Now!* And stop all this self-pitying, wallowing crap.

I take a deep, steadying breath and stand up. *Get it together, Steele.* I head for Kate's car, wiping the tears off my face as I do. I will not think of him again. I can just chalk this incident up to experience and concentrate on my exams.

KATE IS SITTING AT the dining table at her laptop when I arrive. Her welcoming smile fades when she sees me.

"Ana, what's wrong?"

Oh no . . . not the Katherine Kavanagh Inquisition. I shake my head in a back-off-now-Kavanagh way—but I might as well be dealing with a blind, deaf mute.

"You've been crying." She has an exceptional gift for stating the damned obvious sometimes. "What did that bastard do to you?" she growls, and her face—jeez, she's scary.

"Nothing, Kate." That's actually the problem. The thought brings a wry smile to my face.

"Then why have you been crying? You never cry," she says, her voice softening. She stands, her green eyes brimming with concern. She puts her arms around me and hugs me. I need to say something just to get her to back off.

"I was nearly knocked over by a cyclist." It's the best that I can do, but it distracts her momentarily from . . . him.

"Jeez, Ana—are you okay? Were you hurt?" She holds me at arm's length and does a quick visual checkup on me.

"No. Christian saved me," I whisper. "But I was quite shaken."

"I'm not surprised. How was coffee? I know you hate coffee."

"I had tea. It was fine, nothing to report really. I don't know why he asked me."

"He likes you, Ana." She drops her arms.

"Not anymore. I won't be seeing him again." Yes, I manage to sound matter-of-fact.

"Oh?"

Damn it. She's intrigued. I head into the kitchen so that she can't see my face.

"Yeah . . . he's a little out of my league, Kate," I say as dryly as I can manage.

"What do you mean?"

"Oh, Kate, it's obvious." I whirl around and face her as she stands in the kitchen doorway.

"Not to me," she says. "Okay, he's got more money than you, but then he has more money than most people in America!"

"Kate he's—" I shrug.

"Ana! For heaven's sake—how many times do I have to tell you? You're a total babe," she interrupts me. Oh no. She's off on this tirade again.

"Kate, please. I need to study." I cut her short. She frowns.

"Do you want to see the article? It's finished. José took some great pictures."

Do I need a visual reminder of the beautiful Christian I-Don't-Want-You Grey?

"Sure." I magic a smile on my face and stroll over to the laptop. And there he is, staring at me in black and white, staring at me and finding me lacking.

I pretend to read the article, all the time meeting his steady gray gaze, searching the photo for some clue as to why he's not the man for me—his own words to me. And it's suddenly blindingly obvious. He's too gloriously good-looking. We are poles apart and from two very different worlds. I have a vision of myself as Icarus flying too close to the sun and crashing and burning as a result. His words make sense. He's not the man for me. This is what he meant, and it makes his rejection easier to accept . . . almost. I can live with this. I understand.

"Very good, Kate," I manage. "I'm going to study." I am not going to think about him again for now, I vow to myself, and opening my course notes, I start to read.

IT'S ONLY WHEN I'M in bed, trying to sleep, that I allow my thoughts to drift through my strange morning. I keep coming back to the *I don't do the girlfriend thing* quote, and I'm angry that I didn't pounce on this information sooner, before I was in his arms mentally begging him with every fiber of my being to kiss me. He'd said it there and then. He didn't want me as a girlfriend. I turn onto my side. Idly, I wonder if perhaps he's celibate. I close my eyes and begin to drift. Maybe he's saving himself. *Well, not for you.* My sleepy subconscious has a final swipe at me before unleashing itself on my dreams.

And that night, I dream of gray eyes and leafy patterns in milk, and I'm running through dark places with eerie strip lighting, and I don't know if I'm running toward something or away from it . . . it's just not clear.

I put my pen down. Finished. My final exam is over. A Cheshire cat grin spreads over my face. It's probably the first time all week that I've smiled. It's Friday, and we shall be celebrating tonight, really celebrating. I might even get drunk! I've never been drunk before. I glance across the hall at Kate, and she's still scribbling furiously, five minutes to the finish. This is it, the end of my academic career. I shall never have to sit in rows of anxious, isolated students again. Inside I'm doing graceful cartwheels around my head, knowing full well that's the only place I can do graceful cartwheels. Kate stops writing and puts her pen down. She glances across at me, and I catch her Cheshire cat smile, too.

We head back to our apartment together in her Mercedes, refusing to discuss our final paper. Kate is more concerned about what she's going to wear to the bar this evening. I am busily fishing around in my purse for my keys.

"Ana, there's a package for you." Kate is standing on the steps up to the front door holding a brown paper parcel. *Odd.* I haven't ordered anything from Amazon recently. Kate gives me the parcel and takes my keys to open the front door. It's addressed to Miss Anastasia Steele. There's no sender's address or name. Perhaps it's from my mom or Ray.

"It's probably from my folks."

"Open it!" Kate is excited as she heads into the kitchen for our exams-are-finished-hurrah champagne.

I open the parcel, and inside I find a half leather box containing three seemingly identical old cloth-covered books in mint condition and a plain white card. Written on one side, in black ink in neat cursive handwriting, is:

> *Why didn't you tell me there was danger? Why didn't you warn me?*
> *Ladies know what to guard against, because they read novels that tell them of these tricks . . .*

I recognize the quote from *Tess.* I am stunned by the coincidence as I've just spent three hours writing about the novels of Thomas Hardy in my final examination. Perhaps there is no coincidence . . . perhaps it's deliberate. I inspect the books closely, three volumes of *Tess of the d'Urbervilles*. I open the front cover of one of the books. Written in an old typeface on the front plate is:

London: Jack R. Osgood, McIlvaine and Co., 1891.

Holy shit—they are first editions. They must be worth a fortune, and I know immediately who's sent them. Kate is at my shoulder gazing at the books. She picks up the card.

"First editions," I whisper.

"No." Kate's eyes are wide with disbelief. "Grey?"

I nod. "Can't think of anyone else."

"What does this card mean?"

"I have no idea. I think it's a warning—honestly, he keeps warning me off. I have no idea why. It's not like I'm beating his door down." I frown.

"I know you don't want to talk about him, Ana, but he's seriously into you. Warnings or no."

I have not let myself dwell on Christian Grey for the past week. Okay . . . so his gray eyes are still haunting my dreams, and I know it will take an eternity to expunge the feel of his arms around me and his wonderful fragrance from my brain. Why has he sent me this? He told me that I wasn't for him.

"I've found one *Tess* first edition for sale in New York for fourteen thousand dollars. But yours look in much better condition. They must have cost more." Kate is consulting her good friend Google.

"This quote—Tess says it to her mother after Alec d'Urberville has had his wicked way with her."

"I know," muses Kate. "What is he trying to say?"

"I don't know, and I don't care. I can't accept these from him. I'll send them back with an equally baffling quote from some obscure part of the book."

"The bit where Angel Clare says fuck off?" Kate asks with a completely straight face.

"Yes, that bit." I giggle. I love Kate; she's loyal and supportive. I repack the books and leave them on the dining table. Kate hands me a glass of champagne.

"To the end of exams and our new life in Seattle." She grins.

"To the end of exams, our new life in Seattle, and excellent results." We clink glasses and drink.

THE BAR IS LOUD and hectic, full of soon-to-be graduates out to get trashed. José joins us. He won't graduate for another year, but he's in the mood to party and gets us into the spirit of our newfound freedom by buying a pitcher of margaritas for us all. As I down my fifth glass, I know this is not a good idea on top of the champagne.

"So what now, Ana?" José shouts at me over the noise.

"Kate and I are moving to Seattle. Kate's parents have bought a condo there for her."

"*Dios mío,* how the other half live. But you'll be back for my show?"

"Of course, José, I wouldn't miss it for the world." I smile, and he puts his arm around my waist and pulls me close.

"It means a lot to me that you'll be there, Ana," he whispers in my ear. "Another margarita?"

"José Luis Rodriguez—are you trying to get me drunk? Because I think it's working." I giggle. "I think I'd better have a beer. I'll go get us a pitcher."

"More drink, Ana!" Kate bellows.

Kate has the constitution of an ox. She's got her arm draped over Levi, one of our fellow English students and her usual photographer on the student newspaper. He's given up taking photos of the drunkenness that surrounds him. He only has eyes for Kate. She's all tiny camisole, tight jeans, and high heels, hair piled high with tendrils hanging down softly around her face, her usual stunning self. Me, I'm more of a Converse and T-shirt kind of girl, but I'm wearing my most flattering jeans. I move out of José's hold and get up from our table.

Whoa. Head spin.

I have to grab the back of the chair. Tequila-based cocktails are not a good idea.

I make my way to the bar and decide that I should visit the bathroom while I am on my feet. *Good thinking, Ana.* I stagger off through the crowd. Of course, there's a line, but at least it's quiet and cool in the corridor. I reach for my cell phone to relieve the boredom of waiting. *Hmm . . . Who did I last call?* Was it José? Before that, a number I don't recognize. Oh yes. Grey, I think this is his number. I giggle. I have no idea what the time is; maybe I'll wake him. Perhaps he can tell me why he sent me those books and the cryptic message. If he wants me to stay away, he should leave me alone. I suppress a drunken grin and hit the "call" button. He answers on the second ring.

"Anastasia?" He's surprised to hear from me. Well, frankly, I'm surprised to be calling him. Then my befuddled brain registers . . . how does he know it's me?

"Why did you send me the books?" I slur at him.

"Anastasia, are you okay? You sound strange." His voice is filled with concern.

"I'm not the strange one, you are." There—that told him, my courage fuelled by alcohol.

"Anastasia, have you been drinking?"

"What's it to you?"

"I'm . . . curious. Where are you?"

"In a bar."

"Which bar?" He sounds exasperated.

"A bar in Portland."

"How are you getting home?"

"I'll find a way." This conversation is not going how I expected.

"Which bar are you in?"

"Why did you send me the books, Christian?"

"Anastasia, where are you? Tell me now." His tone is so . . . so dictatorial, his usual control freak. I imagine him as an old-time movie director wearing jodhpurs, holding an old-fashioned megaphone and a riding crop. The image makes me laugh out loud.

"You're so . . . domineering." I giggle.

"Ana, so help me, where the fuck are you?"

Christian Grey is swearing at me. I giggle again. "I'm in Portland . . .'s a long way from Seattle."

"Where in Portland?"

"Good night, Christian."

"Ana!"

I hang up. Ha! Though he didn't tell me about the books. I frown. Mission not accomplished. I am really quite drunk—my head swims uncomfortably as I shuffle with the line. Well, the object of the exercise was to get drunk. I have succeeded. This is what it's like—*probably not an experience to be repeated.* The line has moved, and it's now my turn. I stare blankly at the poster on the back of the toilet door that extols the virtues of safe sex. Holy crap, did I just call Christian Grey? Shit. My phone rings and it makes me jump. I yelp in surprise.

"Hi," I bleat timidly in to the phone. I hadn't reckoned on this.

"I'm coming to get you," he says, and hangs up. Only Christian Grey could sound so calm and so threatening at the same time.

Holy crap. I pull my jeans up. My heart is thumping. Coming to get me? *Oh no.* I'm going to be sick . . . no . . . I'm fine. Hang on. He's just messing with my head. I didn't tell him where I was. He can't find me here. Besides, it will take him hours to get here from Seattle, and we'll be long gone by then. I wash my hands and check my face in the mirror. I look flushed and slightly unfocused. *Hmm . . . tequila.*

I wait at the bar for what feels like an eternity for the pitcher of beer and eventually return to the table.

"You've been gone so long," Kate scolds me. "Where were you?"

"I was in line for the restroom."

José and Levi are having some heated debate about our local baseball team. José pauses in his tirade to pour us all beers, and I take a long sip.

"Kate, I think I'd better step outside and get some fresh air."

"Ana, you are such a lightweight."

"I'll be five minutes."

I make my way through the crowd again. I am beginning to feel nauseated, my head is spinning uncomfortably, and I'm a little unsteady on my feet. More unsteady than usual.

Drinking in the cool evening air in the parking lot makes me realize how drunk I am. My vision has been affected, and I'm really seeing double of everything like in old reruns of *Tom and Jerry* cartoons. I think I'm going to be sick. Why did I let myself get this messed up?

"Ana," José has joined me. "You okay?"

"I think I've just had a bit too much to drink." I smile weakly at him.

"Me, too," he murmurs, and his dark eyes are regarding me intently. "Do you need a hand?" he asks and steps closer, putting his arm around me.

"José, I'm okay. I've got this." I try to push him away rather feebly.

"Ana, please," he whispers, and now he's holding me in his arms, pulling me close.

"José, what are you doing?"

"You know I like you Ana, please." He has one hand at the small of my back holding me against him, the other at my chin tipping back my head. *Holy fuck . . . he's going to kiss me.*

"No, José, stop—no." I push him, but he's a wall of hard muscle, and I cannot shift him. His hand has slipped into my hair, and he's holding my head in place.

"Please, Ana, *cariño,*" he whispers against my lips. His breath is soft and smells too sweet—of margarita and beer. He gently trails kisses along my jaw up to the side of my mouth. I feel panicky, drunk, and out of control. The feeling is suffocating.

"José, no," I plead. *I don't want this.* You are my friend, and I think I'm going to throw up.

"I think the lady said no," a voice in the dark says quietly. Holy shit! Christian Grey, he's here. How? José releases me.

"Grey," he says tersely. I glance anxiously up at Christian. He's glowering at José, and he's furious. Crap. My stomach heaves, and I double over, my body no longer able to tolerate the alcohol, and I vomit spectacularly on to the ground.

"Ugh—*Dios mío*, Ana!" José jumps back in disgust. Grey grabs my hair and pulls it out of the firing line and gently leads me over to a raised flowerbed on the edge of the parking lot. I note, with deep gratitude, that it's in relative darkness.

"If you're going to throw up again, do it here. I'll hold you." He has one arm around my shoulders—the other is holding my hair in a makeshift ponytail down my back so it's off my face. I try awkwardly to push him away, but I vomit again . . . and again. *Oh, shit . . . how long is this going to last?* Even when my stomach's empty and nothing is coming up, horrible dry heaves rack my body. I vow silently that I'll never ever drink again. This is just too appalling for words. Finally, it stops.

My hands are resting on the brick wall of the flowerbed, barely holding me up. Vomiting profusely is exhausting. Grey takes his hands off me and passes me a handkerchief. Only he would have a monogrammed, freshly laundered linen handkerchief. *CTG*. I didn't know you could still buy these. Vaguely I wonder what the *T* stands for as I wipe my mouth. I cannot bring myself to look at him. I'm swamped with shame, disgusted with myself. I want to be swallowed up by the azaleas in the flowerbed and be anywhere but here.

José is still hovering by the entrance to the bar, watching us. I groan and put my head in my hands. This has to be the single worst moment of my life. My head is still swimming as I try to remember a worse one—and I can only come up with Christian's rejection—and this is so, so many shades darker in terms of humiliation. I risk a peek at him. He's staring down at me, his face composed, giving nothing away. Turning, I glance at José, who looks pretty shamefaced himself and, like me, intimidated by Grey. I glare at him. I have a few choice words for my so-called friend, none of which I can repeat in front of Christian Grey, CEO. *Ana, who are you kidding? He's just seen you hurl all over the ground and into the local flora. There's no disguising your lack of ladylike behavior.*

"I'll, er . . . see you inside," José mutters, but we both ignore him, and he slinks off back into the building. I'm on my own with Grey. Double crap. What should I say to him? Apologize for the phone call.

"I'm sorry," I mutter, staring at the handkerchief, which I am furiously worrying with my fingers. *It's so soft.*

"What are you sorry for, Anastasia?"

Damn it, he wants his damned pound of flesh.

"The phone call, mainly. Being sick. Oh, the list is endless," I murmur, feeling my skin coloring up. *Please, please, can I die now?*

"We've all been here, perhaps not quite as dramatically as you," he says dryly. "It's about knowing your limits, Anastasia. I mean, I'm all for pushing limits, but really this is beyond the pale. Do you make a habit of this kind of behavior?"

My head buzzes with excess alcohol and irritation. What the hell has it got to do with him? I didn't invite him here. He sounds like a middle-aged man scolding me like an errant child. Part of me wants to say that if I want to get drunk every night like this, then it's my decision and nothing to do with him—but I'm not brave enough. Not now that I've thrown up in front of him. Why is he still standing there?

"No," I say contritely. "I've never been drunk before and right now I have no desire to ever be again."

I just don't understand why he's here. I begin to feel faint. He notices my dizziness and grabs me before I fall and hoists me into his arms, holding me close to his chest like a child.

"Come on, I'll take you home," he murmurs.

"I need to tell Kate." *I'm in his arms again.*

"My brother can tell her."

"What?"

"My brother Elliot is talking to Miss Kavanagh."

"Oh?" I don't understand.

"He was with me when you phoned."

"In Seattle?" I'm confused.

"No, I'm staying at the Heathman."

Still? Why?

"How did you find me?"

"I tracked your cell phone, Anastasia."

Oh, of course he did. How is that possible? Is it legal? *Stalker,* my subconscious whispers at me through the cloud of tequila that's still floating in my brain, but somehow, because it's him, I don't mind.

"Do you have a jacket or a purse?"

"Er . . . yes, I came with both. Christian, please, I need to tell Kate. She'll worry." His mouth presses into a hard line, and he sighs heavily.

"If you must."

He sets me down and, taking my hand, leads me back into the bar. I feel weak, still drunk, embarrassed, exhausted, mortified, and, on some strange level, absolutely off-the-charts thrilled. He's clutching my hand—such a confusing array of emotions. I'll need at least a week to process them all.

It's noisy, crowded, and the music has started so there is a large crowd on the dance floor. Kate is not at our table, and José has disappeared. Levi looks lost and forlorn on his own.

"Where's Kate?" I shout at Levi above the noise. My head is beginning to pound in time to the thumping bass line of the music.

"Dancing," Levi shouts, and I can tell he's mad. He's eyeing Christian suspiciously. I struggle into my black jacket and place my small shoulder bag over my head so it sits at my hip. I'm ready to go, once I've seen Kate.

I touch Christian's arm and lean up and shout in his ear, "She's on the dance floor," brushing his hair with my nose, smelling his clean, fresh smell. All those forbidden, unfamiliar feelings that I have tried to deny surface and run amok through my drained body. I flush, and somewhere deep, deep down my muscles clench deliciously.

He rolls his eyes at me and takes my hand again and leads me to the bar. He's served immediately, no waiting for Mr. Control Freak Grey. Does everything come so easily to him? I can't hear what he orders. He hands me a very large glass of iced water.

"Drink." He shouts his order at me.

The moving lights are twisting and turning in time to the music, casting strange colored light and shadows all over the bar and the clientele. He's alternately green, blue, white, and a demonic red. He's watching me intently. I take a tentative sip.

"All of it," he shouts.

He's so overbearing. He runs his hand through his unruly hair. He looks frustrated, angry. What is his problem? Apart from a silly drunk girl calling him in the middle of the night so he thinks she needs rescuing. And it turns out she does from her over-amorous friend. Then seeing her being violently ill at his feet. *Oh, Ana . . . are you ever going to live this down?* My subconscious is figuratively tutting and glaring at me over her half-moon specs. I sway a little, and he puts his hand on my shoulder to steady me. I do as I'm told and drink the entire glass. It makes me feel queasy. Taking the glass from me, he places it on the bar. I notice through a blur what he's wearing: a loose white linen shirt, snug jeans, black Converse sneakers, and a dark pinstriped jacket. His shirt is unbuttoned at the top, and I see a sprinkling of hair in the gap. In my groggy frame of mind, he looks yummy.

He takes my hand once more. *Holy cow*—he's leading me onto the dance floor. Shit. I do not dance. He can sense my reluctance, and under the colored lights I see his amused, sardonic smile. He gives my hand a sharp tug, and I'm in his arms again, and he starts to move, taking me with him. Boy, he can dance, and I can't believe that I'm following him step for step. Maybe it's because I'm drunk that I can keep up. He's holding me tight against him, his body against mine . . . if he wasn't clutching me so tightly, I'm sure I would swoon at his feet. In the back of my mind, my mother's often-recited warning comes to me: *Never trust a man who can dance.*

He moves us through the crowded throng of dancers to the other side of the dance floor, and we are beside Kate and Elliot, Christian's brother. The music is pounding away, loud and leery, outside and inside my head. Oh no. *Kate is making her moves.* She's dancing her ass off, and she only ever does that if she likes someone. Really likes someone. It means there'll be three of us for breakfast tomorrow morning. *Kate!*

Christian leans over and shouts in Elliot's ear. I cannot hear what he says. Elliot is tall with wide shoulders, curly blond hair, and light, wickedly gleaming eyes. I can't tell their color under the pulsating heat of the flashing lights. Elliot grins and pulls Kate into his arms, where she is more than happy to be . . . *Kate!* Even in my inebriated state, I am shocked. She's only just met him. She nods at whatever Elliot says and grins at me and waves. Christian propels us off the dance floor in double time.

But I never got to talk to her. Is she okay? I can see where things are heading for her and him. *I need to do the safe-sex lecture.* In the back of my mind, I hope she reads one of the posters on the inside of the bathroom door. My thoughts crash through my brain, fighting the drunk, fuzzy feeling. It's so warm in here, so loud, so colorful—too bright. My head begins to swim, oh no . . . and I can feel the floor coming up to meet my face, or so it feels. The last thing I hear before I pass out in Christian Grey's arms is his harsh epithet.

"Fuck!"

CHAPTER FIVE

It's very quiet. The light is muted. I am comfortable and warm, in this bed. *Hmm* . . . I open my eyes, and for a moment I'm tranquil and serene, enjoying the strange, unfamiliar surroundings. I have no idea where I am. The headboard behind me is in the shape of a massive sun. It's oddly familiar. The room is large and airy and plushly furnished in browns and golds and beiges. I have seen it before. Where? My befuddled brain struggles through its recent visual memories. Holy crap. I'm in the Heathman Hotel . . . in a suite. I have stood in a room similar to this with Kate. This looks bigger. Oh, shit. I'm in Christian Grey's suite. How did I get here?

Fractured memories of the previous night come slowly back to haunt me. The drinking—*oh no, the drinking*—the phone call—*oh no, the phone call*—the vomiting—*oh no, the vomiting.* José and then Christian. *Oh no.* I cringe inwardly. I don't remember coming here. I'm wearing my T-shirt, bra, and panties. No socks. No jeans. *Holy shit.*

I glance at the bedside table. On it is a glass of orange juice and two tablets. Advil. Control freak that he is, he thinks of everything. I sit up and take the tablets. Actually, I don't feel that bad, probably much better than I deserve. The orange juice tastes divine. It's thirst-quenching and refreshing.

There's a knock on the door. My heart leaps into my mouth, and I can't seem to find my voice. He opens the door anyway and strolls in.

Holy hell, he's been working out. He's in gray sweatpants that hang, in that way, off his hips and a gray sleeveless T-shirt which is dark with sweat, like his hair. *Christian Grey's sweat; the notion does odd things to me.* I take a deep breath and close my eyes. I feel like a two-year-old; if I close my eyes, then I'm not really here.

"Good morning, Anastasia. How are you feeling?"

"Better than I deserve," I mumble.

I peek up at him. He places a large shopping bag on a chair and grasps each end of the towel that he has around his neck. He's staring at me, gray eyes dark, and as usual, I have no idea what he's thinking. He hides his thoughts and feelings so well.

"How did I get here?" My voice is small, contrite.

He sits down on the edge of the bed. He's close enough for me to touch, for me to smell. Oh my . . . sweat and body wash and Christian. It's a heady cocktail—so much better than a margarita, and now I can speak from experience.

"After you passed out, I didn't want to risk the leather upholstery in my car taking you all the way to your apartment. So I brought you here," he says phlegmatically.

"Did you put me to bed?"

"Yes." His face is impassive.

"Did I throw up again?" My voice is quieter.

"No."

"Did you undress me?" I whisper.

"Yes." He quirks an eyebrow at me as I blush furiously.

"We didn't—?" I whisper, my mouth drying in mortified horror as I can't complete the question. I stare at my hands.

"Anastasia, you were comatose. Necrophilia is not my thing. I like my women sentient and receptive," he says dryly.

"I'm so sorry."

His mouth lifts slightly in a wry smile.

"It was a very diverting evening. Not one that I'll forget in a while."

Me, neither—oh, he's laughing at me, the bastard. I didn't ask him to come and get me. Somehow I've been made to feel like the villain of the piece.

"You didn't have to track me down with whatever James Bond gadgetry you're developing for the highest bidder," I snap. He stares at me, surprised and, if I'm not mistaken, a little wounded.

"First, the technology to track cell phones is available over the Internet. Second, my company does not invest or manufacture any kind of surveillance devices. And third, if I hadn't come to get you, you'd probably be waking up in the photographer's bed, and from what I can remember, you weren't overly enthused about him pressing his suit," he says acidly.

Pressing his suit! I glance up at Christian. He's glaring at me, eyes blazing, aggrieved. I try to bite my lip, but I fail to repress my giggle.

"Which medieval chronicle did you escape from? You sound like a courtly knight."

His mood visibly shifts. His eyes soften and his expression warms, and there's a trace of a smile on his lips.

"Anastasia, I don't think so. Dark knight, maybe." His smile is sardonic, and he shakes his head. "Did you eat last night?" His tone is accusatory. I shake my head. What major transgression have I committed now? His jaw clenches, but his face remains impassive.

"You need to eat. That's why you were so ill. Honestly, it's drinking rule number one." He runs this hand through his hair, and I know it's because he's exasperated.

"Are you going to continue to scold me?"

"Is that what I'm doing?"

"I think so."

"You're lucky I'm just scolding you."

"What do you mean?"

"Well, if you were mine, you wouldn't be able to sit down for a week after the stunt you pulled yesterday. You didn't eat, you got drunk, you put yourself at risk." He closes his eyes, dread etched briefly on his face, and he shudders. When he opens his eyes, he glares at me. "I hate to think what could have happened to you."

I scowl back at him. What is his problem? What's it to him? If I was his . . . *Well, I'm not.* Though maybe part of me would like to be. The thought pierces through the irritation I feel at his high-handed words. I flush at the waywardness of my subconscious—she's doing her happy dance in a bright red hula skirt at the thought of being his.

"I would have been fine. I was with Kate."

"And the photographer?" he snaps at me.

Hmm . . . young José. I'll need to face him at some point.

"José just got out of line." I shrug.

"Well, the next time he gets out of line, maybe someone should teach him some manners."

"You are quite the disciplinarian," I hiss.

"Oh, Anastasia, you have no idea." His eyes narrow, and then he grins wickedly. It's disarming. One minute, I'm confused and angry, the next, I'm gazing at his gorgeous smile. *Wow . . .* I am entranced, and it's because his smile is so rare. I quite forget what he's talking about.

"I'm going to have a shower. Unless you'd like to shower first?" He cocks his head to one side, still grinning. My heartbeat has picked up, and my medulla oblongata has neglected to fire any synapses to make me breathe. His grin widens, and he reaches over and runs his thumb down my cheek and across my lower lip.

"Breathe, Anastasia," he whispers then stands back up. "Breakfast will be here in fifteen minutes. You must be famished." He heads into the bathroom and closes the door.

I let out the breath that I've been holding. Why is he so damned attractive? Right now I want to go and join him in the shower. I have never felt this way about anyone. My hormones are racing. My skin tingles where his thumb traced over my face and lower lip. I'm squirming with a needy, achy . . . discomfort. I don't understand this reaction. *Hmm . . . Desire.* This is desire. This is what it feels like.

I lie back on the soft feather-filled pillows. *If you were mine.* Oh my—what would I do to be his? He's the only man who has ever set the blood racing through my body. Yet he's so antagonizing, too; he's difficult, complicated, and confusing. One minute he rebuffs me, the next he sends me fourteen-thousand-dollar books, then he tracks me like a stalker. And for all that, I have spent the night in his hotel suite, and I feel safe. Protected. He cares enough to come and rescue me from some mistakenly perceived danger.

He's not a dark knight at all but a white knight in shining, dazzling armor—a classic romantic hero—Sir Gawain or Sir Lancelot.

I scramble out of his bed frantically searching for my jeans. He emerges from the bathroom wet and glistening from the shower, still unshaven, with just a towel around his waist, and there am I—all bare legs and awkward gawkiness. He's surprised to see me out of bed.

"If you're looking for your jeans, I've sent them to the laundry." His gaze is dark. "They were spattered with your vomit."

"Oh." I flush scarlet. Why oh why does he always catch me off balance?

"I sent Taylor out for another pair and some shoes. They're in the bag on the chair."

Clean clothes. What an unexpected bonus.

"Um . . . I'll have a shower," I mutter. "Thanks." What else can I say? I grab the bag and dart into the bathroom away from the unnerving proximity of naked Christian. Michelangelo's *David* has nothing on him.

In the bathroom, it's all hot and steamy. I strip off my clothes and quickly clamber into the shower, anxious to be under the cleansing stream of water. It cascades over me, and I hold up my face into the welcoming torrent. I want Christian Grey. I want him badly. Simple fact. For the first time in my life, I want to go to bed with a man. I want to feel his hands and his mouth on me.

He said he likes his women sentient. *He's probably not celibate then.* But he's not made a pass at me, unlike Paul or José. I don't understand. Does he want me? He wouldn't kiss me last week. Am I repellent to him? And yet I'm here and he brought me here. I just don't know what his game is. What's he thinking? *You've slept in his bed all night, and he's not touched you, Ana. You do the math.* My subconscious has reared her ugly, snide head. I ignore her.

The water is warm and soothing. *Hmm . . .* I could stay under this shower, in his bathroom, forever. I reach for the body wash and it smells of him. It's a delicious smell. I rub it all over myself, fantasizing that it's him—him rubbing this heavenly scented soap into my body, across my breasts, over my stomach, between my thighs with his long-fingered hands. *Oh my.* My heartbeat picks up again. This feels so . . . so good.

"Breakfast is here." He knocks on the door, startling me.

"O-okay," I stutter as I'm yanked cruelly out of my erotic daydream.

I climb out of the shower and grab two towels. I put my hair in one and wrap it Carmen Miranda style on my head. Hastily, I dry myself, ignoring the pleasurable feel of the towel rubbing against my oversensitized skin.

I inspect the bag of jeans. Not only has Taylor brought me jeans and new Converse,. but also a pale blue shirt, socks, and underwear. Oh my. A clean bra and panties—actually, to describe them in such a mundane, utilitarian way does not do them justice. They are exquisitely designed fancy European lingerie. All pale blue lace and finery. Wow. I am in awe and slightly daunted by this underwear. What's more, they fit perfectly. But of course they do. I flush to think of Buzz Cut in some lingerie store buying this for me. I wonder what else is in his job description.

I dress quickly. The rest of the clothing is a perfect fit. I brusquely towel-dry my hair and try desperately to bring it under control. But, as usual, it refuses to cooperate, and my only option is to restrain it with a hair tie which I don't have. I should have one in my purse, wherever it is. I take a deep breath. Time to face Mr. Confusing.

I'm relieved to find the bedroom empty. I hunt quickly for my purse—but it's not in here. Taking another deep breath, I enter the living area of the suite. It's huge. There's an opulent, plush seating area, all overstuffed couches and soft cushions, an elaborate coffee table with a stack of large glossy books, a study area with the latest-generation iMac, and an enormous plasma screen TV on the wall. Christian is sitting at a dining table on the other side of the room reading a newspaper. It's the size of a tennis court or something, not that I play tennis, though I have watched Kate a few times. *Kate!*

"Crap, Kate," I croak. Christian peers up at me.

"She knows you're here and still alive. I texted Elliot," he says with just a trace of humor.

Oh no. I remember her fervent dancing of the night before. All her patented moves used with maximum effect to seduce Christian's brother, no less! What's she going to think about me being here? I've never stayed out before. She's still with Elliot. She's only done this twice before, and both times I've had to endure the hideous pink PJs for a week from the fallout. She's going to think I've had a one-night stand, too.

Christian stares at me imperiously. He's wearing a white linen shirt, collar and cuffs undone.

"Sit," he commands, pointing to a place at the table. I make my way across the room and sit down opposite him as I've been directed. The table is laden with food.

"I didn't know what you liked, so I ordered a selection from the breakfast menu." He gives me a crooked, apologetic smile.

"That's very profligate of you," I murmur, bewildered by the choice, though I am hungry.

"Yes, it is." He sounds guilty.

I opt for pancakes, maple syrup, scrambled eggs, and bacon. Christian tries to hide a smile as he returns to his egg white omelet. The food is delicious.

"Tea?" he asks.

"Yes, please."

He passes me a small teapot of hot water and on the saucer is a Twinings English Breakfast teabag. Jeez, he remembers how I like my tea.

"Your hair's very damp," he scolds.

"I couldn't find the hair dryer," I mutter, embarrassed. Not that I looked.

Christian's mouth presses into a hard line, but he doesn't say anything.

"Thank you for the clothes."

"It's a pleasure, Anastasia. That color suits you."

I blush and stare down at my fingers.

"You know, you really should learn to take a compliment." His tone is castigating.

"I should give you some money for these clothes."

He glares at me as if I have offended him on some level. I hurry on.

"You've already given me the books, which, of course, I can't accept. But these clothes . . . please let me pay you back." I smile tentatively at him.

"Anastasia, trust me, I can afford it."

"That's not the point. Why should you buy these for me?"

"Because I can." His eyes flash with a wicked gleam.

"Just because you can doesn't mean that you should," I reply quietly as he arches an eyebrow at me, his eyes twinkling, and suddenly I feel that we're talking about something else, but I don't know what it is. Which reminds me . . .

"Why did you send me the books, Christian?" My voice is soft. He puts down his cutlery and regards me intently, his eyes burning with some unfathomable emotion. Holy crap—my mouth dries.

"Well, when you were nearly run over by the cyclist—and I was holding you and you were looking up at me—all 'kiss me, kiss me, Christian' "—he pauses and shrugs—"I felt I owed you an apology and a warning." He runs his hand through his hair. "Anastasia, I'm not a hearts and flowers kind of man . . . I don't do romance. My tastes are very singular. You should steer clear of me." He closes his eyes as if in defeat. "There's something about you, though, and I'm finding it impossible to stay away. But I think you've figured that out already."

My appetite vanishes. *He can't stay away!*

"Then don't," I whisper.

He gasps, his eyes wide. "You don't know what you're saying."

"Enlighten me, then."

We sit gazing at each other, neither of us touching our food.

"You're not celibate, then?" I breathe.

Amusement lights up his eyes.

"No, Anastasia, I'm not celibate." He pauses for this information to sink in, and I flush scarlet. The mouth-to-brain filter is broken again. I can't believe I've just said that out loud.

"What are your plans for the next few days?" he asks, his voice low.

"I'm working today, from midday. What time is it?" I panic suddenly.

"It's just after ten; you've plenty of time. What about tomorrow?" He has his elbows on the table, and his chin is resting on his long, steepled fingers.

"Kate and I are going to start packing. We're moving to Seattle next weekend, and I'm working at Clayton's all this week."

"You have a place in Seattle already?"

"Yes."

"Where?"

"I can't remember the address. It's in the Pike Market District."

"Not far from me." He smiles. "So what are you going to do for work in Seattle?"

Where is he going with all these questions? The Christian Grey Inquisition is almost as irritating as the Katherine Kavanagh Inquisition.

"I've applied for some internships. I'm waiting to hear."

"Have you applied to my company as I suggested?"

I flush . . . *Of course not.* "Um . . . no."

"And what's wrong with my company?"

"Your company or your *company*?" I smirk.

"Are you smirking at me, Miss Steele?" He tilts his head to one side, and I think he looks amused, but it's hard to tell. I flush and glance down at my unfinished breakfast. I can't look him in the eye when he uses that tone of voice.

"I'd like to bite that lip," he whispers darkly.

I gasp, completely unaware that I am chewing my bottom lip and my mouth pops open. That has to be the sexiest thing anybody has ever said to me. My heartbeat spikes, and I think I'm panting. Jeez, I'm a quivering, mess, and he hasn't even touched me. I squirm in my seat and meet his dark glare.

"Why don't you?" I challenge quietly.

"Because I'm not going to touch you, Anastasia—not until I have your written consent to do so." His lips hint at a smile.

What?

"What does that mean?"

"Exactly what I say." He sighs and shakes his head at me, amused but exasperated, too. "I need to show you, Anastasia. What time do you finish work this evening?"

"About eight."

"Well, we could go to Seattle this evening or next Saturday for dinner at my place, and I'll acquaint you with the facts then. The choice is yours."

"Why can't you tell me now?"

"Because I'm enjoying my breakfast and your company. Once you're enlightened, you probably won't want to see me again."

What does that mean? Does he white-slave small children to some godforsaken part of the planet? Is he part of some underworld crime syndicate? It would explain why he's so rich. Is he deeply religious? Is he impotent? Surely not—he could prove that to me right now. I flush scarlet thinking about the possibilities. This is getting me nowhere. I'd like to solve the riddle that is Christian Grey sooner rather than later. If it means that whatever secret he has is so gross that I don't want to know him anymore, then, quite frankly, it will be a relief. *Don't lie to yourself*—my subconscious yells at me—*it'll have to be pretty damned bad to have you running for the hills.*

"Tonight."

He raises an eyebrow.

"Like Eve, you're so quick to eat from the tree of knowledge." He smirks.

"Are you smirking at me, Mr. Grey?" I ask sweetly. *Pompous ass.*

He narrows his eyes at me and picks up his BlackBerry. He presses one number.

"Taylor. I'm going to need *Charlie Tango.*"

Charlie Tango! Who's he?

"From Portland at, say, twenty thirty . . . No, standby at Escala . . . All night."

All night!

"Yes. On call tomorrow morning. I'll pilot from Portland to Seattle."

Pilot?

"Standby pilot from twenty-two thirty." He puts the phone down. No please or thank you.

"Do people always do what you tell them?"

"Usually, if they want to keep their jobs," he says, deadpan.

"And if they don't work for you?"

"Oh, I can be very persuasive, Anastasia. You should finish your breakfast. And then I'll drop you off at home. I'll pick you up at Clayton's at eight when you finish. We'll fly up to Seattle."

I blink at him rapidly.

"Fly?"

"Yes. I have a helicopter."

I gape at him. I have my second date with Christian Oh-So-Mysterious Grey. From coffee to helicopter rides. Wow.

"We'll go by helicopter to Seattle?"

"Yes."

"Why?"

He grins wickedly. "Because I can. Finish your breakfast."

How can I eat now? I'm going to Seattle by helicopter with Christian Grey. And he wants to bite my lip . . . I squirm at the thought.

"Eat," he says more sharply. "Anastasia, I have an issue with wasted food . . . eat."

"I can't eat all this." I gape at what's left on the table.

"Eat what's on your plate. If you'd eaten properly yesterday, you wouldn't be here, and I wouldn't be declaring my hand so soon." His mouth sets in a grim line. He looks angry.

I frown and return to my now cold food. *I'm too excited to eat, Christian. Don't you understand?* my subconscious explains. But

I'm too much of a coward to voice these thoughts aloud, especially when he looks so sullen. *Hmm*, like a small boy. I find the thought amusing.

"What's so funny?" he asks. I shake my head, not daring tell him, and keep my eyes on my food. Swallowing my last piece of pancake, I peek up at him. He's eyeing me speculatively.

"Good girl," he says. "I'll take you home when you've dried your hair. I don't want you getting ill." There's some kind of unspoken promise in his words. *What does he mean?* I leave the table, wondering for a moment if I should ask permission but dismissing the idea. Sounds like a dangerous precedent to set. I head back to his bedroom. A thought stops me.

"Where did you sleep last night?" I turn to gaze at him still sitting in the dining room chair. I can't see any blankets or sheets out here—perhaps he's had them tidied away.

"In my bed," he says simply, his gaze impassive again.

"Oh."

"Yes, it was quite a novelty for me, too." He smiles.

"Not having . . . sex." There—I said the word. I blush—of course.

"No." He shakes his head and frowns as if recalling something uncomfortable. "Sleeping with someone." He picks up his newspaper and continues to read.

What in heaven's name does that mean? He's never slept with anyone? He's a virgin? Somehow I doubt that. I stand staring at him in disbelief. He is the most mystifying person I've ever met. And it dawns on me that I have slept with Christian Grey, and I kick myself—what would I have given to be conscious to watch him sleep? See him vulnerable. Somehow, I find that hard to imagine. Well, allegedly all will be revealed tonight.

In his bedroom, I hunt through a chest of drawers and find the hair dryer. Using my fingers, I dry my hair the best I can. When I've finished, I head into the bathroom. I want to brush my teeth. I eye Christian's toothbrush. It would be like having him in my mouth. *Hmm* . . . Glancing guiltily over my shoulder at the door, I feel the bristles on the toothbrush. They are damp. He must have used it already. Grabbing it quickly, I squirt toothpaste on it and brush my teeth in double time. I feel so naughty. It's such a thrill.

Grabbing my T-shirt, bra, and panties from yesterday, I put them in the shopping bag that Taylor brought and head back to the living area to hunt for my bag and jacket. Deep joy, there is a hair tie in my bag. Christian is watching me as I tie my hair back, his expression unreadable. I feel his eyes follow me as I sit down and wait for him to finish. He's on his BlackBerry talking to someone.

"They want two? . . . How much will that cost? . . . Okay, and what safety measures do we have in place? . . . And they'll go via Suez? . . . How safe is Ben Sudan? . . . And when do they arrive in Darfur? . . . Okay, let's do it. Keep me abreast of progress." He hangs up.

"Ready to go?"

I nod. I wonder what his conversation was about. He slips on a navy pinstriped jacket, picks up his car keys, and heads for the door.

"After you, Miss Steele," he murmurs, opening the door for me. He looks casually elegant.

I pause, fractionally too long, drinking in the sight of him. And to think I slept with him last night and, after all the tequila and the throwing up, he's still here. What's more, he wants to take me to Seattle. Why me? I don't understand it. I head out the door recalling his words—*There's something about you*—well, the feeling is entirely mutual, Mr. Grey, and I aim to find out what his secret is.

We walk in silence down the corridor toward the elevator. As we wait, I peek up at him through my lashes, and he looks out of the corner of his eyes down at me. I smile, and his lips twitch.

The elevator arrives, and we step in. We're alone. Suddenly, for some inexplicable reason, possibly our proximity in such an enclosed space, the atmosphere between us changes, charged with an electric, exhilarating anticipation. My breathing alters as my heart races. His head turns fractionally toward me, his eyes darkest slate. I bite my lip.

"Oh, fuck the paperwork," he growls. He lunges at me, pushing me against the wall of the elevator. Before I know it, he's got both of my hands in one of his in a viselike grip above my head, and he's pinning me to the wall using his hips. Holy shit. His other hand grabs my hair and yanks down, bringing my face up, and his lips are on mine. It's only just not painful. I moan into his mouth, giving his tongue an opening. He takes full advantage, his tongue expertly exploring my mouth. I have never been kissed like this. My tongue tentatively strokes his and joins his in a slow, erotic dance that's all about touch and sensation, all bump and grind. He brings his hand up to grasp my chin and holds me in place. I'm helpless, my hands pinned, my face held, and his hips restraining me. His erection is against my belly. *Oh my* . . . He wants me. Christian Grey, Greek god, wants me, and I want *him*, here . . . now, in the elevator.

"You. Are. So. Sweet," he murmurs, each word a staccato.

The elevator stops, the doors open, and he pushes away from me in the blink of an eye, leaving me hanging. Three men in business suits look at both of us and smirk as they climb on board. My heart rate is through the roof, I feel like I've run an uphill race. I want to lean over and grasp my knees . . . but that's just too obvious.

I glance up at him. He looks so cool and calm, like he's been doing the *Seattle Times* crossword. *How unfair.* Is he totally unaffected by my presence? He glances at me out of the corner of his eyes, and he gently blows out a deep breath. Oh, he's affected all right—and my very small inner goddess sways in a gentle victorious samba. The businessmen exit on the second floor. We have one more floor to travel.

"You've brushed your teeth," he says, staring at me.

"I used your toothbrush."

His lips quirk up in a half smile. "Oh, Anastasia Steele, what am I going to do with you?"

The doors open at the first floor, and he takes my hand and pulls me out.

"What is it about elevators?" he mutters, more to himself than to me as he strides across the lobby. I struggle to keep up with him because my wits have been thoroughly and royally scattered all over the floor and walls of elevator three in the Heathman Hotel.

CHAPTER SIX

Christian opens the passenger-side door to the black Audi SUV, and I clamber in. It's a beast of a car. He hasn't mentioned the outburst of passion that exploded in the elevator. Should I? Should we talk about it or pretend that it didn't happen? It hardly seems real, my first proper no-holds-barred kiss. As time ticks on, I assign it mythical, Arthurian legend, Lost City of Atlantis status. It never happened, it never existed. *Perhaps I imagined it all.* No. I touch my lips, swollen from his kiss. It definitely happened. I am a changed woman. I want this man desperately, and he wanted me.

I glance at him. Christian is his usual polite, slightly distant self.

How confusing.

He starts the engine and reverses out of his space in the parking lot. He switches on the sound system. The car interior is filled with the sweetest, most magical music of two women singing. Oh wow . . . all my senses are in disarray, so this is doubly affecting. It sends delicious shivers up my spine. Christian pulls out onto Southwest Park Avenue, and he drives with easy, lazy confidence.

"What are we listening to?"

"It's 'The Flower Duet' by Delibes, from the opera *Lakmé*. Do you like it?"

"Christian, it's wonderful."

"It is, isn't it?" He grins, glancing at me. And for a fleeting moment, he seems his age: young, carefree, and heart-stoppingly beautiful. Is this the key to him? Music? I sit and listen to the angelic voices teasing and seducing me.

"Can I hear that again?"

"Of course." Christian pushes a button, and the music is caressing me once more. It's a gentle, slow, sweet, and sure assault on my aural senses.

"You like classical music?" I ask, hoping for a rare insight into his personal preferences.

"My taste is eclectic, Anastasia, everything from Thomas Tallis to the Kings of Leon. It depends on my mood. You?"

"Me, too. Though I don't know who Thomas Tallis is."

He turns and gazes at me briefly before his eyes are back on the road.

"I'll play it for you sometime. He's a sixteenth-century British composer. Tudor, church choral music." Christian grins at me. "Sounds very esoteric, I know, but it's also magical."

He presses a button and the Kings of Leon start singing. Hmm . . . this I know. "Sex on Fire." How appropriate. The music is interrupted by the sound of a cell phone ringing over the sound system speakers. Christian hits a button on the steering wheel.

"Grey," he snaps. He's so brusque.

"Mr. Grey, it's Welch here. I have the information you require." A rasping, disembodied voice comes over the speakers.

"Good. E-mail it to me. Anything to add?"

"No, sir."

He presses the button, then the call ceases and the music is back. No good-bye or thanks. I'm so glad that I never seriously entertained the thought of working for him. I shudder at the very idea. He's just too controlling and cold with his employees. The music cuts off again for the phone.

"Grey."

"The NDA has been e-mailed to you, Mr. Grey." A woman's voice.

"Good. That's all, Andrea."

"Good day, sir."

Christian hangs up by pressing a button on the steering wheel. The music is on very briefly when the phone rings again. Holy hell, is this his life—constant nagging phone calls?

"Grey," he snaps.

"Hi, Christian, d'you get laid?"

"Hello, Elliot—I'm on speakerphone, and I'm not alone in the car." Christian sighs.

"Who's with you?"

Christian rolls his eyes. "Anastasia Steele."

"Hi, Ana!"

Ana!

"Hello, Elliot."

"Heard a lot about you," Elliot murmurs huskily. Christian frowns.

"Don't believe a word Kate says."

Elliot laughs.

"I'm dropping Anastasia off now." Christian emphasizes my full name. "Shall I pick you up?"

"Sure."

"See you shortly." Christian hangs up, and the music is back.

"Why do you insist on calling me Anastasia?"

"Because it's your name."

"I prefer Ana."

"Do you now?"

We are almost at my apartment. It's not taken long.

"Anastasia," he muses. I scowl at him, but he ignores my expression. "What happened in the elevator—it won't happen again, well, not unless it's premeditated."

He pulls up outside my duplex. I belatedly realize he's not asked me where I live—yet he knows. But then he sent the books; of course he knows where I live. What able, cell phone–tracking, helicopter-owning stalker wouldn't?

Why won't he kiss me again? I pout at the thought. I don't understand. Honestly, his surname should be Cryptic, not Grey. He climbs out of the car, walking with easy, long-legged grace around to my side to open the door, ever the gentleman—except perhaps in rare, precious moments in elevators. I flush at the memory of his mouth on mine, and the thought that I'd been unable to touch him enters my mind. I wanted to run my fingers through his decadent, untidy hair, but I'd been unable to move my hands. I am retrospectively frustrated.

"I liked what happened in the elevator," I murmur as I climb out of the car. I'm not sure if I hear an audible gasp, but I choose to ignore it and head up the steps to the front door.

Kate and Elliot are sitting at our dining table. The fourteen-thousand-dollar books have disappeared. Thank heavens. I have plans for them. She has the most un-Kate-like ridiculous grin on her face, and she looks mussed up in a sexy kind of way. Christian follows me into the living room, and in spite of her I've-been-having-a-good-time-all-night grin, Kate eyes him suspiciously.

"Hi, Ana." She leaps up to hug me, then holds me at arm's length so she can examine me. She frowns and turns to Christian.

"Good morning, Christian," she says, and her tone is a little hostile.

"Miss Kavanagh," he says in his stiff, formal way.

"Christian, her name is Kate," Elliot grumbles.

"Kate." Christian gives her a polite nod and glares at Elliot, who grins and rises to hug me, too.

"Hi, Ana." He smiles, his blue eyes twinkling, and I like him immediately. He's obviously nothing like Christian, but then they're adopted brothers.

"Hi, Elliot." I smile at him, and I'm aware that I'm biting my lip.

"Elliot, we'd better go," Christian says mildly.

"Sure." He turns to Kate and pulls her into his arms and gives her a long, lingering kiss.

Jeez . . . get a room. I stare at my feet, embarrassed. I glance up at Christian, and he's watching me intently. I narrow my eyes at him. Why can't you kiss me like that? Elliot continues to kiss Kate, sweeping her off her feet and dipping her in a dramatic hold so that her hair touches the ground as he kisses her hard.

"Laters, baby." He grins.

Kate just melts. I've never seen her melt before—the words

"comely" and "compliant" come to mind. Compliant Kate. Boy, Elliot must be good. Christian rolls his eyes and stares down at me, his expression unreadable, although maybe he's mildly amused. He tucks a stray strand of my hair that has worked its way free from my ponytail behind my ear. My breath hitches at the contact, and I lean my head into his fingers. His eyes soften, and he runs his thumb across my lower lip. My blood sears in my veins. And all too quickly, his touch is gone.

"Laters, baby," he murmurs, and I have to laugh because it's so unlike him. But even though I know he's being irreverent, the endearment tugs at something deep inside me.

"I'll pick you up at eight." He turns to leave, opening the front door and stepping out onto the porch. Elliot follows him to the car but turns and blows Kate another kiss, and I feel an unwelcome pang of jealousy.

"So, did you?" Kate asks as we watch them climb into the car and drive off, the burning curiosity evident in her voice.

"No," I snap irritably, hoping that will halt the questions. We head back into the apartment. "You obviously did, though." I can't contain my envy. Kate always manages to ensnare men. She is irresistible, beautiful, sexy, funny, forward . . . all the things that I'm not. But her answering grin is infectious.

"And I'm seeing him again this evening." She claps her hands and jumps up and down like a small child. She cannot contain her excitement and happiness, and I can't help but feel happy for her. A happy Kate . . . this is going to be interesting.

"Christian is taking me to Seattle this evening."

"Seattle?"

"Yes."

"Maybe you will *then*?"

"Oh, I hope so."

"You like him, then?"

"Yes."

"Like him enough to . . . ?"

"Yes."

She raises her eyebrows.

"Wow. Ana Steele, finally falling for a man, and it's Christian Grey—hot, sexy billionaire."

"Oh yeah—it's all about the money." I smirk, and we both fall into a fit of giggles.

"Is that a new blouse?" she asks, and I let her have all the unexciting details about my night.

"Has he kissed you yet?" she asks as she makes coffee.

I blush.

"Once."

"Once!" she scoffs.

I nod, rather shamefaced. "He's very reserved."

She frowns. "That's odd."

"I don't think odd covers it, really."

"We need to make sure you're simply irresistible for this evening," she says with determination.

Oh no . . . this sounds like it will be time consuming, humiliating, and painful.

"I have to be at work in an hour."

"I can work with that time frame. Come on." Kate grabs my hand and takes me into her bedroom.

THE DAY DRAGS AT Clayton's even though we're busy. We've hit the summer season, so I have to spend two hours restocking the shelves once the shop is closed. It's mindless work, and it gives me too much time to think. I've not really had a chance all day.

Under Kate's tireless and frankly intrusive instruction, my legs and underarms are shaved to perfection, my eyebrows plucked, and I am buffed all over. It has been a most unpleasant experience. But she assures me that this is what men expect these days. What else will he expect? I have to convince Kate that this is what I want to do. For some strange reason, she doesn't trust him, maybe because he's so stiff and formal. She says she can't put her finger on it, but I have promised to text her when I arrive in Seattle. I haven't told her about the helicopter; she'd freak.

I also have the José issue. He's left three messages and seven missed calls on my cell. He's also called home twice. Kate has been very vague as to where I am. He'll know she's covering for me. Kate doesn't do vague. But I have decided to let him stew. I'm still too angry with him.

Christian mentioned some kind of written paperwork, and I don't know if he was joking or if I'm going to have to sign something. It's frustrating trying to guess. And on top of all the angst, I can barely contain my excitement or my nerves. Tonight's the night! After all this time, am I ready for this? My inner goddess glares at me, tapping her small foot impatiently. She's been ready for this for years, and she's ready for anything with Christian Grey, but I still don't understand what he sees in me . . . mousey Ana Steele—it makes no sense.

He is punctual, of course, and waiting for me when I leave Clayton's. He climbs out of the back of the Audi to open the door and smiles warmly at me.

"Good evening, Miss Steele," he says.

"Mr. Grey." I nod politely to him as I climb into the backseat of the car. Taylor is sitting in the driver's seat.

"Hello, Taylor," I say.

"Good evening, Miss Steele." His voice is polite and professional. Christian climbs in the other side and clasps my hand, giving it a gentle squeeze that echoes through my body.

"How was work?" he asks.

"Very long," I reply, and my voice is husky, too low, and full of need.

"Yes, it's been a long day for me, too."

"What did you do?" I manage.

"I went hiking with Elliot." His thumb strokes my knuckles, back and forth, and my heart skips a beat as my breathing accelerates. How does he do this to me? He's only touching a very small area of my body, and the hormones are flying.

The drive to the heliport is short and, before I know it, we arrive. I wonder where the fabled helicopter might be. We're in a built-up area of the city, and even I know helicopters need space to take off and land. Taylor parks, climbs out, and opens the door for me. Christian is beside me in an instant and takes my hand again.

"Ready?" he asks. I nod and want to say, *For anything*, but I can't articulate the words as I'm too nervous, too excited.

"Taylor." He nods curtly at his driver, and we head into the building, straight to a set of elevators. *Elevator!* The memory of our kiss this morning comes back to haunt me. I have thought of nothing else all day, daydreaming at the register at Clayton's. Twice Mr. Clayton had to shout my name to bring me back to Earth. To say I've been distracted would be the understatement of the year. Christian glances down at me, a slight smile on his lips. Ha! He's thinking about it, too.

"It's only three floors," he says dryly, his eyes dancing with amusement. He's telepathic, surely. It's spooky.

I try to keep my face impassive as we enter the elevator. The doors close, and it's there, the weird electrical attraction crackling between us, enslaving me. I close my eyes in a vain attempt to ignore it. He tightens his grip on my hand, and five seconds later the doors open onto the roof of the building. And there it is, a white helicopter with the name GREY ENTERPRISES HOLDINGS, INC. written in blue with the company logo on the side. *Surely this is misuse of company property.*

He leads me to a small office where an old-timer sits behind the desk.

"Here's your flight plan, Mr. Grey. All external checks are done. It's ready and waiting, sir. You're free to go."

"Thank you, Joe." Christian smiles warmly at him.

Oh. Someone deserving of the polite treatment from Christian. Perhaps he's not an employee. I stare at the old guy in awe.

"Let's go," Christian says, and we make our way toward the helicopter. When we're up close, it's much bigger than I thought. I expected it to be a roadster version for two, but it has at least seven seats. Christian opens the door and directs me to one of the seats at the very front.

"Sit—don't touch anything," he orders as he climbs in behind me.

He shuts the door with a slam. I'm glad that the area is floodlit, otherwise I'd find it difficult to see inside the small cockpit. I sit down in my allotted seat, and he crouches beside me to strap me into the harness. It's a four-point harness with all the straps connecting to one central buckle. He tightens both of the upper straps, so I can hardly move. He's so close and intent on what he's doing. If I could only lean forward, my nose would be in his hair. He smells clean, fresh, heavenly, but I'm fastened securely into my seat and effectively immobile. He glances up and smiles, like he's enjoying his usual private joke, his eyes heated. He's so tantalizingly close. I hold my breath as he pulls at one of the upper straps.

"You're secure, no escaping," he whispers. "Breathe, Anastasia," he adds softly. Reaching up, he caresses my cheek, running his long fingers down to my chin, which he grasps between his thumb and forefinger. He leans forward and plants a brief, chaste kiss, leaving me reeling, my insides clenching at the thrilling, unexpected touch of his lips.

"I like this harness," he whispers.

What?

He sits down beside me and buckles himself into his seat, then begins a protracted procedure of checking gauges and flipping switches and buttons from the mind-boggling array of dials and lights and switches in front of me. Little lights wink and flash from various dials, and the whole of the instrument panel lights up.

"Put your cans on," he says, pointing to a set of headphones in front of me. I pull them on, and the rotor blades start. They are deafening. He puts his headphones on and continues flipping various switches.

"I'm just going through all the preflight checks." Christian's disembodied voice is in my ears through the headphones. I turn and grin at him.

"Do you know what you are doing?" I ask. He turns and smiles at me.

"I've been a fully qualified pilot for four years, Anastasia. You're safe with me." He gives me a wolfish grin. "Well, while we're flying," he adds, and winks at me.

Winking . . . Christian!

"Are you ready?"

I nod, wide-eyed.

"Okay, tower. PDX, this is *Charlie Tango* Golf–Golf Echo Hotel, cleared for take-off. Please confirm, over."

"*Charlie Tango*—you are clear. PDX to call, proceed to one four thousand, heading zero one zero, over."

"Roger, tower, *Charlie Tango* set, over and out. Here we go," he adds to me, and the helicopter rises slowly and smoothly into the air.

Portland disappears in front of us as we head into U.S. airspace, though my stomach remains firmly in Oregon. Whoa! All the bright lights shrink until they are twinkling sweetly below us. It's like looking out from inside a fish bowl. Once we're higher, there really is nothing to see. It's pitch-black, not even the moon to shed any light on our journey. How can he see where we're going?

"Eerie, isn't it?" Christian's voice is in my ears.

"How do you know you're going the right way?"

"Here." He points his long index finger at one of the gauges, and it shows an electronic compass. "This is an EC135 Eurocopter. One of the safest in its class. It's equipped for night flight." He glances and grins at me.

"There's a helipad on top of the building I live in. That's where we're heading."

Of course there's a helipad where he lives. I am so out of my league here. His face is softly illuminated by the lights on the instrument panel. He's concentrating hard, and he's continually glancing at the various dials in front of him. I drink in his features from beneath my lashes. He has a beautiful profile. Straight nose, square jawed—I'd like to run my tongue along his jaw. He hasn't shaved, and his stubble makes the prospect doubly tempting. Hmm . . . I'd like to feel how rough it is beneath my tongue, my fingers, against my face.

"When you fly at night, you fly blind. You have to trust the instrumentation," he says, interrupting my erotic reverie.

"How long will the flight be?" I manage breathlessly. I wasn't thinking about sex at all, no, no way.

"Less than an hour—the wind is in our favor."

Hmm, less than an hour to Seattle . . . that's not bad going. No wonder we're flying.

I have less than an hour before the big reveal. All the muscles clench deep in my belly. I have a serious case of butterflies. They are flourishing in my stomach. Holy shit, what has he got in store for me?

"You okay, Anastasia?"

"Yes." My answer is short, clipped, squeezed out through my nerves.

I think he smiles, but it's difficult to tell in the darkness. Christian flicks yet another switch.

"PDX, this is *Charlie Tango* now at one four thousand, over." He exchanges information with air traffic control. It all sounds very professional to me. I think we're moving from Portland's airspace to Seattle International Airport's. "Understood, Sea-Tac, standing by, over and out."

"Look, over there." He points to a small pinpoint of light in the far distance. "That's Seattle."

"Do you always impress women this way? 'Come and fly in my helicopter'?" I ask, genuinely interested.

"I've never brought a girl up here, Anastasia. It's another first for me." His voice is quiet, serious.

Oh, that was an unexpected answer. Another first? Oh, the sleeping thing, perhaps?

"Are you impressed?"

"I'm awed, Christian."

He smiles.

"Awed?" And for a brief moment, he's his age again.

I nod. "You're just so . . . competent."

"Why, thank you, Miss Steele," he says politely. I think he's pleased, but I'm not sure.

We ride in the dark night in silence for a while. The bright spot that is Seattle is slowly getting bigger.

"Sea-Tac tower to *Charlie Tango.* Flight plan to Escala in place. Please proceed. And stand by. Over."

"This is *Charlie Tango,* understood, Sea-Tac. Standing by, over and out."

"You obviously enjoy this," I murmur.

"What?" He glances at me. He looks quizzical in the half light of the instruments.

"Flying," I reply.

"It requires control and concentration . . . how could I not love it? Though my favorite is soaring."

"Soaring?"

"Yes. Gliding, to the layperson. Gliders and helicopters—I fly them both."

"Oh." *Expensive hobbies.* I remember him telling me during the interview. I like reading and occasionally going to the movies. I am out of my depth here.

"*Charlie Tango,* come in, please, over." The disembodied voice of air traffic control interrupts my reverie. Christian answers, sounding in control and confident.

Seattle is getting closer. We are on the very outskirts now. Wow! It looks absolutely stunning. Seattle at night, from the sky . . .

"Looks good, doesn't it?" Christian murmurs.

I nod enthusiastically. It looks otherworldly—unreal—and I feel like I'm on a giant film set; José's favorite film maybe, *Blade Runner.* The memory of José's attempted kiss haunts me. I'm beginning to feel a bit cruel not calling him back. *He can wait until tomorrow . . . surely.*

"We'll be there in a few minutes," Christian mutters, and suddenly my blood is pounding in my ears as my heartbeat accelerates and adrenaline spikes through my system. He starts talking to air traffic control again, but I am no longer listening. I think I'm going to faint. My fate is in his hands.

We are now flying among the buildings, and up ahead I can

see a tall skyscraper with a helipad on top. The word "Escala" is painted in white on top of the building. It's getting nearer and nearer, bigger and bigger . . . like my anxiety. *God, I hope I don't let him down.* He'll find me lacking in some way. I wish I'd listened to Kate and borrowed one of her dresses, but I like my black jeans, and I'm wearing a soft mint-green shirt and Kate's black jacket. I look smart enough. I grip the edge of my seat tighter and tighter. *I can do this. I can do this.* I chant this mantra as the skyscraper looms below us.

The helicopter slows and hovers, and Christian sets it down on the helipad on top of the building. My heart is in my mouth. I can't decide if it's from nervous anticipation, relief that we've arrived alive, or fear that I will fail in some way. He switches the ignition off and the rotor blades slow and quiet until all I hear is the sound of my own erratic breathing. Christian takes his headphones off and reaches across and pulls mine off, too.

"We're here," he says softly.

His look is so intense, half in shadow and half in the bright white light from the landing lights. Dark knight and white knight, it's a fitting metaphor for Christian. He looks strained. His jaw is clenched and his eyes are tight. He unfastens his seatbelt and reaches over to unbuckle mine. His face is inches from mine.

"You don't have to do anything you don't want to do. You know that, don't you?" His tone is so earnest, desperate even, his eyes impassioned. He takes me by surprise.

"I'd never do anything I didn't want to do, Christian." And as I say the words, I don't quite feel their conviction, because at this moment in time, I'd probably do anything for this man seated beside me. But this does the trick. He's mollified.

He eyes me warily for a moment and somehow, even though he's so tall, he manages to ease his way gracefully to the door of the helicopter and open it. He jumps out, waiting for me to follow, and takes my hand as I clamber down on to the helipad. It's very windy on top of the building, and I'm nervous about the fact that I'm standing at least thirty stories high in an unenclosed space.

Christian wraps his arm around my waist, pulling me tightly against him.

"Come," he shouts above the noise of the wind. He drags me over to an elevator and, after tapping a number into a keypad, the doors open. It's warm inside and all mirrored glass. I can see Christian to infinity everywhere I look, and the wonderful thing is he's holding me to infinity, too. Christian taps another code into the keypad, then the doors close and the elevator descends.

Moments later, we're in an all-white foyer. In the middle is a round, dark wood table, and on it is an unbelievably huge bunch of white flowers. On the walls there are paintings everywhere. He opens a set of double doors, and the white theme continues across a wide corridor where directly opposite, is the entrance to a palatial room. It's the main living area, double height. "Huge" is too small a word for it. The far wall is glass and leads onto a balcony that overlooks Seattle.

To the right is an imposing U-shaped sofa that could seat ten adults comfortably. It faces a state-of-the-art stainless-steel—or maybe platinum, for all I know—modern fireplace. The fire is lit and flaming gently. On the left beside us, by the entryway, is the kitchen area. All white with dark wood worktops and a breakfast bar that seats six.

Near the kitchen area, in front of the glass wall, is a dining table surrounded by sixteen chairs. And tucked in the corner is a full-sized, shiny black grand piano. Oh yes . . . he probably plays the piano, too. There is art of all shapes and sizes on all the walls. In fact, this apartment looks more like a gallery than a place to live.

"Can I take your jacket?" Christian asks. I shake my head. I'm still cold from the wind on the helipad.

"Would you like a drink?" he asks. I blink at him. After last night! *Is he trying to be funny?* For one second, I think about asking for a margarita—but I don't have the nerve.

"I'm going to have a glass of white wine. Would you like to join me?"

"Yes, please," I murmur.

I am standing in this enormous room feeling out of place. I walk over to the glass wall, and I realize that the lower half of the wall opens concertina style onto the balcony. Seattle is lit up and lively in the background. I walk back to the kitchen area—it takes a few seconds, it's so far from the glass wall—and Christian is opening a bottle of wine. He's removed his jacket.

"Pouilly Fumé okay with you?"

"I know nothing about wine, Christian. I'm sure it will be fine." My voice is soft and hesitant. My heart is thumping. I want to run. This is seriously rich. Seriously over-the-top Bill Gates–style wealthy. What am I doing here? *You know very well what you're doing here,* my subconscious sneers at me. Yes, I want to be in Christian Grey's bed.

"Here." He hands me a glass of wine. Even the glasses are rich . . . heavy, contemporary crystal. I take a sip, and the wine is light, crisp, and delicious.

"You're very quiet, and you're not even blushing. In fact, I think this is the palest I've ever seen you, Anastasia," he murmurs. "Are you hungry?"

I shake my head. Not for food. "It's a very big place you have here."

"Big?"

"Big."

"It's big," he agrees, and his eyes glow with amusement. I take another sip of wine.

"Do you play?" I point my chin at the piano.

"Yes."

"Well?"

"Yes."

"Of course you do. Is there anything you can't do well?"

"Yes . . . a few things." He takes a sip of his wine. He doesn't take his eyes off me. I feel them following me as I turn and glance around this vast room. "Room" is the wrong word. It's not a room—it's a mission statement.

"Do you want to sit?"

I nod, and he takes my hand and leads me to the large off-white couch. As I sit, I'm struck by the fact that I feel like Tess Durbeyfield looking at the new house that belongs to the notorious Alec d'Urberville. The thought makes me smile.

"What's so amusing?" He sits down beside me, turning to face me. He rests his head on his right hand, his elbow propped on the back of the couch.

"Why did you give me *Tess of the d'Urbervilles* specifically?" I ask. Christian stares at me for a moment. I think he's surprised by my question.

"Well, you said you liked Thomas Hardy."

"Is that the only reason?" Even I can hear the disappointment in my voice. His mouth presses into a hard line.

"It seemed appropriate. I could hold you to some impossibly high ideal like Angel Clare or debase you completely like Alec d'Urberville," he murmurs, and his eyes flash dark and dangerous.

"If there are only two choices, I'll take the debasement." I whisper, gazing at him. My subconscious is staring at me in awe. He gasps.

"Anastasia, stop biting your lip, please. It's very distracting. You don't know what you're saying."

"That's why I'm here."

He frowns.

"Yes. Would you excuse me for a moment?" He disappears through a wide doorway on the far side of the room. He's gone for a couple of minutes and returns with a document.

"This is a nondisclosure agreement." He shrugs and has the grace to look a little embarrassed. "My lawyer insists on it." He hands it to me. I'm completely bemused. "If you're going for option two, debasement, you'll need to sign this."

"And if I don't want to sign anything?"

"Then it's Angel Clare high ideals, well, for most of the book anyway."

"What does this agreement mean?"

"It means you cannot disclose anything about us. Anything, to anyone."

I stare at him in disbelief. Holy shit. It's bad, really bad, and now I'm very curious to know.

"Okay. I'll sign."

He hands me a pen.

"Aren't you even going to read it?"

"No."

He frowns.

"Anastasia, you should always read anything you sign," he admonishes me.

"Christian, what you fail to understand is that I wouldn't talk about us to anyone anyway. Even Kate. So it's immaterial whether I sign an agreement or not. If it means so much to you, or your lawyer . . . whom *you* obviously talk to, then fine. I'll sign."

He gazes down at me, and he nods gravely.

"Fair point well made, Miss Steele."

I lavishly sign on the dotted line of both copies and hand one back to him. Folding the other, I place it my purse and take a large swig of my wine. I'm sounding so much braver than I'm actually feeling.

"Does this mean you're going to make love to me tonight, Christian?" *Holy shit. Did I just say that?* His mouth drops open slightly, but he recovers quickly.

"No, Anastasia, it doesn't. First, I don't make love. I fuck . . . hard. Second, there's a lot more paperwork to do. And third, you don't yet know what you're in for. You could still run for the hills. Come, I want to show you my playroom."

My mouth drops open. *Fuck hard!* Holy shit, that sounds so . . . hot. But why are we looking at a playroom? I am mystified.

"You want to play on your Xbox?" I ask. He laughs loudly.

"No, Anastasia, no Xbox, no Playstation. Come." He stands, holding out his hand. I let him lead me back out to the corridor. On the right of the double doors, where we came in, another door leads to a staircase. We go up to the second floor and turn right.

Producing a key from his pocket, he unlocks yet another door and takes a deep breath.

"You can leave anytime. The helicopter is on standby to take you whenever you want to go; you can stay the night and go home in the morning. It's fine whatever you decide."

"Just open the damn door, Christian."

He opens the door and stands back to let me in. I gaze at him once more. I so want to know what's in here. Taking a deep breath I walk in.

And it feels like I've time-traveled back to the sixteenth century and the Spanish Inquisition.

Holy fuck.

CHAPTER SEVEN

The first thing I notice is the smell: leather, wood, polish with a faint citrus scent. It's very pleasant, and the lighting is soft, subtle. In fact, I can't see the source, but it's around the cornice in the room, emitting an ambient glow. The walls and ceiling are a deep, dark burgundy, giving a womb-like effect to the spacious room, and the floor is old, old varnished wood. There is a large wooden cross like an X fastened to the wall facing the door. It's made of high-polished mahogany, and there are restraining cuffs on each corner. Above it is an expansive iron grid suspended from the ceiling, eight-foot square at least, and from it hang all manner of ropes, chains, and glinting shackles. By the door, two long, polished, ornately carved poles, like spindles from a banister but longer, hang like curtain rods across the wall. From them swing a startling assortment of paddles, whips, riding crops, and funny-looking feathery implements.

Beside the door stands a substantial mahogany chest of drawers, each drawer slim as if designed to contain specimens in a crusty old museum. I wonder briefly what the drawers actually *do* hold. *Do I want to know?* In the far corner is an oxblood leather padded bench, and fixed to the wall beside it is a wooden, polished rack that looks like a pool or billiard cue holder, but on closer inspection, it holds canes of varying lengths and widths. There's a stout six-foot-long table in the opposite corner—polished wood with intricately carved legs—and two matching stools underneath.

But what dominates the room is a bed. It's bigger than king sized, an ornately carved rococo four-poster with a flat top. It looks late nineteenth century. Under the canopy, I can see more gleaming chains and cuffs. There is no bedding . . . just a mattress covered in red leather and red satin cushions piled at one end.

At the foot of the bed, set apart a few feet, is a large oxblood chesterfield couch, just stuck in the middle of the room facing the bed. An odd arrangement . . . to have a couch facing the bed, and I smile to myself—I've picked on the couch as odd, when really it's the most mundane piece of furniture in the room. I glance up and stare at the ceiling. There are carabiners all over the ceiling at odd intervals. I vaguely wonder what they're for. Weirdly, all the wood, dark walls, moody lighting, and oxblood leather makes the room kind of soft and romantic . . . I know it's anything but; this is Christian's version of soft and romantic.

I turn, and he's regarding me intently, as I knew he would be, his expression completely unreadable. I walk farther into the room, and he follows me. The feathery thing has me intrigued. I touch it hesitantly. It's suede, like a small cat-o'-nine-tails but bushier, and there are very small plastic beads on the end.

"It's called a flogger." Christian's voice is quiet and soft.

A flogger . . . hmm. I think I'm in shock. My subconscious has emigrated or been struck dumb or simply keeled over and expired. I am numb. I can observe and absorb but not articulate my feelings about all this, because I'm in shock. What is the appropriate response to finding out a potential lover is a complete freaky sadist or masochist? *Fear* . . . yes . . . that seems to be the overriding feeling. I recognize it now. But weirdly not of him—I don't think he'd hurt me, well, not without my consent. So many questions cloud my mind. Why? How? When? How often? Who? I walk toward the bed and run my hands down one of the intricately carved posts. The post is very sturdy, the craftsmanship outstanding.

"Say something," Christian commands, his voice deceptively soft.

"Do you do this to people or do they do it to you?"

His mouth quirks up, either amused or relieved.

"People?" He blinks a couple of times as he considers his answer. "I do this to women who want me to."

I don't understand.

"If you have willing volunteers, why am I here?"

"Because I want to do this with you, very much."

"Oh," I gasp. *Why?*

I wander to the far corner of the room and pat the waist-high padded bench and run my fingers over the leather. *He likes to hurt women*. The thought depresses me.

"You're a sadist?"

"I'm a Dominant." His eyes are a scorching gray, intense.

"What does that mean?" I whisper.

"It means I want you to willingly surrender yourself to me, in all things."

I frown at him as I try to assimilate this idea.

"Why would I do that?"

"To please me," he whispers as he cocks his head to one side, and I see a ghost of a smile.

Please him! He wants me to please him! I think my mouth drops open. *Please Christian Grey.* And I realize, in that moment, that yes, that's exactly what I want to do. I want him to be damned delighted with me. It's a revelation.

"In very simple terms, I want you to want to please me," he says softly. His voice is hypnotic.

"How do I do that?" My mouth is dry, and I wish I had more wine. Okay, I understand the pleasing bit, but I am puzzled by the soft-boudoir Elizabethan-torture setup. Do I want to know the answer?

"I have rules, and I want you to comply with them. They are for your benefit and for my pleasure. If you follow these rules to my satisfaction, I shall reward you. If you don't, I shall punish you, and you will learn," he whispers. I glance at the rack of canes as he says this.

"And where does all this fit in?" I wave my hand in the general direction of the room.

"It's all part of the incentive package. Both reward and punishment."

"So you'll get your kicks by exerting your will over me."

"It's about gaining your trust and your respect, so you'll let me exert my will over you. I will gain a great deal of pleasure, joy even, in your submission. The more you submit, the greater my joy—it's a very simple equation."

"Okay, and what do I get out of this?"

He shrugs and looks almost apologetic.

"Me," he says simply.

Oh my. Christian rakes his hand through his hair as he gazes at me.

"You're not giving anything away, Anastasia," he murmurs, exasperated. "Let's go back downstairs where I can concentrate better. It's very distracting having you in here." He holds his hand out to me, and now I'm hesitant to take it.

Kate had said he was dangerous; she was so right. *How did she know?* He's dangerous to my health, because I know I'm going to say yes. And part of me doesn't want to. Part of me wants to run screaming from this room and all it represents. I am so out of my depth here.

"I'm not going to hurt you, Anastasia."

I know he speaks the truth. I take his hand, and he leads me out the door.

"If you do this, let me show you." Rather than going back downstairs, he turns right out of the *playroom*, as he calls it, and down a corridor. We pass several doors until we reach the one at the end. Beyond it is a bedroom with a large double bed, all in white . . . everything—furniture, walls, bedding. It's sterile and cold but with the most glorious view of Seattle through the glass wall.

"This will be your room. You can decorate it how you like, have whatever you like in here."

"My room? You're expecting me to move in?" I can't hide the horror in my voice.

"Not full time. Just, say, Friday evening through Sunday. We have to talk about all that, negotiate. If you want to do this," he adds, his voice quiet and hesitant.

"I'll sleep here?"

"Yes."

"Not with you."

"No. I told you, I don't sleep with anyone, except you when you're stupefied with drink." His voice is reprimanding.

My mouth presses in a hard line. This is what I cannot reconcile. Kind, caring Christian, who rescues me from inebriation and holds me gently while I'm throwing up into the azaleas, and the monster who possesses whips and chains in a special room.

"Where do you sleep?"

"My room is downstairs. Come, you must be hungry."

"Weirdly, I seem to have lost my appetite," I murmur petulantly.

"You must eat, Anastasia," he scolds, and, taking my hand, leads me back downstairs.

Back in the impossibly big room, I am filled with deep trepidation. I am on the edge of a precipice, and I have to decide whether to jump.

"I'm fully aware that this is a dark path I'm leading you down, Anastasia, which is why I really want you to think about this. You must have some questions," he says as he wanders into the kitchen area, releasing my hand.

I do. But where to start?

"You've signed your NDA; you can ask me anything you want and I'll answer."

I stand at the breakfast bar watching him as he opens the refrigerator and pulls out a plate of different cheeses with two large bunches of green and red grapes. He sets the plate down on the worktop and proceeds to cut up a French baguette.

"Sit." He points to one of the stools at the breakfast bar, and I obey his command. If I'm going to do this, I'm going to have to get used to it. I realize he's been this bossy since I met him.

"You mentioned paperwork."

"Yes."

"What paperwork?"

"Well, apart from the NDA, a contract saying what we will and won't do. I need to know your limits, and you need to know mine. This is consensual, Anastasia."

"And if I don't want to do this?"

"That's fine," he says carefully.

"But we won't have any sort of relationship?" I ask.

"No."

"Why?"

"This is the only sort of relationship I'm interested in."

"Why?"

He shrugs. "It's the way I am."

"How did you become this way?"

"Why is anyone the way they are? That's kind of hard to answer. Why do some people like cheese and other people hate it? Do you like cheese? Mrs. Jones—my housekeeper—has left this for supper." He takes some large white plates from a cupboard and places one in front of me.

We're talking about cheese . . . Holy crap.

"What are your rules that I have to follow?"

"I have them written down. We'll go through them once we've eaten."

Food. How can I eat now?

"I'm really not hungry," I whisper.

"You will eat," he says simply. *Dominating Christian, it all becomes clear.* "Would you like another glass of wine?"

"Yes, please."

He pours wine into my glass and comes to sit beside me. I take a hasty sip.

"Help yourself to food, Anastasia."

I take a small bunch of grapes. This I can manage. He narrows his eyes.

"Have you been like this for a while?" I ask.

"Yes."

"Is it easy to find women who want to do this?"

He raises an eyebrow at me.

"You'd be amazed," he says dryly.

"Then why me? I really don't understand."

"Anastasia, I've told you. There's something about you. I can't leave you alone." He smiles ironically. "I'm like a moth to a flame." His voice darkens. "I want you very badly, especially now, when you're biting your lip again." He takes a deep breath and swallows.

My stomach somersaults—he wants me . . . in a weird way, true, but this beautiful, strange, kinky man wants me.

"I think you have that cliché the wrong way around," I grumble. I am the moth and he is the flame, and I'm going to get burned. I know.

"Eat!"

"No. I haven't signed anything yet, so I think I'll hang on to my free will for a bit longer, if that's okay with you."

His eyes soften, and his lips turn up in a smile.

"As you wish, Miss Steele."

"How many women?" I blurt out the question, but I'm so curious.

"Fifteen."

Oh . . . not as many as I thought.

"For long periods of time?"

"Some of them, yes."

"Have you ever hurt anyone?"

"Yes."

Holy shit.

"Badly?"

"No."

"Will you hurt me?"

"What do you mean?"

"Physically, will you hurt me?"

"I will punish you when you require it, and it will be painful."

I think I feel a little faint. I take another sip of wine. Alcohol—this will make me brave.

"Have you ever been beaten?" I ask.

"Yes."

Oh . . . that surprises me. Before I can question him on this revelation further, he interrupts my train of thought.

"Let's discuss this in my study. I want to show you something."

This is hard to process. Here I was foolishly thinking that I'd spend a night of unparalleled passion in this man's bed, and we're negotiating this weird arrangement.

I follow him into his study, a spacious room with another floor-to-ceiling window that opens out onto the balcony. He sits on the desk, motions for me to sit on a leather chair in front of him, and hands me a piece of paper.

"These are the rules. They may be subject to change. They form part of the contract, which you can also have. Read these rules and let's discuss."

RULES

<u>*Obedience:*</u>

The Submissive will obey any instructions given by the Dominant immediately without hesitation or reservation and in an expeditious manner. The Submissive will agree to any sexual activity deemed fit and pleasurable by the Dominant excepting those activities that are outlined in hard limits (Appendix 2). She will do so eagerly and without hesitation.

<u>*Sleep:*</u>

The Submissive will ensure she achieves a minimum of seven hours' sleep a night when she is not with the Dominant.

<u>*Food:*</u>

The Submissive will eat regularly to maintain her health and well-being from a prescribed list of foods (Appendix 4). The Submissive will not snack between meals, with the exception of fruit.

<u>*Clothes:*</u>

During the Term, the Submissive will wear clothing only approved by the Dominant. The Dominant will provide a clothing budget for the Submissive, which the Submissive shall utilize. The Dominant shall accompany the Submissive to purchase clothing on an ad hoc basis. If the Dominant so requires, the Submissive shall wear during the Term any adornments the Dominant shall require, in the presence of the Dominant and at any other time the Dominant deems fit.

Exercise:

The Dominant shall provide the Submissive with a personal trainer four times a week in hour-long sessions at times to be mutually agreed between the personal trainer and the Submissive. The personal trainer will report to the Dominant on the Submissive's progress.

Personal Hygiene/Beauty:

The Submissive will keep herself clean and shaved and/or waxed at all times. The Submissive will visit a beauty salon of the Dominant's choosing at times to be decided by the Dominant and undergo whatever treatments the Dominant sees fit.

Personal Safety:

The Submissive will not drink to excess, smoke, take recreational drugs, or put herself in any unnecessary danger.

Personal Qualities:

The Submissive will not enter into any sexual relations with anyone other than the Dominant. The Submissive will conduct herself in a respectful and modest manner at all times. She must recognize that her behavior is a direct reflection on the Dominant. She shall be held accountable for any misdeeds, wrongdoings, and misbehavior committed when not in the presence of the Dominant.

Failure to comply with any of the above will result in immediate punishment, the nature of which shall be determined by the Dominant.

Holy fuck.

"Hard limits?" I ask.

"Yes. What you won't do, what I won't do, we need to specify in our agreement."

"I'm not sure about accepting money for clothes. It feels wrong." I shift uncomfortably, the word "ho" rattling around my head.

"I want to lavish money on you. Let me buy you some clothes. I may need you to accompany me to functions, and I want you dressed well. I'm sure your salary, when you do get a job, won't cover the kind of clothes I'd like you to wear."

"I don't have to wear them when I'm not with you?"

"No."

"Okay." *Think of them as a uniform.*

"I don't want to exercise four times a week."

"Anastasia, I need you supple, strong, and with stamina. Trust me, you need to exercise."

"But surely not four times a week. How about three?"

"I want you to do four."

"I thought this was a negotiation?"

He purses his lips at me. "Okay, Miss Steele, another point well made. How about an hour on three days and one day half an hour?"

"Three days, three hours. I get the impression you're going to keep me exercised when I'm here."

He smiles wickedly, and his eyes glow as if relieved. "Yes, I am. Okay, agreed. Are you sure you don't want to intern at my company? You're a good negotiator."

"No, I don't think that's a good idea." I stare down at his rules. *Waxing! Waxing what? Everything? Ugh.*

"So, limits. These are mine." He hands me another piece of paper.

<u>HARD LIMITS</u>

No acts involving fire play.

No acts involving urination or defecation and the products thereof.

No acts involving needles, knives, piercing, or blood.

No acts involving gynecological medical instruments.

No acts involving children or animals.

No acts that will leave any permanent marks on the skin.

No acts involving breath control.

No activity that involves the direct contact of electric current (whether alternating or direct), fire, or flames to the body.

Ugh. He has to write these down! Of course—they all look very sensible and, frankly, necessary . . . Any sane person wouldn't want to be involved in this sort of thing, surely. Though I now feel a little queasy.

"Is there anything you'd like to add?" he asks kindly.

Crap. I've no idea. I am completely stumped. He gazes at me and furrows his brow.

"Is there anything you won't do?"

"I don't know."

"What do you mean you don't know?"

I squirm uncomfortably and bite my lip.

"I've never done anything like this."

"Well, when you've had sex, was there anything that you didn't like doing?"

For the first time in what seems to be ages, I blush.

"You can tell me, Anastasia. We have to be honest with each other or this isn't going to work."

I squirm uncomfortably again and stare at my knotted fingers.

"Tell me," he commands.

"Well . . . I haven't had sex before, so I don't know." My voice is small. I peek up at him, and he's gaping at me, frozen, and pale—really pale.

"Never?" he whispers. I shake my head.

"You're a virgin?" he breathes. I nod, flushing again. He closes his eyes and looks to be counting to ten. When he opens them again, he's angry, glaring at me.

"Why the fuck didn't you tell me?" he growls.

CHAPTER EIGHT

Christian is running his hands through his hair and pacing up and down his study. Two hands—that's double exasperation. His usual concrete control seems to have slipped a notch.

"I don't understand why you didn't tell me," he castigates me.

"The subject never came up. I'm not in the habit of revealing my sexual status to everyone I meet. I mean, we hardly know each other." I'm staring at my hands. Why am I feeling guilty? Why is he so mad? I peek up at him.

"Well, you know a lot more about me now," he snaps, his mouth presses into a hard line. "I knew you were inexperienced, but a *virgin!*" He says it like it's a really dirty word. "Hell, Ana, I just showed you . . ." he groans. "May God forgive me. Have you ever been kissed, apart from by me?"

"Of course I have." I try my best to look affronted. *Okay . . . maybe twice.*

"And a nice young man hasn't swept you off your feet? I just don't understand. You're twenty-one, nearly twenty-two. You're beautiful." He runs his hand through his hair again.

Beautiful. I flush with pleasure. Christian Grey thinks I'm beautiful. I knot my fingers together, staring at them hard, trying to conceal my goofy grin. *Perhaps he's farsighted.* My subconscious has reared her somnambulant head. Where was she when I needed her?

"And you're seriously discussing what I want to do, when you have no experience." His brows knit together. "How have you avoided sex? Tell me, please."

I shrug.

"No one's really, you know . . ." Come up to scratch, only you. And you turn out to be some kind of monster. "Why are you so angry with me?" I whisper.

"I'm not angry with you, I'm angry with myself. I just assumed . . ." He sighs. He regards me shrewdly and then shakes his head. "Do you want to go?" he asks, his voice gentle.

"No, unless you want me to go," I murmur. *Oh no . . . I don't want to leave.*

"Of course not. I like having you here." He frowns as he says this and then glances at his watch. "It's late." And he turns to look at me. "You're biting your lip." His voice is husky, and he's eyeing me speculatively.

"Sorry."

"Don't apologize. It's just that I want to bite it, too, hard."

I gasp . . . how can he say things like that to me and not expect me to be affected.

"Come," he murmurs.

"What?"

"We're going to rectify the situation right now."

"What do you mean? What situation?"

"Your situation. Ana, I'm going to make love to you, now."

"Oh." The floor has fallen away. *I'm a situation.* I'm holding my breath.

"That's if you want to, I mean, I don't want to push my luck."

"I thought you didn't make love. I thought you fucked hard." I swallow, my mouth suddenly dry.

He gives me a wicked grin, the effects of which travel all the way down *there.*

"I can make an exception, or maybe combine the two, we'll see. I really want to make love to you. Please, come to bed with me. I want our arrangement to work, but you really need to have some idea what you're getting yourself into. We can start your training tonight—with the basics. This doesn't mean I've come over all hearts and flowers; it's a means to an end, but one that I want, and hopefully you do, too." His gaze is intense.

I flush . . . *oh my* . . . wishes do come true.

"But I haven't done all the things you require from your list of rules." My voice is all breathy, hesitant.

"Forget about the rules. Forget about all those details for tonight. I want you. I've wanted you since you fell into my office, and I know you want me. You wouldn't be sitting here calmly discussing punishment and hard limits if you didn't. Please, Ana, spend the night with me." He holds his hand out to me, his eyes are bright, fervent . . . excited, and I put my hand in his. He pulls me up and into his arms so I can feel the length of his body against mine, this swift action taking me by surprise. He runs his fingers around the nape of my neck, winds my ponytail around his wrist, and gently pulls so I'm forced to look up at him. He gazes down at me.

"You are one brave young woman," he whispers. "I am in awe of you."

His words are like some kind of incendiary device; my blood flames. He leans down and kisses my lips gently, and he sucks at my lower lip.

"I want to bite this lip," he murmurs against my mouth, and carefully he tugs at it with his teeth. I moan, and he smiles.

"Please, Ana, let me make love to you."

"Yes," I whisper, because that's why I'm here. His smile is triumphant as he releases me and takes my hand and leads me through the apartment.

His bedroom is vast. The ceiling-height windows look out on lit-up Seattle high-rises. The walls are white, and the furnishings are pale blue. The enormous bed is ultramodern, made of rough, gray wood like driftwood, four posts but no canopy. On the wall above it is a stunning painting of the sea.

I am quaking like a leaf. This is it. Finally, after all this time, I'm going to do it, with none other than Christian Grey. My breath is shallow, and I can't take my eyes off him. He removes his watch and places it on top of a chest of drawers that matches the bed, and removes his jacket, placing it on a chair. He's dressed in his white linen shirt and jeans. He is heart-stoppingly beautiful. His dark copper hair is a mess, his shirt hanging out—his gray eyes bold and dazzling. He steps out of his Converse shoes and reaches down and takes his socks off individually. Christian Grey's feet . . . wow . . . what is it about naked feet? Turning, he gazes at me, his expression soft.

"I assume you're not on the pill."

What? Shit.

"I didn't think so." He opens the top drawer of the chest and removes a packet of condoms. He gazes at me intently.

"Be prepared," he murmurs. "Do you want the blinds drawn?"

"I don't mind," I whisper. "I thought you didn't let anyone sleep in your bed."

"Who says we're going to sleep?" he murmurs.

"Oh." *Holy hell.*

He strolls slowly toward me. Confident, sexy, eyes blazing, and my heart begins to pound. My blood's pumping through my body. Desire, thick and hot, pools in my belly. He stands in front of me, staring down into my eyes. *He's so freaking hot.*

"Let's get this jacket off, shall we?" he says softly, and takes hold of the lapels and gently slides my jacket off my shoulders. He places it on the chair.

"Do you have any idea how much I want you, Ana Steele?" he whispers. My breath hitches. I cannot take my eyes off his. He reaches up and gently runs his fingers down my cheek to my chin.

"Do you have any idea what I'm going to do to you?" he adds, caressing my chin.

The muscles inside the deepest, darkest part of me clench in the most delicious fashion. The pain is so sweet and sharp I want to close my eyes, but I'm hypnotized by his eyes staring fervently into mine. Leaning down, he kisses me. His lips are demanding, firm and slow, molding mine. He starts unbuttoning my shirt while he places feather-like kisses across my jaw, my chin, and the corners of my mouth. Slowly he peels it off me and lets it fall to the floor. He stands back and gazes at me. I'm in the pale blue lacy perfect-fit bra. *Thank heavens.*

"Oh, Ana," he breathes. "You have the most beautiful skin, pale and flawless. I want to kiss every single inch of it."

I flush. *Oh my . . .* Why did he say he couldn't make love? I will do anything he wants. He grasps my hair tie, pulls it free, and gasps as my hair cascades down around my shoulders.

"I like brunettes," he murmurs, and both of his hands are in my hair, grasping each side of my head. His kiss is demanding, his tongue and lips coaxing mine. I moan, and my tongue tentatively meets his. He puts his arms around me and hauls me against his body, squeezing me tightly. One hand remains in my hair, the other travels down my spine to my waist and down to my behind. His hand flexes over my backside and squeezes gently. He holds me against his hips, and I feel his erection, which he languidly pushes into me.

I moan once more into his mouth. I can hardly contain the riotous feelings—or are they hormones?—that rampage through my body. I want him so badly. Gripping his upper arms, I feel his biceps. He's surprisingly strong . . . muscular. Tentatively, I move my hands up to his face and into his hair. It's so soft, unruly. I tug gently, and he groans. He eases me toward the bed, until I feel it behind my knees. I think he's going to push me down on to it, but he doesn't. Releasing me, he suddenly drops to his knees. He grabs my hips with both his hands and runs his tongue around my navel, then gently nips his way to my hipbone, then across my belly to my other hipbone.

"Ah," I groan.

Seeing him on his knees in front of me, feeling his mouth on me, it's so unexpected, and hot. My hands stay in his hair, pulling gently as I try to quiet my too-loud breathing. He gazes up at me through impossibly long lashes, his eyes a scorching smoky gray. His hands reach up and undo the button on my jeans, and he leisurely pulls down the zipper. Without taking his eyes off mine, his hands move beneath the waistband, skimming me and moving to my behind. His hands glide slowly down my backside to my thighs, removing my jeans as they go. I cannot look away.

He stops and licks his lips, never breaking eye contact. He leans forward, running his nose up the apex between my thighs. I feel him. *There.*

"You smell so good," he murmurs, and closes his eyes, a look of pure pleasure on his face, and I practically convulse. He reaches up and tugs the duvet off the bed, then pushes me gently so I fall on to the mattress.

Still kneeling, he grasps my foot and undoes my Converse, pulling off my shoe and sock. I raise myself up on my elbows to see what he's doing. I'm panting . . . wanting. He lifts my foot by the heel and runs his thumbnail up my instep. It's almost painful, but I feel the movement echoed in my groin. I gasp. Not taking his eyes off mine, again he runs his tongue along my instep and then his teeth. *Shit.* I groan . . . how can I feel this *there?* I fall back onto the bed, moaning. I hear his soft chuckle.

"Oh, Ana, what I could do to you," he whispers. He removes my other shoe and sock, then stands and removes my jeans completely. I'm lying on his bed dressed only in my bra and panties, and he's staring down at me.

"You're very beautiful, Anastasia Steele. I can't wait to be inside you."

Holy shit. His words. He's so seductive. He takes my breath away.

"Show me how you pleasure yourself."

What? I frown.

"Don't be coy, Ana, show me," he whispers.

I shake my head. "I don't know what you mean." My voice is hoarse. I hardly recognize it, laced with desire.

"How do you make yourself come? I want to see."

I shake my head.

"I don't," I mumble. He raises his eyebrows, astonished for a moment, and his eyes darken, and he shakes his head in disbelief.

"Well, we'll have to see what we can do about that." His voice is soft, challenging, a delicious sensual threat. He undoes the buttons of his jeans and slowly pulls his jeans down, his eyes on mine the whole time. He leans down over me and, grasping each of my ankles, quickly jerks my legs apart and crawls onto the bed between my legs. He hovers over me. I am squirming with need.

"Keep still," he murmurs, and then he leans down and kisses the inside of my thigh, trailing kisses up, over the thin lacy material of my panties, kissing me.

Oh . . . I can't keep still. How can I not move? I wriggle beneath him.

"We're going to have to work on keeping you still, baby." He trails kisses up my belly, and his tongue dips into my navel. Still he's heading north, kissing me across my torso. My skin is burning. I'm flushed, too hot, too cold, and I'm clawing at the sheet beneath me. He lies down beside me and his hand trails up from my hip, to my waist, and up to my breast. He gazes down at me, his expression unreadable, and gently cups my breast.

"You fit my hand perfectly, Anastasia," he murmurs, and dips his index finger into the cup of my bra and gently yanks it down, freeing my breast, but the underwire and fabric of the cup force it upward. His finger moves to my other breast and repeats the process. My breasts swell, and my nipples harden under his steady gaze. I am trussed up by my own bra.

"Very nice," he whispers appreciatively, and my nipples harden even more.

He blows very gently on one as his hand moves to my other breast, and his thumb slowly rolls the end of my nipple, elongating it. I groan, feeling the sweet sensation all the way to my groin. I am so wet. *Oh, please,* I beg internally as my fingers clasp the sheet tighter. His lips close around my other nipple, and when he tugs, I nearly convulse.

"Let's see if we can make you come like this," he whispers, continuing his slow, sensual assault. My nipples bear the delicious brunt of his deft fingers and lips, setting alight every single nerve ending so that my whole body sings with sweet agony. He just doesn't stop.

"Oh . . . please," I beg, and I pull my head back, my mouth

open as I groan, my legs stiffening. Holy hell, what's happening to me?

"Let go, baby," he murmurs. His teeth close round my nipple, and his thumb and finger pull hard, and I fall apart in his hands, my body convulsing and shattering into a thousand pieces. He kisses me, deeply, his tongue in my mouth absorbing my cries.

Oh my. That was extraordinary. Now I know what all the fuss is about. He gazes down at me, a satisfied smile on his face, while I'm sure there's nothing but gratitude and awe on mine.

"You are very responsive," he breathes. "You're going to have to learn to control that, and it's going to be so much fun teaching you how." He kisses me again.

My breathing is still ragged as I come down from my orgasm. His hand moves down my waist, to my hips, and then cups me, intimately . . . *Jeez.* His finger slips through the fine lace and slowly circles around me—*there.* Briefly he closes his eyes, and his breathing hitches.

"You're so deliciously wet. God, I want you." He thrusts his finger inside me, and I cry out as he does it again and again. He palms my clitoris, and I cry out once more. He pushes inside me harder and harder still. I groan.

Suddenly, he sits up and tugs my panties off and throws them on the floor. Pulling off his boxer briefs, his erection springs free. *Holy cow . . .* He reaches over to his bedside table and grabs a foil packet, and then he moves between my legs, spreading them farther apart. He kneels up and pulls a condom onto his considerable length. *Oh no . . . Will it? How?*

"Don't worry," he breathes, his eyes on mine. "You expand, too." He leans down, his hands on either side of my head, so he's hovering over me, staring down into my eyes, his jaw clenched, eyes burning. It's only now that I register he's still wearing his shirt.

"You really want to do this?" he asks softly.

"Please," I beg.

"Pull your knees up," he orders softly, and I'm quick to obey.

"I'm going to fuck you now, Miss Steele," he murmurs as he positions the head of his erection at the entrance of my sex. "Hard," he whispers, and he slams into me.

"Aargh!" I cry as I feel a weird pinching sensation deep inside me as he rips through my virginity. He stills, gazing down at me, his eyes bright with ecstatic triumph.

His mouth is open slightly, and his breathing is harsh. He groans.

"You're so tight. You okay?"

I nod, my eyes wide, my hands on his forearms. I feel so full. He stays still, letting me acclimatize to the intrusive, overwhelming feeling of him inside me.

"I'm going to move, baby," he breathes after a moment, his voice tight.

Oh.

He eases back with exquisite slowness. And he closes his eyes and groans, and thrusts into me again. I cry out a second time, and he stills.

"More?" he whispers, his voice raw.

"Yes," I breathe. He does it once more, and stills again.

I groan, my body accepting him . . . Oh, I want this.

"Again?" he breathes.

"Yes." It's a plea.

And he moves, but this time he doesn't stop. He shifts onto his elbows so I can feel his weight on me, holding me down. He moves slowly at first, easing himself in and out of me. And as I grow accustomed to the alien feeling, my hips move tentatively to meet his. He speeds up. I moan, and he pounds on, picking up speed, merciless, a relentless rhythm, and I keep up, meeting his thrusts. He grasps my head between his hands and kisses me hard, his teeth pulling at my lower lip again. He shifts slightly, and I can feel something building deep inside me, like before. I start to stiffen as he thrusts on and on. My body quivers, bows; a sheen of sweat gathers over me. *Oh my* . . . I didn't know it would feel like this . . . didn't know it could feel as good as this. My thoughts are scattering . . . there's only sensation . . . only him . . . only me . . . oh, please . . . I stiffen.

"Come for me, Ana," he whispers breathlessly, and I unravel at his words, exploding around him as I climax and splinter into a million pieces underneath him. And as he comes, he calls out my name, thrusting hard, then stilling as he empties himself into me.

I am still panting, trying to slow my breathing, my thumping heart, and my thoughts are in riotous disarray. *Wow . . . that was astounding.* I open my eyes, and he has his forehead pressed against mine, his eyes closed, his breathing ragged. Christian's eyes flicker open and gaze down at me, dark but soft. He's still inside me. Leaning down, he gently presses a kiss against my forehead then slowly pulls out of me.

"Ooh." I wince at the unfamiliarity.

"Did I hurt you?" Christian asks as he lies down beside me propped on one elbow. He tucks a stray strand of my hair behind my ear. And I have to grin, widely.

"*You* are asking me if you hurt me?"

"The irony is not lost on me," he smiles sardonically. "Seriously, are you okay?" His eyes are intense, probing, demanding even.

I stretch out beside him, feeling loose-limbed, my bones like jelly, but I'm relaxed, deeply relaxed. I grin at him. I can't stop grinning. Now I know what all the fuss is about. Two orgasms . . . coming apart at the seams, like the spin cycle on a washing machine, wow. I had no idea what my body was capable of, could be wound so tightly and released so violently, so gratifyingly. The pleasure was indescribable.

"You're biting your lip, and you haven't answered me." He's frowning. I grin up at him impishly. He looks glorious with his tousled hair, burning narrowed gray eyes, and serious, dark expression.

"I'd like to do that again," I whisper. For a moment, I think I see a fleeting look of relief on his face, before the shutters come down, and he gazes at me through hooded eyes.

"Would you now, Miss Steele?" he murmurs dryly. He leans down and kisses me very gently at the corner of my mouth. "Demanding little thing, aren't you? Turn on your front."

I blink at him momentarily, and then I turn over. He unhooks my bra and runs his hand down my back to my behind.

"You really have the most beautiful skin," he murmurs. He shifts so that one of his legs pushes between mine, and he's half lying across my back. I can feel the buttons of his shirt pressing into me as he gathers my hair off my face and kisses my bare shoulder.

"Why are you wearing your shirt?" I ask. He stills. After a beat, he shuffles out of his shirt, and he lies back down on me. I feel his warm skin against mine. *Hmm . . .* it feels heavenly. He has a light dusting of hair across his chest, which tickles my back.

"So you want me to fuck you again?" he whispers in my ear, and he begins to trail featherlight kisses around my ear and down my neck.

His hand moves down, skimming my waist, over my hip, and down my thigh to the back of my knee. He pushes my knee up higher, and my breath hitches . . . *What's he doing now?* He shifts so he's between my legs, pressed against my back, and his hand travels up my thigh to my behind. He caresses my cheek slowly, and then trails his fingers down between my legs.

"I'm going to take you from behind, Anastasia," he murmurs, and with his other hand, he grasps my hair at the nape in a fist and pulls gently, holding me in place. I cannot move my head. I am pinioned beneath him, helpless.

"You are mine," he whispers. "Only mine. Don't forget it." His voice is intoxicating, his words heady, seductive. I feel his growing erection against my thigh.

His long fingers reach around to gently massage my clitoris, circling slowly. His breath is soft against my face as he slowly nips me along my jaw.

"You smell divine." He nuzzles behind my ear. His hand rubs against me, around and around. Reflexively, my hips start to circle, mirroring his hand, as excruciating pleasure spikes through my blood like adrenaline.

"Keep still," he orders, his voice soft but urgent, and slowly he inserts his thumb inside me, rotating it around and around, stroking the front wall of my vagina. The effect is mind-blowing—all my energy concentrating on this one small space inside my body. I moan.

"You like this?" he asks softly, his teeth grazing my outer ear, and he starts to flex his thumb slowly, in, out, in, out . . . his fingers still circling.

I close my eyes, trying to keep my breathing under control, trying to absorb the disordered, chaotic sensations that his fingers are unleashing on me, fire coursing through my body. I moan again.

"You're so wet, so quickly. So responsive. Oh, Anastasia, I like that. I like that a lot," he whispers.

I want to stiffen my legs, but I can't move. He's pinning me down, keeping up a constant, slow, tortuous rhythm. It's absolutely exquisite. I moan again, and he moves suddenly.

"Open your mouth," he commands, and thrusts his thumb in my mouth. My eyes fly open, blinking wildly.

"See how you taste," he breathes against my ear. "Suck me, baby." His thumb presses on my tongue, and my mouth closes around him, sucking wildly. I taste the saltiness on his thumb and the faint metallic tang of blood. *Holy fuck*. This is wrong, but holy hell is it erotic.

"I want to fuck your mouth, Anastasia, and I will soon," his voice is hoarse, raw, his breathing more disjointed.

Fuck my mouth! I moan, and I bite down on him. He gasps, and he pulls my hair tighter, painfully, so I release him.

"Naughty, sweet girl," he whispers, and then reaches over to the bedside table for a foil packet. "Stay still, don't move," he orders as he releases my hair.

He rips the foil while I'm breathing hard, my blood singing in my veins. The anticipation is exhilarating. He leans down, his weight on me again, and he grabs my hair, holding my head immobile. I cannot move. I'm enticingly ensnared by him, and he's poised and ready to take me once more.

"We're going to go real slow this time, Anastasia," he breathes.

And slowly he eases into me, slowly, slowly, until he's buried in me. Stretching, filling, relentless. I groan loudly. It feels deeper this time, delectable. I groan again, and he deliberately circles his hips and pulls back, pauses a beat, and then eases his way back in. He repeats this motion again and again. It's driving me insane—his teasing, deliberately slow thrusts, and the intermittent feeling of fullness is overwhelming.

"You feel so good," he groans, and my insides start to quiver. He pulls back and waits. "Oh no, baby, not yet," he murmurs, and as the quivering ceases, he starts the whole delicious process again.

"Oh, please," I beg. I'm not sure I can take much more. My body is wound so tight, craving release.

"I want you sore, baby," he murmurs, and he continues his sweet, leisurely torment, backward, forward. "Every time you move tomorrow, I want you to be reminded that I've been here. Only me. You are mine."

I groan.

"Please, Christian," I whisper.

"What do you want, Anastasia? Tell me."

I groan again. He pulls out and moves slowly back into me, circling his hips once more.

"Tell me," he murmurs.

"You, please."

He increases the rhythm infinitesimally, and his breathing becomes more erratic. My insides start quickening, and Christian picks up the rhythm.

"You. Are. So. Sweet," he murmurs between each thrust. "I. Want. You. So. Much."

I moan.

"You. Are. Mine. Come for me, baby," he growls.

His words are my undoing, tipping me over the precipice. My

body convulses around him, and I come, loudly calling out a garbled version of his name into the mattress. Christian follows with two sharp thrusts, and he freezes, pouring himself into me as he finds his release. He collapses on top of me, his face in my hair.

"Fuck. Ana," he breathes. He pulls out of me immediately and rolls onto his side of the bed. I pull my knees up to my chest, utterly spent, and immediately drift off or pass out into an exhausted sleep.

WHEN I WAKE, IT'S still dark. I have no idea how long I've slept. I stretch out beneath the duvet, and I feel sore, deliciously sore. Christian is nowhere to be seen. I sit up, staring out at the cityscape in front of me. There are fewer lights on among the skyscrapers, and there's a whisper of dawn in the east. I hear music. The lilting notes of the piano, a sad, sweet lament. Bach, I think, but I'm not sure.

I wrap the duvet around me and quietly pad down the corridor toward the big room. Christian is at the piano, completely lost in the melody he's playing. His expression is sad and forlorn, like the music. His playing is stunning. Leaning against the wall at the entrance, I listen, enraptured. He's such an accomplished musician. He sits naked, his body bathed in the warm light cast by a solitary freestanding lamp beside the piano. With the rest of the large room in darkness, it's like he's in his own isolated little pool of light, untouchable . . . lonely, in a bubble.

I pad quietly toward him, enticed by the sublime, melancholy music. I'm mesmerized, watching his long, skilled fingers as they find and gently press the keys, thinking how those same fingers have expertly handled and caressed my body. I flush and gasp at the memory and press my thighs together. He glances up, his unfathomable gray eyes bright, his expression unreadable.

"Sorry," I whisper. "I didn't mean to disturb you."

A frown flits across his face.

"Surely, I should be saying that to you," he murmurs. He finishes playing and puts his hands on his legs.

I notice now that he's wearing PJ pants. He runs his fingers through his hair and stands. His pants hang from his hips, in that way . . . *oh my.* My mouth goes dry as he casually strolls around the piano toward me. He has broad shoulders, narrow hips, and his abdominal muscles ripple as he walks. He really is stunning.

"You should be in bed," he admonishes.

"That was a beautiful piece. Bach?"

"Transcription by Bach, but it's originally an oboe concerto by Alessandro Marcello."

"It was exquisite, but very sad, such a melancholy melody."

His lips quirk up in a half smile.

"Bed," he orders. "You'll be exhausted in the morning."

"I woke and you weren't there."

"I find it difficult to sleep, and I'm not used to sleeping with anyone," he murmurs. I can't fathom his mood. He seems a little despondent, but it's difficult to tell in the darkness. Perhaps it was the tone of the piece he was playing. He puts his arm around me and gently walks me back to the bedroom.

"How long have you been playing? You play beautifully."

"Since I was six."

"Oh." Christian as a six-year-old boy . . . my mind conjures an image of a beautiful, copper-haired little boy with gray eyes and my heart melts—a moppet-haired kid who likes impossibly sad music.

"How are you feeling?" he asks when we are back in the room. He switches on a sidelight.

"I'm good."

We both glance down at the bed at the same time. There's blood on the sheets—evidence of my lost virginity. I flush, embarrassed, pulling the duvet tighter around me.

"Well, that's going to give Mrs. Jones something to think about," Christian mutters as he stands in front of me. He puts his hand under my chin and tips my head back, staring down at me. His eyes are intense as he examines my face. I realize that I've not seen his naked chest before. Instinctively, I reach out to run my fingers through the smattering of dark hair on his chest to see how it feels. Immediately, he steps back out of my reach.

"Get into bed," he says sharply. His voice softens. "I'll come and lie down with you." I drop my hand and frown. I don't think I've ever touched his torso. He opens a chest of drawers and pulls out a T-shirt and quickly slips it on.

"Bed," he orders again. I climb back onto the bed, trying not to think about the blood. He clambers in beside me and pulls me into his embrace, wrapping his arms around me so that I'm facing away from him. He kisses my hair gently, and he inhales deeply.

"Sleep, sweet Anastasia," he murmurs, and I close my eyes, but I can't help feel a residual melancholy either from the music or his demeanor. Christian Grey has a sad side.

CHAPTER NINE

Light fills the room, coaxing me from deep sleep to wakefulness. I stretch out and open my eyes. It's a beautiful May morning, Seattle at my feet. Wow, what a view. Beside me, Christian Grey is fast asleep. Wow, what a view. I'm surprised he's still in bed. He's facing me, and I have an unprecedented opportunity to study him. His lovely face looks younger, relaxed in sleep. His sculptured, pouty lips are parted slightly, and his shiny, clean hair is a glorious mess. How could anyone look this good and still be legal? I remember his room upstairs . . . perhaps he's not legal. I shake my head, so much to think about. It's tempting to reach out and touch him, but like a small child, he's so lovely when he's asleep. I don't have to worry about what I'm saying, what he's saying, what plans he has, especially his plans for me.

I could gaze at him all day, but I have needs—bathroom needs. Slipping out of bed, I find his white shirt on the floor and shrug it on. I walk through a door thinking that it might be the bathroom, but I'm in a vast walk-in closet as big as my bedroom. Lines and lines of expensive suits, shirts, shoes, and ties. How can anyone need this many clothes? I tut with disapproval. Actually, Kate's wardrobe probably rivals this. Kate! *Oh no.* I didn't think about her all evening. I was supposed to text her. Crap. I'm going to be in trouble. I wonder briefly how she's getting on with Elliot.

Returning to the bedroom, Christian is still asleep. I try the other door. It's the bathroom, and it's bigger than my bedroom. Why does one man need so much space? Two sinks, I notice with irony. Given he doesn't sleep with anyone, one of them can't have been used.

I stare at myself in the gigantic mirror above the sinks. Do I look different? I feel different. I feel a little sore, if I'm honest, and my muscles—jeez, it's like I've never done any exercise in my life. *You don't do any exercise in your life.* My subconscious has woken. She's staring at me with pursed lips, tapping her foot. *So you've just slept with him, given him your virginity, a man who doesn't love you. In fact, he has very odd ideas about you, wants to make you some sort of kinky sex slave.*

ARE YOU CRAZY? She's shouting at me.

I wince as I look in the mirror. I am going to have to process all this. Honestly, fancy falling for a man who's beyond beautiful, richer than Croesus, and has a Red Room of Pain waiting for me. I shudder. I'm bewildered and confused. My hair is its usual wayward self. Just-fucked hair doesn't suit me. I try to bring order to the chaos with my fingers but fail miserably and give up—maybe I'll find hair ties in my purse.

I'm starving. I head back out to the bedroom. Sleeping beauty is still sleeping, so I leave him and head for the kitchen.

Oh no . . . Kate. I left my purse in Christian's study. I fetch it and reach for my cell phone. Three texts.

RU OK Ana
Where RU Ana
Damn it Ana

I call Kate. When she doesn't answer, I leave her a groveling message to tell her I am alive and have not succumbed to Bluebeard, well, not in the sense she would be worried about—*or perhaps I have.* Oh, this is so confusing. I have to try to categorize and analyze my feelings for Christian Grey. It's an impossible task. I shake my head in defeat. I need alone time, away from here to think.

I find two welcome hair ties at the same time in my bag and quickly tie my hair in pigtails. Yes! The more girly I look perhaps the safer I'll be from Bluebeard. I take my iPod out of the bag and plug my headphones in. There's nothing like music to cook by. I slip it into the breast pocket of Christian's shirt, turn it up loud, and start dancing.

Holy hell, I'm hungry.

I am daunted by his kitchen. It's so sleek and modern, and none of the cupboards has handles. It takes me a few seconds to deduce that I have to push the cupboard doors to open them. Perhaps I should cook Christian breakfast. He was eating an omelet the other day . . . um, yesterday at the Heathman. Jeez, so much has happened since then. I check in the fridge, where there are plenty of eggs, and decide I want pancakes and bacon. I set about making some batter, dancing my way around the kitchen.

Being busy is good. It allows a bit of time to think but not too deeply. Music blaring in my ears also helps to stave off deep thought. I came here to spend the night in Christian Grey's bed and managed it, even though he doesn't let anyone in his bed. I smile, mission accomplished. Big time. I grin. Big, big time, and I'm distracted by the memory of last night. His words, his body, his lovemaking . . . I close my eyes as my body hums at the recollection, and my muscles contract deliciously deep in my belly. My subconscious scowls at me . . . *Fucking—not lovemaking,* she screams at me like a harpy. I ignore her, but deep down I know she has a point. I shake my head to concentrate on the task at hand.

There is a state-of-the-art range. I think I have the hang of it. I need somewhere to keep the pancakes warm, and I start on the bacon. Amy Studt is singing in my ear about misfits. This song used to mean so much to me; that's because I'm a misfit. I have never fitted in anywhere and now . . . I have an indecent proposal to consider from King Misfit himself. Why is he this way? Nature or nurture? It's so alien to anything I know.

I put the bacon under the grill, and while it's cooking, I whisk some eggs. I turn, and Christian is sitting on one of the barstools at the breakfast bar, leaning on it, his face supported by his steepled hands. He's still wearing the T-shirt he slept in. Just-fucked hair really, really suits him, as does his designer stubble. He looks both amused and bewildered. I freeze, flush, then gather myself and pull the headphones out of my ears, my knees weak at the sight of him.

"Good morning, Miss Steele. You're very energetic this morning," he says dryly.

"I-I slept well," I stutter my explanation. His lips try to mask his smile.

"I can't imagine why." He pauses and frowns. "So did I after I came back to bed."

"Are you hungry?"

"Very," he says with an intense look, and I don't think he's referring to food.

"Pancakes, bacon, and eggs?"

"Sounds great."

"I don't know where you keep your placemats." I shrug, trying desperately hard not to look flustered.

"I'll do that. You cook. Would you like me to put some music on so you can continue your . . . er . . . dancing?"

I stare down at my fingers, knowing that I am turning puce.

"Please, don't stop on my account. It's very entertaining." His tone is one of wry amusement.

I purse my lips. Entertaining, eh? My subconscious has doubled over in laughter at me. I turn and continue to whisk the eggs, probably beating them a little harder than necessary. In a moment, he's beside me. He gently pulls my pigtail.

"I love these," he whispers. "They won't protect you." *Hmm, Bluebeard . . .*

"How would you like your eggs?" I ask tartly. He smiles.

"Thoroughly whisked and beaten." He smirks.

I turn back to the task at hand, trying to hide my smile. He's hard to stay mad at. Especially when he's being so uncharacteristically playful. He opens a drawer and takes out two slate black placemats for the breakfast bar. I pour the egg mix into a pan, pull out the bacon, turn it over, and put it back under the grill.

When I turn back around, there is orange juice on the table, and he's making coffee.

"Would you like some tea?"

"Yes, please. If you have some."

I find a couple of plates and place them in the warming tray of the range. Christian reaches into a cupboard and pulls out some Twinings English Breakfast tea. I purse my lips.

"Bit of a foregone conclusion, wasn't I?"

"Are you? I'm not sure we've concluded anything yet, Miss Steele," he murmurs.

What does he mean by that? Our negotiations? Our, er . . . relationship . . . whatever that is? He's still so cryptic. I serve up the breakfast onto the heated plates and lay them on the placemats. I hunt in the refrigerator and find some maple syrup.

I glance up at Christian, and he's waiting for me to sit down.

"Miss Steele." He motions to one of the barstools.

"Mr. Grey." I nod in acknowledgment. I climb up and wince slightly as I sit down.

"Just how sore are you?" he asks as he sits down. I flush. *Why does he ask such personal questions?*

"Well, to be truthful, I have nothing to compare this to," I snap at him. "Did you wish to offer your commiserations?" I ask too sweetly. I think he's trying to stifle a smile, but I can't be sure.

"No. I wondered if we should continue your basic training."

"Oh." I stare at him dumbfounded as I stop breathing and everything inside me clenches tight. *Ooh . . . that's so nice.* I suppress my groan.

"Eat, Anastasia." My appetite has become uncertain again . . . more . . . more sex . . . yes, please.

"This is delicious, incidentally." He grins at me.

I try a forkful of omelet but can barely taste it. Basic training! *I want to fuck your mouth.* Does that form part of basic training?

"Stop biting your lip. It's very distracting, and I happen to know you're not wearing anything under my shirt, which makes it even more distracting."

I dunk my teabag in the small pot that Christian has provided. My mind is in a whirl.

"What sort of basic training did you have in mind?" I ask, my voice slightly too high, betraying my wish to sound as natural, disinterested, and calm as I can with my hormones wreaking havoc through my body.

"Well, as you're sore, I thought we could stick to oral skills."

I choke on my tea, and I stare at him, eyes wide and mouth gaping. He pats me gently on the back and passes me some orange juice. I cannot tell what he's thinking.

"That's if you want to stay," he adds. I glance up at him, trying to recover my equilibrium. His expression is unreadable. It's so frustrating.

"I'd like to stay for today. If that's okay. I have to work tomorrow."

"What time do you have to be at work tomorrow?"

"Nine."

"I'll get you to work by nine tomorrow."

I frown. *Does he want me to stay another night?*

"I'll need to go home tonight—I need clean clothes."

"We can get you some here."

I don't have spare cash to spend on clothes. His hand comes up, and he grasps my chin, tugging it so my lip is released from the grip of my teeth. I'm not even aware I've been biting my lip.

"What is it?" he asks.

"I need to be home this evening."

His mouth is a hard line.

"Okay, this evening," he acquiesces. "Now eat your breakfast."

My thoughts and my stomach are in turmoil. My appetite has vanished. I stare at my half-eaten breakfast. I'm just not hungry.

"Eat, Anastasia. You didn't eat last night."

"I'm really not hungry," I whisper.

His eyes narrow. "I would really like you to finish your breakfast."

"What is it with you and food?" I blurt out. His brow knits.

"I told you, I have issues with wasted food. Eat," he snaps. His eyes are dark, pained.

Holy crap. What is that all about? I pick up my fork and eat slowly, trying to chew. I must remember not to put so much on my plate if he's going to be weird about food. His expression softens as I carefully make my way through my breakfast. I note that he cleans his plate. He waits for me to finish, and then he clears my plate.

"You cooked, I'll clear."

"That's very democratic."

"Yes." He frowns. "Not my usual style. After I've done this, we'll take a bath."

"Oh, okay." *Oh my . . . I'd much rather have a shower.* My cell rings, interrupting my reverie. It's Kate.

"Hi." I wander over to the glass doors of the balcony, away from him.

"Ana, why didn't you text last night?" She's angry.

"I'm sorry, I was overtaken by events."

"You're okay?"

"Yes, I'm fine."

"Did you?" She's fishing for information. I roll my eyes at the expectation in her voice.

"Kate, I don't want to talk over the phone." Christian glances up at me.

"You did . . . I can tell."

How can she tell? She's bluffing, and I can't talk about this. I've signed a damned agreement.

"Kate, please."

"What was it like? Are you okay?"

"I've told you I'm okay."

"Was he gentle?"

"Kate, please!" I can't hide my exasperation.

"Ana, don't hold out on me, I've been waiting for this day for nearly four years."

"I'll see you this evening." I hang up.

That is going to be one difficult square to circle. She's so tenacious, and she wants to know—in detail, and I can't tell her because I've signed a—what was it called? NDA. She'll freak and rightly so. I need a plan. I head back to watch Christian move gracefully around his kitchen.

"The NDA, does it cover everything?" I ask tentatively.

"Why?" He turns and gazes at me while putting the Twinings away. I flush.

"Well, I have a few questions, you know, about sex." I stare down at my fingers. "And I'd like to ask Kate."

"You can ask me."

"Christian, with all due respect . . ." My voice fades. *I can't ask you.* I'll get your biased, kinky-as-hell, distorted worldview regarding sex. I want an impartial opinion. "It's just about mechanics. I won't mention the Red Room of Pain."

He raises his eyebrows.

"Red Room of Pain? It's mostly about pleasure, Anastasia. Believe me," he says. "Besides," his tone is harsher, "your roommate is making the beast with two backs with my brother. I'd really rather you didn't."

"Does your family know about your . . . um, predilection?"

"No. It's none of their business." He saunters toward me until he's standing in front of me.

"What do you want to know?" he asks, and raising his hand runs his fingers gently down my cheek to my chin, tilting my head back so he can look directly into my eyes. I squirm inwardly. I cannot lie to this man.

"Nothing specific at the moment," I whisper.

"Well, we can start with: How was last night for you?" His eyes burn, filled with curiosity. *He's anxious to know. Wow.*

"Good," I murmur.

His lips lift slightly.

"Me, too," he murmurs. "I've never had vanilla sex before. There's a lot to be said for it. But then, maybe it's because it's with you." He runs his thumb across my lower lip.

I inhale sharply. *Vanilla sex?*

"Come, let's have a bath." He leans down and kisses me.

My heart leaps and desire pools way down low . . . way down *there*.

THE BATH IS A white stone, deep, egg-shaped affair, very designer. Christian leans over and fills it from the faucet on the tiled wall. He pours some expensive-looking bath oil into the water. It foams as the bath fills and smells of sweet, sultry jasmine. He stands and gazes at me, his eyes dark, then peels his T-shirt off and casts it on the floor.

"Miss Steele." He holds his hand out.

I'm standing in the doorway, wide-eyed and wary, my arms wrapped around myself. I step forward while surreptitiously admiring his physique. I take his hand, and he bids me to step into the bath while I am still wearing his shirt. I do as I'm told. I'll have to get used to it if I'm going to take him up on his outrageous offer . . . *if!* The water is enticingly hot.

"Turn around, face me," he orders, his voice soft. I do as I'm told. He's watching me intently.

"I know that lip is delicious, I can attest to that, but will you stop biting it?" he says through clenched teeth. "Your chewing it makes me want to fuck you, and you're sore, okay?"

I gasp, automatically unlocking my lip, shocked.

"Yeah," he challenges. "Get the picture?" He glares at me. I nod frantically. *I had no idea I could affect him so.*

"Good." He reaches forward and takes my iPod out of the breast pocket, and he puts it by the sink.

"Water and iPods—not a clever combination," he mutters. He reaches down, grasps the hem of my white shirt, lifts it above my head, and discards it on the floor.

He stands back to gaze at me. *I'm naked for heaven's sake.* I flush crimson and stare down at my hands, level with the base of my belly, and I desperately want to disappear into the hot water and foam, but I know he won't want that.

"Hey," he summons me. I peek up at him, and his head is cocked to one side. "Anastasia, you're a very beautiful woman, the whole package. Don't hang your head like you're ashamed. You have nothing to be ashamed of, and it's a real joy to stand here and gaze at you." He takes my chin in his hand and tilts my head up to reach his eyes. They are soft and warm, heated even. He's so close. I could just reach up and touch him.

"You can sit down now." He halts my scattered thoughts, and I scoot down into the warm, welcoming water. Ooh . . . it stings and that takes me by surprise, but it smells heavenly, too. The initial smarting pain soon ebbs away. I lie back and briefly close my eyes, relaxing in the soothing warmth. When I open them, he is gazing down at me.

"Why don't you join me?" I ask, bravely I think—my voice husky.

"I think I will. Move forward," he orders.

He strips out of his PJ pants and climbs in behind me. The water rises as he sits and pulls me against his chest. He places his long legs over mine, his knees bent and his ankles level with mine, and he pulls his feet apart, opening my legs. I gasp in surprise. His nose is in my hair and he inhales deeply.

"You smell so good, Anastasia."

A tremor runs through my whole body. *I am naked in a bath with Christian Grey. He's naked.* If someone had told me I'd be doing this when I woke up in his hotel suite yesterday, I would not have believed them.

He reaches for a bottle of body wash from the built-in shelf beside the bath and squirts some into his hand. He rubs his hands together, creating a soft, foaming lather, and he closes his hands around my neck and starts to rub the soap into my neck and shoulders, massaging firmly with his long, strong fingers. I groan. His hands on me feel good.

"You like that?" I can almost hear his smile.

"Hmm."

He moves down my arms, then beneath them to my underarms, washing gently. I'm so glad Kate insisted I shave. His hands glide across to my breasts, and I inhale sharply as his fingers encircle them and start kneading gently, taking no prisoners. My body bows instinctively, pushing my breasts into his hands. My nipples are tender. Very tender, no doubt, from his less-than-delicate treatment of them last night. He doesn't linger long and glides his hands down to my stomach and belly. My breathing increases and my heart is racing. His growing erection presses against my behind. It's such a turn-on knowing that it's my body making him feel this way. *Ha . . . not your mind,* my subconscious sneers. I shake off the unwelcome thought.

He stops and reaches for a washcloth as I pant against him, wanting . . . needing. My hands rest on his firm, muscular thighs. Squirting more soap onto the washcloth, he leans down and washes between my legs. I hold my breath. His fingers skillfully stimulating me through the cloth, it's heavenly, and my hips start moving at their own rhythm, pushing against his hand. As the sensations take over, I tilt my head back, my eyes rolling to the back of my head, my mouth slack, and I groan. The pressure is building slowly, inexorably inside me . . . *oh my.*

"Feel it, baby," Christian whispers in my ear, and very gently grazes my earlobe with his teeth. "Feel it for me." My legs are pinioned by his to the side of the bath, holding me prisoner, giving him easy access to this most private part of myself.

"Oh . . . please," I whisper. I try to stiffen my legs as my body goes rigid. I am in a sexual thrall to this man, and he doesn't let me move.

"I think you're clean enough now," he murmurs, and he stops. *What! No! No! No!* My breathing is ragged.

"Why are you stopping?" I gasp.

"Because I have other plans for you, Anastasia."

What . . . oh my . . . but . . . I was . . . that's not fair.

"Turn around. I need washing, too," he murmurs.

Oh! Turning to face him, I'm shocked to find he has his erection firmly in his grasp. My mouth drops open.

"I want you to become well acquainted, on first name terms if you will, with my favorite and most cherished part of my body. I'm very attached to this."

It's so big and growing. His erection is above the water line, the water lapping at his hips. I glance up at him and come face-to-face with his wicked grin. He's enjoying my astounded expression. I realize that I'm staring. I swallow. *That was inside me!* It doesn't seem possible. He wants me to touch him. *Hmm* . . . okay, bring it on.

I smile at him and reach for the body wash, squirting some soap onto my hand. I do as he's done, lathering the soap in my hands until they are foamy. I do not take my eyes off his. My lips are parted to accommodate my breathing . . . very deliberately I gently bite my bottom lip and then run my tongue across it, tracing where my teeth have been. His eyes are serious and dark, and they widen as my tongue skims my lower lip. I reach forward and place one of my hands around him, mirroring how he's holding himself. His eyes close briefly. Wow . . . feels much firmer than I expected. I squeeze, and he places his hand over mine.

"Like this," he whispers, and he moves his hand up and down with a firm grip around my fingers, and my fingers tighten around him. He closes his eyes again, and his breath hitches in his throat. When he opens them again, his gaze is scorching molten gray. "That's right, baby."

He releases my hand, leaving me to continue alone, and closes his eyes as I move up and down his length. He flexes his hips slightly into my hand and reflexively I grasp him tighter. A low groan escapes from deep within his throat. *Fuck my mouth . . . hmm.* I remember him pushing his thumb in my mouth and asking me to suck, hard. His mouth drops open as his breathing increases. I lean forward, while he has his eyes closed, and place my lips around him and tentatively suck, running my tongue over the tip.

"Whoa . . . Ana." His eyes fly open, and I suck harder.

Hmm . . . he's hard and soft at once, like steel encased in velvet, and surprisingly tasty—salty and smooth.

"Christ," he groans, and he closes his eyes again.

Moving down, I push him into my mouth. He groans again. *Ha!* My inner goddess is thrilled. I can do this. *I* can fuck *him* with my mouth. I twirl my tongue around the tip again, and he flexes and raises his hips. His eyes are open now, blistering with heat. His teeth are clenched as he flexes again, and I push him deeper into my mouth, supporting myself on his thighs. I feel his legs tense beneath my hands. He reaches up and grabs my pigtails and starts to really move.

"Oh . . . baby . . . that feels good," he murmurs. I suck harder, flicking my tongue across the head of his impressive erection. Wrapping my teeth behind my lips, I clamp my mouth around him. His breath hisses between his teeth, and he groans.

"Jesus. How far can you go?" he whispers.

Hmm . . . I pull him deeper into my mouth so I can feel him at the back of my throat and then to the front again. My tongue swirls around the end. He's my very own Christian Grey–flavored popsicle. I suck harder and harder, pushing him deeper and deeper, swirling my tongue around and around. *Hmm* . . . I had no idea giving pleasure could be such a turn-on, watching him writhe subtly with carnal longing. My inner goddess is doing the merengue with some salsa moves.

"Anastasia, I'm going to come in your mouth," his breathy tone is warning. "If you don't want me to, stop now." He thrusts his hips again, his eyes are wide, wary, and filled with salacious need—need for me. Need for my mouth . . . *oh my.*

His hands are really gripping my hair. I can do this. I push even harder and, in a moment of extraordinary confidence, I bare my teeth. It tips him over the edge. He cries out and stills, and I can feel warm, salty liquid oozing down my throat. I swallow quickly. Ugh . . . I'm not sure about this. But one look at him, and I don't care—he's come apart in the bath because of me. I sit back and watch him, a triumphant, gloating smile tugging at the corners of my lips. His breathing is ragged. Opening his eyes, he glares at me.

"Don't you have a gag reflex?" he asks, astonished. "Christ, Ana . . . that was . . . good, really good. Unexpected, though." He frowns. "You know, you never cease to amaze me."

I smile and consciously bite my lip. He eyes me speculatively.

"Have you done that before?"

"No." And I can't help the small tinge of pride in my denial.

"Good," he says complacently and, I think, relieved. "Yet another first, Miss Steele." He looks appraisingly at me. "Well, you get an A in oral skills. Come, let's go to bed, I owe you an orgasm."

Orgasm! Another one!

Quickly, he clambers out of the bath, giving me my first full glimpse of the Adonis, divinely formed, that is Christian Grey. My inner goddess has stopped dancing and is staring, too, open-mouthed and drooling slightly. His erection tamed but still substantial . . . wow. He wraps a small towel around his waist, covering the essentials, and holds out a larger fluffy white towel for me. Climbing out of the bath, I take his proffered hand. He wraps me in the towel, pulls me into his arms, and kisses me hard, pushing his tongue into my mouth. I long to reach around and embrace him . . . touch him . . . but he has my arms trapped in the towel. I'm soon lost in his kiss. He cradles my head, his tongue exploring my mouth, and I get a sense he's expressing his gratitude—maybe—for my first blow job? *Whoa.*

He pulls away, his hands on either side of my face, staring intently into my eyes. He looks lost.

"Say yes," he whispers fervently.

I frown, not understanding.

"To what?"

"Yes to our arrangement. To being mine. Please, Ana," he whispers pleading, emphasizing the last word and my name. He kisses me again, sweetly, passionately, before he stands back and stares at me, blinking slightly. He takes my hand and leads me back to his bedroom, leaving me reeling, so I follow him meekly. Stunned. *He really wants this.*

In his bedroom, he stares down at me as we stand by his bed.

"Trust me?" he asks suddenly. I nod, wide-eyed with the sudden realization that I do trust him. *What's he going to do to me now?* An electric thrill hums through me.

"Good girl," he breathes, his thumb brushing my bottom lip.

He steps away into his closet and comes back with a silver-gray silk woven tie.

"Hold your hands together in front of you," he orders as he peels the towel off me and throws it on the floor.

I do as he asks, and he binds my wrists together with his tie, knotting it firmly. His eyes are bright with excitement. He tugs at the binding. It's secure. *Some Boy Scout he must have been to learn this knot.* What now? My pulse has gone through the roof, my heart beating a frantic rhythm. He runs his fingers down my pigtails.

"You look so young with these," he murmurs, and moves forward. Instinctively, I move back until I feel the bed against the back of my knees. He drops his towel, but I can't take my eyes off his face. His expression is ardent, full of desire.

"Oh, Anastasia, what shall I do to you?" he whispers as he lowers me onto the bed, lying beside me and raising my hands above my head.

"Keep your hands up here, don't move them, understand?" His eyes burn into mine, and I'm breathless from their intensity. This is not a man I want to cross . . . ever.

"Answer me," he demands, his voice soft.

"I won't move my hands." I'm breathless.

"Good girl," he murmurs, and deliberately licks his lips slowly. I'm mesmerized by his tongue as it sweeps slowly over his upper lip. He's staring into my eyes, watching me, appraising. He leans down and plants a chaste, swift kiss on my lips.

"I'm going to kiss you all over, Miss Steele," he says softly, and he cups my chin, pushing it up, giving him access to my throat. His lips glide down my throat, kissing, sucking, and nipping, to the small dip at the base of my neck. My body leaps to attention . . . everywhere. My recent bath experience has made my skin hypersensitive. My heated blood pools low in my belly, between my legs, right down *there*. I groan.

I want to touch him. I move my hands and rather awkwardly, given I'm restrained, feel his hair. He stops kissing me and glares up at me, shaking his head from side to side, tutting as he does. He reaches for my hands and places them above my head again.

"Don't move your hands, or we just have to start all over again," he scolds me mildly. Oh, he's such a tease.

"I want to touch you." My voice is all breathy and out of control.

"I know," he murmurs. "Keep your hands above your head," he orders, his voice forceful.

He cups my chin again and starts to kiss my throat as before. Oh . . . he's so frustrating. His hands run down my body and over my breasts as he reaches the dip at the base of my neck with his lips. He swirls the tip of his nose around it then begins a very leisurely cruise with his mouth, heading south, following the path of his hands, down my sternum to my breasts. Each one is kissed and nipped gently and my nipples tenderly sucked. *Holy crap.* My hips start swaying and moving of their own accord, grinding to the rhythm of his mouth on me, and I'm desperately trying to remember to keep my hands above my head.

"Keep still," he warns, his breath warm against my skin. Reaching my navel, he dips his tongue inside, and then gently grazes my belly with his teeth. My body bows off the bed.

"Hmm. You are so sweet, Miss Steele." His nose glides along the line between my belly and my pubic hair, biting me gently, teasing me with his tongue. Sitting up suddenly, he kneels at my feet, grasping both my ankles and spreading my legs wide.

Holy shit. He grabs my left foot, bends my knee, and brings my foot up to his mouth. Watching and assessing my every reaction, he tenderly kisses each of my toes, then bites each one of them softly on the pads. When he reaches my little toe, he bites harder, and I convulse, whimpering. He glides his tongue up my instep—and I can no longer watch him. It's too erotic. I'm going to combust. I squeeze my eyes shut and try to absorb and manage all the sensations he's creating. He kisses my ankle and trails kisses up my calf to my knee, stopping just above. He then starts on my right foot, repeating the whole, seductive, mind-blowing process.

"Oh, please," I moan as he bites my little toe, the action resonating deep in my belly.

"All good things, Miss Steele," he breathes.

This time he doesn't stop at my knee, he continues up the inside of my thigh, pushing my thighs apart as he does. And I know what he's going to do, and part of me wants to push him off because I'm mortified and embarrassed. He's going to kiss me *there!* I know it. And part of me is glorying in the anticipation. He turns to my other knee and kisses his way up my thigh, kissing, licking, sucking, and then he's between my legs, running his nose up and down my sex, very softly, very gently. I writhe . . . *oh my.*

He stops, waiting for me to calm. I do and raise my head to gaze at him, my mouth open as my pounding heart struggles to calm.

"Do you know how intoxicating you smell, Miss Steele?" he murmurs, and keeping his eyes on mine, he pushes his nose into my pubic hair and inhales.

I flush scarlet everywhere, feeling faint, and I instantly close my eyes. I can't watch him do that!

He blows gently up the length of my sex. *Oh, fuck . . .*

"I like this." He gently tugs at my pubic hair. "Perhaps we'll keep this."

"Oh . . . please," I beg.

"Hmm, I like it when you beg me, Anastasia."

I groan.

"Tit for tat is not my usual style, Miss Steele," he whispers as he gently blows up and down me. "But you've pleased me today, and you should be rewarded." I hear the wicked grin in his voice, and while my body is singing from his words, his tongue starts to slowly circle my clitoris as his hands hold down my thighs.

"Aargh!" I moan as my body bows and convulses at the touch of his tongue.

He swirls his tongue around and around, again and again, keeping up the torture. I'm losing all sense of self, every atom of my being concentrating hard on that small, potent powerhouse at the apex of my thighs. My legs go rigid, and he slips his finger inside me, and I hear his growling groan.

"Oh, baby. I love that you're so wet for me."

He moves his finger in a wide circle, stretching me, pulling at me, his tongue mirroring his actions, around and around. I groan. It is too much . . . My body begs for relief, and I can no longer deny it. I let go, losing all cogent thought as my orgasm seizes me, wringing my insides again and again. *Holy fuck.* I cry out, and the world dips and disappears from view as the force of my climax renders everything null and void.

I am panting and vaguely hear the rip of foil. Very slowly he eases into me and starts to move. Oh . . . my. The feeling is sore and sweet and bold and gentle all at once.

"How's this?" he breathes.

"Fine. Good," I breathe. And he really starts to move, fast, hard, and large, thrusting into me over and over, implacable, pushing me and pushing me until I am close to the edge again. I whimper.

"Come for me, baby." His voice is harsh, hard, raw at my ear, and I explode around him as he pounds rapidly into me.

"Thank fuck," he whispers, and he thrusts hard once more and groans as he reaches his climax, pressing himself into me. Then he stills, his body rigid.

Collapsing on top of me, I feel his full weight forcing me into the mattress. I pull my tied hands over his neck and hold him the best I can. I know in that moment I would do anything for this man. I am his. The wonder that he's introduced me to, it's beyond anything I could have imagined. And he wants to take it further, so much further, to a place I can't, in my innocence, even imagine. *Oh . . . what to do?*

He leans up on his elbows and stares down at me, gray eyes intense.

"See how good we are together?" he murmurs. "If you give yourself to me, it will be so much better. Trust me, Anastasia, I can take you places you don't even know exist." His words echo my thoughts. He strokes his nose against mine. I am still reeling from my extraordinary physical reaction to him, and I gaze up at him blankly, grasping for a coherent thought.

Suddenly we both become aware of voices in the hall outside his bedroom door. It takes a moment to process what I can hear.

"But if he's still in bed, then he must be ill. He's never in bed at this time. Christian never sleeps in."

"Mrs. Grey, please."

"Taylor. You cannot keep me from my son."

"Mrs. Grey, he's not alone."

"What do you mean he's not alone?"

"He has someone with him."

"Oh . . ." Even I hear the disbelief in her voice.

Christian blinks rapidly, staring down at me, wide-eyed with humored horror.

"Shit! It's my mother."

CHAPTER TEN

He pulls out of me suddenly. I wince. He sits up on the bed and throws the used condom in a wastebasket.

"Come on, we need to get dressed—that's if you want to meet my mother." He grins, leaps up off the bed, and pulls on his jeans—no underwear! I struggle to sit up as I'm still tethered.

"Christian—I can't move."

His grin widens, and leaning down, he undoes the tie. The woven pattern has made an indentation around my wrists. It's . . . sexy. He gazes at me. He's amused, his eyes dancing with mirth. He kisses my forehead quickly and beams at me.

"Another first," he acknowledges, but I have no idea what he's talking about.

"I have no clean clothes in here." I am filled with sudden panic, and considering what I've just experienced, I'm finding the panic overwhelming. His mother! *Holy crap.* I have no clean clothes, and she's practically walked in on us in flagrante delicto. "Perhaps I should stay here."

"Oh no, you don't," Christian threatens. "You can wear something of mine." He's slipped on a white T-shirt and runs his hand through his just-fucked hair. In spite of my anxiety, I lose my train of thought. His beauty is derailing.

"Anastasia, you could be wearing a sack and you'd look lovely. Please don't worry. I'd like you to meet my mother. Get dressed. I'll just go and calm her down." His mouth presses into a hard line. "I will expect you in that room in five minutes, otherwise I'll come and drag you out of here myself in whatever you're wearing. My T-shirts are in this drawer. My shirts are in the closet. Help yourself." He eyes me speculatively for a moment, then leaves the room.

Holy shit. Christian's mother. This is so much more than I bargained for. Perhaps meeting her will help put a little part of the jigsaw in place. Might help me understand why Christian is the way he is . . . Suddenly, I want to meet her. I pick up my shirt off the floor, and I'm pleased to discover that it has survived the night well with hardly any creases. I find my blue bra under the bed and dress quickly. But if there's one thing I hate, it's not wearing clean panties. I rifle through Christian's chest of drawers and come across his boxer briefs. After pulling on a pair of tight gray Calvin Kleins, I tug on my jeans and my Converse.

Grabbing my jacket, I dash into the bathroom and stare at my too-bright eyes, my flushed face—and my hair! Holy crap . . . just-fucked pigtails do not suit me, either. I hunt in the vanity unit for a brush and find a comb. It will have to do. I quickly tie back my hair while I despair at my clothes. Maybe I should take Christian up on his offer of clothes. My subconscious purses her lips and mouths the word "ho." I ignore her. Struggling into my jacket, pleased that the cuffs cover the telltale patterns from his tie, I take a last anxious glance at myself in the mirror. This will have to do. I make my way into the main living room.

"Here she is." Christian stands from where he's lounging on the couch.

His expression is warm and appreciative. The sandy-haired woman beside him turns and beams at me, a full megawatt smile. She stands, too. She's impeccably attired in a camel-colored fine knit sweater dress with matching shoes. She looks groomed, elegant, beautiful, and inside I die a little, knowing I look such a mess.

"Mother, this is Anastasia Steele. Anastasia, this is Grace Trevelyan-Grey."

Dr. Trevelyan-Grey holds her hand out to me. *T . . . for Trevelyan? His initial.*

"What a pleasure to meet you," she murmurs. If I'm not mistaken, there is wonder and maybe stunned relief in her voice and a warm glow in her hazel eyes. I grasp her hand, and I can't help but smile, returning her warmth.

"Dr. Trevelyan-Grey," I murmur.

"Call me Grace." She grins, and Christian frowns. "I am usually Dr. Trevelyan, and Mrs. Grey is my mother-in-law." She winks. "So how did you two meet?" She looks questioningly at Christian, unable to hide her curiosity.

"Anastasia interviewed me for the student paper at WSU because I'm conferring the degrees there this week."

Double crap. I'd forgotten that.

"So you are graduating this week?" Grace asks.

"Yes."

My cell phone starts ringing. *Kate, I bet.*

"Excuse me." It's in the kitchen. I wander over and lean across the breakfast bar, not checking the number.

"Kate."

"*Dios mío!* Ana!" *Holy crap, it's José.* He sounds desperate. "Where are you? I've been trying to contact you. I need to see you, to apologize for my behavior on Friday. Why haven't you returned my calls?"

"Look, José, now's not a good time." I glance anxiously over at Christian, who's watching me intently, his face impassive as he murmurs something to his mom. I turn my back to him.

"Where are you? Kate is being so evasive," he whines.

"I'm in Seattle."

"What are you doing in Seattle? Are you with him?"

"José, I'll call you later. I can't talk to you now." I hang up.

I walk nonchalantly back to Christian and his mother. Grace is in full flow.

" . . . and Elliot called to say you were around—I haven't seen you for two weeks, darling."

"Did he now?" Christian murmurs, gazing at me, his expression unreadable.

"I thought we might have lunch together, but I can see you have other plans, and I don't want to interrupt your day." She gathers up her long cream coat and turns to him, offering him her cheek. He kisses her briefly, sweetly. She doesn't touch him.

"I have to drive Anastasia back to Portland."

"Of course, darling. Anastasia, it's been such a pleasure. I do hope we meet again." She holds her hand out to me, her eyes glowing, and we shake.

Taylor appears from . . . *where?*

"Mrs. Grey?" he asks.

"Thank you, Taylor." He escorts her from the room and through the double doors to the foyer. Taylor was here the whole time? How long has he been here? Where has he been?

Christian glares at me.

"So the photographer called?"

Crap.

"Yes."

"What did he want?"

"Just to apologize, you know—for Friday."

Christian narrows his eyes.

"I see," he says simply.

Taylor reappears.

"Mr. Grey, there's an issue with the Darfur shipment."

Christian nods curtly at him.

"*Charlie Tango* back at Boeing Field?"

"Yes, sir."

Taylor nods at me.

"Miss Steele."

I smile tentatively back at him, and he turns and leaves.

"Does he live here? Taylor?"

"Yes." His tone is clipped. *What is his problem?*

Christian heads over to the kitchen and picks up his BlackBerry, scrolling through some e-mails, I assume. His mouth presses in a hard line, and he makes a call.

"Ros, what's the issue?" he snaps. He listens, watching me, eyes speculative, as I stand in the middle of the huge room wondering what to do with myself, feeling extraordinarily self-conscious and out of place.

"I'm not having either crew put at risk. No, cancel . . . We'll air-drop instead . . . Good." He hangs up. The warmth in his eyes has disappeared. He looks forbidding, and with one quick glance at me, he heads into his study and returns a moment later.

"This is the contract. Read it, and we'll discuss it next weekend. May I suggest you do some research, so you know what's involved." He pauses. "That's if you agree, and I really hope you do," he adds, his tone softer, anxious.

"Research?"

"You'll be amazed what you can find on the Internet," he murmurs.

Internet! I don't have access to a computer, only Kate's laptop, and I couldn't use the one at Clayton's, not for this sort of "research" surely.

"What is it?" he asks, cocking his head to one side.

"I don't have a computer. I usually use the computers at school. I'll see if I can use Kate's laptop."

He hands me a manila envelope.

"I'm sure I can . . . er, lend you one. Get your things, we'll drive back to Portland and grab some lunch on the way. I need to dress."

"I'll just make a call," I murmur. I just want to hear Kate's voice. He frowns.

"The photographer?" His jaw clenches and his eyes burn. I blink at him. "I don't like to share, Miss Steele. Remember that." His quiet, chilling tone is a warning, and with one long, cold look at me, he heads back to the bedroom.

Holy crap. *I just wanted to call Kate*, I want to call after him, but his sudden aloofness has left me paralyzed. What happened to the generous, relaxed, smiling man who was making love to me not half an hour ago?

"READY?" CHRISTIAN ASKS AS we stand by the double doors to the foyer.

I nod uncertainly. He's resumed his distant, polite, uptight persona, his mask back up and on show. He's carrying a leather messenger bag. Why does he need that? Perhaps he's staying in Portland, and then I remember graduation. Oh yes . . . he'll be there on Thursday. He's wearing a black leather jacket. He certainly doesn't look like the multi-multimillionaire, billionaire, whatever-aire, in these clothes. He looks like a boy from the wrong side of the tracks, maybe a badly behaved rock star or a catwalk model. I sigh inwardly, wishing I had a tenth of his poise. He's so calm and controlled. I frown, recalling his outburst about José . . . Well, he seems to be.

Taylor is hovering in the background.

"Tomorrow, then," he says to Taylor, who nods.

"Yes, sir. Which car are you taking, sir?"

He looks down at me briefly.

"The R8."

"Safe trip, Mr. Grey. Miss Steele." Taylor looks kindly at me, though perhaps there's a hint of pity hidden in the depths of his eyes.

No doubt he thinks I've succumbed to Mr. Grey's dubious sexual habits. Not yet, just his exceptional sexual habits, or perhaps sex is like that for everyone. I frown at the thought. I have no comparison, and I can't ask Kate. That's something I am going to have to address with Christian. It's perfectly natural that I should talk to someone—and I can't talk to him if he's open one minute and standoffish the next.

Taylor holds the door open for us and ushers us through. Christian summons the elevator.

"What is it, Anastasia?" he asks. How does he know I'm chewing something over in my mind? He reaches up and pulls my chin.

"Stop biting your lip, or I will fuck you in the elevator, and I don't care who gets in with us."

I blush, but there's a hint of a smile around his lips. Finally his mood seems to be shifting.

"Christian, I have a problem."

"Oh?" I have his full attention.

The elevator arrives. We walk in, and Christian presses the button marked "G."

"Well," I flush. *How to say this?* "I need to talk to Kate. I've so many questions about sex, and you're too involved. If you want me to do all these things, how do I know—?" I pause, struggling to find the right words. "I just don't have any terms of reference."

He rolls his eyes at me.

"Talk to her if you must." He sounds exasperated. "Make sure she doesn't mention anything to Elliot."

I bristle at his insinuation. *Kate isn't like that.*

"She wouldn't do that, and I wouldn't tell you anything she tells me about Elliot—if she were to tell me anything," I add quickly.

"Well, the difference is that I don't want to know about his sex life," Christian murmurs dryly. "Elliot's a nosy bastard. But only about what we've done so far," he warns. "She'd probably have my balls if she knew what I wanted to do to you," he adds so softly I'm not sure I'm supposed to hear it.

"Okay," I agree readily, smiling up at him, relieved. The thought of Kate with Christian's balls is not something I want to dwell on.

His lip quirks up at me, and he shakes his head.

"The sooner I have your submission the better, and we can stop all this," he murmurs.

"Stop all what?"

"You, defying me." He reaches down and cups my chin and plants a swift, sweet kiss on my lips as the doors to the elevator open. He grabs my hand and leads me into the underground garage.

Me, defying him . . . how?

Beside the elevator, I can see the black 4x4 Audi, but it's the sleek black sporty number that blips open and lights up when he points the key fob at it. It's one of those cars that should have a very leggy blonde, wearing nothing but a sash, sprawled across the hood.

"Nice car," I murmur dryly.

He glances up and grins.

"I know," he says, and for a split second sweet, young, carefree Christian is back. It warms my heart. He's so excited. *Boys and their toys.* I roll my eyes at him but can't stifle my smile. He opens the door for me and I climb in. Whoa . . . it's low. He moves around the car with easy grace, and folds his long frame elegantly in beside me. *How does he do that?*

"So what sort of car is this?"

"It's an Audi R8 Spyder. It's a lovely day; we can take the top down. There's a baseball cap in there. In fact there should be two." He points to the glove box. "And sunglasses if you want them."

He starts the ignition, and the engine roars behind us. He places his bag in the space behind our seats, presses a button, and the roof slowly retracts. With the flick of a switch, Bruce Springsteen surrounds us.

"Gotta love Bruce." He grins at me and eases the car out of the parking space and up the steep ramp, where we pause for the gate to lift.

Then we're out into the bright Seattle May morning. I reach into the glove box and retrieve the baseball caps. The Mariners. He likes baseball? I pass him a cap, and he puts it on. I pull my hair through the back of mine and pull the peak down low.

People stare at us as we drive through the streets. For a moment, I think it's at him . . . and then a very paranoid part thinks everyone is looking at me because they know what I've been doing during the last twelve hours, but finally I realize it's the car. Christian seems oblivious, lost in thought.

The traffic is light and we're soon on Interstate 5 heading south, the wind sweeping over our heads. Bruce is singing about being on fire and his desire. How apt. I flush as I listen to the words. Christian glances at me. He's got his Ray-Bans on so I can't see what he's feeling. His mouth twitches slightly, and he reaches across and places his hand on my knee, squeezing gently. My breath hitches.

"Hungry?" he asks.

Not for food.

"Not particularly."

His mouth tightens into that hard line.

"You must eat, Anastasia," he chides. "I know a great place near Olympia. We'll stop there." He squeezes my knee again, and then returns his hand to the steering wheel as he puts his foot down on the gas. I'm pressed into the back of my seat. Boy, this car can move.

THE RESTAURANT IS SMALL and intimate, a wooden chalet in the middle of a forest. The décor is rustic: random chairs and tables with gingham tablecloths, wild flowers in little vases. CUISINE SAUVAGE, it boasts above the door.

"I've not been here for a while. We don't get a choice—they cook whatever they've caught or gathered." He raises his eyebrows in mock horror, and I have to laugh. The waitress takes our drinks order. She flushes when she sees Christian, avoiding eye contact with him, hiding under her long blond bangs. She likes him! *It's not just me!*

"Two glasses of the Pinot Grigio," Christian says with a voice of authority. I purse my lips, exasperated.

"What?" he snaps.

"I wanted a Diet Coke," I whisper.

His gray eyes narrow, and he shakes his head.

"The Pinot Grigio here is a decent wine. It will go well with the meal, whatever we get," he says patiently.

"Whatever we get?"

"Yes." He smiles his dazzling head-cocked-to-one-side smile, and my stomach pole vaults over my spleen. I can't help but reflect his glorious smile back at him.

"My mother liked you," he says dryly.

"Really?" His words make me flush with pleasure.

"Oh yes. She's always thought I was gay."

My mouth drops open, and I remember *that question . . . from the interview. Oh no.*

"Why did she think you were gay?" I whisper.

"Because she's never seen me with a girl."

"Oh . . . not even one of the fifteen?"

He smiles.

"You remembered. No, none of the fifteen."

"Oh."

"You know, Anastasia, it's been a weekend of firsts for me, too," he says quietly.

"It has?"

"I've never slept with anyone, never had sex in my bed, never flown a girl in *Charlie Tango*, never introduced a woman to my mother. What are you doing to me?" His eyes burn, their intensity takes my breath away.

The waitress arrives with our glasses of wine, and I immediately take a quick sip. Is he opening up or just making a casual observation?

"I've really enjoyed this weekend," I murmur. He narrows his eyes at me again.

"Stop biting that lip," he growls. "Me, too," he adds.

"What's vanilla sex?" I ask, if anything to distract myself from the intense, burning, sexy look he's giving me. He laughs.

"Just straightforward sex, Anastasia. No toys, no add-ons." He shrugs. "You know . . . well, actually you don't, but that's what it means."

"Oh." I thought it was chocolate fudge brownie sex that we had, with a cherry on the top. But hey, what do I know?

The waitress brings us soup. We both stare at it rather dubiously.

"Nettle soup," the waitress informs us before turning and flouncing back into the kitchen. I don't think she likes to be ignored by Christian. I take a tentative taste. It's delicious. Christian and I look up at each other at the same time with relief. I giggle, and he cocks his head to one side.

"That's a lovely sound," he murmurs.

"Why have you never had vanilla sex before? Have you always done . . . er, what you've done?" I ask, intrigued.

He nods slowly.

"Sort of." His voice is wary. He frowns for a moment and seems to be engaged in some kind of internal struggle. Then he glances up, a decision made. "One of my mother's friends seduced me when I was fifteen."

"Oh." *Holy shit, that's young!*

"She had very particular tastes. I was her submissive for six years." He shrugs.

"Oh." My brain has frozen, stunned into inactivity by this admission.

"So I do know what it involves, Anastasia." His eyes glow with insight.

I stare at him, unable to articulate anything—even my subconscious is silent.

"I didn't really have a run-of-the-mill introduction to sex."

Curiosity kicks in big time.

"So you never dated anyone at college?"

"No." He shakes his head to emphasize the point.

The waitress takes our bowls, interrupting us for a moment.

"Why?" I ask when she's gone.

He smiles sardonically.

"Do you really want to know?"

"Yes."

"I didn't want to. She was all I wanted, needed. And besides, she'd have beaten the shit out of me." He smiles fondly at the memory.

Oh, this is way too much information—but I want more.

"So if she was a friend of your mother's, how old was she?"

He smirks. "Old enough to know better."

"Do you still see her?"

"Yes."

"Do you still . . . er . . . ?" I flush.

"No." He shakes his head and smiles indulgently at me. "She's a very good friend."

"Oh. Does your mother know?"

He gives me a don't-be-stupid stare.

"Of course not."

The waitress returns with venison, but my appetite has vanished. What a revelation. *Christian the submissive . . . Holy shit.* I take a large slug of Pinot Grigio—he's right, of course, it's delicious. Jeez, all these revelations, it's so much to think about. I need time to process this, when I'm on my own, not when I'm distracted by his presence. He's so overwhelming, so alpha male, and now he's thrown this bombshell into the equation. *He knows what it's like.*

"But it can't have been full time?" I'm confused.

"Well, it was, though I didn't see her all the time. It was . . . difficult. After all, I was still at school and then at college. Eat up, Anastasia."

"I'm really not hungry, Christian." *I am reeling from your disclosure.*

His expression hardens. "Eat," he says quietly, too quietly.

I stare at him. This man—sexually abused as an adolescent—his tone is so threatening.

"Give me a moment," I mutter quietly. He blinks a couple of times.

"Okay," he murmurs, and he continues with his meal.

This is what it will be like if I sign, him ordering me around. I frown. *Do I want this?* Reaching for my knife and fork, I tentatively cut into the venison. It's very tasty.

"Is this what our, er . . . relationship will be like?" I whisper. "You ordering me around?" I can't quite bring myself to look at him.

"Yes," he murmurs.

"I see."

"And what's more, you'll want me to," he adds, his voice low.

I sincerely doubt that. I slice another piece of venison, holding it against my mouth.

"It's a big step," I murmur, and eat.

"It is." He closes his eyes briefly. When he opens them, they are wide and grave. "Anastasia, you have to go with your gut. Do the research, read the contract—I'm happy to discuss any aspect. I'll be in Portland until Friday if you want to talk about it before then." His words are coming at me in a rush. "Call me—maybe we can have dinner—say, Wednesday? I really want to make this work. In fact, I've never wanted anything as much as I want this to work."

His burning sincerity, his longing, is reflected in his eyes. This is fundamentally what I don't grasp. *Why me?* Why not one of the fifteen? Oh no . . . Will that be me—a number? Sixteen of many?

"What happened to the fifteen?" I blurt out.

He raises his eyebrows in surprise, then looks resigned, shaking his head.

"Various things, but it boils down to . . ." He pauses, struggling to find the words I think. "Incompatibility." He shrugs.

"And you think that I might be compatible with you?"

"Yes."

"So you're not seeing any of them anymore?"

"No, Anastasia, I'm not. I am monogamous in my relationships."

Oh . . . *this is news.*

"I see."

"Do the research, Anastasia."

I put my knife and fork down. I cannot eat any more.

"That's it? That's all you're going to eat?"

I nod. He scowls at me but chooses not to say anything. I breathe a small sigh of relief. My stomach is churning with all this new information, and I'm feeling a little lightheaded from the wine. I watch as he devours everything on his plate. He eats like a horse. He must work out to stay in such great shape. The memory of the way his pajamas hung from his hips comes unbidden to my mind. The image is totally distracting. I squirm uncomfortably. He glances up at me, and I blush.

"I'd give anything to know what you're thinking right at this moment," he murmurs. I blush further.

He smiles a wicked smile at me.

"I can guess," he teases softly.

"I'm glad you can't read my mind."

"Your mind, no, Anastasia, but your body—*that* I've gotten to know quite well since yesterday." His voice is suggestive. How does he switch so quickly from one mood to the next? He's so mercurial . . . It's hard to keep up.

He motions for the waitress and asks for the check. Once he's paid, he stands and holds out his hand.

"Come." Taking my hand in his, he leads me back to the car. This contact, flesh to flesh, it's what is so unexpected from him, normal, intimate. I can't reconcile this ordinary, tender gesture with what he wants to do in that room . . . the Red Room of Pain.

We are quiet on the drive from Olympia to Vancouver, both lost in our own thoughts. When he parks outside my apartment, it's five in the evening. The lights are on—Kate is at home. Packing, no doubt, unless Elliot is still there. He switches off the engine, and I realize I'm going to have to leave him.

"Do you want to come in?" I ask. I don't want him to go. I want to prolong our time together.

"No. I have work to do," he says simply, gazing at me, his expression unfathomable.

I stare down at my hands, as I knot my fingers together. Suddenly I feel emotional. He's leaving. Reaching over, he takes one of my hands and slowly pulls it to his mouth, tenderly kissing the back of my hand, such an old-fashioned, sweet gesture. My heart leaps into my mouth.

"Thank you for this weekend, Anastasia. It's been . . . the best. Wednesday? I'll pick you up from work, from wherever?" he says softly.

"Wednesday," I whisper.

He kisses my hand again and places it back in my lap. He climbs out of the car, comes around to my side, and opens the passenger-side door. Why do I feel suddenly bereft? A lump forms in my throat. I must not let him see me like this. Fixing a smile on my face, I clamber out of the car and head up the path, knowing I have to face Kate, dreading facing Kate. I turn and gaze at him midway. *Chin up, Steele,* I chide myself.

"Oh . . . by the way, I'm wearing your underwear." I give him a small smile and pull up the waistband of the boxer briefs I'm wearing so he can see. Christian's mouth drops open, shocked. What a great reaction. My mood shifts immediately, and I sashay into the house, part of me wanting to jump and punch the air. *YES!* My inner goddess is thrilled.

Kate is in the living room packing up her books into crates.

"You're back. Where's Christian? How are you?" Her voice is fevered, anxious, and she bounds up to me, grabbing my shoulders, minutely analyzing my face before I've even said hello.

Crap . . . I have to deal with Kate's persistence and tenacity, and I'm in possession of a signed legal document saying I can't talk. It's not a healthy mix.

"Well, how was it? I couldn't stop thinking about you, after Elliot left, that is." She grins mischievously.

I can't help but smile at her concern and her burning curiosity, but suddenly I feel shy. I blush. It was very private. All of it. Seeing and knowing what Christian has to hide. But I have to give her some details, because she won't leave me alone until I do.

"It was good, Kate. Very good, I think," I say quietly, trying to hide my embarrassed tell-all smile.

"You think?"

"I've got nothing to compare it to, do I?" I shrug apologetically.

"Did he make you come?"

Holy crap. She's so blunt. I go scarlet.

"Yes," I mumble, exasperated.

Kate pulls me to the couch and we sit. She clasps my hands.

"That *is* good." Kate looks at me in disbelief. "It was your first time. Wow, Christian must really know what he's doing."

Oh, Kate, if only you knew.

"My first time was horrid," she continues, making a sad comedy face.

"Oh?" This has me interested, something she's never divulged before.

"Yes, Steve Patrone. High school, dickless jock." She shudders. "He was rough. I wasn't ready. We were both drunk. You know—typical teenage post-prom disaster. Ugh—it took me months before I decided to have another go. And not with him, the gutless wonder. I was too young. You were right to wait."

"Kate, that sounds awful."

Kate looks wistful.

"Yeah, took almost a year to have my first orgasm through penetrative sex, and here you are . . . first time?"

I nod shyly. My inner goddess sits in the lotus position looking serene except for the sly, self-congratulatory smile on her face.

"I'm glad you lost it to someone who knows his ass from his elbow." She winks at me. "So when are you seeing him again?"

"Wednesday. We're having dinner."

"So you still like him?"

"Yes. But I don't know about . . . the future."

"Why?"

"He's complicated, Kate. You know—he inhabits a very different world to mine." Great excuse. Believable, too. Much better than: *He's got a Red Room of Pain, and he wants to make me his sex slave.*

"Oh, please, don't let this be about money, Ana. Elliot said it's very unusual for Christian to date anyone."

"Did he?" My voice hitches up several octaves.

Too obvious, Steele! My subconscious glares at me, wagging her long, skinny finger, then morphs into the scales of justice to remind me he could sue if I disclose too much. *Ha . . . what's he going to do—take all my money?* I must remember to Google "*penalties for breaching a nondisclosure agreement*" while I'm doing the rest of my "research." It's like I've been given a school assignment. Maybe I'll be graded. I flush, remembering my A for this morning's bath experiment.

"Ana, what is it?"

"I'm just remembering something Christian said."

"You look different," Kate says fondly.

"I feel different. Sore," I confess.

"Sore?"

"A little." I flush.

"Me, too. Men," she says in mock disgust. "They're animals." We both laugh.

"You're sore?" I exclaim.

"Yes . . . overuse."

I giggle.

"Tell me about Elliot the overuser," I ask when I've stopped giggling. Oh, I can feel myself relaxing for the first time since I was in line at the bar . . . before the phone call that started all this—when I was admiring Mr. Grey from afar. Happy, uncomplicated days.

Kate blushes. *Oh my* . . . Katherine Agnes Kavanagh goes all Anastasia Rose Steele on me. She gives me a dewy-eyed look. I've never seen her react this way to a man before. My jaw drops to the floor. *Where's Kate; what have you done with her?*

"Oh, Ana," she gushes. "He's just so . . . everything. And when we . . . oh . . . really good." She can hardly string a sentence together, she's got it so bad.

"I think you're trying to tell me that you like him."

She nods, grinning like a lunatic.

"And I'm seeing him on Saturday. He's going to help us move." She clasps her hands together, leaps up off the couch, and pirouettes to the window. Moving. Crap—I'd forgotten all about that, even with the packing cases surrounding us.

"That's helpful of him," I say appreciatively. I can get to know him, too. Perhaps he can give me more insight into his strange, disturbing brother.

"So what did you do last night?" I ask. She cocks her head at me and raises her eyebrows in a what-do-you-think-stupid look.

"Pretty much what you did, though we had dinner first." She grins at me. "Are you okay really? You look kind of overwhelmed."

"I feel overwhelmed. Christian is very intense."

"Yeah, I could see how he could be. But he was good to you?"

"Yes," I reassure her. "I'm really hungry, shall I cook?"

She nods and picks up two more books to pack.

"What do you want to do with the fourteen-thousand-dollar books?" she asks.

"I'm going to return them to him."

"Really?"

"It's a completely over-the-top gift. I can't accept it, especially now." I grin at Kate, and she nods.

"I understand. A couple of letters came for you, and José has been calling every hour on the hour. He sounded desperate."

"I'll call him," I mutter evasively. If I tell Kate about José, she'll have him for breakfast. I collect the letters from the dining table and open them.

"Hey, I have interviews! The week after next, in Seattle, for intern placements!"

"For which publishing house?"

"For both of them!"

"I told you your GPA would open doors, Ana."

Kate, of course, already has an internship set up at *The Seattle Times*. Her father knows someone who knows someone.

"How does Elliot feel about you going away?" I ask.

Kate wanders into the kitchen, and for the first time this evening, she's disconsolate.

"He's understanding. Part of me doesn't want to go, but it's tempting to lie in the sun for a couple of weeks. Besides, Mom is hanging in there, thinking this will be our last real family holiday before Ethan and I head off into the world of paid employment."

I have never left the continental U.S. Kate is off to Barbados with her parents and her brother, Ethan, for two whole weeks. I'll be Kateless in our new apartment. That will be weird. Ethan has been traveling the world since he graduated last year. I wonder briefly if I'll see him before they go on vacation. He's such a lovely guy. The phone rings, jolting me from my reverie.

"That'll be José."

I sigh. I know I have to talk to him. I grab the phone.

"Hi."

"Ana, you're back!" José shouts his relief at me.

"Obviously." Sarcasm drips from my voice, and I roll my eyes at the phone.

He's silent for a moment.

"Can I see you? I'm sorry about Friday night. I was drunk . . . and you . . . well. Ana—please forgive me."

"Of course, I forgive you José. Just don't do it again. You know I don't feel like that about you."

He sighs heavily, sadly.

"I know, Ana. I just thought if I kissed you, it might change how you feel."

"José, I love you dearly, you mean so much to me. You're like the brother I never had. That's not going to change. You know that." I hate to let him down, but it's the truth.

"So you're with him now?" His tone is full of disdain.

"José, I'm not with anybody."

"But you spent the night with him."

"That's none of your business!"

"Is it the money?"

"José! How dare you!" I shout, staggered by his audacity.

"Ana," he whines and apologizes simultaneously. I cannot deal with his petty jealousy now. I know he's hurt, but my plate is overflowing dealing with Christian Grey.

"Maybe we can have a coffee or something tomorrow. I'll call you." I am conciliatory. He is my friend, and I'm very fond of him. But right now, I don't need this.

"Tomorrow, then. You'll call?" The hope in his voice twists my heart.

"Yes . . . good night, José." I hang up, not waiting for his response.

"What was that all about?" Katherine demands, her hands on her hips. I decide honesty is the policy. She's looking more intractable than ever.

"He made a pass at me on Friday."

"José? *And* Christian Grey? Ana, your pheromones must be working overtime. What was the stupid fool thinking?" She shakes her head in disgust and returns to packing crates.

Forty-five minutes later, we pause our packing for the house specialty, my lasagna. Kate opens a bottle of wine, and we sit among the boxes eating, quaffing cheap red wine, and watching crap TV. This is normality. It's so grounding and welcome after the last forty-eight hours of . . . madness. I eat my first unhurried, no-nagging, peaceful meal in that time. *What is it about him and food?* Kate clears the dishes and I finish packing up the living room. We are left with the couch, the TV, and the dining table. What more could we need? Just the kitchen and our bedrooms left to pack up, and we have the rest of the week.

The phone rings again. It's Elliot. Kate winks at me and skips off to her bedroom like she's fourteen. I know that she should be writing her valedictorian speech, but it seems Elliot is more important. What is it about the Grey men? What is it that makes them totally distracting, all-consuming, and irresistible? I take another slug of wine.

I flick through the TV channels, but deep down I know I'm procrastinating. Burning a bright red hole in the side of my purse is that contract. Do I have the strength and the wherewithal to read it tonight?

I put my head in my hands. José and Christian, they both want something from me. José is easy to deal with. But Christian . . . Christian takes a whole different league of handling, of understanding. Part of me wants to run and hide. What am I going to do? His burning gray eyes and that intense smoldering stare come into my mind's eye, and my body tightens at the thought. I gasp. He's not even here and I'm turned on. It just can't be about sex, can it? I recall his gentle banter this morning at breakfast, his joy at my delight with the helicopter ride, him playing the piano—the sweet, soulful, oh-so-sad music.

He's such a complicated person. And now I have an insight as to why. A young man deprived of his adolescence, sexually abused by some evil Mrs. Robinson figure . . . no wonder he's old before his time. My heart fills with sadness at the thought of what he must have been through. I'm too naïve to know exactly what, but the research should shed some light. But do I really want to know? Do I want to explore this world I know nothing about? It's such a big step.

If I'd not met him, I'd still be sweetly and blissfully oblivious. My mind drifts to last night and this morning . . . and the incredible, sensual sexuality I'd experienced. Do I want to say good-bye to that? *No!* screams my subconscious . . . my inner goddess nods in silent Zen-like agreement with her.

Kate wanders back into the living room, grinning from ear to ear. *Perhaps she's in love.* I gape at her. She's never behaved like this.

"Ana, I'm off to bed. I'm pretty tired."

"Me, too, Kate."

She hugs me.

"I'm glad you're back in one piece. There's something about Christian," she adds quietly, apologetically. I give her a small, reassuring smile—all the while thinking . . . *How the hell does she know?* This is what will make her a great journalist, her unfaltering intuition.

COLLECTING MY PURSE, I wander listlessly into my bedroom. I am weary from all the carnal exertions of the last day and from the complete and utter dilemma that I'm faced with. I sit on my bed and gingerly extract the manila envelope from my bag, turning it over and over in my hands. Do I really want to know the extent of Christian's depravity? It's so daunting. I take a deep breath, and with my heart in my throat, I rip open the envelope.

CHAPTER ELEVEN

There are several papers inside the envelope. I fish them out, my heart still pounding, and I sit back on my bed and begin to read.

CONTRACT

Made this day ____of 2011 ("The Commencement Date")

BETWEEN

MR. CHRISTIAN GREY of 301 Escala, Seattle, WA 98889

("The Dominant")

MISS ANASTASIA STEELE of 1114 SW Green Street, Apartment 7, Haven Heights, Vancouver, WA 98888

("The Submissive")

THE PARTIES AGREE AS FOLLOWS

1 The following are the terms of a binding contract between the Dominant and the Submissive.

FUNDAMENTAL TERMS

2 The fundamental purpose of this contract is to allow the Submissive to explore her sensuality and her limits safely, with due respect and regard for her needs, her limits, and her well-being.

3 The Dominant and the Submissive agree and acknowledge that all that occurs under the terms of this contract will be consensual, confidential, and subject to the agreed limits and safety procedures set out in this contract. Additional limits and safety procedures may be agreed in writing.

4 The Dominant and the Submissive each warrant that they

suffer from no sexual, serious, infectious, or life-threatening illnesses, including but not limited to HIV, herpes, and hepatitis. If during the Term (as defined below) or any extended term of this contract either party should be diagnosed with or become aware of any such illness, he or she undertakes to inform the other immediately and in any event prior to any form of physical contact between the parties.

5 Adherence to the above warranties, agreements, and undertakings (and any additional limits and safety procedures agreed under clause 3 above) are fundamental to this contract. Any breach shall render it void with immediate effect and each party agrees to be fully responsible to the other for the consequence of any breach.

6 Everything in this contract must be read and interpreted in the light of the fundamental purpose and the fundamental terms set out in clauses 2–5 above.

ROLES

7 The Dominant shall take responsibility for the well-being and the proper training, guidance, and discipline of the Submissive. He shall decide the nature of such training, guidance, and discipline and the time and place of its administration, subject to the agreed terms, limitations, and safety procedures set out in this contract or agreed additionally under clause 3 above.

8 If at any time the Dominant should fail to keep to the agreed terms, limitations, and safety procedures set out in this contract or agreed additionally under clause 3 above, the Submissive is entitled to terminate this contract forthwith and to leave the service of the Dominant without notice.

9 Subject to that proviso and to clauses 2–5 above, the Submissive is to serve and obey the Dominant in all things. Subject to the agreed terms, limitations, and safety procedures set out in this contract or agreed additionally under clause 3 above, she shall without query or hesitation offer the Dominant such pleasure as he may require and she shall accept

without query or hesitation his training, guidance, and discipline in whatever form it may take.

COMMENCEMENT AND TERM

10 The Dominant and Submissive enter into this contract on the Commencement Date fully aware of its nature and undertake to abide by its conditions without exception.

11 This contract shall be effective for a period of three calendar months from the Commencement Date ("the Term"). On the expiry of the Term the parties shall discuss whether this contract and the arrangements they have made under this contract are satisfactory and whether the needs of each party have been met. Either party may propose the extension of this contract subject to adjustments to its terms or to the arrangements they have made under it. In the absence of agreement to such extension this contract shall terminate and both parties shall be free to resume their lives separately.

AVAILABILITY

12 The Submissive will make herself available to the Dominant from Friday evenings through to Sunday afternoons each week during the Term at times to be specified by the Dominant ("the Allotted Times"). Further allocated time can be mutually agreed on an ad hoc basis.

13 The Dominant reserves the right to dismiss the Submissive from his service at any time and for any reason. The Submissive may request her release at any time, such request to be granted at the discretion of the Dominant subject only to the Submissive's rights under clauses 2–5 and 8 above.

LOCATION

14 The Submissive will make herself available during the Allotted Times and agreed additional times at locations to be determined by the Dominant. The Dominant will ensure that all travel costs incurred by the Submissive for that purpose are met by the Dominant.

SERVICE PROVISIONS

15 The following service provisions have been discussed and

agreed and will be adhered to by both parties during the Term. Both parties accept that certain matters may arise that are not covered by the terms of this contract or the service provisions, or that certain matters may be renegotiated. In such circumstances, further clauses may be proposed by way of amendment. Any further clauses or amendments must be agreed, documented, and signed by both parties and shall be subject to the fundamental terms set out under clauses 2–5 above.

DOMINANT

15.1 The Dominant shall make the Submissive's health and safety a priority at all times. The Dominant shall not at any time require, request, allow, or demand the Submissive to participate at the hands of the Dominant in the activities detailed in Appendix 2 or in any act that either party deems to be unsafe. The Dominant will not undertake or permit to be undertaken any action which could cause serious injury or any risk to the Submissive's life. The remaining subclauses of this clause 15 are to be read subject to this proviso and to the fundamental matters agreed in clauses 2–5 above.

15.2 The Dominant accepts the Submissive as his, to own, control, dominate, and discipline during the Term. The Dominant may use the Submissive's body at any time during the Allotted Times or any agreed additional times in any manner he deems fit, sexually or otherwise.

15.3 The Dominant shall provide the Submissive with all necessary training and guidance in how to properly serve the Dominant.

15.4 The Dominant shall maintain a stable and safe environment in which the Submissive may perform her duties in service of the Dominant.

15.5 The Dominant may discipline the Submissive as necessary to ensure the Submissive fully appreciates her role of subservience to the Dominant and to discourage unacceptable conduct. The Dominant may flog, spank, whip, or corporally punish the Submissive as he sees fit, for purposes of discipline, for his own personal enjoyment, or for any other reason, which he is not obliged to provide.

15.6 In training and in the administration of discipline the Dominant shall ensure that no permanent marks are made upon the Submissive's body nor any injuries incurred that may require medical attention.

15.7 In training and in the administration of discipline the Dominant shall ensure that the discipline and the instruments used for the purposes of discipline are safe, shall not be used in such a way as to cause serious harm, and shall not in any way exceed the limits defined and detailed in this contract.

15.8 In case of illness or injury the Dominant shall care for the Submissive, seeing to her health and safety, encouraging and, when necessary, ordering medical attention when it is judged necessary by the Dominant.

15.9 The Dominant shall maintain his own good health and seek medical attention when necessary in order to maintain a risk-free environment.

15.10 The Dominant shall not loan his Submissive to another Dominant.

15.11 The Dominant may restrain, handcuff, or bind the Submissive at any time during the Allotted Times or any agreed additional times for any reason and for extended periods of time, giving due regard to the health and safety of the Submissive.

15.12 The Dominant will ensure that all equipment used for the purposes of training and discipline shall be maintained in a clean, hygienic, and safe state at all times.

SUBMISSIVE

15.13 The Submissive accepts the Dominant as her master, with the understanding that she is now the property of the Dominant, to be dealt with as the Dominant pleases during the Term generally but specifically during the Allotted Times and any additional agreed allotted times.

15.14 The Submissive shall obey the rules ("the Rules") set out in Appendix 1 to this agreement.

15.15 The Submissive shall serve the Dominant in any way the Dominant sees fit and shall endeavor to please the Dominant at all times to the best of her ability.

15.16 The Submissive shall take all measures necessary to maintain her good health and shall request or seek medical attention whenever it is needed, keeping the Dominant informed at all times of any health issues that may arise.

15.17 The Submissive will ensure that she procures oral contraception and ensure that she takes it as and when prescribed to prevent any pregnancy.

15.18 The Submissive shall accept without question any and all disciplinary actions deemed necessary by the Dominant and remember her status and role in regard to the Dominant at all times.

15.19 The Submissive shall not touch or pleasure herself sexually without permission from the Dominant.

15.20 The Submissive shall submit to any sexual activity demanded by the Dominant and shall do so without hesitation or argument.

15.21 The Submissive shall accept whippings, floggings, spankings, canings, paddlings, or any other discipline the Dominant should decide to administer, without hesitation, inquiry, or complaint.

15.22 The Submissive shall not look directly into the eyes of the Dominant except when specifically instructed to do so. The Submissive shall keep her eyes cast down and maintain a quiet and respectful bearing in the presence of the Dominant.

15.23 The Submissive shall always conduct herself in a respectful manner to the Dominant and shall address him only as Sir, Mr. Grey, or such other title as the Dominant may direct.

15.24 The Submissive will not touch the Dominant without his express permission to do so.

ACTIVITIES

16 The Submissive shall not participate in activities or any sexual acts that either party deems to be unsafe or any activities detailed in Appendix 2.

17 The Dominant and the Submissive have discussed the activities set out in Appendix 3 and recorded in writing on Appendix 3 their agreement in respect of them.

SAFEWORDS

18 The Dominant and the Submissive recognize that the Dominant may make demands of the Submissive that cannot be met without incurring physical, mental, emotional, spiritual, or other harm at the time the demands are made to the Submissive. In such circumstances related to this, the Submissive may make use of a safeword ("the Safeword[s]"). Two Safewords will be invoked depending on the severity of the demands.

19 The Safeword "Yellow" will be used to bring to the attention of the Dominant that the Submissive is close to her limit of endurance.

20 The Safeword "Red" will be used to bring to the attention of the Dominant that the Submissive cannot tolerate any further demands. When this word is said, the Dominant's action will cease completely with immediate effect.

CONCLUSION

21 We the undersigned have read and understood fully the provisions of this contract. We freely accept the terms of this contract and have acknowledged this by our signatures below.

____

The Dominant: Christian Grey
Date

____

The Submissive: Anastasia Steele
Date

APPENDIX 1
RULES

Obedience:

The Submissive will obey any instructions given by the Dominant immediately without hesitation or reservation and in an expeditious manner. The Submissive will agree to any sexual activity deemed fit and pleasurable by the Dominant excepting those activities that are outlined in hard limits (Appendix 2). She will do so eagerly and without hesitation.

Sleep:

The Submissive will ensure she achieves a minimum of eight hours' sleep a night when she is not with the Dominant.

Food:

The Submissive will eat regularly to maintain her health and well-being from a prescribed list of foods (Appendix 4). The Submissive will not snack between meals, with the exception of fruit.

Clothes:

During the Term the Submissive will wear clothing only approved by the Dominant. The Dominant will provide a clothing budget for the Submissive, which the Submissive shall utilize. The Dominant shall accompany the Submissive to purchase clothing on an ad hoc basis. If the Dominant so requires, the Submissive shall, during the Term, wear adornments the Dominant shall require, in the presence of the Dominant and at any other time the Dominant deems fit.

Exercise:

The Dominant shall provide the Submissive with a personal trainer four times a week in hour-long sessions at times to be mutually agreed between the personal trainer and the Submissive. The personal trainer will report to the Dominant on the Submissive's progress.

Personal Hygiene/Beauty:

The Submissive will keep herself clean and shaved and/or waxed at all times. The Submissive will visit a beauty salon of the Dominant's choosing at times to be decided by the Dominant and undergo whatever treatments the Dominant sees fit. All costs will be met by the Dominant.

Personal Safety:

The Submissive will not drink to excess, smoke, take recreational drugs, or put herself in any unnecessary danger.

Personal Qualities:

The Submissive will not enter into any sexual relations with anyone other than the Dominant. The Submissive will conduct herself in a respectful and modest manner at all times. She must recognize that her behavior is a direct reflection on the Dominant. She shall be held accountable for any misdeeds, wrongdoings, and misbehavior committed when not in the presence of the Dominant.

Failure to comply with any of the above will result in immediate punishment, the nature of which shall be determined by the Dominant.

APPENDIX 2

Hard Limits

No acts involving fire play.

No acts involving urination or defecation and the products thereof.

No acts involving needles, knives, cutting, piercing, or blood.

No acts involving gynecological medical instruments.

No acts involving children or animals.

No acts that will leave any permanent marks on the skin.

No acts involving breath control.

No activity that involves the direct contact of electric current (whether alternating or direct), fire, or flames to the body.

APPENDIX 3

Soft Limits

To be discussed and agreed between both parties:

Does the Submissive consent to:

- Masturbation
- Cunnilingus
- Fellatio
- Swallowing Semen
- Vaginal intercourse
- Vaginal fisting
- Anal intercourse
- Anal fisting

Does the Submissive consent to the use of:

- Vibrators
- Butt plugs
- Dildos
- Other vaginal/anal toys

Does the Submissive consent to:

- Bondage with rope
- Bondage with leather cuffs
- Bondage with handcuffs/shackles/manacles
- Bondage with tape
- Bondage with other

Does the Submissive consent to be restrained with:

- Hands bound in front
- Ankles bound
- Elbows bound
- Hands bound behind back
- Knees bound
- Wrists bound to ankles
- Binding to fixed items, furniture, etc.
- Binding with spreaderbar
- Suspension

Does the Submissive consent to be blindfolded?

Does the Submissive consent to be gagged?

How much pain is the Submissive willing to experience?

Where 1 is likes intensely and 5 is dislikes intensely:
1—2—3—4—5

Does the Submissive consent to accept the following forms of pain/punishment/discipline:

- Spanking
- Paddling
- Whipping
- Caning
- Biting
- Nipple clamps
- Genital clamps
- Ice
- Hot wax
- Other types/methods of pain

Holy fuck. I can't bring myself to even consider the food list. I swallow hard, my mouth dry, and read it again.

My head is buzzing. How can I possibly agree to all this? And apparently it's for my benefit, *to explore my sensuality, my limits—safely*—oh, please! I scoff angrily. *Serve and obey in all things*. All things! I shake my head in disbelief. Actually, don't the marriage vows use those words . . . *obey*? This throws me. Do couples still say that? Only three months—is that why there have been so many? He doesn't keep them for long? Or have they had enough after three months? *Every weekend?* That's too much. I'll never see Kate or whatever friends I may make at my new job, provided I get one. Perhaps I should have one weekend a month to myself. Perhaps when I have my period—that sounds . . . practical. He's my master! I'm to be dealt with as he pleases! *Holy shit*.

I shudder at the thought of being flogged or whipped. Spanking probably wouldn't be so bad; humiliating, though. And tied up? Well, he did tie my hands together. That was . . . well, it was hot, really hot, so perhaps that won't be so bad. He won't loan me to another Dominant—damn right he won't. That would be totally unacceptable. *Why am I even thinking about this?*

I can't look him in the eye. *How weird is that?* The only way I ever have any chance to see what he's thinking. Actually, who am I kidding? I never know what he's thinking, but I like looking into his eyes. He has beautiful eyes—captivating, intelligent, deep, and dark, dark with dominant secrets. I recall his burning smoky gaze and press my thighs together, squirming.

And I can't touch him. Well, no surprise there. And these silly rules . . . No, no, I can't do this. I put my head in my hands. This is no way to have a relationship. I need some sleep. I'm shattered. All the physical shenanigans I've been engaged in over the last twenty-four hours have been, frankly, exhausting. And mentally . . . oh, man, this is so much to handle. As José would say, a real mind-fuck. Perhaps in the morning this might not read like a bad joke.

I scramble up and change quickly. Perhaps I should borrow Kate's pink flannel pajamas. I want something cuddly and reassuring around me. I head to the bathroom in my T-shirt and sleep shorts and brush my teeth.

I stare at myself in the bathroom mirror. *You can't seriously be considering this* . . . My subconscious sounds sane and rational, not her usual snarky self. My inner goddess is jumping up and down, clapping her hands like a five-year-old. *Please, let's do this . . . otherwise we'll end up alone with lots of cats and your classic novels to keep you company.*

The only man I've ever been attracted to, and he comes with a bloody contract, a flogger, and a whole world of issues. Well, at least I got my way this weekend. My inner goddess stops jumping and smiles serenely. *Oh yes* . . . she mouths, nodding at me smugly. I flush at the memory of his hands and his mouth on me, his body inside mine. Closing my eyes, I feel the familiar delicious pull of my muscles from deep, deep down. I want to do that again and again. Maybe if I just sign up for the sex . . . would he go with that? I suspect not.

Am I submissive? Maybe I come across that way. Maybe I misled him in the interview. I'm shy, yes . . . but submissive? I let Kate bully me—is that the same? And those soft limits, jeez. My mind boggles, but I'm reassured that they are up for discussion.

I wander back to my bedroom. This is too much to think about.

I need a clear head—a fresh morning approach to the problem. I put the offending documents in my backpack. Tomorrow . . . tomorrow is another day. Clambering into bed, I switch off the light and lie staring up at the ceiling. Oh, I wish I'd never met him. My inner goddess shakes her head at me. She and I know it's a lie. I have never felt as alive as I do now.

I close my eyes, and I drift into a heavy sleep with occasional dreams of four-poster beds and shackles and intense gray eyes.

KATE WAKES ME THE next day.

"Ana, I've been calling you. You must have been out cold."

My eyes reluctantly open. She's not just up—she's been for a run. I glance at my alarm. It's eight in the morning. Holy Moses, I've slept for a solid nine hours.

"What is it?" I mumble sleepily.

"There's a man here with a delivery for you. You have to sign for it."

"What?"

"Come on. It's big. It looks interesting." She hops from foot to foot excitedly and bounds back into the living room. I clamber out of bed and grab my robe hanging on the back of my door. A smart young man with a ponytail is standing in our living room clasping a large box.

"Hi," I mumble.

"I'll make you some tea." Kate scuttles off to the kitchen.

"Miss Steele?"

And I immediately know who the parcel is from.

"Yes," I answer cautiously.

"I have a package for you here, but I have to set it up and show you how to use it."

"Really? At this time?"

"Only following orders, ma'am." He smiles in a charming but professional he's-not-taking-any-crap way.

Did he just call me ma'am? Have I aged ten years overnight? If I have, it's that contract. My mouth puckers in disgust.

"Okay, what is it?"

"It's a MacBook Pro."

"Of course it is." I roll my eyes.

"These aren't available in the shops yet, ma'am; the very latest from Apple."

How come that does not surprise me? I sigh heavily.

"Just set it up on the dining table over there."

I wander into the kitchen to join Kate.

"What is it?" she says inquisitively, bright-eyed and bushy-tailed. She's slept well, too.

"It's a laptop from Christian."

"Why's he sent you a laptop? You know you can use mine." She frowns.

Not for what he has in mind.

"Oh, it's only on loan. He wanted me to try it out." My excuse sounds feeble. But Kate nods her assent. *Oh my* . . . I have hoodwinked Katherine Kavanagh. A first. She hands me my tea.

The Mac laptop is sleek and silver and rather beautiful. It has a very large screen. Christian Grey likes scale—I think of his living area, in fact, his whole apartment.

"It's got the latest OS and a full suite of programs, plus a one-point-five terabyte hard drive so you'll have plenty of room, thirty-two gigs of RAM—what are you planning to use it for?"

"Uh . . . e-mail."

"E-mail!" he chokes, raising his eyebrows with a slightly sick look on his face.

"And maybe Internet research?" I shrug apologetically.

He sighs.

"Well, this has full wireless N, and I've set it up with your Me account details. This baby is all ready to go, practically anywhere on the planet." He looks longingly at it.

"Me account?"

"Your new e-mail address."

I have an e-mail address?

He points to an icon on the screen and continues to talk at me, but it's like white noise. I haven't got a clue what he's saying, and in all honestly, I'm not interested. *Just tell me how to switch it on and off*—I'll figure out the rest. After all, I've been using Kate's for four years. Kate whistles, impressed when she sees it.

"This is next-generation tech." She raises her eyebrows at me. "Most women get flowers or maybe jewelry," she says suggestively, trying to suppress a smile.

I scowl at her but can't keep a straight face. We both burst into a fit of giggles, and computer man gapes at us, bemused. He finishes up and asks me to sign the delivery note.

As Kate shows him out, I sit with my cup of tea and open the e-mail program, and waiting for me is an e-mail from Christian. My heart leaps into my mouth. *I have an e-mail from Christian Grey*. Nervously, I open it.

From: Christian Grey
Subject: Your New Computer
Date: May 22 2011 23:15
To: Anastasia Steele

Dear Miss Steele,
I trust you slept well. I hope that you put this laptop to good use, as discussed.

I look forward to dinner Wednesday.

Happy to answer any questions before then, via e-mail, should you so desire.

Christian Grey
CEO, Grey Enterprises Holdings, Inc.

I hit "reply."

From: Anastasia Steele
Subject: Your New Computer (on loan)
Date: May 23 2011 08:20
To: Christian Grey

I slept very well, thank you—for some strange reason—*Sir*.
I understood that this computer was on loan, ergo not mine.

Ana

Almost instantaneously there is a response.

From: Christian Grey
Subject: Your New Computer (on loan)
Date: May 23 2011 08:22
To: Anastasia Steele

The computer is on loan. Indefinitely, Miss Steele.
I note from your tone that you have read the documentation I gave you.

Do you have any questions so far?

Christian Grey
CEO, Grey Enterprises Holdings, Inc.

I can't help but grin.

From: Anastasia Steele
Subject: Inquiring Minds

Date: May 23 2011 08:25
To: Christian Grey

I have many questions, but not suitable for e-mail, and some of us have to work for a living.

I do not want or need a computer indefinitely.

Until later, good day. *Sir.*

Ana

His reply again is instant, and it makes me smile.

From: Christian Grey
Subject: Your New Computer (again on loan)
Date: May 23 2011 08:26
To: Anastasia Steele

Laters, baby.
P.S.: I work for a living, too.

Christian Grey
CEO, Grey Enterprises Holdings, Inc.

I shut the computer down, grinning like an idiot. How can I resist playful Christian? I am going to be late for work. Well, it is my last week—Mr. and Mrs. Clayton will probably cut me some slack. I race into the shower, unable to shake my face-splitting grin. *He e-mailed me.* I'm like a small, giddy child. And all the contract angst fades. As I wash my hair, I try to think of what I could possibly ask him via e-mail. Surely it's better to talk these things through. Suppose someone hacked into his account? I flush at the thought. I dress quickly, shout a hasty good-bye to Kate, and I'm off to work my last week at Clayton's.

JOSÉ PHONES AT ELEVEN.

"Hey, are we doing coffee?" He sounds like the old José. José my friend, not a—what did Christian call him? Suitor. Ugh.

"Sure. I'm at work. Can you make it here for, say, twelve?"

"See you then."

He hangs up, and I go back to restocking the paintbrushes and thinking about Christian Grey and his contract.

José is punctual. He comes bounding into the shop like a gamboling dark-eyed puppy.

"Ana." He smiles his dazzling toothy all-Hispanic-American smile, and I can't be angry with him anymore.

"Hi, José." I hug him. "I'm starving. I'll just let Mrs. Clayton know I'm going for lunch."

As we stroll to the local coffee shop, I slip my arm through José's. I'm so grateful for his . . . normality. Someone I know and understand.

"Hey, Ana," he murmurs. "You've really forgiven me?"

"José, you know I can never stay mad at you for long."

He grins.

I CAN'T WAIT TO get home, the lure of e-mailing Christian, and maybe I can begin my research project. Kate is out somewhere, so I fire up the new laptop and open my e-mail. Sure enough, there's a message from Christian sitting in the inbox. I'm practically bouncing out of my seat with glee.

From: Christian Grey
Subject: Working for a Living
Date: May 23 2011 17:24
To: Anastasia Steele

Dear Miss Steele,
I do hope you had a good day at work.

Christian Grey
CEO, Grey Enterprises Holdings, Inc.

I hit "reply."

From: Anastasia Steele
Subject: Working for Living
Date: May 23 2011 17:48
To: Christian Grey

Sir . . . I had a very good day at work.
Thank you.

Ana

From: Christian Grey
Subject: Do the Work!
Date: May 23 2011 17:50
To: Anastasia Steele

Miss Steele,
Delighted you had a good day.

While you are e-mailing, you are not researching.

Christian Grey
CEO, Grey Enterprises Holdings, Inc.

From: Anastasia Steele
Subject: Nuisance
Date: May 23 2011 17:53
To: Christian Grey

Mr. Grey, stop e-mailing me, and I can start my assignment.
I'd like another A.

Ana

I hug myself.

From: Christian Grey
Subject: Impatient
Date: May 23 2011 17:55
To: Anastasia Steele

Miss Steele,
Stop e-mailing *me*—and do your assignment.

I'd like to award another A.

The first one was so well deserved. ;)

Christian Grey
CEO, Grey Enterprises Holdings, Inc.

Christian Grey just sent me a winking smiley . . . *Oh my.* I fire up Google.

From: Anastasia Steele
Subject: Internet Research

Date: May 23 2011 17:59
To: Christian Grey

Mr. Grey,
What would you suggest I put into a search engine?

Ana

From: Christian Grey
Subject: Internet Research
Date: May 23 2011 18:02
To: Anastasia Steele

Miss Steele,
Always start with Wikipedia.

No more e-mails unless you have questions.

Understood?

Christian Grey
CEO, Grey Enterprises Holdings, Inc.

From: Anastasia Steele
Subject: Bossy!
Date: May 23 2011 18:04
To: Christian Grey

Yes . . . *Sir.*
You are so bossy.

Ana

From: Christian Grey
Subject: In Control
Date: May 23 2011 18:06
To: Anastasia Steele

Anastasia, you have no idea.
Well, maybe an inkling now.

Do the work.

Christian Grey
CEO, Grey Enterprises Holdings, Inc.

I type "Submissive" into Wikipedia.

Half an hour later, I feel slightly queasy and frankly shocked to my core. Do I really want this stuff in my head? Jeez—is this what he gets up to in the Red Room of Pain? I sit staring at the screen, and part of me, a very moist and integral part of me that I've only become acquainted with very recently, is seriously turned on. Oh my, some of this stuff is HOT. But is it for me? Holy shit . . . could I do this? I need space. I need to think.

CHAPTER TWELVE

For the first time in my life, I voluntarily go for a run. I find my nasty, never-used sneakers, some sweatpants, and a T-shirt. I put my hair in pigtails, blushing at the memories they bring back, and I plug in my iPod. I can't sit in front of that marvel of technology and look at or read any more disturbing material. I need to expend some of this excess, enervating energy. Quite frankly, I have a mind to run to the Heathman Hotel and just demand sex from the control freak. But that's five miles, and I don't think I'll be able to run one mile, let alone five, and, of course, he might turn me down, which would be beyond humiliating.

Kate is walking from her car as I head out of the door. She nearly drops her shopping bags when she sees me. Ana Steele in sneakers. I wave and don't stop for the inquisition. I need some serious alone time. Snow Patrol blaring in my ears, I set off into the opal and aquamarine dusk.

I pace through the park. *What am I going to do?* I want him, but on his terms? I just don't know. Perhaps I should negotiate what I want. Go through that ridiculous contract line by line and say what is acceptable and what isn't. My research has told me that legally it's unenforceable. He must know that. I figure that it just sets up the parameters of the relationship. It illustrates what I can expect from him and what he expects from me—my total submission. Am I prepared to give him that? Am I even capable?

I am plagued by one question—why is he like this? Is it because he was seduced at such a young age? I just don't know. He's still such a mystery.

I stop beside a large spruce and put my hands on my knees,

breathing hard, dragging precious air into my lungs. Oh, this feels good, cathartic. I feel my resolve hardening. Yes. I need to tell him what's okay and what isn't. I need to e-mail him my thoughts, and then we can discuss these on Wednesday. I take a deep, cleansing breath, then jog back to the apartment.

Kate has been shopping, as only she can, for clothes for her vacation to Barbados. Mainly bikinis and matching sarongs. She will look fabulous in all of them, yet she still makes me sit and comment while she tries on each and every one. There are only so many ways one can say, "You look fabulous, Kate." She has a curvy, slim figure to die for. She doesn't do it on purpose, I know, but I haul my sorry, perspiration-clad ass into my room on the pretext of packing more boxes. Could I feel any more inadequate? Taking the awesome free technology with me, I set the laptop up on my desk. I e-mail Christian.

From: Anastasia Steele
Subject: Shocked of WSUV
Date: May 23 2011 20:33
To: Christian Grey

Okay, I've seen enough.
It was nice knowing you.

Ana

I press "send," hugging myself, laughing at my little joke. Will he find it as funny? *Oh, shit*—probably not. Christian Grey is not famed for his sense of humor. But I know it exists, I've experienced it. Perhaps I've gone too far. I wait for his answer.

I wait . . . and wait. I glance at my alarm clock. Ten minutes have passed.

To distract myself from the anxiety that blooms in my belly,

I start doing what I told Kate I would be doing—packing up my room. I begin by cramming my books into a crate. By nine, I've heard nothing. *Perhaps he's out.* I pout petulantly as I plug my iPod earbuds in, listen to Snow Patrol, and sit down at my small desk to reread the contract and make my comments.

I don't know why I glance up, maybe I catch a slight movement from the corner of my eye, I don't know, but when I do, he's standing in the doorway of my bedroom, watching me intently. He's wearing his gray flannel pants and a white linen shirt, gently twirling his car keys. I pull my earbuds out and freeze. *Fuck!*

"Good evening, Anastasia." His voice is cool, his expression completely guarded and unreadable. The capacity to speak deserts me. Damn Kate for letting him in here with no warning. Vaguely, I'm aware that I'm still in my sweats, unshowered, yucky, and he's just gloriously yummy, his pants doing that hanging from the hips thing, and what's more, he's here in my bedroom.

"I felt that your e-mail warranted a reply in person," he explains dryly.

I open my mouth and then close it again, twice. The joke is on me. Never in this or any alternative universe did I expect him to drop everything and turn up here.

"May I sit?" he asks, his eyes now dancing with humor—*thank heavens—maybe he'll see the funny side?*

I nod. The power of speech remains elusive. *Christian Grey is sitting on my bed.*

"I wondered what your bedroom would look like," he says.

I glance around it, plotting an escape route. No—there's still only the door or window. My room is functional but cozy—sparse white wicker furniture and a white iron double bed with a patchwork quilt, made by my mother when she was in her folksy Americana quilting phase. It's all pale blue and cream.

"It's very serene and peaceful in here," he murmurs. *Not at the moment . . . not with you here.*

Finally, my medulla oblongata recalls its purpose. I breathe. "How . . . ?"

He smiles at me. "I'm still at the Heathman."

I know that.

"Would you like a drink?" Politeness wins out over everything else I'd like to say.

"No thank you, Anastasia." He smiles a dazzling, crooked smile, his head cocked slightly to one side.

Well, I might need one.

"So, it was *nice* knowing me?"

Holy cow, is he *offended*? I stare down at my fingers. How am I going to dig myself out of this? If I tell him it was a joke, I don't think he'll be impressed.

"I thought you'd reply by e-mail." My voice is small, pathetic.

"Are you biting your lower lip deliberately?" he asks darkly.

I blink up at him, gasping, freeing my lip.

"I wasn't aware I was biting my lip," I murmur softly.

My heart is pounding. I can feel that pull, that delicious electricity between us charging, filling the space with static. He's sitting so close to me, his eyes dark smoky gray, his elbows resting on his knees, his legs apart. Leaning forward, he slowly undoes one of my pigtails, his fingers freeing my hair. My breathing is shallow, and I cannot move. I watch hypnotized as his hand moves to my second pigtail, and pulling the hair tie, he loosens the braid with his long, skilled fingers.

"So you decided on some exercise," he breathes, his voice soft and melodious. His fingers gently tuck my hair behind my ear. "Why, Anastasia?" His fingers circle my ear, and very softly, rhythmically, he tugs my earlobe. It's so sexual.

"I needed time to think," I whisper. I'm all deer/headlights, moth/flame, bird/snake . . . and he knows exactly what he's doing to me.

"Think about what, Anastasia?"

"You."

"And you decided that it was nice knowing me? Do you mean knowing me in the biblical sense?"

Oh, shit. I flush.

"I didn't think you were familiar with the Bible."

"I went to Sunday school, Anastasia. It taught me a great deal."

"I don't remember reading about nipple clamps in the Bible. Perhaps you were taught from a modern translation."

His lips arch with a trace of a smile, and my eyes are drawn to his mouth.

"Well, I thought I should come and remind you how *nice* it was knowing me."

Holy crap. I stare at him openmouthed, and his fingers move from my ear to my chin.

"What do you say to that, Miss Steele?"

His eyes blaze at me, his challenge intrinsic in his stare. His lips are parted—he's waiting, coiled to strike. Desire—acute, liquid, and smoldering—combusts deep in my belly. I take preemptive action and launch myself at him. Somehow he moves, I have no idea how, and in the blink of an eye I'm on the bed, pinned beneath him, my arms stretched out and held above my head, his free hand clutching my face, and his mouth finding mine.

His tongue is in my mouth, claiming and possessing me, and I revel in the force he uses. I feel him against the length of my body. He wants *me*, and this does strange, delicious things to my insides. Not Kate in her little bikinis, not one of the fifteen, not evil Mrs. Robinson. Me. This beautiful man wants me. My inner goddess glows so bright she could light up Portland. He stops kissing me, and opening my eyes, I find him gazing down at me.

"Trust me?" he breathes.

I nod, wide-eyed, my heart bouncing off my ribs, my blood thundering through my body.

He reaches down, and from his pants pocket, he takes out his silver-gray silk tie . . . *that* silver-gray woven tie that leaves small impressions of its weave on my skin. He moves so quickly, sitting astride me as he fastens my wrists together, but this time, he ties the other end of the tie to one of the spokes of my white iron headboard. He pulls at my binding, checking it's secure.

I'm not going anywhere. I'm tied, literally, to my bed, and I'm so aroused.

He slides off me and stands beside the bed, staring down at me, his eyes dark with want. His look is triumphant mixed with relief.

"That's better," he murmurs, and smiles a wicked, knowing smile. He bends and starts undoing one of my sneakers. Oh no . . . no . . . my feet. No. I've just been running.

"No," I protest, trying to kick him off.

He stops.

"If you struggle, I'll tie your feet, too. If you make a noise, Anastasia, I will gag you. Keep quiet. Katherine is probably outside listening right now."

Gag me! Kate! I shut up.

He removes my shoes and my socks efficiently and slowly peels off my sweatpants. Oh—*what panties am I wearing?* He lifts me and pulls the quilt and my duvet out from underneath me and places me back down, this time on the sheets.

"Now then." He licks his bottom lip slowly. "You're biting that lip, Anastasia. You know the effect it has on me." He places his long index finger over my mouth, a warning.

Oh my. I can barely contain myself, lying helpless, watching him move gracefully around my room. It's a heady aphrodisiac. Slowly, almost leisurely, he removes his shoes and socks, undoes his pants, and lifts his shirt off over his head.

"I think you've seen too much." He chuckles slyly. He sits astride me again, pulls my T-shirt up, and I think he's going to take it off me, but he rolls it up to my neck and then pulls it up over my head so he can see my mouth and my nose, but it covers my eyes. And because it's folded over, I cannot see a thing through it.

"Mmm," he breathes appreciatively. "This just gets better and better. I'm going to get a drink."

Leaning down, he kisses me, his lips tender against mine, and his weight shifts off the bed. I hear the quiet creak of the bedroom door. Get a drink. *Where? Here? Portland? Seattle?* I strain to hear him. I can make out low rumblings, and I know he's talking to Kate—oh no . . . *he's practically naked.* What's she going to say? I hear a faint popping sound. What's that? He returns, the door creaking once more, his feet padding across the bedroom floor, and ice tinkling against glass as it swirls in liquid. What kind of drink? He shuts the door and shuffles around removing his pants. They drop to the floor, and I know he's naked. He sits astride me again.

"Are you thirsty, Anastasia?" he asks, his voice teasing

"Yes," I breathe, because my mouth is suddenly parched. I hear the ice clink against the glass, and he leans down and kisses me, pouring a delicious, crisp liquid into my mouth as he does. It's white wine. It's so unexpected, so *hot*, though it's chilled and Christian's lips are cool.

"More?" he whispers.

I nod. It tastes all the more divine because it's been in *his* mouth. He leans down, and I drink another mouthful from his lips . . . *oh my.*

"Let's not go too far; we know your capacity for alcohol is limited, Anastasia."

I can't help it. I grin, and he leans down to deliver another delicious mouthful. He shifts so he's lying beside me, his erection at my hip. Oh, I want him inside me.

"Is this *nice*?" he asks, but I hear the edge in his voice.

I tense. He moves the glass again and leans down, kissing me and depositing a small shard of ice in my mouth with a little wine. He slowly and leisurely trails chilled kisses down the center of my body, from the base of my throat to between my breasts, down my torso to my belly. He pops a fragment of ice in my navel in a pool of cool, cold wine. It burns all the way down to the depths of my belly. Wow.

"Now you have to keep still," he whispers. "If you move, Anastasia, you'll get wine all over the bed."

My hips flex automatically.

"Oh no. If you spill the wine, I will punish you, Miss Steele."

I groan and desperately fight the urge to tilt my hips, pulling on my restraint. Oh no . . . *please.*

With one finger, he pulls down my bra cups in turn, my breasts pushed up, exposed and vulnerable. Leaning down, he kisses and tugs at each of my nipples in turn with cool, cold lips. I fight my body as it tries to arch in response.

"How *nice* is this?" he breathes, blowing on one of my nipples.

I hear another clink of ice, and then I can feel it around my right nipple as he tugs the left one with his lips. I moan, struggling not to move. It's sweet, agonizing torture.

"If you spill the wine, I won't let you come."

"Oh . . . please . . . Christian . . . Sir . . . Please." He's driving me insane. I *hear* him smile.

The ice in my navel is melting. I am beyond warm—warm and chilled and wanting. Wanting him, inside me. Now.

His cool fingers trail languidly across my belly. My skin is oversensitive, my hips flex automatically, and the now-warmer liquid from my navel seeps over my belly. Christian moves quickly, lapping it up with his tongue, kissing, biting me softly, sucking.

"Oh dear, Anastasia, you moved. What am I going to do to you?"

I'm panting loudly. All I can concentrate on is his voice and his touch. Nothing else is real. Nothing else matters, nothing else registers on my radar. His fingers slip into my panties, and I'm rewarded with his unguarded sharp intake of air.

"Oh, baby," he murmurs, and he pushes two fingers inside me.

I gasp.

"Ready for me so soon," he says. He moves his fingers tantalizingly slowly, in, out, and I push against him, tilting my hips up.

"You are a greedy girl," he scolds softly, and his thumb circles my clitoris and then presses down.

I groan loudly as my body bucks beneath his expert fingers. He reaches up and pushes the T-shirt over my head so I can see him. I blink in the soft light of my sidelight. I long to touch him.

"I want to touch you," I breathe.

"I know," he murmurs. He leans down and kisses me, his fingers still moving rhythmically inside me, his thumb circling and pressing. His other hand scoops my hair off my head and holds my head in place. His tongue mirrors the actions of his fingers, claiming me. My legs begin to stiffen as I push against his hand. He gentles his hand, so I'm brought back from the brink. He does this again and again. It's so frustrating . . . *Oh, please, Christian*, I scream in my head.

"This is your punishment, so close and yet so far. Is this *nice*?" he breathes in my ear. I whimper, exhausted, pulling against my restraint. I'm helpless, lost in an erotic torment.

"Please," I beg, and he finally takes pity on me.

"How shall I fuck you, Anastasia?"

Oh . . . my body starts to quiver. He stills again.

"Please."

"What do you want, Anastasia?"

"You . . . now," I cry.

"Shall I fuck you this way, or this way, or this way? There's an endless choice," he breathes against my lips. He withdraws his hand and reaches over to the bedside table for a foil packet. He kneels up between my legs, and very slowly he pulls my panties off, staring down at me, his eyes gleaming. He puts on the condom. I watch fascinated, mesmerized.

"How *nice* is this?" he says as he strokes himself.

"I meant it as a joke," I whimper. *Please fuck me, Christian*.

He raises his eyebrows as his hand moves up and down his impressive length.

"A joke?" His voice is menacingly soft.

"Yes. Please, Christian," I beseech him.

"Are you laughing now?"

"No," I mewl.

I'm a ball of sexual tense need. He stares down at me for a moment, measuring my need, then he grabs me suddenly and flips me over. It takes me by surprise, and because my hands are tied, I have to support myself on my elbows. He pushes both my knees up the bed so my behind is in the air, and he slaps me hard. Before I can react, he plunges inside me. I cry out—from the slap and from his sudden assault, and I come instantly again and again, falling apart beneath him as he continues to slam deliciously into me. He doesn't stop. I'm spent. I can't take this . . . and he pounds on and on and on . . . then I'm building again . . . surely not . . . . no . . .

"Come on, Anastasia, again," he growls through clenched teeth, and unbelievably, my body responds, convulsing around him as I climax anew, calling out his name. I shatter again into tiny fragments, and Christian stills, finally letting go, silently finding his release. He collapses on top of me, breathing hard.

"How *nice* was that?" he asks through his gritted teeth.

Oh my.

I lie panting and spent on the bed, eyes closed as he slowly pulls out of me. He rises immediately and dresses. When he's fully clothed, he climbs back on the bed and gently undoes my binding and pulls my T-shirt off. I flex my fingers and rub my wrists, smiling at the woven pattern imprinted on my wrists from the tie. I readjust my bra as he pulls the duvet and quilt over me. I stare up at him completely dazed, and he smirks down at me.

"That was really nice," I whisper, smiling coyly.

"There's that word again."

"You don't like that word?"

"No. It doesn't do it for me at all."

"Oh—I don't know . . . it seems to have a very beneficial effect on you."

"I'm a beneficial effect, now am I? Could you wound my ego any further, Miss Steele?"

"I don't think there's anything wrong with your ego." But even as I say it, I don't feel the conviction of my words—something elusive crosses my mind, a fleeting thought, but it's lost before I can grasp it.

"You think?" His voice is soft. He's lying beside me, fully

clothed, his head propped up on his elbow, and I am only wearing my bra.

"Why don't you like to be touched?"

"I just don't." He reaches over and plants a soft kiss on my forehead. "So, that e-mail was your idea of a joke."

I smile apologetically at him and shrug.

"I see. So you are still considering my proposition?"

"Your indecent proposal . . . yes, I am. I have issues though."

He grins down at me as if relieved.

"I'd be disappointed if you didn't."

"I was going to e-mail them to you, but you kind of interrupted me."

"Coitus interruptus."

"See, I knew you had a sense of humor somewhere in there." I smile.

"Only certain things are funny, Anastasia. I thought you were saying no, no discussion at all." His voice drops.

"I don't know yet. I haven't made up my mind. Will you collar me?"

He raises his eyebrows. "You have been doing your research. I don't know, Anastasia. I've never collared anyone."

Oh . . . should I be surprised by this? I know so little about *the scene* . . . I don't know.

"Were you collared?" I whisper.

"Yes."

"By Mrs. Robinson?"

"Mrs. Robinson!" He laughs loudly, freely, and he looks so young and carefree, his head thrown back, his laughter infectious.

I grin back at him.

"I'll tell her you said that; she'll love it."

"You still talk to her regularly?" I can't keep the shock out of my voice.

"Yes." He's serious now.

Oh . . . and part of me is suddenly insanely jealous—I'm disturbed by the depth of my feeling.

"I see." My voice is tight. "So you have someone you can discuss your alternative lifestyle with, but I'm not allowed."

He frowns.

"I don't think I've ever thought about it like that. Mrs. Robinson was part of that lifestyle. I told you, she's a good friend now. If you'd like, I can introduce you to one of my former subs. You could talk to her."

What? Is he deliberately trying to upset me?

"Is this *your* idea of a joke?

"No, Anastasia." He's bemused as he shakes his head.

"No—I'll do this on my own, thank you very much," I snap at him, pulling the duvet up to my chin.

He stares at me, at sea, surprised.

"Anastasia, I . . ." He's lost for words. A first, I think. "I didn't mean to offend you."

"I'm not offended. I'm appalled."

"Appalled?"

"I don't want to talk to one of your ex-girlfriends . . . slave . . . sub . . . whatever you call them."

"Anastasia Steele—are you jealous?"

I flush, crimson.

"Are you staying?"

"I have a breakfast meeting tomorrow at the Heathman. Besides, I told you, I don't sleep with girlfriends, slaves, subs, or anyone. Friday and Saturday were exceptions. It won't happen again." I can hear the resolve behind his soft, husky voice.

I purse my lips at him.

"Well, I'm tired now."

"Are you kicking me out?" He raises his eyebrows, amused and a little dismayed.

"Yes."

"Well, that's another first." He eyes me speculatively. "So nothing you want to discuss now? About the contract."

"No." I reply petulantly.

"God, I'd like to give you a good hiding. You'd feel a lot better, and so would I."

"You can't say things like that . . . I haven't signed anything yet."

"A man can dream, Anastasia." He leans over me and grasps my chin. "Wednesday?" he murmurs, and he kisses me lightly on my lips.

"Wednesday," I agree. "I'll see you out. If you give me a minute." I sit up and grab my T-shirt, pushing him out of the way. Reluctantly, he gets up off the bed.

"Please pass me my sweatpants."

He collects them from the floor and hands them to me.

"Yes, ma'am." He's trying unsuccessfully to hide his smile.

I narrow my eyes at him as I slip the pants on. My hair is a mess, and I know I'll have to face the Katherine Kavanagh Inquisition after he's gone. Grabbing a hair tie, I walk to my bedroom door, opening it to check for Kate. She is not in the living room. I think I can hear her on the phone in her room. Christian follows me out. During the short walk from bedroom to front door, my thoughts and feelings ebb and flow, transforming. I'm no longer angry with him, I feel suddenly unbearably shy. I don't want him to go. For the first time, I'm wishing he was *normal*—wanting a normal relationship that doesn't need a ten-page agreement, a flogger, and carabiners in his playroom ceiling.

I open the door for him and stare down at my hands. This is the first time I have ever had sex in my home, and as sex goes, I think it was pretty damn fine. But now I feel like a receptacle—an empty vessel to be filled at his whim. My subconscious shakes her head. *You wanted to run to the Heathman for sex—you had it express delivered.* She crosses her arms and taps her foot with a what-are-you-complaining-about look on her face. Christian stops in the doorway and clasps my chin, forcing my eyes to meet his. His brow creases.

"You okay?" he asks tenderly as his thumb lightly caresses my bottom lip.

"Yes," I reply, though in all honesty I'm just not sure. I feel a paradigm shift. I know that if I do this thing with him, I will get hurt. He's not capable, interested, or willing to offer me any more . . . and I want more. *Much more.* The surge of jealousy I felt only moments ago tells me that I have deeper feelings for him than I have admitted to myself.

"Wednesday," he confirms, and he leans forward and kisses me softly. Something changes while he's kissing me; his lips grow more urgent against mine, his hand moves up from my chin and he's holding the side of my head, his other hand on the other side. His breathing accelerates. He deepens the kiss, leaning into me. I put my hands on his arms. I want to run them through his hair, but I resist, knowing that he won't like it. He leans his forehead against mine, his eyes closed, his voice strained.

"Anastasia," he whispers. "What are you doing to me?"

"I could say the same to you," I whisper back.

Taking a deep breath, he kisses my forehead and leaves. He strolls purposefully down the path toward his car as he runs his hand through his hair. Glancing up as he opens his car door, he smiles his breathtaking smile. My answering smile is weak, completely dazzled by him, and I'm reminded once more of Icarus soaring too close to the sun. I close the front door as he climbs into his sports car. I have an overwhelming urge to cry; a sad and lonely melancholy grips and tightens around my heart. Dashing back to my bedroom, I close the door and lean against it, trying to rationalize my feelings. I can't. Sliding to the floor, I put my head in my hands as my tears begin to flow.

Kate knocks gently.

"Ana?" she whispers. I open the door. She takes one look at me and throws her arms around me.

"What's wrong? What did that creepy good-looking bastard do?"

"Oh, Kate, nothing I didn't want him to."

She pulls me to my bed and we sit.

"You have dreadful sex hair."

In spite of my poignant sadness, I laugh.

"It was good sex, not dreadful at all."

Kate smiles.

"That's better. Why are you crying? You never cry." She retrieves my brush from the side table and, sitting behind me, very slowly starts brushing out the knots.

"I just don't think our relationship is going to go anywhere." I stare down at my fingers.

"I thought you said you were going to see him on Wednesday?"

"I am. That was our original plan."

"So, why did he turn up here today?"

"I sent him an e-mail."

"Asking him to drop by?"

"No, saying I didn't want to see him anymore."

"And he turns up? Ana, that's genius."

"Actually, it was a joke."

"Oh. Now I'm really confused."

Patiently, I explain the essence of my e-mail without giving anything away.

"So you thought he'd reply by e-mail."

"Yes."

"But instead he turns up here."

"Yes."

"I'd say he's completely smitten with you."

I frown. *Christian smitten with me? Hardly.* He's just looking for a new toy—a convenient new toy that he can bed and do unspeakable things to. My heart tightens painfully. This is the reality.

"He came here to fuck me, that's all."

"Who said romance was dead?" she whispers, horrified. I've shocked Kate. I didn't think that was possible. I shrug apologetically.

"He uses sex as a weapon."

"Fuck you into submission?" She shakes her head disapprovingly. I blink rapidly at her, and I feel the blush as it spreads across my face. *Oh . . . spot on, Katherine Kavanagh, Pulitzer Prize–winning journalist.*

"Ana, I don't understand, you just let him make love to you?"

"No, Kate, we don't make love—we fuck—Christian's terminology. He doesn't do the love thing."

"I knew there was something weird about him. He has commitment issues."

I nod, as if in agreement. Inwardly, I pine. Oh, Kate . . . I wish I could tell you everything, everything about this strange, sad, kinky guy, and you could tell me to forget about him. Stop me from being a fool.

"I guess it's all a little overwhelming," I murmur. *That's the understatement of the year.*

Because I don't want to talk about Christian anymore, I ask her about Elliot. Katherine's whole demeanor changes at the mere mention of his name. She lights up from within, beaming at me.

"He's coming over early Saturday to help load up." She hugs the hairbrush—boy, has she got it bad—and I feel a familiar faint stab of envy. Kate has found herself a normal man, and she looks so happy.

I turn and hug her.

"Oh, I meant to say. Your dad called while you were . . . er, occupied. Apparently Bob has sustained some injury, so your mom and he can't make graduation. But your dad will be here Thursday. He wants you to call."

"Oh . . . my mom never called me. Is Bob okay?"

"Yes. Call her in the morning. It's late now."

"Thanks, Kate. I'm okay now. I'll call Ray in the morning, too. I think I'll just turn in."

She smiles, but her eyes crinkle at the corners with concern.

After she's gone, I sit and read the contract again, making more notes as I go. When I've finished, I fire up the laptop, ready to respond.

There's an e-mail from Christian in my inbox.

From: Christian Grey
Subject: This Evening
Date: May 23 2011 23:16
To: Anastasia Steele

Miss Steele,
I look forward to receiving your notes on the contract.

Until then, sleep well, baby.

Christian Grey
CEO, Grey Enterprises Holdings, Inc.

From: Anastasia Steele
Subject: Issues
Date: May 24 2011 00:02
To: Christian Grey

Dear Mr. Grey,
Here is my list of issues. I look forward to discussing them more fully at dinner on Wednesday.

The numbers refer to clauses:

2: Not sure why this is solely for MY benefit—i.e., to explore MY sensuality and limits. I'm sure I wouldn't need a ten-page contract to do that! Surely this is for YOUR benefit.

4: As you are aware, you are my only sexual partner. I don't take drugs, and I've not had any blood transfusions. I'm probably safe. What about you?

8: I can terminate at any time if I don't think you're sticking to the agreed limits. Okay—I like this.

9: Obey you in all things? Accept without hesitation your discipline? We need to talk about this.

11: One-month trial period. Not three.

12: I cannot commit every weekend. I do have a life, or will have. Perhaps three out of four?

15.2: Using my body as you see fit sexually or otherwise—please define "or otherwise."

15.5: This whole discipline clause. I'm not sure I want to be whipped, flogged, or corporally punished. I am sure this would be in breach of clauses 2–5. And also "for any other reason." That's just mean—and you told me you weren't a sadist.

15.10: Like loaning me out to someone else would ever be an option. But I'm glad it's here in black and white.

15.14: The Rules. More on those later.

15.19: Touching myself without your permission. What's the problem with this? You know I don't do it anyway.

15.21: Discipline—please see clause 15.5 above.

15.22: I can't look into your eyes? Why?

15.24: Why can't I touch you?

Rules:

Sleep—I'll agree to six hours.

Food—I am not eating food from a prescribed list. The food list goes or I do—deal breaker.

Clothes—as long as I only have to wear your clothes when I'm with you . . . okay.

Exercise—We agreed on three hours, this still says four.

Soft Limits:

Can we go through all of these? No fisting of any kind. What is suspension? Genital clamps—you have got to be kidding me.

Can you please let me know the arrangements for Wednesday? I am working until five p.m. that day.

Good night.

Ana

From: Christian Grey
Subject: Issues
Date: May 24 2011 00:07
To: Anastasia Steele

Miss Steele,
That's a long list. Why are you still up?

Christian Grey
CEO, Grey Enterprises Holdings, Inc.

From: Anastasia Steele
Subject: Burning the Midnight Oil
Date: May 24 2011 00:10
To: Christian Grey

Sir,
If you recall, I was going through this list when I was distracted and bedded by a passing control freak.

Good night.

Ana

From: Christian Grey
Subject: Stop Burning the Midnight Oil
Date: May 24 2011 00:12
To: Anastasia Steele

GO TO BED, ANASTASIA.

Christian Grey
CEO & Control Freak, Grey Enterprises Holdings, Inc.

Oh . . . shouty capitals! I switch off. How can he intimidate me when he's six miles away? I shake my head. My heart still heavy, I climb into bed and fall instantly into a deep but troubled sleep.

CHAPTER THIRTEEN

The following day, I call my mom after I get home from work. It's been a relatively peaceful day at Clayton's, allowing me far too much time to think. I'm restless, nervous about my showdown with Mr. Control Freak tomorrow, and at the back of my mind, I'm worried that perhaps I've been too negative in my response to the contract. Perhaps he'll call the whole thing off.

My mom is oozing contrition, desperately sorry not to make my graduation. Bob has twisted some ligament, which means he's hobbling all over the place. Honestly, he's as accident-prone as I am. He's expected to make a full recovery, but it means he's resting up, and my mother has to wait on him hand and sore foot.

"Ana, honey, I'm so sorry," my mom whines into the phone.

"Mom, it's fine. Ray will be there."

"Ana, you sound distracted—are you okay, baby?"

"Yes, Mom," *Oh, if only you knew.* There's an obscenely rich guy I've met and he wants some kind of strange kinky sexual relationship, in which I don't get a say in things.

"Have you met someone?"

"No, Mom." I am so not going there right now.

"Well, darling, I'll be thinking of you on Thursday. I love you . . . you know that, honey?"

I close my eyes. Her precious words give me a warm glow inside.

"Love you, too, Mom. Say hi to Bob, and I hope he gets better fast."

"Will do, honey. Bye."

"Bye."

I have strayed into my bedroom with the phone. Idly, I switch the mean machine on and fire up the e-mail program. There's an e-mail from Christian from late last night or very early this morning, depending on your point of view. My heart rate spikes instantly, and I hear the blood pumping in my ears. Holy crap . . . perhaps he's said no—that's it—maybe he's canceling dinner. The thought is so painful. I dismiss it quickly and open the e-mail.

From: Christian Grey
Subject: Your Issues
Date: May 24 2011 01:27
To: Anastasia Steele

Dear Miss Steele,
Following my more thorough examination of your issues, may I bring to your attention the definition of submissive.

submissive [s*uh*b-mis-iv]—*adjective*

1. inclined or ready to submit; unresistingly or humbly obedient: *submissive servants.*

2. marked by or indicating submission: *a submissive reply.*

Origin: 1580–90; submiss + -ive

Synonyms: 1. tractable, compliant, pliant, amenable. 2. passive, resigned, patient, docile, tame, subdued. *Antonyms: 1.* rebellious, disobedient.

Please bear this in mind for our meeting on Wednesday.

Christian Grey
CEO, Grey Enterprises Holdings, Inc.

My initial feeling is one of relief. He's willing to discuss my issues at least, and he still wants to meet tomorrow. After some thought, I reply.

From: Anastasia Steele
Subject: My Issues . . . What about Your Issues?
Date: May 24 2011 18:29
To: Christian Grey

Sir,

Please note the date of origin: 1580–90. I would respectfully remind Sir that the year is 2011. We have come a long way since then.

May I offer a definition for *you* to consider for our meeting:

compromise [kom-pr*uh*-mahyz]—*noun*

1. a settlement of differences by mutual concessions; an agreement reached by adjustment of conflicting or opposing claims, principles, etc., by reciprocal modification of demands. 2. the result of such a settlement. 3. something intermediate between different things: *The split-level is a compromise between a ranch house and a multistoried house.* 4. an endangering, esp. of reputation; exposure to danger, suspicion, etc.: *a compromise of one's integrity.*

Ana

From: Christian Grey
Subject: What about My Issues?
Date: May 24 2011 18:32
To: Anastasia Steele

Good point, well made, as ever, Miss Steele. I will collect you from your apartment at 7:00 tomorrow.

Christian Grey
CEO, Grey Enterprises Holdings, Inc.

From: Anastasia Steele
Subject: 2011—Women Can Drive
Date: May 24 2011 18:40
To: Christian Grey

Sir,
I have a car. I can drive.

I would prefer to meet you somewhere.

Where shall I meet you?

At your hotel at 7:00?

Ana

From: Christian Grey
Subject: Stubborn Young Women
Date: May 24 2011 18:43
To: Anastasia Steele

Dear Miss Steele,
I refer to my e-mail dated May 24, 2011, sent at 1:27 and the definition contained therein.

Do you ever think you'll be able to do what you're told?

Christian Grey
CEO, Grey Enterprises Holdings, Inc.

From: Anastasia Steele
Subject: Intractable Men

Date: May 24 2011 18:49
To: Christian Grey

Mr. Grey,
I would like to drive.

Please.

Ana

From: Christian Grey
Subject: Exasperated Men
Date: May 24 2011 18:52
To: Anastasia Steele

Fine.
My hotel at 7:00.

I'll meet you in the Marble Bar.

Christian Grey
CEO, Grey Enterprises Holdings, Inc.

He's even grumpy by e-mail. Doesn't he understand that I may need to make a quick getaway? Not that my Beetle is quick . . . but still—I need a means of escape.

From: Anastasia Steele
Subject: Not So Intractable Men
Date: May 24 2011 18:55
To: Christian Grey

Thank you.
Ana x

From: Christian Grey
Subject: Exasperating Women
Date: May 24 2011 18:59
To: Anastasia Steele

You're welcome.

Christian Grey
CEO, Grey Enterprises Holdings, Inc.

I call Ray, who is just about to watch the Sounders play some soccer team from Salt Lake City, so our conversation is mercifully brief. He's driving down on Thursday for graduation. He wants to take me out afterward for a meal. My heart swells talking to Ray, and a huge lump forms in my throat. He has been my constant through all Mom's romantic ups and downs. We have a special bond that I treasure. Even though he's my stepdad, he's always treated me as his own, and I can't wait to see him. It's been too long. His quiet fortitude is what I need now, what I miss. Maybe I can channel my inner Ray for my meeting tomorrow.

Kate and I concentrate on packing, sharing a bottle of cheap red wine as we do. When I finally go to bed, having almost finished packing my room, I feel calmer. The physical activity of boxing everything up has been a welcome distraction, and I'm tired. I want a good night's rest. I snuggle into my bed and am soon asleep.

PAUL IS BACK FROM Princeton before he sets off for New York to start an internship with a financing company. He follows me around the store all day asking me for a date. It's annoying.

"Paul, for the hundredth time, I have a date this evening."

"No, you don't, you're just saying that to avoid me. You're always avoiding me."

Yes . . . you'd think you'd take the hint.

"Paul, I never thought it was a good idea to date the boss's brother."

"You're finishing here on Friday. You're not working tomorrow."

"And I'll be in Seattle as of Saturday and you'll be in New York soon. We couldn't get much farther apart if we tried. Besides, I do have a date this evening."

"With José?"

"No."

"Who then?"

"Paul . . . oh." My sigh is exasperated. He's not going to let this go. "Christian Grey." I cannot help the annoyance in my voice. But it does the trick. Paul's mouth falls open, and he gapes at me, struck dumb. Humph—even his *name* renders people speechless.

"You have a date with Christian Grey?" he says finally, once he's over the shock. Disbelief is evident in his voice.

"Yes."

"I see." Paul looks positively crestfallen, stunned even, and a very small part of me resents that he should find this a surprise. My inner goddess does, too. She makes a very vulgar and unattractive gesture at him with her fingers.

After that, he ignores me, and at five I am out the door, pronto.

Kate has lent me two dresses and two pairs of shoes for tonight and for graduation tomorrow. I wish I could feel more enthused about clothes and make an extra effort, but clothes are just not my thing. *What is your thing, Anastasia?* Christian's softly spoken question haunts me. Shaking my head and endeavoring to quell my nerves, I decide on the plum-colored sheath dress for this evening. It's demure and vaguely businesslike—after all, I am negotiating a contract.

I shower, shave my legs and underarms, wash my hair, and then spend a good half hour drying it so that it falls in soft waves to my breasts and down my back. I slip a comb in to keep one side off my face and apply mascara and some lip gloss. I rarely wear makeup—it intimidates me. None of my literary heroines had to deal with makeup—maybe I'd know more about it if they had. I slip on the plum-colored stilettos that match the dress, and I'm ready by six thirty.

"Well?" I ask Kate.

She grins.

"Boy, you scrub up well, Ana." She nods with approval. "You look hot."

"Hot! I'm aiming for demure and businesslike."

"That, too, but most of all hot. The dress really suits you and your coloring. The way it clings." She smirks.

"Kate!" I scold.

"Just keeping it real, Ana. The whole package—looks good. Keep the dress. You'll have him eating out of your hand."

My mouth presses in a hard line. *Oh, you so have that the wrong way around.*

"Wish me luck."

"You need luck for a date?" Her brow furrows, puzzled.

"Yes, Kate."

"Well, then—good luck." She hugs me, and I am out the front door.

I have to drive in my bare feet—Wanda, my sea-blue Beetle, wasn't built to be driven by stiletto-wearers. I pull up outside the Heathman at six fifty-eight precisely and hand my car keys to the valet for parking. He looks askance at my Beetle, but I ignore him. Taking a deep breath and mentally girding my loins, I head into the hotel.

Christian is leaning casually against the bar, drinking a glass of white wine. He's dressed in his customary white linen shirt, black jeans, black tie, and black jacket. His hair is as tousled as ever. I sigh. I stand for a few seconds in the entrance of the bar, gazing at him, admiring the view. He glances, nervously I think, toward the entrance and stills when he sees me. Blinking a couple of times, he then smiles a slow, lazy, sexy smile that renders me speechless and all molten inside. Making a supreme effort not to bite my lip,

I move forward, aware that I, Anastasia Steele of Clumsyville, am in high stilettos. He walks gracefully over to meet me.

"You look stunning," he murmurs as he leans down to briefly kiss my cheek. "A dress, Miss Steele. I approve." Taking my arm, he leads me to a secluded booth and signals for the waiter.

"What would you like to drink?"

My lips quirk up in a quick, sly smile as I sit and slide into the booth—well, at least he's asking me.

"I'll have what you're having, please." See! I can play nice and behave myself. Amused, he orders another glass of Sancerre and slides in opposite me.

"They have an excellent wine cellar here," he says. Putting his elbows on the table, he steeples his fingers in front of his mouth, his eyes alive with some unreadable emotion. And there it is . . . that familiar pull and charge from him, it connects somewhere deep inside me. I shift uncomfortably under his scrutiny, my heart palpitating. I must keep my cool.

"Are you nervous?" he asks softly.

"Yes."

He leans forward.

"Me, too," he whispers conspiratorially. My eyes shoot up to meet his. *Him? Nervous? Never.* I blink, and he smiles his adorable lopsided smile at me. The waiter arrives with my wine, a small dish of mixed nuts, and another of olives.

"So, how are we going to do this?" I ask. "Run through my points one by one?"

"Impatient as ever, Miss Steele."

"Well, I could ask you what you thought of the weather today."

He smiles, and his long fingers reach down to collect an olive. He pops it in his mouth, and my eyes linger on his mouth, that mouth, that's been on me . . . all parts of me. I flush.

"I thought the weather was particularly unexceptional today." He smirks.

"Are you smirking at me, Mr. Grey?"

"I am, Miss Steele."

"You know this contract is legally unenforceable."

"I am fully aware of that, Miss Steele."

"Were you going to tell me that at any point?"

He frowns. "You'd think I'd coerce you into something you don't want to do, and then pretend that I have a legal hold over you?"

"Well . . . yes."

"You don't think very highly of me, do you?"

"You haven't answered my question."

"Anastasia, it doesn't matter if it's legal or not. It represents an arrangement that I would like to make with you—what I would like from you and what you can expect from me. If you don't like it, then don't sign. If you do sign and then decide you don't like it, there are enough get-out clauses so you can walk away. Even if it were legally binding, do you think I'd drag you through the courts if you did decide to run?"

I take a long sip of my wine. My subconscious taps me hard on the shoulder. You must keep your wits about you. *Don't drink too much.*

"Relationships like this are built on honesty and trust," he continues. "If you don't trust me—trust me to know how I'm affecting you, how far I can go with you, how far I can take you—if you can't be honest with me, then we really can't do this."

Oh my, we've cut to the chase quickly. *How far he can take me.* Holy shit. What does that mean?

"So it's quite simple, Anastasia. Do you trust me or not?" His eyes are burning, fervent.

"Did you have similar discussions with, um . . . the fifteen?"

"No."

"Why not?"

"Because they were all established submissives. They knew what they wanted out of a relationship with me and generally what I expected. With them, it was just a question of fine-tuning the soft limits, details like that."

"Is there a store you go to? Submissives 'Я' Us?"

He laughs. "Not exactly."

"Then how?"

"Is that what you want to discuss? Or shall we get down to the nitty-gritty? Your issues, as you say."

I swallow. *Do I trust him?* Is that what this all comes down to—trust? Surely that should be a two-way thing. I remember his snit when I phoned José.

"Are you hungry?" he asks, distracting me from my thoughts.

Oh no . . . food.

"No."

"Have you eaten today?"

I stare at him. *Honesty . . .* Holy crap, he's not going to like my answer.

"No." My voice is small.

He narrows his eyes.

"You have to eat, Anastasia. We can eat down here or in my suite. What would you prefer?"

"I think we should stay in public, on neutral ground."

He smiles sardonically.

"Do you think that would stop me?" he says softly, a sensual warning.

My eyes widen, and I swallow again.

"I hope so."

"Come, I have a private dining room booked. No public." He smiles at me enigmatically and climbs out of the booth, holding his hand out to me.

"Bring your wine," he murmurs.

Placing my hand in his, I slide out and stand up beside him. He releases me, and his hand reaches for my elbow. He leads me back through the bar and up the grand stairs to a mezzanine floor. A young man in full Heathman livery approaches us.

"Mr. Grey, this way, sir."

We follow him through a plush seating area to an intimate dining room. *Just one secluded table.* The room is small but sumptuous. Beneath a shimmering chandelier, the table is all starched linen, crystal glasses, silver cutlery, and white rose bouquet. An old-world, sophisticated charm pervades the wood-paneled room. The waiter pulls out my chair, and I sit. He places my napkin in my lap. Christian sits opposite me. I peek up at him.

"Don't bite your lip," he whispers.

I frown. Damn it. I don't even know that I'm doing it.

"I've ordered already. I hope you don't mind."

Frankly, I'm relieved. I'm not sure I can make any further decisions.

"No, that's fine," I acquiesce.

"It's good to know that you can be amenable. Now, where were we?"

"The nitty-gritty." I take another large sip of wine. It really is delicious. Christian Grey does wine well. I remember the last sip of wine he gave me, in my bed. I blush at the intrusive thought.

"Yes, your issues." He fishes into his inside jacket pocket and pulls out a piece of paper. My e-mail.

"Clause 2. Agreed. This is for the benefit of us both. I shall redraft."

I blink at him. Holy shit . . . we are going to go through each of these points one at a time. I just don't feel so brave face-to-face. He looks so earnest. I steel myself with another sip of my wine. Christian continues.

"My sexual health. Well, all of my previous partners have had blood tests, and I have regular tests every six months for all the health risks you mention. All my recent tests are clear. I have never taken drugs. In fact, I'm vehemently antidrug. I have a strict no-tolerance policy with regards to drugs for all my employees, and I insist on random drug testing."

Wow . . . control freakery gone mad. I blink at him, shocked.

"I have never had any blood transfusions. Does that answer your question?"

I nod, impassive.

"Your next point I mentioned earlier. You can walk away any time, Anastasia. I won't stop you. If you go, however—that's it. Just so you know."

"Okay," I answer softly. If I go, that's it. The thought is surprisingly painful.

The waiter arrives with our first course. How can I possibly eat? Holy Moses—he's ordered oysters on a bed of ice.

"I hope you like oysters." Christian's voice is soft.

"I've never had one." Ever.

"Really? Well." He reaches for one. "All you do is tip and swallow. I think you can manage that." He gazes at me, and I know what he's referring to. I blush scarlet. He grins at me, squirts some lemon juice onto his oyster, and then tips it into his mouth.

"Hmm, delicious. Tastes of the sea." He grins at me. "Go on," he encourages.

"So, I don't chew it?"

"No, Anastasia, you don't." His eyes are alight with humor. He looks so young like this.

I bite my lip and his expression changes instantly. He looks sternly at me. I reach across and pick up my first-ever oyster. Okay . . . here goes nothing. I squirt some lemon juice on it and tip it up. It slips down my throat, all sea water, salt, the sharp tang of citrus, and fleshiness . . . ooh. I lick my lips, and he's watching me intently, his eyes hooded.

"Well?"

"I'll have another," I say dryly.

"Good girl," he says proudly.

"Did you choose these deliberately? Aren't they known for their aphrodisiac qualities?"

"No, they are the first item on the menu. I don't need an aphrodisiac near you. I think you know that, and I think you react the same way near me," he says simply. "So where were we?" He glances at my e-mail as I reach for another oyster.

He reacts the same way. I affect him . . . wow.

"Obey me in all things. Yes, I want you to do that. I need you to do that. Think of it as role-play, Anastasia."

"But I'm worried you'll hurt me."

"Hurt you how?"

"Physically." *And emotionally.*

"Do you really think I would do that? Go beyond any limit you can't take?"

"You've said you've hurt someone before."

"Yes, I have. It was a long time ago."

"How did you hurt her?"

"I suspended her from my playroom ceiling. In fact, that's one of your questions. Suspension—that's what the carabiners are for in the playroom. Rope play. One of the ropes was tied too tightly."

I hold my hand up, begging him to stop.

"I don't need to know any more. So you won't suspend me then?"

"Not if you really don't want to. You can make that a hard limit."

"Okay."

"So obeying, do you think you can manage that?"

He stares at me, his gaze intense,. The seconds tick by.

"I could try," I whisper.

"Good." He smiles. "Now term. One month instead of three is no time at all, especially if you want a weekend away from me each month. I don't think I'll be able to stay away from you for that length of time. I can barely manage it now." He pauses.

He can't stay away from me? What?

"How about one day over one weekend per month you get to yourself—but I get a midweek night that week?"

"Okay."

"And please, let's try it for three months. If it's not for you, then you can walk away anytime."

"Three months?" I'm feeling railroaded. I take another large sip of wine and treat myself to another oyster. I could learn to like these.

"The ownership thing, that's just terminology and goes back to the principle of obeying. It's to get you into the right frame of mind, to understand where I'm coming from. And I want you to know that as soon as you cross my threshold as my submissive, I will do what I like to you. You have to accept that and willingly. That's why you have to trust me. I will fuck you, any time, any way

I want—anywhere I want. I will discipline you, because you will screw up. I will train you to please me.

"But I know you've not done this before. Initially, we'll take it slowly, and I will help you. We'll build up to various scenarios. I want you to trust me, but I know I have to earn your trust, and I will. The 'or otherwise'—again it's to help you get into the mindset; it means anything goes."

He's so passionate, mesmerizing. This is obviously his obsession, the way he is . . . I can't take my eyes off him. He really, really wants this. He stops talking and gazes at me.

"Still with me?" he whispers, his voice rich, warm, and seductive. He takes a sip of his wine, his penetrating stare holding mine.

The waiter comes to the door, and Christian subtly nods, permitting the waiter to clear our table.

"Would you like some more wine?"

"I have to drive."

"Some water then?"

I nod.

"Still or sparkling?"

"Sparkling, please."

The waiter leaves.

"You're very quiet," Christian whispers.

"You're very verbose."

He smiles.

"Discipline. There's a very fine line between pleasure and pain, Anastasia. They are two sides of the same coin, one not existing without the other. I can show you how pleasurable pain can be. You don't believe me now, but this is what I mean about trust. There will be pain, but nothing that you can't handle. Again, it comes down to trust. *Do* you trust me, Ana?"

Ana!

"Yes, I do." I respond spontaneously, not thinking . . . because it's true—I *do* trust him.

"Well, then," he looks relieved. "The rest of this stuff is just details."

"Important details."

"Okay, let's talk through those."

My head is swimming with all his words. I should have brought Kate's digital recorder so I can listen to this again later. There is so much information, so much to process. The waiter re-emerges with our entrees: black cod, asparagus, and crushed potatoes with a hollandaise sauce. I have never felt less like food.

"I hope you like fish," Christian says mildly.

I make a stab at my food and take a long drink of my sparkling water. I vehemently wish it was wine.

"The rules. Let's talk about them. The food is a deal breaker?"

"Yes."

"Can I modify to say that you will eat at least three meals a day?"

"No." I am so not backing down on this. No one is going to dictate to me what I eat. How I fuck, yes, but eat . . . no, no way.

He purses his lips. "I need to know that you're not hungry."

I frown. *Why?* "You'll have to trust me."

He gazes at me for a moment, and he relaxes.

"Touché, Miss Steele," he says quietly. "I concede the food and the sleep."

"Why can't I look at you?"

"That's a Dom/sub thing. You'll get used to it."

Will I?

"Why can't I touch you?"

"Because you can't."

His mouth sets in a mulish line.

"Is it because of Mrs. Robinson?"

He looks quizzically at me. "Why would you think that?" And immediately he understands. "You think she traumatized me?"

I nod.

"No, Anastasia. She's not the reason. Besides, Mrs. Robinson wouldn't take any of that shit from me."

Oh . . . but I have to. I pout.

"So nothing to do with her."

"No. And I don't want you touching yourself, either."

What? Ah yes, the no masturbation clause.

"Out of curiosity . . . why?"

"Because I want all your pleasure." His voice is husky but determined.

Oh . . . I have no answer for that. On one level it's up there with "I want to bite that lip"; on another, it's so selfish. I frown and take a bite of cod, trying to assess mentally what concessions I've gained. The food, the sleep. He's going to take it slow, and we haven't discussed soft limits. But I'm not sure I can face that over food.

"I've given you a great deal to think about, haven't I?"

"Yes."

"Do you want to go through the soft limits now, too?"

"Not over dinner."

He smiles. "Squeamish?"

"Something like that."

"You've not eaten very much."

"I've had enough."

"Three oysters, four bites of cod, and one asparagus stalk, no potatoes, no nuts, no olives, and you've not eaten all day. You said I could trust you."

Jeez. He's kept an inventory.

"Christian, please, it's not every day I sit through conversations like this."

"I need you fit and healthy, Anastasia."

"I know."

"And right now, I want to peel you out of that dress."

I swallow. *Peel me out of Kate's dress.* I feel the pull deep in my belly. Muscles that I'm now more acquainted with clench at his words. But I can't have this. His most potent weapon, used against me again. He's so good at sex—even I've figured this out.

"I don't think that's a good idea," I murmur quietly. "We haven't had dessert."

"You want dessert?" he snorts.

"Yes."

"You could be dessert," he murmurs suggestively.

"I'm not sure I'm sweet enough."

"Anastasia, you're deliciously sweet. I know."

"Christian. You use sex as a weapon. It really isn't fair," I whisper, staring down at my hands, and then looking directly at him. He raises his eyebrows, surprised, and I see he's considering my words. He strokes his chin thoughtfully.

"You're right. I do. In life you use what you know, Anastasia. Doesn't change how much I want you. Here. Now."

How can he seduce me solely with his voice? I'm panting already—my heated blood rushing through my veins, my nerves tingling.

"I'd like to try something," he breathes.

I frown. He's just given me a shitload of ideas to process and now this.

"If you were my sub, you wouldn't have to think about this. It would be easy." His voice is soft, seductive. "All those decisions—all the wearying thought processes behind them. The 'is this the right thing to do? Should this happen here? Can it happen now?' You wouldn't have to worry about any of that detail. That's what I'd do as your Dom. And right now, I know you want me, Anastasia."

My frown deepens. How can he tell?

"I can tell because . . ."

Holy shit, he's answering my unspoken question. Is he psychic as well?

" . . . your body gives you away. You're pressing your thighs together, you're flushed, and your breathing has changed."

Okay, this is too much.

"How do you know about my thighs?" My voice is low, disbelieving. They're under the table, for heaven's sake.

"I felt the tablecloth move, and it's a calculated guess based on years of experience. I'm right, aren't I?"

I flush and stare down at my hands. That's what I'm hindered by in this game of seduction. He's the only one who knows and understands the rules. I'm just too naïve and inexperienced. My only sphere of reference is Kate, and she doesn't take any shit from men. My other references are all fictional: Elizabeth Bennet would be outraged, Jane Eyre too frightened, and Tess would succumb, just as I have.

"I haven't finished my cod."

"You'd prefer cold cod to me?"

My head jerks up to glare at him, and his eyes burn molten silver with compelling need.

"I thought you liked me to clear my plate."

"Right now, Miss Steele, I couldn't give a fuck about your food."

"Christian. You just don't fight fair."

"I know. I never have."

My inner goddess frowns at me. You can do this, she coaxes—play this sex god at his own game. *Can I?* Okay. What to do? My inexperience is an albatross around my neck. Picking up a spear of asparagus, I gaze at him and bite my lip. Then very slowly put the tip of my cold asparagus in my mouth and suck it.

Christian's eyes widen infinitesimally, but I notice.

"Anastasia. What are you doing?"

I bite off the tip.

"Eating my asparagus."

Christian shifts in his seat.

"I think you're toying with me, Miss Steele."

I feign innocence. "I'm just finishing my food, Mr. Grey."

The waiter chooses this moment to knock and, unbidden, enter. He glances briefly at Christian, who frowns at him but then nods, so the waiter clears our plates. The waiter's arrival has broken the spell. And I grasp this precious moment of clarity. I have to go. Our meeting will only end one way if I stay, and I need some boundaries after such an intense conversation. As much as my body craves his touch, my mind is rebelling. I need some distance to think about all he's said. I still haven't made a decision, and his sexual allure and prowess doesn't make it any easier.

"Would you like some dessert?" Christian asks, ever the gentleman, but his eyes still blaze.

"No thank you. I think I should go." I stare down at my hands.

"Go?" He can't hide his surprise.

The waiter leaves hastily.

"Yes." It's the right decision. If I stay here, in this room with him, he will fuck me. I stand, purposefully. "We both have the graduation ceremony tomorrow."

Christian stands automatically, revealing years of ingrained civility.

"I don't want you to go."

"Please . . . I have to."

"Why?"

"Because you've given me so much to consider . . . and I need some distance."

"I could make you stay," he threatens.

"Yes, you could easily, but I don't want you to."

He runs his hand through his hair, regarding me carefully.

"You know, when you fell into my office to interview me, you were all 'yes, sir,' 'no, sir.' I thought you were a natural-born submissive. But quite frankly, Anastasia, I'm not sure you have a submissive bone in your delectable body." He moves slowly toward me as his speaks, his voice tense.

"You may be right," I breathe.

"I want the chance to explore the possibility that you do," he murmurs, staring down at me. He reaches up and caresses my face, his thumb tracing my lower lip. "I don't know any other way, Anastasia. This is who I am."

"I know."

He leans down to kiss me but pauses before his lips touch mine, his eyes searching mine, wanting, asking permission. I raise my lips to his, and he kisses me, and because I don't know if I'll ever kiss him again, I let go—my hands moving of their own accord and twisting into his hair, pulling him to me, my mouth opening, my tongue stroking his. His hand grasps the nape of my neck as he deepens the kiss, responding to my ardor. His other hand slides down my back and flattens at the base of my spine as he pushes me against his body.

"I can't persuade you to stay?" he breathes between kisses.

"No."

"Spend the night with me."

"And not touch you? No."

He groans.

"You impossible girl." He pulls back, gazing down at me. "Why do I think you're telling me good-bye?"

"Because I'm leaving now."

"That's not what I mean, and you know it."

"Christian, I have to think about this. I don't know if I can have the kind of relationship you want."

He closes his eyes and presses his forehead against mine, giving us both the opportunity to slow our breathing. After a moment, he kisses my forehead, inhales deeply, his nose in my hair, and then he releases me, stepping back.

"As you wish, Miss Steele," he says, his face impassive. "I'll escort you to the lobby." He holds out his hand. Leaning down, I grab my purse and place my hand in his. *Holy crap, this could be it*. I follow him meekly down the grand stairs and into the lobby, my scalp prickling, my blood pumping. This could be the last good-bye if I decide to say no. My heart contracts painfully in my chest. What a turnaround. What a difference a moment of clarity can make to a girl.

"Do you have your valet ticket?"

I fish into my clutch purse and hand him the ticket, which he gives to the doorman. I peek up at him as we stand waiting.

"Thank you for dinner," I murmur.

"It's a pleasure as always, Miss Steele," he says politely, though he looks deep in thought, completely distracted.

As I peer up at him, I commit his beautiful profile to memory. The idea that I might not see him again haunts me, unwelcome and too painful to contemplate. He turns suddenly, staring down at me, his expression intense.

"You're moving this weekend to Seattle. If you make the right decision, can I see you on Sunday?" He sounds hesitant.

"We'll see. Maybe," I breathe. Momentarily, he looks relieved, and then he frowns.

"It's cooler now, don't you have a jacket?"

"No."

He shakes his head in irritation and takes off his jacket.

"Here. I don't want you catching cold."

I blink up at him as he holds it open, and as I hold my arms out behind me, I'm reminded of the time in his office when he slipped my coat onto my shoulders—the first time I met him—and the effect he had on me then. Nothing's changed; in fact, it's more intense. His jacket is warm, far too big, and it smells of him. . . . delicious.

My car pulls up outside. Christian's mouth drops open.

"That's what you drive?" He's appalled. Taking my hand, he leads me outside. The valet jumps out and hands me my keys, and Christian coolly palms him some money.

"Is this roadworthy?" He's glaring at me now.

"Yes."

"Will it make it to Seattle?"

"Yes. She will."

"Safely?"

"Yes," I snap, exasperated. "Okay, she's old. But she's mine, and she's roadworthy. My stepdad bought it for me."

"Oh, Anastasia, I think we can do better than this."

"What do you mean?" Realization dawns. "You are *not* buying me a car."

He glowers at me, his jaw tense.

"We'll see," he says tightly.

He grimaces as he opens the driver's-side door and helps me

in. I take my shoes off and roll down the window. He's gazing at me, his expression unfathomable, eyes dark.

"Drive safely," he says quietly.

"Good-bye, Christian." My voice is hoarse from unbidden, unshed tears—*jeez, I'm not going to cry.* I give him a small smile.

As I drive away, my chest constricts, my tears start to fall, and I choke back a sob. Soon tears are streaming down my face, and I really don't understand why I'm crying. I was holding my own. He explained everything. He was clear. He wants me, but the truth is I need more. I need him to want me like I want and need him, and deep down I know that's not possible. I am just overwhelmed.

I don't even know how to categorize him. If I do this thing . . . will he be my boyfriend? Will I be able to introduce him to my friends? Go out to bars, the cinema, bowling even, with him? The truth is I don't think I will. He won't let me touch him and he won't let me sleep with him. I know I've not had these things in my past, but I want them in my future. And that's not the future he envisages.

What if I do say yes, and in three months' time he says no, he's had enough of trying to mold me into something I'm not? How will I feel? I'll have emotionally invested three months, doing things that I'm not sure I want to do. And if he then says no, agreement over, how could I cope with that level of rejection? Perhaps it's best to back away now with what self-esteem I have reasonably intact.

But the thought of not seeing him again is agonizing. How has he gotten under my skin so quickly? It can't just be the sex . . . can it? I dash the tears from my eyes. I don't want to examine my feelings for him. I'm frightened what I'll uncover if I do. *What am I going to do?*

I park outside our duplex. No lights on. Kate must be out. I'm relieved. I don't want her to catch me crying again. As I undress, I wake up the mean machine and sitting in my inbox is a message from Christian.

From: Christian Grey
Subject: Tonight
Date: May 25 2011 22:01
To: Anastasia Steele

I don't understand why you ran this evening. I sincerely hope I answered all your questions to your satisfaction. I know I have given you a great deal to contemplate, and I fervently hope that you will give my proposal your serious consideration. I really want to make this work. We will take it slow.
Trust me.

Christian Grey
CEO, Grey Enterprises Holdings, Inc.

His e-mail makes me weep more. I am not a merger. I am not an acquisition. Reading this, I might as well be. I don't reply. I just don't know what to say to him. I fumble into my PJs and, wrapping his jacket around me, I climb into bed. As I lie staring into the darkness, I think of all the times he warned me to stay away.

Anastasia, you should steer clear of me. I'm not the man for you.

I don't do the girlfriend thing.

I'm not a hearts and flowers kind of guy.

I don't make love.

This is all I know.

And as I weep into my pillow silently, it's this last idea I cling to. This is all I know, too. Perhaps together we can chart a new course.

CHAPTER FOURTEEN

Christian is standing over me grasping a plaited leather riding crop. He's wearing old, faded, ripped Levis and that's all. He flicks the crop slowly into his palm as he gazes down at me. He's smiling, triumphant. I cannot move. I am naked and shackled, spread-eagled on a large four-poster bed. Reaching forward, he trails the tip of the crop from my forehead down the length of my nose, so I can smell the leather, and over my parted, panting lips. He pushes the tip into my mouth so I can taste the smooth, rich leather.

"Suck," he commands, his voice soft. My mouth closes over the tip as I obey.

"Enough," he snaps.

I'm panting once more as he tugs the crop out of my mouth, trails it down and under my chin, on down my neck to the hollow at the base of my throat. He swirls it slowly there and then continues to drag the tip down my body, along my sternum, between my breasts, over my torso, down to my navel. I'm panting, squirming, pulling against my restraints that are biting into my wrists and my ankles. He swirls the tip around my navel then continues to trail the leather tip south, through my pubic hair to my clitoris. He flicks the crop and it hits my sweet spot with a sharp slap, and I come, gloriously, shouting my release.

Abruptly, I wake, gasping for breath, covered in sweat and feeling the aftershocks of my orgasm. Holy hell. I'm completely disorientated. *What the hell just happened?* I'm in my bedroom alone. How? Why? I sit bolt upright, shocked . . . wow. It's morning. I glance at my alarm clock—eight o'clock. I put my head in my hands. I didn't know I could dream sex. Was it something I ate?

Perhaps the oysters and my Internet research manifesting itself in my first wet dream. It's bewildering. I had no idea that I could orgasm in my sleep.

Kate is skipping around the kitchen when I stagger in.

"Ana, are you okay? You look odd. Is that Christian's jacket you're wearing?"

"I'm fine." Damn, should have checked in the mirror. I avoid her piercing green eyes. I'm still reeling from my morning's event. "Yes, this is Christian's jacket."

She frowns. "Did you sleep?"

"Not very well."

I head for the kettle. I need tea.

"How was dinner?"

So it begins.

"We had oysters. Followed by cod, so I'd say it was fishy."

"Ugh . . . I hate oysters, and I don't want to know about the food. How was Christian? What did you talk about?"

"He was attentive." I pause. What can I say? His HIV status is clear, he's heavily into role-play, wants me to obey his every command, he hurt someone he tied to his playroom ceiling, and he wanted to fuck me in the private dining room. Would that be a good summary? I try desperately to remember something from my encounter with Christian that I can discuss with Kate.

"He doesn't approve of Wanda."

"Who does, Ana? That's old news. Why are you being so coy? Give it up, girlfriend."

"Oh, Kate, we talked about lots things. You know—how fussy he is about food. Incidentally, he liked your dress." The kettle has boiled, so I make myself some tea. "Do you want tea? Would you like me to hear your speech for today?"

"Yes, please. I worked on it last night over at Becca's. I'll go fetch it. And yes, I'd love some tea." Kate races out of the kitchen.

Phew, Katherine Kavanagh sidetracked. I slice a bagel and pop it into the toaster. I flush, remembering my vivid dream. What on Earth was that about?

Last night I found it hard to sleep. My head was buzzing with various options. I am so confused. Christian's idea of a relationship is more like a job offer. It has set hours, a job description, and a rather harsh grievance procedure. It's not how I envisaged my first romance—but, of course, Christian doesn't do romance. If I tell him I want more, he may say no . . . and I could jeopardize what he has offered. And this is what concerns me most, because I don't want to lose him. But I'm not sure I have the stomach to be his submissive—deep down, it's the canes and whips that put me off. I'm a physical coward, and I will go a long way to avoid pain. I think of my dream *. . . is that what it would be like?* My inner goddess jumps up and down with cheerleading pom-poms shouting yes at me.

Kate comes back into the kitchen with her laptop. I concentrate on my bagel and listen patiently as she runs through her valedictorian speech.

I AM DRESSED AND ready when Ray arrives. I open the front door, and he's standing on the porch in his ill-fitting suit. A warm surge of gratitude and love for this uncomplicated man streaks through me, and I throw my arms around him in an uncharacteristic display of affection. He's taken aback, bemused.

"Hey, Annie, I'm pleased to see you, too," he mutters as he hugs me. Setting me back down, his hands on my shoulders, he looks me up and down, his brow furrowed. "You okay, kid?"

"Of course, Dad. Can't a girl be pleased to see her old man?"

He smiles, his dark eyes crinkling at the corners, and follows me into the living room.

"You look good," he says.

"This is Kate's dress." I glance down at the gray chiffon halterneck dress.

He frowns.

"Where is Kate?"

"She's gone to campus. She's giving a speech, so she has to be early."

"Should we head on over?"

"Dad, we have half an hour. Would you like some tea? And you can tell me how everyone in Montesano is getting along. How was the drive down?"

RAY PULLS HIS CAR into the campus parking lot, and we follow the stream of humanity dotted with ubiquitous black and red gowns heading toward the gym.

"Good luck, Annie. You seem awfully nervous. Do you have to do anything?"

Holy crap . . . why has Ray picked today to be observant?

"No, Dad. It's a big day." *And I'm going to see him.*

"Yeah, my baby girl has gotten a degree. I'm proud of you, Annie."

"Aw . . . thanks, Dad." Oh, I love this man.

The gym is crowded. Ray has gone to sit with the other parents and well-wishers in the tiered seating, while I make my way to my seat. I'm wearing my black gown and my cap, and I feel protected by them, anonymous. There is no one on the stage yet, but I can't seem to steady my nerves. My heart is pounding, and my breathing is shallow. He's here, somewhere. I wonder if Kate is talking to him, interrogating him maybe. I make my way to my seat amongst fellow students whose surnames also begin with S. I am in the second row, affording me yet more anonymity. I glance behind me and spot Ray high up in the bleachers. I give him a wave. He self-consciously gives me a half-wave, half-salute back. I sit and wait.

The auditorium fills quickly, and the buzz of excited voices gets louder and louder. The row of seats in front fills. On either side of me, I am joined by two girls whom I don't know from a different department. They're obviously close friends and talk across me excitedly.

At eleven precisely, the chancellor appears from behind the stage, followed by the three vice chancellors and then the senior professors, all decked out in their black and red regalia. We stand and applaud our teaching staff. Some professors nod and wave, others look bored. Professor Collins, my tutor and my favorite teacher, looks like he's just fallen out of bed, as usual. Last on to the stage are Kate and Christian. Christian stands out in his bespoke gray suit, copper highlights glinting in his hair under the auditorium lights. He looks so serious and self-contained. As he sits, he undoes his single-breasted jacket, and I glimpse his tie. *Holy shit . . . that tie!* I rub my wrists reflexively. I cannot take my eyes off him. He's wearing that tie, on purpose no doubt. My mouth presses into a hard line. The audience sits down and the applause ceases.

"Look at him!" one of the girls beside me hisses enthusiastically to her friend.

"He's hot."

I stiffen. I'm sure they're not talking about Professor Collins.

"Must be Christian Grey."

"Is he single?"

I bristle. "I don't think so," I murmur.

"Oh." Both girls look at me in surprise.

"I think he's gay," I mutter.

"What a shame," one of the girls groans.

As the chancellor gets to his feet and kicks off the proceedings with his speech, I watch Christian subtly scanning the hall. I sink into my seat, hunching my shoulders, trying to make myself as inconspicuous as possible. I fail miserably as a second later his eyes find mine. He stares at me, his face impassive, completely inscrutable. I squirm uncomfortably, hypnotized by his glare as a slow flush spreads across my face. Unbidden, I recall my dream from this morning, and the muscles in my belly do the delectable clench thing. I inhale sharply. The shadow of a smile crosses his lips, but it's fleeting. He briefly closes his eyes and, on opening them, resumes his indifferent expression. Following a swift glance up at the chancellor, he stares ahead, focusing on the WSUV emblem hung above the entrance. He doesn't turn his eyes toward me again. The chancellor drones on, and Christian still doesn't look at me. He just stares fixedly ahead.

Why won't he look at me? Perhaps he's changed his mind? A wave of unease washes over me. Perhaps walking out on him last night was the end for him, too. He's bored of waiting for me to make up my mind. Oh no, I could have completely blown it. I remember his e-mail last night. Maybe he's mad that I haven't replied.

Suddenly, the room erupts into applause as Miss Katherine Kavanagh has taken the stage. The chancellor sits, and Kate tosses her lovely long hair behind her as she places her papers on the lectern. She takes her time, not intimidated by a thousand people staring at her. She smiles when she's ready, looks up at the captivated throng, and launches eloquently into her speech. She's composed and funny, the girls beside me erupt on cue at her first joke. *Oh, Katherine Kavanagh, you can deliver a good line.* I am so proud of her at that moment, my errant thoughts of Christian pushed to one side. Even though I have heard her speech before, I listen carefully. She commands the room and takes her audience with her.

Her theme is "What Next After College?" Oh, what next indeed. Christian is watching Kate, his eyebrows raised—in surprise, I think. Yes, it could have been Kate who went to interview him. And it could have been Kate who he was now making indecent proposals to. Beautiful Kate and beautiful Christian, together. I could be like the two girls beside me, admiring him from afar. I know Kate wouldn't have given him the time of day. What did she call him the other day? Creepy. The thought of a confrontation between Kate and Christian makes me uncomfortable. I have to say I don't know which of them I would put my money on.

Kate concludes her speech with a flourish, and spontaneously everyone stands, applauding and cheering, her first standing ovation. I beam at her and cheer, and she grins back at me. *Good job, Kate.* She sits, as does the audience, and the chancellor rises and introduces Christian . . . *Holy shit,* Christian's going to give a speech. The chancellor touches briefly on Christian's achievements: CEO of his own extraordinarily successful company, a real self-made man.

" . . . and also a major benefactor to our university. Please welcome Mr. Christian Grey."

The chancellor pumps Christian's hand, and there is a swell of polite applause. My heart's in my throat. He approaches the lectern and surveys the hall. He looks so confident standing in front of us all, as Kate did before him. The two girls beside me lean in, enraptured. In fact, I think most of the female members of the audience inch closer and a few of the men. He begins, his voice soft, measured, and mesmerizing.

"I'm profoundly grateful and touched by the great compliment accorded to me by the authorities of WSU today. It offers me a rare opportunity to talk about the impressive work of the environmental science department here at the university. Our aim is to develop viable and ecologically sustainable methods of farming for third world countries; our ultimate goal is to help eradicate hunger and poverty across the globe. Over a billion people, mainly in sub-Saharan Africa, South Asia, and Latin America, live in abject poverty. Agricultural dysfunction is rife within these parts of the world, and the result is ecological and social destruction. I have known what it's like to be profoundly hungry. This is a very personal journey for me . . ."

My jaw falls to the floor. *What?* Christian was hungry once. *Holy crap.* Well, that explains a great deal. And I recall the interview; he really *does* want to feed the world. I desperately rack my brains to remember what Kate had written in her article. Adopted at age four, I think. I can't imagine that Grace starved him, so it must have been before then, as a little boy. I swallow, my heart constricting at the thought of a hungry, gray-eyed toddler. *Oh no.* What kind of life did he have before the Greys got hold of him and rescued him?

I'm seized by a sense of raw outrage. Poor, fucked-up, kinky, philanthropic Christian—though I'm sure he wouldn't see himself this way and would repel any thoughts of sympathy or pity.

Abruptly, everyone bursts into applause and stands. I follow, though I haven't heard half his speech. He's doing all of these good works, running a huge company, and chasing me at the same time. It's overwhelming. I remember the brief snippets of conversations he's had about Darfur . . . it all falls into place. *Food.*

He smiles briefly at the warm applause—even Kate is clapping—then he resumes his seat. He doesn't look my way, and I'm off-kilter trying to assimilate this new information about him.

One of the vice chancellors rises, and we begin the long, tedious process of collecting our degrees. There are more than four hundred to be given out, and it takes just over an hour before I hear my name. I make my way up to the stage between the two giggling girls. Christian gazes down at me, his look warm but guarded.

"Congratulations, Miss Steele," he says as he shakes my hand, squeezing it gently. I feel the charge of his flesh on mine. "Do you have a problem with your laptop?"

I frown as he hands me my degree.

"No."

"Then you *are* ignoring my e-mails?"

"I only saw the mergers and acquisitions one."

He looks quizzically at me.

"Later," he says, and I have to move on because I'm holding up the line.

I go back to my seat. E-mails? He must have sent another. What did it say?

The ceremony takes another hour to conclude. It's interminable. Finally, the chancellor leads the faculty members off the stage to yet more rousing applause, preceded by Christian and Kate. Christian does not glance at me, even though I'm willing him to do it. My inner goddess is not pleased.

As I stand and wait for our row to disperse, Kate calls to me. She's heading my way from behind the stage.

"Christian wants to talk to you," she shouts. The two girls who are now standing beside me turn and gape at me.

"He's sent me out here," she continues.

Oh . . .

"Your speech was great, Kate."

"It was, wasn't it?" She beams. "Are you coming? He can be very insistent." She rolls her eyes, and I grin.

"You have no idea. I can't leave Ray for long." I glance up at Ray and hold my fingers up indicating five minutes. He nods, giving me an okay sign, and I follow Kate into the corridor behind the stage. Christian is talking to the chancellor and two of the teaching staff. He looks up when he sees me.

"Excuse me, gentlemen," I hear him murmur. He comes toward me and smiles briefly at Kate.

"Thank you," he says, and before she can reply, he takes my elbow and steers me into what looks like a men's locker room. He checks to see if it's empty, and then he locks the door.

Holy shit, what does he have in mind? I blink up at him as he turns on me.

"Why haven't you e-mailed me? Or texted me back?" He glares. I'm nonplussed.

"I haven't looked at my computer today, or my phone." Crap, has he been trying to call? I try my distraction technique that's so effective on Kate. "That was a great speech."

"Thank you."

"Explains your food issues to me."

He runs a hand through his hair, exasperated.

"Anastasia, I don't want to go there at the moment." He closes his eyes, looking pained. "I've been worried about you."

"Worried, why?"

"Because you went home in that deathtrap you call a car."

"What? It's not a deathtrap. It's fine. José regularly services it for me."

"José, the photographer?" Christian's eyes narrow, his face frosting. *Oh, crap.*

"Yes, the Beetle used to belong to his mother."

"Yes, and probably her mother and her mother before her. It's not safe."

"I've been driving it for over three years. I'm sorry you were worried. Why didn't you call?" Jeez, he's completely overreacting.

He takes a deep breath.

"Anastasia, I need an answer from you. This waiting around is driving me crazy."

"Christian, I . . . look, I've left my stepdad on his own."

"Tomorrow. I want an answer by tomorrow."

"Okay. Tomorrow, I'll tell you then."

He steps back, regarding me coolly, and his shoulders relax.

"Are you staying for drinks?" he asks.

"I don't know what Ray wants to do."

"Your stepfather? I'd like to meet him."

Oh no . . . why?

"I'm not sure that's a good idea."

Christian unlocks the door, his mouth in a grim line.

"Are you ashamed of me?"

"No!" It's my turn to sound exasperated. "Introduce you to my dad as what? 'This is the man who deflowered me and wants us to start a BDSM relationship'? You're not wearing running shoes."

Christian glares down at me, and then his lips twitch up in a smile. And in spite of the fact I'm mad at him, my face is unwillingly pulled into an answering grin.

"Just so you know, I can run quite fast. Just tell him I'm your friend, Anastasia."

He opens the door, and I head out. My mind is whirling. The chancellor, the three vice chancellors, four professors, and Kate stare at me as I walk hastily past them. *Crap.* Leaving Christian with the faculty, I go in search of Ray.

Tell him I'm your friend.

Friend with benefits, my subconscious scowls. I know, I know. I shake the unpleasant thought away. How will I introduce him to

Ray? The hall is still at least half full, and Ray has not moved from his spot. He sees me, waves, and makes his way down.

"Hey, Annie. Congratulations." He puts his arm around me.

"Would you like to come and have a drink in the marquee?"

"Sure. It's your day. Lead the way."

"We don't have to if you don't want to." *Please say no . . .*

"Annie, I've just sat for two and half hours listening to all kinds of jabbering. I need a drink."

I put my arm through his, and we stroll out with the throng into the warmth of the early afternoon. We pass the line for the official photographer.

"Oh, that reminds me." Ray drags a digital camera out of his pocket. "One for the album, Annie." I roll my eyes at him as he snaps a picture of me.

"Can I take the cap and gown off now? I feel kind of dorky."

You look kinda dorky . . . My subconscious is at her snarky best. *So are you going to introduce Ray to the man you're fucking?* She is glaring at me over her wing-shaped spectacles. *He'd be so proud.* God, I hate her sometimes.

The marquee is immense and crowded—students, parents, teachers, and friends, all chattering happily. Ray hands me a glass of champagne, or cheap fizzy wine, I suspect. It's not chilled, and it tastes sweet. My thoughts turn to Christian . . . *he won't like this.*

"Ana!" I turn, and Ethan Kavanagh scoops me into his arms. He twirls me around, without spilling my wine—some feat.

"Congratulations!" He beams down at me, green eyes twinkling.

What a surprise. His dirty blond hair is tousled and sexy. He's as beautiful as Kate. The family resemblance is striking.

"Wow—Ethan! How lovely to see you. Dad, this is Ethan, Kate's brother. Ethan, this is my dad, Ray Steele." They shake hands, my dad coolly assessing Mr. Kavanagh.

"When did you get back from Europe?" I ask.

"I've been back for a week, but I wanted to surprise my little sister," he says conspiratorially.

"That's so sweet." I grin.

"She is valedictorian, couldn't miss that." He looks immensely proud of his sister.

"She gave a great speech."

"That she did," Ray agrees.

Ethan has his arm around my waist when I look up into the frosty gray eyes of Christian Grey. Kate is beside him.

"Hello, Ray." Kate kisses Ray on both cheeks, making him blush. "Have you met Ana's boyfriend? Christian Grey."

Holy shit . . . Kate! Fuck! All the blood drains from my face.

"Mr. Steele, it's a pleasure to meet you," Christian says smoothly, warmly, completely unflustered by Kate's introduction. He holds out his hand, which Ray, all credit to him, takes, not showing a hint of the drop-dead surprise he's just had thrust upon him.

Thank you very much, Katherine Kavanagh, I fume. I think my subconscious has fainted.

"Mr. Grey," Ray murmurs, his expression indecipherable except perhaps for the slight widening of his big brown eyes. They slide over to my face with a when-were-you-going-to-give-me-this-news look. I bite my lip.

"And this is my brother, Ethan Kavanagh," says Kate to Christian.

Christian turns his arctic glare on Ethan, who still has one arm around me.

"Mr. Kavanagh."

They shake hands. Christian holds his hand out to me.

"Ana, baby," he murmurs, and I nearly expire at the endearment.

I walk out of Ethan's grasp, while Christian smiles icily at him, and I take my place at his side. Kate grins at me. She knows exactly what she's doing, the vixen!

"Ethan, Mom and Dad wanted a word." Kate drags Ethan away.

"So how long have you kids known each other?" Ray looks impassively from Christian to me.

The power of speech has deserted me. I want the ground to swallow me up. Christian puts his arm around me, his thumb skimming my naked back in a caress, before his hand clasps my shoulder.

"Couple of weeks or so now," he says smoothly. "We met when Anastasia came to interview me for the student newspaper."

"Didn't know you worked on the student newspaper, Ana." Ray's voice is a quiet admonishment, revealing his irritation. *Shit.*

"Kate was ill," I murmur. It's all I can manage.

"Fine speech you gave, Mr. Grey."

"Thank you, sir. I understand that you're a keen fisherman."

Ray raises his eyebrows and smiles—a rare, genuine, bona fide Ray Steele smile—and off they go, talking fish. In fact, I soon feel surplus to requirements. He's charming the pants off my dad . . . *like he did you,* my subconscious snaps at me. His power knows no bounds. I excuse myself to go and find Kate.

She's talking to her parents, who are delightful as ever and greet me warmly. We exchange brief pleasantries, mostly about their up and coming vacation to Barbados and about our move.

"Kate, how could you out me to Ray?" I hiss at the first opportunity we won't be overheard.

"Because I knew you never would, and I want to help with Christian's commitment issues." Kate smiles at me sweetly.

I scowl. *It's me that won't commit to him, silly!*

"He seems très cool about it, Ana. Don't sweat it. Look at him now—Christian cannot take his eyes off you." I glance up, and both Ray and Christian are looking at me. "He's been watching you like a hawk."

"I'd better go rescue Ray, or Christian. I don't know which. You haven't heard the last of this, Katherine Kavanagh!" I glare at her.

"Ana, I did you a favor," she calls after me.

"Hi." I smile at both of them on my return.

They seem okay. Christian is enjoying some private joke, and my dad looks unbelievably relaxed given he's in a social situation. *What have they been discussing apart from fish?*

"Ana, where are the restrooms?"

"Back out front of the marquee and to the left."

"See you in a moment. You kids enjoy yourselves."

Ray heads out. I glance nervously up at Christian. We pause briefly as a photographer takes a picture of both of us.

"Thank you, Mr. Grey." The photographer scurries off. I blink from the flash.

"So you've charmed my father as well?"

"As well?" Christian's eyes burn and he raises a questioning eyebrow. I flush. He lifts his hand and traces my cheek with his fingers.

"Oh, I wish I knew what you were thinking, Anastasia," he whispers darkly, cupping my chin and raising my head so that we gaze intently into each other's eyes.

My breath hitches. How can he have this effect on me, even in this crowded tent?

"Right now, I'm thinking, *Nice tie*," I breathe.

He chuckles. "It's recently become my favorite."

I blush scarlet.

"You look lovely, Anastasia. This halter-neck dress suits you, and I get to stroke your back, feel your beautiful skin."

Suddenly, it's like we're on our own in the room. Just the two of us. My whole body has come alive, every nerve ending singing softly, that electricity pulling me to him, charging between us.

"You know it's going to be good, don't you, baby?" he whispers. I close my eyes as my insides uncoil and melt.

"But I want more," I whisper.

"More?" he looks down at me puzzled, his eyes darkening. I nod and swallow. *Now he knows.*

"More," he says again softly. Testing the word—a small, simple word, but so full of promise. His thumb traces my lower lip. "You want hearts and flowers."

I nod again. He blinks down at me, and I watch his internal struggle played out in his eyes.

"Anastasia." His voice is soft. "It's not something I know."

"Me, either."

He smiles slightly.

"You don't know much," he murmurs.

"You know all the wrong things."

"Wrong? Not to me." He shakes his head. He looks so sincere. "Try it," he whispers. A challenge, daring me, and he cocks his head to one side and smiles his crooked, dazzling smile.

I gasp, and I'm Eve in the Garden of Eden, and he's the serpent, and I cannot resist.

"Okay," I whisper.

"What?" I have his full, undivided attention. I swallow.

"Okay. I'll try."

"You're agreeing?" His disbelief is evident.

"Subject to the soft limits, yes. I'll try." My voice is so small. Christian closes his eyes and pulls me into an embrace.

"Jesus, Ana, you're so unexpected. You take my breath away."

He steps back, and suddenly Ray's returned, and the volume in the marquee gradually rises and fills my ears. We are not alone. *Holy shit, I've just agreed to be his sub.* Christian smiles at Ray and his eyes are dancing with joy.

"Annie, should we get some lunch?"

"Okay." I blink up at Ray, trying to find my equilibrium. *What have you done?* my subconscious screams at me. My inner goddess is doing backflips in a routine worthy of a Russian Olympic gymnast.

"Would you like to join us, Christian?" Ray asks.

Christian! I stare up at him, imploring him to refuse. I need space to think . . . what the fuck have I done?

"Thank you, Mr. Steele, but I have plans. It's been great to meet you, sir."

"Likewise," Ray responds. "Look after my baby girl."

"Oh, I fully intend to."

They shake hands. I feel sick. Ray has no idea how Christian intends to look after me. Christian takes my hand and brings it to his lips and kisses my knuckles tenderly, his scorching eyes intent on mine.

"Later, Miss Steele," he breathes, his voice full of promise.

My belly curls at the thought. *Hang on . . . later?*

Ray takes my elbow and leads me toward the entrance to the tent.

"Seems a solid young man. Well off, too. You could do a lot worse, Annie. Though why I had to hear about him from Katherine . . ." he scolds.

I shrug apologetically.

"Well, any man who likes and knows his fly-fishing is okay with me."

Holy cow—Ray approves. If only he knew.

RAY DROPS ME BACK at the house at dusk.

"Call your mom," he says.

"I will. Thanks for coming, Dad."

"Wouldn't have missed it for the world, Annie. You make me so proud."

Oh no. I'm not going to get emotional. A huge lump forms in my throat, and I hug him, hard. He puts his arms around me, bemused, and I can't help it—tears pool in my eyes.

"Hey, Annie, sweetheart," Ray croons. "Big old day . . . eh? Want me to come in and make you some tea?"

I laugh, in spite of my tears. Tea is always the answer, according to Ray. I remember my mother complaining about him, saying that when it came to tea and sympathy, he was always good at the tea, not so hot on the sympathy.

"No, Dad, I'm good. It's been so great to see you. I'll visit real soon once I'm settled in Seattle."

"Good luck with the interviews. Let me know how they go."

"Sure thing, Dad."

"Love you, Annie."

“Love you, too, Dad.”

He smiles, his brown eyes warm, glowing, and he climbs back into his car. I wave him off as he drives into the dusk, and I wander listlessly back into the apartment.

First thing I do is check my cell phone. It needs recharging, so I have to hunt down the charger and plug it in before I can collect my messages. Four missed calls, one voice message, and two texts. Three missed calls from Christian . . . no messages. One missed call from José and a voice mail from him wishing me all the best for graduation.

I open the texts.

Are you home safe?
Call me

They are both from Christian. Why didn’t he call the house? I head into my bedroom and fire up the mean machine.

From: Christian Grey
Subject: Tonight
Date: May 25 2011 23:58
To: Anastasia Steele

I hope you made it home in that car of yours.
Let me know if you’re okay.

Christian Grey
CEO, Grey Enterprises Holdings, Inc.

Jeez . . . why is he so worried about my Beetle? It has given me three years of loyal service, and José has always been on hand to maintain it for me. Christian’s next e-mail is from today.

From: Christian Grey
Subject: Soft Limits
Date: May 26 2011 17:22
To: Anastasia Steele

What can I say that I haven't already?
Happy to talk these through anytime.

You looked beautiful today.

Christian Grey
CEO, Grey Enterprises Holdings, Inc.

I want to see him. I hit "reply."

From: Anastasia Steele
Subject: Soft Limits
Date: May 26 2011 19:23
To: Christian Grey

I can come over this evening to discuss if you'd like.

Ana

From: Christian Grey
Subject: Soft Limits
Date: May 26 2011 19:27
To: Anastasia Steele

I'll come to you. I meant it when I said I wasn't happy about you driving that car.
I'll be with you shortly.

Christian Grey
CEO, Grey Enterprises Holdings, Inc.

Holy crap . . . he's coming over now. I have to get one thing ready for him—the first edition Thomas Hardy books are still on the shelves in the living room. I cannot keep them. I wrap them in brown paper, and I scrawl on the wrapping a direct quote from Tess from the book:

"I agree to the conditions, Angel; because you know best what my punishment ought to be; only—only—don't make it more than I can bear!"

CHAPTER FIFTEEN

"Hi." I feel unbearably shy when I open the door. Christian is standing on the porch in his jeans and leather jacket.

"Hi," he says, and his face lights up with his radiant smile. I take a moment to admire the pretty. Oh my, he's hot in leather.

"Come in."

"If I may," he says, amused. He holds up a bottle of champagne as he walks in. "I thought we'd celebrate your graduation. Nothing beats a good Bollinger."

"Interesting choice of words," I comment dryly.

He grins. "Oh, I like your ready wit, Anastasia."

"We only have teacups. We've packed all the glasses."

"Teacups? Sounds good to me."

I head into the kitchen. Nervous, butterflies flooding my stomach, it's like having a panther or mountain lion all unpredictable and predatory in my living room.

"Do you want saucers as well?"

"Teacups will be fine, Anastasia," Christian calls distractedly from the living room.

When I return, he's staring at the brown parcel of books. I place the cups on the table.

"That's for you," I murmur anxiously.

Crap . . . this is probably going to be a fight.

"Hmm, I figured as much. Very apt quote." His long index finger absently traces the writing. "I thought I was d'Urberville, not Angel. You decided on the debasement." He gives me a brief wolfish smile. "Trust you to find something that resonates so appropriately."

"It's also a plea," I whisper. *Why am I so nervous?* My mouth is dry.

"A plea? For me to go easy on you?"

I nod.

"I bought these for you," he says quietly, his gaze impassive. "I'll go easier on you if you accept them."

I swallow convulsively.

"Christian, I can't accept them, they're just too much."

"You see, this is what I was talking about, you defying me. I want you to have them, and that's the end of the discussion. It's very simple. You don't have to think about this. As a submissive you would just be grateful for them. You just accept what I buy you because it pleases me for you to do so."

"I wasn't a submissive when you bought them for me," I whisper.

"No . . . but you've agreed, Anastasia." His eyes turn wary.

I sigh. I am not going to win this, so over to plan B.

"So they are mine to do with as I wish?"

He eyes me suspiciously but concedes.

"Yes."

"In that case, I'd like to give them to a charity, one working in Darfur since that seems to be close to your heart. They can auction them."

"If that's what you want to do." His mouth sets into a hard line. He's disappointed.

I flush.

"I'll think about it," I murmur. I don't want to disappoint him, and his words come back to me. *I want you to want to please me.*

"Don't think, Anastasia. Not about this." His tone is quiet and serious.

How can I not think? *You can pretend to be a car, like his other possessions.* My subconscious makes an unwelcome vitriolic return. I ignore her. Oh, can't we rewind? The atmosphere between us is now tense. I don't know what to do. I stare down at my fingers. How do I retrieve this situation?

He puts the champagne bottle on the table and stands in front of me. Putting his hand under my chin, he tilts my head up. He gazes down at me, his expression grave.

"I will buy you lots of things, Anastasia. Get used to it. I can afford it. I'm a very wealthy man." He leans down and plants a swift, chaste kiss on my lips. "Please." He releases me.

Ho, my subconscious mouths at me.

"It makes me feel cheap," I murmur.

Christian runs his hand through his hair, exasperated.

"It shouldn't. You're overthinking it, Anastasia. Don't place some vague moral judgment on yourself based on what others might think. Don't waste your energy. It's only because you have reservations about our arrangement; that's perfectly natural. You don't know what you're getting yourself into."

I frown, trying to process his words.

"Hey, stop this," he commands softly, cupping my chin again and pulling at it gently so I release my lower lip from my teeth. "There is nothing about you that is cheap, Anastasia. I won't have you thinking that. I just bought you some old books that I thought might mean something to you, that's all. Have some champagne." His eyes warm and soften, and I smile tentatively up at him. "That's better," he murmurs. He picks up the champagne, takes off the foil top and cage, twists the bottle rather than the cork, and opens it with a small pop and a practiced flourish that doesn't spill a drop. He half fills the cups.

"It's pink," I murmur, surprised.

"Bollinger Grande Année Rosé 1999, an excellent vintage," he says with relish.

"In teacups."

He grins.

"In teacups. Congratulations on your degree, Anastasia." We clink cups, and he takes a drink, but I can't help thinking this is really about my capitulation.

"Thank you," I murmur, and take a sip. Of course it's delicious. "Shall we go through the soft limits?"

He smiles, and I blush.

"Always so eager." Christian takes my hand and leads me to the couch, where he sits and tugs me down beside him.

"Your stepfather's a very taciturn man."

Oh . . . not soft limits, then. I just want to get this out of the way; the anxiety is gnawing at me.

"You managed to get him eating out of your hand." I pout.

Christian laughs softly.

"Only because I know how to fish."

"How did you know he liked fishing?"

"You told me. When we went for coffee."

"Oh . . . did I?" I take another sip. Wow, he has a memory for detail. Hmm . . . this champagne really is very good. "Did you try the wine at the reception?"

Christian makes a face.

"Yes. It was foul."

"I thought of you when I tasted it. How did you get to be so knowledgeable about wine?"

"I'm not knowledgeable, Anastasia, I just know what I like." His eyes shine, almost silver, and it makes me flush. "Some more?" he asks, referring to the champagne.

"Please."

Christian rises gracefully and collects the bottle. He fills my cup. Is he getting me tipsy? I eye him suspiciously.

"This place looks pretty bare. Are you ready for the move?"

"More or less."

"Are you working tomorrow?"

"Yes, my last day at Clayton's."

"I'd help you move, but I promised to meet my sister at the airport."

Oh . . . this is news.

"Mia arrives from Paris very early Saturday morning. I'm heading back to Seattle tomorrow, but I hear Elliot is giving you two a hand."

"Yes, Kate is very excited about that."

Christian frowns. "Yes, Kate and Elliot, who would have thought?" he murmurs, and for some reason he doesn't look pleased. "So what are you doing about work in Seattle?"

When are we going to talk about the limits? What's his game?

"I have a couple of interviews for intern places."

"You were going tell me this when?" He arches a brow.

"Er . . . I'm telling you now."

He narrows his eyes.

"Where?"

For some reason, possibly because he might use his influence, I don't want to tell him.

"A couple of publishing houses."

"Is that what you want to do, something in publishing?"

I nod warily.

"Well?" He looks at me patiently wanting more information.

"Well what?"

"Don't be obtuse, Anastasia, which publishing houses?" he scolds.

"Just small ones," I murmur.

"Why don't you want me to know?"

"Undue influence."

He frowns.

"Oh, now *you're* being obtuse."

He laughs. "Obtuse? Me? God, you're challenging. Drink up, let's talk about these limits." He fishes out another copy of my e-mail and the list. Does he wander about with these lists in his pockets? I think there's one in his jacket that I have. Shit, I'd better not forget that. I drain my cup.

He glances quickly at me.

"More?"

"Please."

He smiles that oh-so-smug private smile of his, holds the champagne bottle up, and pauses.

"Have you eaten anything?"

Oh no . . . not this old chestnut.

"Yes. I had a three-course meal with Ray." I roll my eyes at him. The champagne is making me bold.

He leans forward and holds my chin, staring intently into my eyes.

"Next time you roll your eyes at me, I will take you across my knee."

What?

"Oh," I breathe, and I can see the excitement in his eyes.

"Oh," he responds, mirroring my tone. "So it begins, Anastasia."

My heart slams against my chest, and the butterflies escape from my stomach into my constricting throat. *Why is that hot?*

He fills my cup, and I drink practically all of it. Chastened, I stare up at him.

"Got your attention now, haven't I?"

I nod.

"Answer me."

"Yes . . . you've got my attention."

"Good," he smiles a knowing smile. "So sexual acts. We've done most of this."

I move closer to him on the couch and glance down at the list.

APPENDIX 3

Soft Limits

To be discussed and agreed between both parties:

Does the Submissive consent to:

- Masturbation
- Cunnilingus
- Fellatio
- Swallowing Semen
- Vaginal intercourse
- Vaginal fisting
- Anal intercourse
- Anal fisting

"No fisting, you say. Anything else you object to?" he asks softly.

I swallow.

"Anal intercourse doesn't exactly float my boat."

"I'll agree to the fisting, but I'd really like to claim your ass, Anastasia. But we'll wait for that. Besides, it's not something we can dive into." He smirks at me. "Your ass will need training."

"Training?" I whisper.

"Oh yes. It'll need careful preparation. Anal intercourse can be very pleasurable, trust me. But if we try it and you don't like it, we don't have to do it again." He grins down at me.

I blink up at him. He thinks I'll enjoy it? How does he know it's pleasurable?

"Have you done that?" I whisper.

"Yes."

Holy crap. I gasp.

"With a man?"

"No. I've never had sex with a man. Not my scene."

"Mrs. Robinson?"

"Yes."

Holy shit . . . how? I frown. He moves on down the list.

"And . . . swallowing semen. Well, you get an A in that."

I flush, and my inner goddess smacks her lips together, glowing with pride.

"So." He looks down at me grinning. "Swallowing semen okay?"

I nod, not able to look him in the eye, and drain my cup again.

"More?" he asks.

"More." And I'm suddenly reminded of our conversation earlier today as he refills my cup. Is he referring to that or just the champagne? Is this whole champagne thing more?

"Sex toys?" he asks.

I shrug, glancing down the list.

Does the Submissive consent to the use of:

- Vibrators
- Butt plugs
- Dildos
- Other vaginal/anal toys

"Butt plug? Does it do what it says on the box?" I scrunch my nose up in distaste.

"Yes," he smiles. "And I refer to anal intercourse above. Training."

"Oh . . . what's in other?"

"Beads, eggs . . . that sort of stuff."

"Eggs?" I'm alarmed.

"Not real eggs." He laughs loudly, shaking his head.

I purse my lips at him.

"I'm glad you find me funny." I can't keep my injured feelings out of my voice.

He stops laughing.

"I apologize. Miss Steele, I'm sorry," he says, trying to look contrite, but his eyes are still dancing with humor. "Any problem with toys?"

"No," I snap.

"Anastasia," he cajoles. "I am sorry. Believe me. I don't mean to laugh. I've never had this conversation in so much detail. You're just so inexperienced. I'm sorry." His eyes are big and gray and sincere.

I thaw a little and take another sip of champagne.

"Right—bondage," he says, returning to the list. I examine the list, and my inner goddess bounces up and down like a small child waiting for ice cream.

Does the Submissive consent to:

- Bondage with rope
- Bondage with leather cuffs
- Bondage with handcuffs/shackles/manacles
- Bondage with tape
- Bondage with other

Christian raises his eyebrow. "Well?"

"Fine," I whisper and quickly look back at the list.

Does the Submissive consent to be restrained with:

- Hands bound in front
- Ankles bound
- Elbows bound
- Hands bound behind back
- Knees bound
- Wrists bound to ankles
- Binding with spreadbar
- Binding to fixed items, furniture, etc.
- Suspension

Does the Submissive consent to be blindfolded?

Does the Submissive consent to be gagged?

"We've talked about suspension. And it's fine if you want to set that up as a hard limit. It takes a great deal of time, and I only have you for short periods of time anyway. Anything else?"

"Don't laugh at me, but what's a spreader bar?"

"I promise not to laugh. I've apologized twice." He glares at me. "Don't make me do it again," he warns. And I think I visibly shrink . . . oh, he's so bossy. "A spreader is a bar with cuffs for ankles and/or wrists. They're fun."

"Okay . . . Well, gagging me. I'd be worried I wouldn't be able to breathe."

"*I'd* be worried if you couldn't breathe. I don't want to suffocate you."

"And how will I use safewords if I'm gagged?"

He pauses.

"First of all, I hope you never have to use them. But if you're gagged, we'll use hand signals," he says simply.

I blink up at him. But if I'm trussed up, how's that going to work? My brain is beginning to fog . . . *hmm, alcohol.*

"I'm nervous about the gagging."

"Okay. I'll take note."

I stare up at him, realization dawning.

"Do you like tying your submissives up so they can't touch you?"

He gazes at me, his eyes widening.

"That's one of the reasons," he says quietly.

"Is that why you've tied my hands?"

"Yes."

"You don't like talking about that," I murmur.

"No, I don't. Would you like another drink? It's making you brave, and I need to know how you feel about pain."

Holy crap . . . this is the tricky part. He refills my teacup, and I sip.

"So, what's your general attitude to receiving pain?" Christian looks expectantly at me. "You're biting your lip," he says darkly.

I stop immediately, but I don't know what to say. I flush and stare down at my hands.

"Were you physically punished as a child?"

"No."

"So you have no sphere of reference at all?"

"No."

"It's not as bad as you think. Your imagination is your worst enemy in this," he whispers.

"Do you have to do it?"

"Yes."

"Why?"

"Goes with the territory, Anastasia. It's what I do. I can see you're nervous. Let's go through methods."

He shows me the list. My subconscious runs, screaming, and hides behind the couch.

- Spanking
- Whipping
- Biting
- Genital clamps
- Hot wax
- Paddling
- Caning
- Nipple clamps
- Ice
- Other types/methods of pain

"Well, you said no to genital clamps. That's fine. It's caning that hurts the most."

I blank.

"We can work up to that."

"Or not do it at all," I whisper.

"This is part of the deal, baby, but we'll work up to all of this. Anastasia, I won't push you too far."

"This punishment thing, it worries me the most." My voice is very small.

"Well, I'm glad you've told me. We'll keep caning off the list for now. And as you get more comfortable with everything else, we'll increase intensity. We'll take it slow."

I swallow, and he leans forward and kisses me on my lips.

"There, that wasn't so bad was it?"

I shrug, my heart in mouth again.

"Look, I want to talk about one more thing, then I'm taking you to bed."

"Bed?" I blink rapidly, and my blood pounds through my body, warming places I didn't know existed until very recently.

"Come on, Anastasia, talking through all this, I want to fuck you into next week, right now. It must be having some effect on you, too."

I squirm. My inner goddess is panting.

"See? Besides, there's something I want to try."

"Something painful?"

"No—stop seeing pain everywhere. It's mainly pleasure. Have I hurt you yet?"

I flush. "No."

"Well, then. Look, earlier today you were talking about wanting more," he halts, uncertain all of a sudden.

Oh my . . . where's this going?

He clasps my hand.

"Outside of the time you're my sub, perhaps we could try. I don't know if it will work. I don't know about separating everything. It may not work. But I'm willing to try. Maybe one night a week. I don't know."

Holy cow . . . my mouth drops open, my subconscious is in shock. *Christian Grey is up for more!* He's willing to try! My subconscious peeks out from behind the couch, still registering shock on her harpy face.

"I have one condition." He looks warily at my stunned expression.

"What?" I breathe. Anything. I'll give you anything.

"You graciously accept my graduation present to you."

"Oh." And deep down I know what it is. Dread spawns in my gut.

He's staring down at me, gauging my reaction.

"Come," he murmurs and rises, dragging me up. Taking his jacket off, he drapes it over my shoulders and heads for the door.

Parked outside is a red hatchback car, a two-door compact Audi.

"It's for you. Happy graduation," he murmurs, pulling me into his arms and kissing my hair.

He's bought me a damned car, brand-new by the looks of it. Jeez . . . I've had enough trouble with the books. I stare at it blankly, trying desperately to determine how I feel about this. I am appalled on one level, grateful on another, shocked that he's actually done it, but the overriding emotion is anger. Yes, I'm angry, especially after everything I told him about the books . . . but then he'd already bought this. Taking my hand, he leads me down the path toward this new acquisition.

"Anastasia, that Beetle of yours is old and frankly dangerous. I would never forgive myself if something happened to you when it's so easy for me to make it right . . ."

His eyes are on me, but at the moment I cannot bring myself to look at him. I stand silently staring at its awesome bright red newness.

"I mentioned it to your stepfather. He was all for it," he murmurs.

Turning, I glare at him, my mouth open in horror.

"You mentioned this to Ray? How could you?" I can barely spit the words out. *How dare he?* Poor Ray. I feel sick, mortified for my dad.

"It's a gift, Anastasia. Can't you just say thank you?"

"But you know it's too much."

"Not to me it isn't, not for my peace of mind."

I frown at him, at a loss what to say. He just doesn't get it! He's had money all his life. Okay, not all his life—not as a small child—and my worldview shifts. The thought is very sobering, and I soften toward the car, feeling guilty about my fit of pique. His intentions are good, misguided, but not from a bad place.

"I'm happy for you to loan this to me, like the laptop."

He sighs heavily. "Okay. On loan. Indefinitely." He looks warily at me.

"No, not indefinitely, but for now. Thank you."

He frowns. I reach up and kiss him on his cheek.

"Thank you for the car, sir," I say as sweetly as I can manage.

He grabs me suddenly and yanks me up against him, one hand at my back holding me to him and the other fisting in my hair.

"You are one challenging woman, Ana Steele." He kisses me passionately, forcing my lips apart with his tongue, taking no prisoners.

My blood heats immediately, and I'm returning his kiss with my own passion. I want him badly—in spite of the car, the books, the soft limits . . . the caning . . . I want him.

"It's taking all my self-control not to fuck you on the hood of this car right now, just to show you that you are mine, and if I want to buy you a fucking car, I'll buy you a fucking car," he growls. "Now let's get you inside and naked." He plants a swift rough kiss on me.

Boy, he's angry. He grabs my hand and leads me back into the apartment and straight into my bedroom . . . no passing go. My subconscious is behind the sofa again, head hidden under her hands. He switches on the sidelight and halts, staring at me.

"Please don't be angry with me," I whisper.

His gaze is impassive; his eyes cold shards of smoky glass.

"I'm sorry about the car and the books . . ." I trail off. He remains silent and brooding. "You scare me when you're angry," I breathe, staring at him.

He closes his eyes and shakes his head. When he opens them, his expression has softened. He takes a deep breath and swallows.

"Turn around," he whispers. "I want to get you out of that dress."

Another mercurial mood swing; it's so hard to keep up. Obediently, I turn, and my heart is thumping, desire instantly replacing unease, coursing through my blood and settling dark and yearning, low, low in my belly. He scoops my hair off my back so it hangs down my right side, curling at my breast. He places his index finger at the nape of my neck and achingly slowly drags it down my spine, his fingernail grazing my skin.

"I like this dress," he murmurs. "I like to see your flawless skin."

His finger reaches the back of my halter dress midway down my spine, and hooking his finger beneath the top, he pulls me closer so that I step back against him so that he's flush against my body. Leaning down, he inhales my hair.

"You smell so good, Anastasia. So sweet." His nose skims past my ear down my neck, and he trails soft, featherlight kisses along my shoulder.

My breathing changes, becoming shallow, rushed, full of expectation. His fingers are at my zipper. Achingly slow, once more he eases it down while his lips move, licking and kissing and sucking their way across to my other shoulder. He is so tantalizingly good at this. My body resonates, and I start to squirm languidly beneath his touch.

"You. Are. Going. To. Have. To. Learn. To. Keep. Still," he whispers, kissing me around my nape between each word.

He tugs at the fastening at the halter neck, and the dress drops and pools at my feet.

"No bra, Miss Steele. I like that."

His hands reach around and cup my breasts, and my nipples pucker at his touch.

"Lift your arms and put them around my head," he murmurs against my neck.

I obey immediately, and my breasts rise and push into his

hands, my nipples hardening further. My fingers weave into his hair, and very gently I tug his soft, sexy hair. I roll my head to one side to give him easier access to my neck.

"Mmm . . ." he murmurs into that space behind my ear as he starts to extend my nipples with his long fingers, mirroring my hands in his hair.

I groan as the sensation registers sharp and clear in my groin.

"Shall I make you come this way?" he whispers.

I arch my back to force my breasts into his expert hands.

"You like this, don't you, Miss Steele?"

"Mmm . . ."

"Tell me." He continues the slow, sensuous torture, pulling gently.

"Yes."

"Yes, what."

"Yes . . . Sir."

"Good girl." He pinches me hard, and my body writhes convulsively against his front.

I gasp at the exquisite, acute pleasure/pain. I feel him against me. I moan and my hands clench in his hair pulling harder.

"I don't think you're ready to come yet," he whispers, stilling his hands, and he gently bites my earlobe and tugs at it. "Besides, you have displeased me."

Oh . . . no, what will this mean? My brain registers through the fog of needy desire as I groan.

"So perhaps I won't let you come after all." He returns the attention of his fingers to my nipples, pulling, twisting, kneading. I grind my behind against him . . . moving side to side.

I feel his grin against my neck as his hands move down to my hips. His fingers hook into my panties at the back, stretching them, and he pushes his thumbs through the material, shredding them and tossing them in front of me so I can see . . . *holy shit.* His hands move down to my sex, and from behind, he slowly inserts his finger.

"Oh yes. My sweet girl is ready," he breathes as he whirls me around so I'm facing him. His breathing has quickened. He puts his finger in his mouth. "You taste so fine, Miss Steele." He sighs.

Holy shit. His finger tastes salty . . . from me.

"Undress me," he commands quietly, staring down at me, eyes hooded.

All I'm wearing are my shoes—well, Kate's high-heeled pumps. I'm taken aback. I've never undressed a man.

"You can do it," he cajoles softly.

I blink rapidly. Where to start? I reach for his T-shirt, and he grabs my hands, smiling slyly at me.

"Oh no." He shakes his head, grinning. "Not the T-shirt. You may need to touch me for what I have planned." His eyes are alive with excitement.

Oh . . . this is news . . . I can touch with clothes. He takes one of my hands and places it against his erection.

"This is the effect you have on me, Miss Steele."

I gasp and flex my fingers around his girth, and he grins.

"I want to be inside you. Take my jeans off. You're in charge."

Holy fuck . . . me in charge. My mouth drops open.

"What are you going to do with me?" he teases.

Oh, the possibilities . . . my inner goddess roars, and from somewhere born of frustration, need, and sheer Steele bravery, I push him on to the bed. He laughs as he falls, and I gaze down at him, feeling victorious. My inner goddess is going to explode. I yank off his shoes, quickly, clumsily, and his socks. He's staring up at me, his eyes luminous with amusement and desire. He looks . . . glorious . . . *mine.* I crawl up the bed and sit astride him to undo his jeans, sliding my fingers under the waistband, feeling the hair in his oh-so-happy trail. He closes his eyes and flexes his hips.

"You'll have to learn to keep still," I scold, and I tug at the hair under his waistband.

His breath hitches, and he grins at me.

"Yes, Miss Steele," he murmurs, eyes burning bright. "In my pocket, condom," he breathes.

I search in his pocket slowly, watching his face as I feel around. His mouth is open. I fish out both foil packets that I find and lay them on the bed by his hips. *Two!* My over-eager fingers reach for the button of his waistband and undo it, fumbling a little. I am beyond excited.

"So eager, Miss Steele," he murmurs, his voice laced with humor. I tug down the zipper, and now I'm faced with the problem of removing his pants . . . *hmm.* I shuffle down and pull. They hardly move. I frown. How can this be so difficult?

"I can't keep still if you're going to bite that lip," he warns, then arches his pelvis up off the bed so I'm able to tug down his trousers and his boxers at the same time, whoa . . . freeing him. He kicks his clothes to the floor.

Holy Moses, he's all mine to play with, and suddenly it's Christmas.

"Now what are you going to do?" he breathes, all trace of humor gone. I reach up and touch him, watching his expression as I do. His mouth shapes like a letter O as he takes a sharp breath. His skin is so smooth and velvety . . . and hard . . . hmm, what a delicious combination. I lean forward, my hair falling around me, and he's in my mouth. I suck, hard. He closes his eyes, his hips jerking beneath me.

"Jeez, Ana, steady," he groans.

I feel so powerful; it's such an exhilarating feeling, teasing and testing him with my mouth and tongue. He tenses underneath me as I run my mouth up and down him, pushing him to the back of my throat, my lips tight . . . again and again.

"Stop, Ana, stop. I don't want to come."

I sit up, blinking at him, and I'm panting like him, but confused. *I thought I was in charge?* My inner goddess looks like someone snatched her ice cream.

"Your innocence and enthusiasm is very disarming," he gasps. "You, on top . . . that's what we need to do."

Oh.

"Here, put this on." He hands me a foil packet.

Holy crap. How? I rip the packet open, and the rubbery condom is all tacky in my fingers.

"Pinch the top and then roll it down. You don't want any air in the end of that sucker," he pants.

And very slowly, concentrating hard, I do as I'm told.

"Christ, you're killing me here, Anastasia," he groans.

I admire my handiwork and him. He really is a fine specimen of a man. Looking at him is very, very arousing.

"Now. I want to be buried inside you," he murmurs. I stare down at him, daunted, and he sits up suddenly, so we're nose to nose.

"Like this," he breathes, and he snakes one hand around my hips, lifting me, and with the other he positions himself beneath me and, very slowly, eases me onto him.

I groan as he stretches me open, filling me, my mouth hanging open in surprise at the sweet, sublime, agonizing, over-full feeling. *Oh . . . please.*

"That's right, baby, feel me, all of me," he growls, and briefly closes his eyes.

And he's inside me, sheathed to the hilt, and he holds me in place, for seconds . . . minutes . . . I have no idea, staring intently into my eyes.

"It's deep this way," he murmurs. He flexes and swivels his hips in the same motion, and I groan . . . oh my—the sensation radiates throughout my belly . . . everywhere. *Fuck!*

"Again," I whisper. He grins a lazy grin and obliges.

Moaning, I throw my head up, my hair tumbling down my back, and very slowly, he sinks down on to the bed.

"You move, Anastasia, up and down, how you want. Take my hands," he breathes, his voice hoarse and low and oh-so-sexy.

I clasp his hands, holding on for life. Gently I push off him and back down. His eyes are burning with wild anticipation. His breathing is ragged, matching mine, and he lifts his pelvis as I come down, bouncing me back up. We pick up the rhythm . . . up, down, up, down . . . over and over . . . and it feels so . . . good.

Between my panting breaths, the deep down, brimming fullness . . . the vehement sensation pulsing through me that's building quickly, I watch him, our eyes locked . . . and I see wonder there, wonder at me.

I am fucking him. I am in charge. He's mine, and I'm his. The thought pushes me, weighted with concrete, over the edge, and I climax around him . . . shouting incoherently. He grabs my hips, and closing his eyes, tipping his head back, his jaw strained, he comes quietly. I collapse on to his chest, overwhelmed, somewhere between fantasy and reality, a place where there are no hard or soft limits.

CHAPTER SIXTEEN

Slowly the outside world invades my senses, and oh my, what an invasion. I am floating, my limbs soft and languid, utterly spent. I'm lying on top of him, my head on his chest, and he smells divine: freshly laundered linen and some expensive body wash and the best, most seductive scent on the planet . . . Christian. I don't want to move, I want to breathe this elixir for eternity. I nuzzle him, wishing I didn't have the barrier of his T-shirt. And as rhyme and reason return to the rest of my body, I stretch my hand out on his chest. This is the first time I've touched him here. He's firm . . . strong. His hand swoops up and grabs mine, but he softens the blow by pulling it to his mouth and sweetly kissing my knuckles. He rolls over so he's gazing down at me.

"Don't," he murmurs, then kisses me lightly.

"Why don't you like to be touched?" I whisper, staring up into soft gray eyes.

"Because I'm fifty shades of fucked up, Anastasia."

Oh . . . his honesty is completely disarming. I blink up at him.

"I had a very tough introduction to life. I don't want to burden you with the details. Just don't." He strokes his nose against mine, and then he pulls out of me and sits up.

"I think that's all the very basics covered. How was that?"

He looks thoroughly pleased with himself and sounds very matter-of-fact at the same time, like he's just marked off another item on a checklist. I'm still reeling from the "tough introduction to life" comment. It's so frustrating—I am desperate to know more. But he won't tell me. I cock my head to one side, like he does, and make an enormous effort to smile at him.

"If you imagine for one minute that I think you ceded control to me, well you haven't taken into account my GPA." I smile shyly at him. "But thank you for the illusion."

"Miss Steele, you are not just a pretty face. You've had six orgasms so far and all of them belong to me," he boasts, playful again.

I flush and blink at the same time, as he stares down at me. *He's keeping count!* His brow furrows.

"Do you have something to tell me?" his voice is suddenly stern.

I frown. *Crap.*

"I had a dream this morning."

"Oh?" He glares at me.

Double crap. Am I in trouble?

"I came in my sleep." I throw my arm over my eyes. He says nothing. I peek up at him from under my arm, and he looks amused.

"In your sleep?"

"Woke me up."

"I'm sure it did. What were you dreaming about?"

Crap.

"You."

"What was I doing?"

I throw my arm over my eyes again. And like a small child, I briefly entertain the thought that if I can't see him, then he can't see me.

"Anastasia, what was I doing? I won't ask you again."

"You had a riding crop."

He moves my arm.

"Really?"

"Yes." I am crimson.

"There's hope for you yet," he murmurs. "I have several riding crops."

"Brown plaited leather?"

He laughs. "No, but I'm sure I could get one."

Leaning down, he gives me a brief kiss, then stands and grabs his boxers. *Oh no . . . he's going.* I glance quickly at the time—it's only nine forty. I scoot out of bed, too, and grab my sweatpants and a cami top, then sit back on the bed, cross-legged, watching him. I don't want him to go. What can I do?

"When is your period due?" He interrupts my thoughts.

What?

"I hate wearing these things," he grumbles. He holds up the condom, then puts it on the floor and slips on his jeans.

"Well?" he prompts when I don't reply, and he looks at me expectantly as if he's waiting for my opinion on the weather. Holy crap . . . this is personal stuff.

"Next week." I stare down at my hands.

"You need to sort out some contraception."

He is so bossy. I stare at him blankly. He sits back on the bed as he puts on his shoes and socks.

"Do you have a doctor?"

I shake my head. We are back to mergers and acquisitions—another 180-degree mood swing.

He frowns. "I can have mine come and see you at your apartment—Sunday morning before you come and see me. Or he can see you at my place. Which would you prefer?"

No pressure then. Something else that he's paying for . . . but actually this is for his benefit.

"Your place." That means I am guaranteed to see him Sunday.

"Okay. I'll let you know the time."

"Are you leaving?"

Don't go . . . stay with me, please.

"Yes."

Why?

"How are you getting back?" I whisper.

"Taylor will pick me up."

"I can drive you. I have a lovely new car."

He gazes at me, his expression warm.

"That's more like it. But I think you've had too much to drink."

"Did you get me tipsy on purpose?"

"Yes."

"Why?"

"Because you overthink everything, and you're reticent like your stepdad. A drop of wine in you and you start talking, and I need you to communicate honestly with me. Otherwise you clam up and I have no idea what you're thinking. In vino veritas, Anastasia."

"And you think you're always honest with me?"

"I endeavor to be." He looks down at me warily. "This will only work if we're honest with each other."

"I'd like you to stay and use this." I hold up the second condom.

He smiles and his eyes glow with humor.

"Anastasia, I have crossed so many lines here tonight. I have to go. I'll see you on Sunday. I'll have the revised contract ready for you, and then we can really start to play."

"Play?" *Holy shit.* My heart leaps into my mouth.

"I'd like to do a scene with you. But I won't until you've signed, so I know you're ready."

"Oh. So I could stretch this out if I don't sign?"

He gazes at me assessing, and then his lips twitch into a smile. "Well, I suppose you could, but I may crack under the strain."

"Crack? How?" My inner goddess has woken and is paying attention.

He nods slowly, and then he grins, teasing. "Could get really ugly."

His grin is infectious.

"Ugly, how?"

"Oh, you know, explosions, car chases, kidnapping, incarceration."

"You'd kidnap me?"

"Oh yes." He grins.

"Hold me against my will?" *Jeez, this is hot.*

"Oh yes." He nods. "And then we're talking TPE 24/7."

"You've lost me," I breathe, my heart is pounding . . . *is he serious?*

"Total Power Exchange—around the clock." His eyes are shining, and his excitement is palpable even from where I sit.

Holy shit.

"So you have no choice," he says sardonically.

"Clearly." I can't keep the sarcasm out of my voice as my eyes reach for the heavens.

"Oh, Anastasia Steele, did you just roll your eyes at me?"

Crap.

"No," I squeak.

"I think you did. What did I say I'd do to you if you rolled your eyes at me again?"

Shit. He sits down on the edge of the bed.

"Come here," he says softly.

I blanch. Jeez . . . he's serious. I sit staring at him, completely immobile.

"I haven't signed," I whisper.

"I told you what I'd do. I'm a man of my word. I'm going to spank you, and then I'm going to fuck you very quick and very hard. Looks like we'll need that condom after all."

His voice is so soft, menacing, and *it's damned hot*. My insides practically contort with potent, needy, liquid, desire. He gazes at me, waiting, eyes blazing. Tentatively, I uncurl my legs. *Should I run?* This is it; our relationship hangs in the balance, right here, right now. Do I let him do this or do I say no, and then that's it? Because I know it will be over if I say no. *Do it!* my inner goddess pleads with me. My subconscious is as paralyzed as I am.

"I'm waiting," he says. "I'm not a patient man."

Oh, for the love of all that's holy. I'm panting, afraid, turned on. Blood pounding through my body, my legs like jelly. Slowly, I crawl over to him until I am beside him.

"Good girl," he murmurs. "Now stand up."

Oh, shit . . . can't he just get this over with? I'm not sure if I can stand. Hesitantly, I clamber to my feet. He holds his hand out, and I place the condom in his palm. Suddenly he grabs me, tipping me across his lap. With one smooth movement, he angles his body so my torso is resting on the bed beside him. He throws his right leg over both of mine and plants his left forearm on the small of my back, holding me down so I cannot move. *Oh, fuck.*

"Put your hands up on either side of your head," he orders.

I obey immediately.

"Why am I doing this, Anastasia?" he asks.

"Because I rolled my eyes at you," I can barely speak.

"Do you think that's polite?"

"No."

"Will you do it again?"

"No."

"I will spank you each time you do it, do you understand?"

Very slowly, he pulls down my sweatpants. Oh, how demeaning is this? Demeaning and scary and hot. He's making such a meal of this. My heart is in my mouth. I can barely breathe. *Shit, is this going to hurt?*

He places his hand on my naked behind, softly fondling me, stroking around and around with his flat palm. And then his hand is no longer there . . . and he hits me—hard. *Ow!* My eyes spring open in response to the pain, and I try to rise, but his hand moves between my shoulder blades, keeping me down. He caresses me again where he's hit me, and his breathing's changed—it's louder, harsher. He hits me again and again, quickly in succession. *Holy fuck it hurts.* I make no sound, my face screwed up against the pain. I try to wriggle away from the blows—spurred on by adrenaline spiking and coursing through my body.

"Keep still," he growls, "or I'll spank you for longer."

He's rubbing me now, and the blow follows. A rhythmic pattern emerges: caress, fondle, hard slap. I have to concentrate to handle this pain. My mind empties as I endeavor to absorb the grueling sensation. He doesn't hit me in the same place twice in succession—he's spreading the pain.

"Aargh!" I cry out on the tenth slap—and I'm unaware that I have been mentally counting the blows.

"I'm just getting warmed up."

He hits me again, then he strokes me softly. The combination of the hard stinging blow and his gentle caress is so mind-numbing. He hits me again . . . this is getting harder to take. My face hurts, it's screwed up so tight. He strokes me gently and then the blow comes. I cry out again.

"No one to hear you, baby, just me."

And he hits me again and again. From somewhere deep inside, I want to beg him to stop. But I don't. I don't want to give him the satisfaction. He continues the unrelenting rhythm. I cry out six more times. Eighteen slaps in total. My body is singing, singing from his merciless assault.

"Enough," he breathes hoarsely. "Well done, Anastasia. Now I'm going to fuck you."

He caresses my behind gently, and it burns as he strokes me around and around and down. Suddenly, he inserts two fingers inside me, taking me completely by surprise. I gasp, this new assault breaking through the numbness around my brain.

"Feel this. See how much your body likes this, Anastasia. You're soaking just for me." There is awe in his voice. He moves his fingers in and out in quick succession.

I groan. *No, surely not*. And then his fingers are gone . . . and I'm left wanting.

"Next time, I will get you to count. Now where's that condom?"

He reaches beside him for the condom and lifts me gently, pushing me face down onto the bed. I hear the sound of his zipper and the rip of the foil. He pulls my sweatpants completely off and then guides me into a kneeling position, gently caressing my now very sore behind.

"I'm going to take you now. You can come," he murmurs.

What? Like I have a choice.

And he's inside me, quickly filling me. I moan loudly. He moves, pounding into me, a fast, intense pace against my sore behind. The feeling is beyond exquisite, raw and debasing and mind-blowing. My senses are ravaged, disconnected, solely concentrating on what he's doing to me. How he's making me feel that familiar pull deep in my belly, tightening, quickening. NO . . . and my traitorous body explodes in an intense, body-shattering orgasm.

"Oh, Ana!" he cries out loudly as he finds his release, holding me in place as he pours himself into me. He collapses, panting hard beside me, and he pulls me on top of him and buries his face in my hair, holding me close.

"Oh, baby," he breathes. "Welcome to my world."

We lie there, panting together, waiting for our breathing to slow. He gently strokes my hair. I'm on his chest again. But this time, I don't have the strength to lift my hand and feel him. *Boy . . . I survived.* That wasn't so bad. I'm more stoic than I thought. My inner goddess is prostrate . . . well, at least she's quiet. Christian nuzzles my hair again, inhaling deeply.

"Well done, baby," he whispers, quiet joy in his voice. His words curl around me like a soft, fluffy towel from the Heathman Hotel, and I'm so pleased that he's happy.

He picks at the strap on my camisole.

"Is this what you sleep in?" he asks gently.

"Yes," I breathe sleepily.

"You should be in silks and satins, you beautiful girl. I'll take you shopping."

"I like my sweats," I murmur, trying and failing to sound irritated.

He kisses my head again.

"We'll see," he says.

We lie for a few more minutes, hours, who knows, and I think I doze.

"I have to go," he says, and leaning down, he kisses my forehead gently. "Are you okay?" His voice is soft.

I think about his question. My backside is sore. Well, glowing now, and amazingly I feel, apart from exhausted, radiant. The realization is humbling, unexpected. I don't understand.

"I'm okay," I whisper. I don't want to say more than that.

He rises.

"Where's your bathroom?"

"Down the hall to the left."

He scoops up the other condom and heads out of the bedroom. I rise stiffly and put my sweatpants back on. They chafe a little against my still-smarting behind. I'm so confused by my reaction. I remember him saying—I can't remember when—that I would feel so much better after a good hiding. *How can that be so?* I really don't get it. But strangely, I do. I can't say that I enjoyed the experience. In fact, I would still go a long way to avoid it, but now . . . I have this safe, weird, bathed in afterglow, sated feeling. I put my head in my hands. I just don't understand.

Christian reenters the room. I can't look him in the eye. I stare down at my hands.

"I found some baby oil. Let me rub it into your behind."

What?

"No. I'll be fine."

"Anastasia," he warns, and I want to roll my eyes but quickly stop myself. I stand facing the bed. Sitting beside me, he gently pulls my sweatpants down again. *Up and down like whores' drawers*, my subconscious remarks bitterly. In my head, I tell her where to go. Christian squirts baby oil into his hand and then rubs my behind with careful tenderness—from makeup remover to soothing balm for a spanked ass, who would have thought it was such a versatile liquid.

"I like my hands on you," he murmurs, and I have to agree; me, too.

"There," he says when he's finished, and he pulls my pants up again.

I glance over at my clock. It's ten thirty.

"I'm leaving now."

"I'll see you out." I still can't look at him.

Taking my hand, he leads me to the front door. Fortunately, Kate is still not home. She must still be having dinner with her folks and Ethan. I'm really glad she's not been around to hear my chastisement.

"Don't you have to call Taylor?" I ask, avoiding eye contact.

"Taylor's been here since nine. Look at me," he breathes.

I struggle to meet his eyes, but when I do, he's gazing down at me with wonder.

"You didn't cry," he murmurs, then grabs me suddenly and kisses me fervently. "Sunday," he whispers against my lips, and it's both a promise and a threat.

I watch him walk down the path and climb into the big black Audi. He doesn't look back. I close the door and stand helpless in the living room of an apartment that I shall only spend another two nights in. A place I have lived happily for almost four years . . . yet today, for the first time ever, I feel lonely and uncomfortable here, unhappy with my own company. Have I strayed so far from who I am? I know that lurking, not very far under my rather numb exterior, is a well of tears. What am I doing? The irony is I can't even sit down and enjoy a good cry. I'll have to stand. I know it's late, but I decide to call my mom.

"Honey, how are you? How was graduation?" she enthuses down the phone. Her voice is a soothing balm.

"Sorry it's so late," I whisper.

She pauses.

"Ana? What's wrong?" She's all seriousness now.

"Nothing, Mom, I just wanted to hear your voice."

She's silent for a moment.

"Ana, what is it? Please tell me." Her voice is soft and comforting, and I know that she cares. Uninvited, my tears begin to flow. I have cried so often in the last few days.

"Please, Ana," she says, and her anguish reflects mine.

"Oh, Mom, it's a man."

"What's he done to you?" Her alarm is palpable.

"It's not like that." *Although it is* . . . Oh, crap. I don't want to worry her. I just want someone else to be strong for me at the moment.

"Ana, please, you're worrying me."

I take a big breath. "I've kind of fallen for this guy, and he's so different from me, and I don't know if we should be together."

"Oh, darling. I wish I could be with you. I am so sorry I missed your graduation. You've fallen for someone, finally. Oh, honey, men, they are tricky. They're a different species, honey. How long have you known him?"

Christian is definitely a different species . . . *different planet.*

"Oh, nearly three weeks or so."

"Ana, darling, that's no time at all. How can you possibly know someone in that kind of time frame? Just take it easy with him and keep him at arm's length until you decide whether he's worthy of you."

Wow . . . it's unnerving when my mother is so insightful, but she's just too late on this. Is he *worthy* of me? That's an interesting concept. I always wonder whether I am worthy of him.

"Honey, you sound so unhappy. Come home—visit with us. I miss you, darling. Bob would love to see you, too. You can get some distance and maybe some perspective. You need a break. You've been working so hard."

Oh boy, is this tempting. Run away to Georgia. Grab some sunshine, some cocktails. My mother's good humor . . . her loving arms.

"I have two job interviews in Seattle on Monday."

"Oh, that's wonderful news."

The door opens and Kate appears, grinning at me. Her face falls when she sees I've been crying.

"Mom, I have to go. I'll think about a visit. Thank you."

"Honey, please, don't let a man get under your skin. You're far too young. Go and enjoy yourself."

"Yes, Mom, love you."

"Oh, Ana, I love you, too, so much. Stay safe, honey." I hang up and face Kate, who glares at me.

"Has that obscenely rich fucker upset you again?"

"No . . . sort of . . . er . . . yes."

"Just tell him to take a hike, Ana. You've been so up and down since you met him. I've never seen you like this."

The world of Katherine Kavanagh is very clear, very black and white. Not the intangible, mysterious, vague hues of gray that color my world. *Welcome to my world.*

"Sit, let's talk. Let's have some wine. Oh, you've had champagne." She spies the bottle. "Some good stuff, too."

I smile ineffectually, looking apprehensively at the couch. I approach it with caution. *Hmm . . . sitting.*

"Are you okay?"

"I fell over and landed on my behind."

She doesn't think to question my explanation, because I am one of the most uncoordinated people in Washington State. I never thought I'd see that as a blessing. I sit down gingerly, pleasantly surprised that I'm okay, and turn my attention to Kate but my mind glazes over and I'm pulled back to the Heathman—*Well, if you were mine you wouldn't be able to sit down for a week after the stunt you pulled yesterday.* He said it then, and all I could concentrate on at the time was being his. All the warning signs were there, I was just too clueless and too enamored to notice.

Kate comes back into the living area with a bottle of red wine and washed teacups.

"Here we go." She hands me a cup of wine. It won't taste as good as the Bolly.

"Ana, if he's a jerk with commitment issues, dump him. Though I don't really understand his commitment issues. He couldn't take his eyes off you in the marquee, watched you like a hawk. I'd say he was completely smitten, but maybe he has a funny way of showing it."

Smitten? Christian? Funny way of showing it? I'll say.

"Kate, it's complicated. How was your evening?" I ask.

I can't talk this through with Kate without revealing too much, but one question on her day and Kate is off. It's reassuring to sit and listen to her normal chatter. The hot news is that Ethan may be coming to live with us after their vacation. That will be fun—Ethan is a hoot. I frown. I don't think Christian will approve.

Well . . . tough. He'll just have to suck it up. I have a couple of teacups of wine and decide to call it a night. It's been one very long day. Kate hugs me, and then grabs the phone to call Elliot.

I check the mean machine after I brush my teeth. There's an e-mail from Christian.

From: Christian Grey
Subject: You
Date: May 26 2011 23:14
To: Anastasia Steele

Dear Miss Steele,
You are quite simply exquisite. The most beautiful, intelligent, witty, and brave woman I have ever met. Take some Advil—this is not a request. And don't drive your Beetle again. I will know.

Christian Grey
CEO, Grey Enterprises Holdings, Inc.

Oh, not drive my car again! I type out my reply.

From: Anastasia Steele
Subject: Flattery
Date: May 26 2011 23:20
To: Christian Grey

Dear Mr. Grey,
Flattery will get you nowhere, but since you've been *everywhere* the point is moot.

I will need to drive my Beetle to a garage so I can sell it—so will not graciously accept any of your nonsense over that.

Red wine is always more preferable to Advil.

Ana

P.S.: Caning is a HARD limit for me.

I hit "send."

From: Christian Grey
Subject: Frustrating Women Who Can't Take Compliments
Date: May 26 2011 23:26
To: Anastasia Steele

Dear Miss Steele,
I am not flattering you. You should go to bed.

I accept your addition to the hard limits.

Don't drink too much.

Taylor will dispose of your car and get a good price for it, too.

Christian Grey
CEO, Grey Enterprises Holdings, Inc.

From: Anastasia Steele
Subject: Taylor—Is He the Right Man for the Job?
Date: May 26 2011 23:40
To: Christian Grey

Dear Sir,
I am intrigued that you are happy to risk letting your right-

hand man drive my car but not some woman you fuck occasionally. How can I be sure that Taylor is the man to get me the best deal for said car? I have, in the past, probably before I met you, been known to drive a hard bargain.

Ana

From: Christian Grey
Subject: Careful!
Date: May 26 2011 23:44
To: Anastasia Steele

Dear Miss Steele,
I am assuming it is the RED WINE talking, and that you've had a very long day.

Though I am tempted to drive back over there to ensure that you don't sit down for a week, rather than an evening.

Taylor is ex-army and capable of driving anything from a motorcycle to a Sherman tank. Your car does not present a hazard to him.

Now please do not refer to yourself as "some woman I fuck occasionally" because, quite frankly, it makes me MAD, and you really wouldn't like me when I'm angry.

Christian Grey
CEO, Grey Enterprises Holdings, Inc.

From: Anastasia Steele
Subject: Careful Yourself
Date: May 26 2011 23:57
To: Christian Grey

Dear Mr. Grey,

I'm not sure I like you anyway, especially at the moment.

Miss Steele

From: Christian Grey
Subject: Careful Yourself
Date: May 27 2011 00:03
To: Anastasia Steele

Why don't you like me?

Christian Grey
CEO, Grey Enterprises Holdings, Inc.

From: Anastasia Steele
Subject: Careful Yourself
Date: May 27 2011 00:09
To: Christian Grey

Because you never stay with me.

There, that's given him something to think about. I shut the machine down with a flourish I don't really feel and crawl into my bed. I switch off my sidelight and stare up at the ceiling. It's been one long day, one emotional wrench after another. It was heartwarming to spend some time with Ray. He looked well, and weirdly, he approved of Christian. Jeez, Kate and her gargantuan mouth. Hearing Christian speak about being hungry. What the hell is that all about? God, and the car. I haven't even told Kate about the new car. What was Christian thinking?

And then this evening, he actually hit me. I've never been hit in my life. What have I gotten myself into? Very slowly, my tears, halted by Kate's arrival, begin to slide down the side of my face and into my ears. I have fallen for someone who's so emotionally shut down, I will only get hurt—deep down I know this—someone who by his own admission is completely fucked up. *Why* is he so fucked up? It must be awful to be as affected as he is, and the thought that as a toddler he suffered some unbearable cruelty makes me cry harder. *Perhaps if he was more normal he wouldn't want you,* my subconscious contributes snidely to my musings . . . and in my heart of hearts I know this is true. I turn into my pillow and the sluice gates open . . . and for the first time in years, I am sobbing uncontrollably into my pillow.

I am momentarily distracted from my dark night of the soul by Kate shouting.

"*What the fuck do you think you're doing here?*"

"*Well, you can't!*"

"*What the fuck have you done to her now?*"

"*Since she's met you she cries all the time.*"

"*You can't come in here!*"

Christian bursts into my bedroom and unceremoniously switches on the overhead light, making me squint.

"Jesus, Ana," he mutters. He flicks the switch off again and is at my side in a moment.

"What are you doing here?" I gasp between sobs. Crap. I can't stop crying.

He switches on the sidelight, making me squint again. Kate comes and stands in the doorway.

"Do you want me to throw this asshole out?" she asks, radiating thermonuclear hostility.

Christian raises his eyebrows at her, no doubt surprised by her flattering epithet and her feral antagonism. I shake my head, and she rolls her eyes at me. *Oh . . . I wouldn't do that near Mr. G.*

"Just holler if you need me," she says more gently. "Grey—you're on my shit list and I'm watching you," she hisses at him. He blinks at her, and she turns and pulls the door closed but doesn't shut it.

Christian gazes down at me, his expression grave, his face ashen. He's wearing his pinstriped jacket, and from his inside pocket he pulls out a handkerchief and hands it to me. I think I still have his other one somewhere.

"What's going on?" he asks quietly.

"Why are you here?" I ask, ignoring his question. My tears have miraculously ceased, but I'm left with dry heaves racking my body.

"Part of my role is to look after your needs. You said you wanted me to stay, so here I am. And yet I find you like this." He blinks at me, truly bewildered. "I'm sure I'm responsible, but I have no idea why. Is it because I hit you?"

I pull myself up, wincing from my sore behind. I sit and face him.

"Did you take some Advil?"

I shake my head. He narrows his eyes, stands, and leaves the room. I hear him talking to Kate but not what they are saying. He's back a few moments later with pills and a teacup of water.

"Take these," he orders gently as he sits on my bed beside me.

I do as I'm told.

"Talk to me," he whispers. "You told me you were okay. I'd never have left you if I thought you were like this."

I stare down at my hands. What can I say that I haven't said already? I want more. I want him to stay because *he* wants to stay with me, not because I'm a blubbering mess, and I don't want him to beat me, is that so unreasonable?

"I take it that when you said you were okay, you weren't."

I flush. "I thought I was fine."

"Anastasia, you can't tell me what you think I want to hear. That's not very honest," he admonishes me. "How can I trust anything you've said to me?"

I peek up at him, and he's frowning, a bleak look in his eye. He runs both hands through his hair.

"How did you feel while I was hitting you and after?"

"I didn't like it. I'd rather you didn't do it again."

"You weren't meant to like it."

"Why do you like it?" I stare up at him.

My question surprises him.

"You really want to know?"

"Oh, trust me, I'm fascinated." And I can't quite keep the sarcasm out of my voice.

He narrows his eyes again.

"Careful," he warns.

I blanch. "Are you going to hit me again?"

"No, not tonight."

Phew . . . my subconscious and I both breathe a silent sigh of relief.

"So," I prompt.

"I like the control it gives me, Anastasia. I want you to behave in a particular way, and if you don't, I shall punish you, and you will learn to behave the way I desire. I enjoy punishing you. I've wanted to spank you since you asked me if I was gay."

I flush at the memory. *Jeez, I wanted to spank myself after that question.* So Katherine Kavanagh is responsible for all this, and if she'd gone to that interview and asked her gay question, she'd be sitting here with the sore ass. I don't like that thought. How confusing is this?

"So you don't like the way I am."

He stares at me, bewildered again. "I think you're lovely the way you are."

"So why are you trying to change me?"

"I don't want to change you. I'd like you to be courteous and to follow the set of rules I've given you and not defy me. Simple," he says.

"But you want to punish me?"

"Yes, I do."

"That's what I don't understand."

He sighs and runs his hands through his hair again.

"It's the way I'm made, Anastasia. I need to control you. I need you to behave in a certain way, and if you don't—I love to watch your beautiful alabaster skin pink and warm up under my hands. It turns me on."

Holy shit. Now we're getting somewhere.

"So it's not the pain you're putting me through?"

He swallows.

"A bit, to see if you can take it, but that's not the whole reason. It's the fact that you are mine to do with as I see fit—ultimate control over someone else. And it turns me on. Big time, Anastasia. Look, I'm not explaining myself very well . . . I've never had to before. I've not really thought about this in any great depth. I've always been with like-minded people." He shrugs apologetically. "And you still haven't answered my question—how did you feel afterward?"

"Confused."

"You were sexually aroused by it, Anastasia." He closes his eyes briefly, and when he reopens them and gazes at me, they are blazing.

His expression pulls at that dark part of me, buried in the depths of my belly—my libido, woken and tamed by him but, even now, insatiable.

"Don't look at me like that," he murmurs.

I frown. *Jeez, what have I done now?*

"I don't have any condoms, Anastasia, and you know, you're upset. Contrary to what your roommate believes, I'm not a priapic monster. So, you felt confused?"

I squirm under his intense gaze.

"You have no problem being honest with me in print. Your e-mails always tell me exactly how you feel. Why can't you do that in conversation? Do I intimidate you that much?"

I pick at an imaginary spot on my mother's blue-and-cream quilt.

"You beguile me, Christian. Completely overwhelm me. I feel like Icarus flying too close to the sun," I whisper.

He gasps. "Well, I think you've got that the wrong way around," he whispers.

"What?"

"Oh, Anastasia, you've bewitched me. Isn't it obvious?"

No, not to me. *Bewitched* . . . my inner goddess is staring openmouthed. Even she doesn't believe this.

"You've still not answered my question. Write me an e-mail, please. But right now, I'd really like to sleep. Can I stay?"

"Do you want to stay?" I can't hide the hope in my voice.

"You wanted me here."

"You haven't answered my question."

"I'll write you an e-mail," he mutters petulantly.

Standing, he empties his jeans pockets of BlackBerry, keys, wallet, and money. Holy cow, men carry a lot of crap in their pockets. He strips off his watch, shoes, socks, and jeans and places his jacket over my chair. He walks around to the other side of the bed and slides in.

"Lie down," he orders.

I slip slowly under the covers, wincing, staring at him. Jeez . . . he's staying. I think I'm numb with elated shock. He leans up on one elbow, staring down at me.

"If you are going to cry, cry in front of me. I need to know."

"Do you want me to cry?"

"Not particularly. I just want to know how you're feeling. I don't want you slipping through my fingers. Switch the light off. It's late, and we both have to work tomorrow."

So here . . . and still so bossy, but I can't complain; he's in my bed. I don't quite understand why . . . maybe I should weep more often in front of him. I switch off the bedside light.

"Lie on your side, facing away from me," he murmurs in the darkness.

I roll my eyes in the full knowledge that he cannot see me, but I do as I'm told. Gingerly, he moves over and puts his arms around me and pulls me to his chest.

"Sleep, baby," he whispers, and I feel his nose in my hair as he inhales deeply.

Holy cow. Christian Grey is sleeping with me, and in the comfort and solace of his arms, I drift into a peaceful sleep.

CHAPTER SEVENTEEN

The candle flame is too hot. It flickers and dances in the over-warm breeze, a breeze that brings no respite from the heat. Soft gossamer wings flutter to and fro in the dark, sprinkling dusty scales in the circle of light. I'm struggling to resist, but I'm drawn. And then it's so bright, and I am flying too close to the sun, dazzled by the light, fried and melting from the heat, weary in my endeavors to stay airborne. I am so warm. The heat . . . it's stifling, overpowering. It wakes me.

I open my eyes, and I'm draped in Christian Grey. He's wrapped around me like a victory flag. He's fast asleep with his head on my chest, his arm over me, holding me close, one of his legs thrown over and hooked around both of mine. He's suffocating me with his body heat, and he's heavy. I take a moment to absorb that he's still in my bed and fast asleep, and it's light outside—morning. He has spent the whole night with me.

My right arm is stretched, no doubt in search of a cool spot, and as I process the fact that he's still with me, the thought occurs that I can touch him. He's asleep. Tentatively, I lift my hand and run the tips of my fingers down his back. Deep in his throat, I hear a faint, distressed groan, and he stirs. He nuzzles my chest, inhaling deeply as he wakes. Sleepy, blinking gray eyes meet mine beneath his tousled mop of hair.

"Good morning," he mumbles, and frowns. "Jesus, even in my sleep I'm drawn to you." He moves slowly, unpeeling his limbs from me as he gets his bearings. I become aware of his erection against my hip. He notices my wide-eyed reaction, and he smiles a slow, sexy smile.

"Hmm . . . this has possibilities, but I think we should wait until Sunday." He leans down and nuzzles my ear with his nose.

I flush, but then I feel seven shades of scarlet from his heat.

"You're very hot," I murmur.

"You're not so bad yourself," he murmurs, and presses himself against me, suggestively.

I flush some more. *That's not what I meant*. He props himself up on his elbow, gazing down at me, amused. He bends and, to my surprise, plants a gentle kiss on my lips.

"Sleep well?" he asks.

I nod, staring up at him, and I realize that I've slept very well except maybe for the last half hour when I was too hot.

"So did I." He frowns. "Yes, really well." He raises his eyebrows in confused surprise. "What's the time?"

I glance at my alarm.

"It's seven thirty."

"Seven thirty . . . shit." He scrambles out of bed and drags on his jeans.

It is my turn to look amused as I sit up. Christian Grey is late and flustered. This is something I have never seen before. I belatedly realize that my behind is no longer sore.

"You are such a bad influence on me. I have a meeting. I have to go—I have to be in Portland at eight. Are you smirking at me?"

"Yes."

He grins. "I'm late. I don't do late. Another first, Miss Steele." He pulls on his jacket and then bends down and grasps my head, his hands on either side.

"Sunday," he says, and the word is pregnant with an unspoken promise. Everything deep in my body uncurls and then clenches in delicious anticipation. The feeling is exquisite.

Holy hell, if my mind could just keep up with my body. He leans forward and kisses me quickly. He grabs his stuff from my side table and his shoes—which he doesn't put on.

"Taylor will come and sort your Beetle. I was serious. Don't drive it. I'll see you at my place on Sunday. I'll e-mail you a time." And like a whirlwind, he's gone.

Christian Grey spent the night with me, and I feel rested. And there was no sex, only cuddling. He told me he never slept with anyone—but he's slept three times with me. I grin and slowly climb out of my bed. I feel more optimistic than I have for the last day or so. I head for the kitchen, needing a cup of tea.

After breakfast, I shower and dress quickly for my last day at Clayton's. It is the end of an era—good-bye to Mr. and Mrs. Clayton, WSU, Vancouver, the apartment, my Beetle. I glance at the mean machine—it's only 7:52. I have time.

From: Anastasia Steele
Subject: Assault and Battery: The After-Effects
Date: May 27 2011 08:05
To: Christian Grey

Dear Mr. Grey,
You wanted to know why I felt confused after you—which euphemism should we apply—spanked, punished, beat, assaulted me. Well, during the whole alarming process, I felt demeaned, debased, and abused. And much to my mortification, you're right, I was aroused, and that was unexpected. As you are well aware, all things sexual are new to me—I only wish I was more experienced and therefore more prepared. I was shocked to feel aroused.

What really worried me was how I felt afterward. And that's more difficult to articulate. I was happy that you were happy. I felt relieved that it wasn't as painful as I thought it would be. And when I was lying in your arms, I felt . . . sated. But I feel very uncomfortable, guilty even, feeling that way. It doesn't sit well with me, and I'm confused as a result. Does that answer your question?

I hope the world of Mergers and Acquisitions is as stimulating as ever . . . and that you weren't too late.

Thank you for staying with me.

Ana

From: Christian Grey
Subject: Free Your Mind
Date: May 27 2011 08:24
To: Anastasia Steele

Interesting . . . if slightly overstated title heading, Miss Steele.

To answer your points:

- I'll go with spanking—as that's what it was.
- So you felt demeaned, debased, abused, and assaulted—how very Tess Durbeyfield of you. I believe it was you who decided on the debasement, if I remember correctly. Do you really feel like this or do you think you ought to feel like this? Two very different things. If that *is* how you feel, do you think you could just try to embrace these feelings, deal with them, for me? That's what a submissive would do.
- I am grateful for your inexperience. I value it, and I'm only beginning to understand what it means. Simply put . . . it means that you are mine in every way.
- Yes, you were aroused, which in turn was very arousing, there's nothing wrong with that.
- Happy does not even begin to cover how I felt. Ecstatic joy comes close.

- Punishment spanking hurts far more than sensual spanking—so that's about as hard as it gets, unless, of course, you commit some major transgression, in which case I'll use some implement to punish you with. My hand was very sore. But I like that.

- I felt sated, too—more so than you could ever know.

- Don't waste your energy on guilt, feelings of wrongdoing, etc. We are consenting adults and what we do behind closed doors is between ourselves. You need to free your mind and listen to your body.

- The world of M&A is not nearly as stimulating as you are, Miss Steele.

Christian Grey
CEO, Grey Enterprises Holdings, Inc.

Holy crap . . . *mine in every way.* My breath hitches.

From: Anastasia Steele
Subject: Consenting Adults!
Date: May 27 2011 08:26
To: Christian Grey

Aren't you in a meeting?
I'm very glad your hand was sore.

And if I listened to my body, I'd be in Alaska by now.

Ana

P.S.: I will think about embracing these feelings.

From: Christian Grey
Subject: You Didn't Call the Cops
Date: May 27 2011 08:35
To: Anastasia Steele

Miss Steele,
I am in a meeting discussing the futures market, if you're really interested.

For the record, you stood beside me knowing what I was going to do.

You didn't at any time ask me to stop—you didn't use either safeword.

You are an adult—you have choices.

Quite frankly, I'm looking forward to the next time my palm is ringing with pain.

You're obviously not listening to the right part of your body.

Alaska is very cold and no place to run. I would find you.

I can track your cell phone—remember?

Go to work.

Christian Grey
CEO, Grey Enterprises Holdings, Inc.

I scowl at the screen. He's right, of course. It's my choice. *Hmm.* Is he serious about coming to find me? Should I decide to escape for a while? My mind flits briefly to my mother's offer. I hit "reply."

From: Anastasia Steele
Subject: Stalker

Date: May 27 2011 08:36
To: Christian Grey

Have you sought therapy for your stalker tendencies?
Ana

From: Christian Grey
Subject: Stalker? Me?
Date: May 27 2011 08:38
To: Anastasia Steele

I pay the eminent Dr. Flynn a small fortune with regard to my stalker and other tendencies.
Go to work.

Christian Grey
CEO, Grey Enterprises Holdings, Inc.

From: Anastasia Steele
Subject: Expensive Charlatans
Date: May 27 2011 08:40
To: Christian Grey

May I humbly suggest you seek a second opinion?
I am not sure that Dr. Flynn is very effective.

Miss Steele

From: Christian Grey
Subject: Second Opinions
Date: May 27 2011 08:43
To: Anastasia Steele

Not that it's any of your business, humble or otherwise, but Dr. Flynn is the second opinion.

You will have to speed, in your new car, putting yourself at unnecessary risk—I think that's against the rules.

GO TO WORK.

Christian Grey
CEO, Grey Enterprises Holdings, Inc.

From: Anastasia Steele
Subject: SHOUTY CAPITALS
Date: May 27 2011 08:47
To: Christian Grey

As the object of your stalker tendencies, I think it is my business, actually.

I haven't signed yet. So rules, schmules. And I don't start until 9:30.

Miss Steele

From: Christian Grey
Subject: Descriptive Linguistics
Date: May 27 2011 08:49
To: Anastasia Steele

"Schmules"? Not sure where that appears in Webster's Dictionary.

Christian Grey
CEO, Grey Enterprises Holdings, Inc.

From: Anastasia Steele
Subject: Descriptive Linguistics
Date: May 27 2011 08:52
To: Christian Grey

It's between control freak and stalker.
And descriptive linguistics is a hard limit for me.

Will you stop bothering me now?

I'd like to go to work in my new car.

Ana

From: Christian Grey
Subject: Challenging but Amusing Young Women
Date: May 27 2011 08:56
To: Anastasia Steele

My palm is twitching.
Drive safely, Miss Steele.

Christian Grey
CEO, Grey Enterprises Holdings, Inc.

The Audi is a joy to drive. It has power steering. Wanda, my Beetle, has no power in it at all—anywhere—so my daily workout, which was driving my Beetle, will cease. Oh, but I will have a personal trainer to contend with, according to Christian's rules. I frown. I hate exercising.

While I am driving, I try to analyze our e-mail exchange. He's a patronizing son of a bitch sometimes. And then I think of Grace and I feel guilty. But of course, she wasn't his birth mother. *Hmm*, that's a whole world of unknown pain. Well, patronizing son of a bitch works well, then. Yes. I'm an adult, thank you for reminding me, Christian Grey, and it is my choice. The problem is, I just want Christian, not all his . . . baggage—and right now he has a 747 cargo hold's worth of baggage. Could I just lie back and embrace it? Like a submissive? I've said I'd try. It's an awfully big ask.

I pull into the parking lot at Clayton's. As I make my way in, I can hardly believe it's my last day. Fortunately, the store is busy and time passes quickly. At lunchtime, Mr. Clayton summons me from the stockroom. He's standing beside a motorcycle courier.

"Miss Steele?" the courier asks. I frown questioningly at Mr. Clayton, who shrugs, as puzzled as me. My heart sinks. What has Christian sent me now? I sign for the small package and open it immediately. It's a BlackBerry. My heart sinks further. I switch it on.

From: Christian Grey
Subject: BlackBerry ON LOAN
Date: May 27 2011 11:15
To: Anastasia Steele

I need to be able to contact you at all times, and since this is your most honest form of communication, I figured you needed a BlackBerry.

Christian Grey
CEO, Grey Enterprises Holdings, Inc.

From: Anastasia Steele
Subject: Consumerism Gone Mad
Date: May 27 2011 13:22
To: Christian Grey

I think you need to call Dr. Flynn right now.
Your stalker tendencies are running wild.

I am at work. I will e-mail you when I get home.

Thank you for yet another gadget.

I wasn't wrong when I said you were the ultimate consumer.

Why do you do this?

Ana

From: Christian Grey
Subject: Sagacity from One So Young
Date: May 27 2011 13:24
To: Anastasia Steele

Fair point well made, as ever, Miss Steele.
Dr. Flynn is on vacation.

And I do this because I can.

Christian Grey
CEO, Grey Enterprises Holdings, Inc.

I put the thing in my back pocket, hating it already. E-mailing Christian is addictive, but I am supposed to be working. It buzzes once against my behind . . . *How apt*, I think ironically, but summoning all my willpower, I ignore it.

At four, Mr. and Mrs. Clayton gather all the other employees in the shop and, during a hair-curlingly embarrassing speech, present me with a check for three hundred dollars. In that moment, all the events from the past three weeks well up inside of me: exams, graduation, an intense, fucked-up billionaire, deflowering, hard and soft limits, playrooms with no consoles, helicopter rides, and the fact that I will move tomorrow. Amazingly, I hold myself together. My subconscious is in awe. I hug the Claytons hard.

They have been kind and generous employers, and I will miss them.

KATE IS CLIMBING OUT of her car when I arrive home.

"What's that?" she says accusingly, pointing at the Audi. I can't resist.

"It's a car," I quip. She narrows her eyes, and for a brief moment, I wonder if she's going to put me across her knee, too. "My graduation present." I try to act nonchalant. *Yes, I get expensive cars given to me every day.* Her mouth drops open.

"Generous, over-the-top bastard, isn't he?"

I nod. "I did try not to accept it, but frankly, it's just not worth the fight."

Kate purses her lips. "No wonder you're overwhelmed. I did note that he stayed."

"Yeah." I smile wistfully.

"Shall we finish packing?"

I nod and follow her inside. I check the e-mail from Christian.

From: Christian Grey
Subject: Sunday
Date: May 27 2011 13:40
To: Anastasia Steele

Shall I see you at 1 p.m. Sunday?
The doctor will be at Escala to see you at 1:30.

I'm leaving for Seattle now.

I hope your move goes well, and I look forward to Sunday.

Christian Grey
CEO, Grey Enterprises Holdings, Inc.

Jeez, he could be discussing the weather. I decide to e-mail him once we've finished packing. He can be such fun one minute, and then he can be so formal and stuffy the next. It's difficult to keep up. Honestly, it's like an e-mail to an employee. I roll my eyes at it defiantly and join Kate to pack.

KATE AND I ARE in the kitchen when there's a knock at the door. Taylor stands on the porch, looking immaculate in his suit. I notice the trace of ex-army in his buzz cut, his trim physique, and his cool stare.

"Miss Steele," he says, "I've come for your car."

"Oh yes, of course. Come in, I'll get the keys."

Surely this is above and beyond the call of duty. I wonder again at Taylor's job description. I hand him the keys, and we walk in an uncomfortable silence—for me—toward the light blue Beetle. I open the door and remove the flashlight from the glove box. That's it. I have nothing else that's personal in Wanda. *Good-bye, Wanda. Thank you.* I caress her roof as I close the passenger door.

"How long have you worked for Mr. Grey?" I ask.

"Four years, Miss Steele."

Suddenly, I have an overwhelming urge to bombard him with questions. What this man must know about Christian, all his secrets. But then he's probably signed an NDA. I look nervously at him. He has the same taciturn expression as Ray, and I warm to him.

"He's a good man, Miss Steele," he says with a smile. Then he gives me a little nod, climbs into my car, and drives away.

Apartment, Beetle, Clayton's—it's all change now. I shake my head as I wander back inside. And the biggest change of all is Christian Grey. Taylor thinks he's a *good man*. Can I believe him?

JOSÉ JOINS US WITH Chinese takeout at eight. We're done. We're packed and ready to go. He brings several bottles of beer, and Kate and I sit on the couch while he's cross-legged on the floor between us. We watch crap TV, drink beer, and, as the evening wears on, we fondly and loudly reminisce as the beer takes effect. It's been a good four years.

The atmosphere between José and me has returned to normal, the attempted kiss forgotten. Well, it's been swept under the rug that my inner goddess is lying on, eating grapes and tapping her fingers, waiting not so patiently for Sunday. There's a knock on the door, and my heart leaps into my throat. Is it . . . ?

Kate answers the door and is nearly knocked off her feet by Elliot. He seizes her in a Hollywood-style clinch that moves quickly into a European art house embrace. *Honestly . . . get a room*. José and I stare at each other. I'm appalled at their lack of modesty.

"Shall we walk down to the bar?" I ask José, who nods frantically. We are too uncomfortable with the unrestrained sexing unfolding in front of us. Kate looks up at me, flushed and bright-eyed.

"José and I are going for a quick drink." I roll my eyes at her. Ha! I can still roll my eyes in my own time.

"Okay." She grins.

"Hi, Elliot. Bye, Elliot."

He winks a big blue eye at me, and José and I are out the door, giggling like teenagers.

As we stroll down to the bar, I put my arm through José's. God, he's so uncomplicated—I hadn't really appreciated that before.

"You'll still come to the opening of my show, won't you?"

"Of course, José, when is it?"

"June ninth."

"What day is that?" I suddenly panic.

"It's a Thursday."

"Yeah, I should make that . . . and you will visit us in Seattle?"

"Try to stop me." He grins.

IT'S LATE WHEN I arrive back from the bar. Kate and Elliot are nowhere to be seen, but boy, can they be heard. *Holy shit.* I hope I'm not that loud. I know Christian isn't. I flush at the thought and escape to my room. After a brief not-at-all-awkward-thank-goodness hug, José has gone. I don't know when I'll see him again, probably his photography show, and once again, I'm blown away that he finally has an exhibition. I shall miss him and his boyish charm. I couldn't bring myself to tell him about the Beetle. I know he'll freak when he finds out, and I can only deal with one man at a time freaking out at me. Once in my room, I check the mean machine, and of course, there's an e-mail from Christian.

From: Christian Grey
Subject: Where Are You?
Date: May 27 2011 22:14
To: Anastasia Steele

"*I am at work. I will e-mail you when I get home.*"
Are you still at work or have you packed your phone, Black-Berry, and MacBook?

Call me, or I may be forced to call Elliot.

Christian Grey
CEO, Grey Enterprises Holdings, Inc.

Crap . . . *José . . . shit.*

I grab my phone. Five missed calls and one voice message. Tentatively, I listen to the message. It's Christian.

"I think you need to learn to manage my expectations. I am not a patient man. If you say you are going to contact me when you finish work, then you should have the decency to do so. Otherwise, I worry, and it's not an emotion I'm familiar with, and I don't tolerate it very well. Call me."

Double crap. Will he ever give me a break? I scowl at the phone. He is suffocating me. With a deep dread uncurling in my stomach, I scroll down to his number and press "call." My heart is in my mouth as I wait for him to answer. He'd probably like to beat seven shades of shit out of me. The thought is depressing.

"Hi," he says softly, and his response knocks me off balance because I am expecting his anger, but if anything, he sounds relieved.

"Hi," I murmur.

"I was worried about you."

"I know. I'm sorry I didn't reply, but I'm fine."

He pauses for a beat.

"Did you have a pleasant evening?" He is crisply polite.

"Yes. We finished packing and Kate and I had Chinese takeout with José." I close my eyes tightly as I say José's name. Christian says nothing.

"How about you?" I ask to fill the sudden deafening chasm of silence. I will not let him make me feel guilty about José.

Eventually, he sighs.

"I went to a fund-raising dinner. It was deathly dull. I left as soon as I could."

He sounds so sad and resigned. My heart clenches. I picture him all those nights ago sitting at the piano in his huge living room and the unbearable bittersweet melancholy of the music he was playing.

"I wish you were here," I whisper, because I have an urge to hold him. Soothe him. Even though he won't let me. I want his proximity.

"Do you?" he murmurs blandly. *Holy shit.* This doesn't sound like him, and my scalp prickles with dawning apprehension.

"Yes," I breathe. After an eternity, he sighs.

"I'll see you Sunday?"

"Yes, Sunday," I murmur, and a thrill courses through my body.

"Good night."

"Good night, Sir."

My address catches him unawares, I can tell by his sharp intake of breath.

"Good luck with your move tomorrow, Anastasia." His voice is soft. And we're both hanging on the phone like teenagers, neither wanting to hang up.

"You hang up," I whisper. Finally, I sense his smile.

"No, you hang up." And I know he's grinning.

"I don't want to."

"Neither do I."

"Were you very angry with me?"

"Yes."

"Are you still?"

"No."

"So you're not going to punish me?"

"No. I'm an in-the-moment kind of guy."

"I've noticed."

"You can hang up now, Miss Steele."

"Do you really want me to, Sir?"

"Go to bed, Anastasia."

"Yes, Sir."

We both stay on the line.

"Do you ever think you'll be able to do what you're told?" He's amused and exasperated at once.

"Maybe. We'll see after Sunday." And I press "end" on the phone.

Elliot stands and admires his handiwork. He has replugged our TV into the satellite system in our Pike Place Market apartment. Kate and I flop onto the couch giggling, impressed by his prowess with a power drill. The flat screen looks odd against the brickwork of the converted warehouse, but no doubt I will get used to it.

"See, baby, easy." He grins a wide, white-toothed smile at Kate, and she almost literally dissolves into the couch.

I roll my eyes at the pair of them.

"I'd love to stay, baby, but my sister is back from Paris. It's a compulsory family dinner tonight."

"Can you come by after?" Kate asks tentatively, all soft and un-Kate-like.

I stand and make my way over to the kitchen area on the pretense of unpacking one of the crates. They are going to get icky.

"I'll see if I can escape," he promises.

"I'll come down with you." Kate smiles.

"Laters, Ana." Elliot grins.

"Bye, Elliot. Say hi to Christian from me."

"Just hi?" His eyebrows shoot up suggestively.

"Yes." I flush. He winks at me, and I go crimson as he follows Kate out of the apartment.

Elliot is adorable and so different from Christian. He's warm, open, physical, very physical, too physical, with Kate. They can barely keep their hands off each other—to be honest it's embarrassing—and I am pea green with envy.

Kate returns about twenty minutes later with pizza, and we sit, surrounded by crates, in our new open space, eating straight from the box. Kate's dad has done us proud. The apartment is not large, but it's big enough, three bedrooms and a large living space that looks out onto Pike Place Market itself. It's all solid wood floors and red brick, and the kitchen tops are smooth concrete, very utilitarian, very now. We both love that we will be in the heart of the city.

At eight, the entry-phone buzzes. Kate leaps up—and my heart leaps into my mouth.

"Delivery, Miss Steele, Miss Kavanagh." Disappointment flows freely and unexpectedly through my veins. It's not Christian.

"Second floor, apartment two."

Kate buzzes the delivery boy in. His mouth falls open when he sees Kate, all tight jeans, T-shirt, and hair piled high with escaping tendrils. She has that effect on men. He holds a bottle of champagne with a helicopter-shaped balloon attached. She gives him a dazzling smile to send him on his way and proceeds to read the card out to me.

Ladies,
Good luck in your new home.
Christian Grey

Kate shakes her head in disapproval.

"Why can't he just write 'from Christian'? And what's with the weird helicopter balloon?"

"*Charlie Tango.*"

"What?"

"Christian flew me to Seattle in his helicopter." I shrug.

Kate stares at me openmouthed. I have to say I love these occasions—Katherine Kavanagh, silent and floored—they are so rare. I take a brief and luxurious moment to enjoy it.

"Yep, he has a helicopter, which he flew himself," I state proudly.

"Of course the obscenely rich bastard has a helicopter. Why didn't you tell me?" Kate looks accusingly at me, but she's smiling, shaking her head in disbelief.

"I've had a lot on my mind lately."

She frowns.

"Are you going to be okay while I'm away?"

"Of course," I answer reassuringly. *New city, no job . . . nut-job boyfriend.*

"Did you give him our address?

"No, but stalking is one of his specialties," I muse matter-of-factly.

Kate's brow knits further.

"Somehow I'm not surprised. He worries me, Ana. At least it's a good champagne and it's chilled."

Of course. Only Christian would send chilled champagne, or get his secretary to do it . . . or maybe Taylor. We open it there and then and find our teacups—they were the last items to be packed.

"Bollinger Grande Année Rosé 1999, an excellent vintage." I grin at Kate, and we clink teacups.

I WAKE EARLY TO a gray Sunday morning after a surprisingly refreshing night's sleep and lie awake staring at my crates. *You should really be unpacking these,* my subconscious nags, pursing her harpy lips together. *No . . . today's the day.* My inner goddess is beside herself, hopping from foot to foot. Anticipation hangs heavy and portentous over my head like a dark tropical storm cloud. Butterflies flood my belly—as well as a darker, carnal, captivating ache as I try to imagine what he will do to me . . . and of course, I have to sign that damned contract, or do I? I hear the ping of incoming mail from the mean machine on the floor beside my bed.

From: Christian Grey
Subject: My Life in Numbers
Date: May 29 2011 08:04
To: Anastasia Steele

If you drive you'll need this access code for the underground garage at Escala: 146963.
Park in bay five—it's one of mine.

Code for the elevator: 1880.

Christian Grey
CEO, Grey Enterprises Holdings, Inc.

From: Anastasia Steele
Subject: An Excellent Vintage
Date: May 29 2011 08:08
To: Christian Grey

Yes, Sir. Understood.
Thank you for the champagne and the blow-up *Charlie Tango,* which is now tied to my bed.

Ana

From: Christian Grey
Subject: Envy
Date: May 29 2011 08:11
To: Anastasia Steele

You're welcome.
Don't be late.

Lucky *Charlie Tango.*

Christian Grey
CEO, Grey Enterprises Holdings, Inc.

I roll my eyes at his bossiness, but his last line makes me smile. I head for the bathroom, wondering if Elliot made it back last night and trying hard to rein in my nerves.

I CAN DRIVE THE Audi in high heels! At 12:55 p.m. precisely, I pull into the garage at Escala and park in bay five. How many bays does he own? The Audi SUV and R8 are there, along with two smaller Audi SUVs . . . *hmm.* I check my seldom-worn mascara in the light-up vanity mirror on my visor. Didn't have one of these in the Beetle.

Go girl! My inner goddess has her pom-poms in hand—she's in cheerleading mode. In the infinity mirrors of the elevator, I check out my plum dress—well, Kate's plum dress. The last time I wore this, he wanted to peel it off me. My body clenches at the thought. The feeling is just exquisite, and I catch my breath. I'm wearing the underwear that Taylor bought for me. I flush at the thought of his buzz cut roaming the aisles of Agent Provocateur or wherever he bought it. The doors open, and I'm facing the foyer of apartment number one.

Taylor stands at the double doors as I step out of the elevator.

"Good afternoon, Miss Steele," he says.

"Oh, please, call me Ana."

"Ana." He smiles. "Mr. Grey is expecting you."

I bet he is.

Christian is seated on his living room couch reading the Sunday papers. He glances up as Taylor directs me into the living area. The room is exactly as I remember it—it's been a whole week since I've been here, but it feels so much longer. Christian looks cool and calm—actually, he looks heavenly. He's in a loose white linen shirt and jeans, no shoes or socks. His hair is tousled and unkempt, and his eyes twinkle wickedly. He rises and strolls toward me, an amused appraising smile on his beautiful sculptured lips.

I stand immobilized at the entrance of the room, paralyzed by his beauty and the sweet anticipation of what's to come. The familiar charge between us is there, sparking slowly in my belly, drawing me to him.

"Hmm . . . that dress," he murmurs approvingly as he gazes down at me. "Welcome back, Miss Steele," he whispers and, clasping my chin, he leans down and proffers a gentle, light kiss on my lips. The touch of his lips to mine reverberates throughout my body. My breath hitches.

"Hi," I whisper as I flush.

"You're on time. I like punctual. Come." He takes my hand and leads me to the couch. "I wanted to show you something," he says as we sit. He hands me the *Seattle Times*. On page eight, there's a photograph of the two of us together at the graduation ceremony. *Holy crap*. I'm in the paper. I check the caption.

Christian Grey and friend at the graduation ceremony at WSU Vancouver.

I laugh. "So I'm your 'friend' now."

"So it would appear. And it's in the newspaper, so it must be true." He smirks.

Sitting beside me, his whole body is turned toward me, one of his legs tucked under the other. Reaching over, he tucks my hair behind my ear with his long index finger. My body comes alive at his touch, waiting and needful.

"So, Anastasia, you have a much better idea of what I'm about since you were last here."

"Yes." *Where's he going with this?*

"And yet you've returned."

I nod shyly, and his eyes blaze. He shakes his head as if he's struggling with the idea.

"Have you eaten?" he asks out of the blue.

Shit.

"No."

"Are you hungry?" He's really trying not to look annoyed.

"Not for food," I whisper, and his nostrils flare in reaction.

He leans forward and whispers in my ear. "You are as eager as ever, Miss Steele, and just to let you in on a little secret, so am I. But Dr. Greene is due here shortly." He sits up. "I wish you'd eat," he scolds me mildly. My heated blood cools. Holy cow—the doctor. I'd forgotten.

"What can you tell me about Dr. Greene?" I ask to distract us both.

"She's the best ob-gyn in Seattle. What more can I say?" He shrugs.

"I thought I was seeing your doctor, and don't tell me you're really a woman, because I won't believe you."

He gives me a don't-be-ridiculous look.

"I think it's more appropriate that you see a specialist. Don't you?" he says mildly.

I nod. Holy Moses, if she's the best ob-gyn, he's scheduled her to see me on a Sunday—at lunchtime! I cannot begin to imagine how much that costs. Christian frowns suddenly as if recalling something unpleasant.

"Anastasia, my mother would like you to come to dinner this evening. I believe Elliot is asking Kate, too. I don't know how you feel about that. It will be odd for me to introduce you to my family."

Odd? Why?

"Are you ashamed of me?" I can't keep the wounded hurt out of my voice.

"Of course not." He rolls his eyes.

"Why is it odd?"

"Because I've never done it before."

"Why are you allowed to roll your eyes, and I'm not?"

He blinks at me. "I wasn't aware that I was."

"Neither am I, usually," I snap.

Christian glares at me, speechless. Taylor appears at the doorway.

"Dr. Greene is here, sir."

"Show her up to Miss Steele's room."

Miss Steele's room!

"Ready for some contraception?" he asks as he stands and holds out his hand to me.

"You're not going to come as well, are you?" I gasp, shocked.

He laughs. "I'd pay very good money to watch, believe me, Anastasia, but I don't think the good doctor would approve."

I take his hand, and he pulls me up into his arms and kisses me deeply. I clutch his arms, taken by surprise. His hand is in my hair, holding my head, and he pulls me against him, his forehead against mine.

"I'm so glad you're here," he whispers. "I can't wait to get you naked."

CHAPTER EIGHTEEN

Dr. Greene is tall, blond, and immaculate, dressed in a royal-blue suit. I'm reminded of the women who work in Christian's office. She's like an identikit model—another Stepford blonde. Her long hair is swept up in an elegant chignon. She must be in her early forties.

"Mr. Grey." She shakes Christian's outstretched hand.

"Thank you for coming on such short notice," Christian says.

"Thank you for making it worth my while, Mr. Grey. Miss Steele." She smiles, her eyes cool and assessing.

We shake hands, and I know she's one of those women who doesn't tolerate fools gladly. Like Kate. I like her immediately. She gives Christian a pointed stare, and after an awkward beat, he takes his cue.

"I'll be downstairs," he mutters, and he leaves what will be my bedroom.

"Well, Miss Steele. Mr. Grey is paying me a small fortune to attend to you. What can I do for you?"

AFTER A THOROUGH EXAMINATION and lengthy discussion, Dr. Greene and I decide on the mini pill. She writes me a prepaid prescription and instructs me to pick the pills up tomorrow. I love her no-nonsense attitude—she has lectured me until she's as blue as her dress about taking it at the same time every day. And I can tell she's burning with curiosity about my so-called relationship with Mr. Grey. I don't give her any details. Somehow I don't think she'd look so calm and collected if she'd seen his Red Room of Pain. I flush as we pass its closed door and head back downstairs to the art gallery that is Christian's living room.

Christian is reading, seated on his couch. A breathtaking aria is playing on the music system, swirling around him, cocooning him, filling the room with a sweet, soulful song. For a moment, he looks serene. He turns and glances at us when we enter and smiles warmly at me.

"Are you done?" he asks as if he's genuinely interested. He points the remote at a sleek white box beneath the fireplace that houses his iPod, and the exquisite melody fades but continues in the background. Standing, he strolls toward us.

"Yes, Mr. Grey. Look after her; she's a beautiful, bright young woman."

Christian is taken aback—as am I. What an inappropriate thing for a doctor to say. Is she giving him some kind of not-so-subtle warning? Christian recovers himself.

"I fully intend to," he mutters, bemused.

Gazing at him, I shrug, embarrassed.

"I'll send you my bill," she says crisply as she shakes his hand.

"Good day, and good luck to you, Ana." She smiles, her eyes crinkling, as we shake hands.

Taylor appears from nowhere to escort her through the double doors and out to the elevator. How does he do that? Where does he lurk?

"How was that?" Christian asks.

"Fine, thank you. She said that I had to abstain from all sexual activity for the next four weeks."

Christian's mouth drops open in shock, and I cannot keep a straight face any longer and grin at him like an idiot.

"Gotcha!"

He narrows his eyes, and I immediately stop laughing. In fact, he looks rather forbidding. *Oh, shit.* My subconscious quails in the corner as all the blood drains from my face, and I imagine him putting me across his knee again.

"Gotcha!" he says, and smirks. He grabs me around my waist and pulls me up against him. "You are incorrigible, Miss Steele," he murmurs, staring down into my eyes as he weaves his fingers into my hair, holding me firmly in place. He kisses me, hard, and I cling on to his muscular arms for support.

"As much as I'd like to take you here and now, you need to eat and so do I. I don't want you passing out on me later," he murmurs against my lips.

"Is that all you want me for—my body?" I whisper.

"That and your smart mouth," he breathes.

He kisses me again passionately, and then abruptly releases me, taking my hand and leading me to the kitchen. I am reeling. One minute we're joking and the next . . . I fan my heated face. He's just sex on legs, and now I have to recover my equilibrium and eat something. The aria is still playing in the background.

"What's the music?"

"'Villa Lobos,' an aria from *Bachianas Brasileiras*. Good, isn't it?"

"Yes," I murmur in total agreement.

The breakfast bar is laid for two. Christian takes a salad bowl from the fridge.

"Chicken caesar salad okay with you?"

Oh, thank heavens, nothing too heavy.

"Yes, fine, thank you."

I watch as he moves gracefully through his kitchen. He's so at ease with his body on one level, but then he doesn't like to be touched . . . so maybe deep down he isn't. No man is an island, I muse—except perhaps Christian Grey.

"What are you thinking?" he asks, pulling me from my reverie. I flush.

"I was just watching the way you move."

He raises an eyebrow, amused.

"And?" he says dryly.

I flush some more.

"You're very graceful."

"Why thank you, Miss Steele," he murmurs. He sits down beside me, holding a bottle of wine. "Chablis?"

"Please."

"Help yourself to salad," he says, his voice soft. "Tell me—what method did you opt for?"

I am momentarily thrown by his question, when I realize he's talking about Dr. Greene's visit.

"Mini pill."

He frowns.

"And will you remember to take it regularly, at the right time, every day?"

Jeez . . . of course I will. How does he know? I blush at the thought—probably from one or more of the fifteen.

"I'm sure you'll remind me," I murmur dryly.

He glances at me with amused condescension.

"I'll put an alarm on my calendar." He smirks. "Eat."

The chicken caesar is delicious. To my surprise, I'm famished, and for the first time since I've been with him, I finish my meal before he does. The wine is crisp, clean, and fruity.

"Eager as ever, Miss Steele?" he smiles down at my empty plate.

I look at him from beneath my lashes.

"Yes," I whisper.

His breath hitches. And as he stares down at me, the atmosphere between us slowly shifting, evolving . . . charging. His look goes from dark to smoldering, taking me with him. He stands, closing the distance between us, and tugs me off my barstool into his arms.

"Do you want to do this?" he breathes, looking down at me intently.

"I haven't signed anything."

"I know—but I'm breaking all the rules these days."

"Are you going to hit me?"

"Yes, but it won't be to hurt you. I don't want to punish you right now. If you'd caught me yesterday evening, well, that would have been a different story."

Holy cow. He *wants* to hurt me . . . how do I deal with this? I can't hide the horror on my face.

"Don't let anyone try to convince you otherwise, Anastasia. One of the reasons people like me do this is because we either like to give or receive pain. It's very simple. You don't, so I spent a great deal of time yesterday thinking about that."

He pulls me against him, and his erection presses into my belly. I should run, but I can't. I'm drawn to him on some deep, elemental level that I can't begin to understand.

"Did you reach any conclusions?" I whisper.

"No, and right now, I just want to tie you up and fuck you senseless. Are you ready for that?"

"Yes," I breathe as everything in my body tightens at once . . . *wow.*

"Good. Come." He takes my hand and, leaving all the dirty dishes on the breakfast bar, we head upstairs.

My heart starts pounding. This is it. I'm really going to do this. My inner goddess is spinning like a world-class ballerina, pirouette after pirouette. He opens the door to his playroom, standing back for me to walk through, and I am once more in the Red Room of Pain.

It's the same, the smell of leather, citrus-scented polish, and dark wood, all very sensual. My blood is running heated and scared through my system—adrenaline mixed with lust and longing. It's a heady, potent cocktail. Christian's stance has changed completely, subtly altered, harder and meaner. He gazes down at me and his eyes are heated, lustful . . . hypnotic.

"When you're in here, you are completely mine," he breathes, each word slow and measured. "To do with as I see fit. Do you understand?"

His gaze is so intense. I nod, my mouth dry, my heart feeling as if it will jump out of my chest.

"Take your shoes off," he orders softly.

I swallow, and rather clumsily, I take them off. He bends and picks them up and deposits them beside the door.

"Good. Don't hesitate when I ask you to do something. Now I'm going to peel you out of this dress. Something I've wanted to do for a few days, if I recall. I want you to be comfortable with your body, Anastasia. You have a beautiful body, and I like to look at it. It is a joy to behold. In fact, I could gaze at you all day, and I want you unembarrassed and unashamed of your nakedness. Do you understand?"

"Yes."

"Yes, what?" He leans over me, glaring.

"Yes, Sir."

"Do you mean that?" he snaps.

"Yes, Sir."

"Good. Lift your arms up over your head."

I do as instructed, and he reaches down and grabs the hem. Slowly, he pulls my dress up over my thighs, my hips, my belly, my breasts, my shoulders, and up over my head. He stands back to examine me and absentmindedly folds my dress, not taking his eyes off me. He places it on the large chest beside the door. Reaching up, he pulls at my chin, his touch searing me.

"You're biting your lip," he breathes. "You know what that does to me," he adds darkly. "Turn around."

I turn immediately, no hesitation. He unclasps my bra and then, taking both straps, he slowly pulls it down my arms, brushing my skin with his fingers and the tip of his thumbnails as he slides my bra off. His touch sends shivers down my spine, waking every nerve ending in my body. He's standing behind me, so close that I feel the heat radiating from him, warming me, warming me all over. He pulls my hair so it's all hanging down my back, grasps a handful at my nape, and angles my head to one side. He runs his nose down my exposed neck, inhaling all the way, then back up to my ear. The muscles in my belly clench, carnal and wanting. Jeez, he's hardly touched me, and I want him.

"You smell as divine as ever, Anastasia," he whispers as he places a soft kiss beneath my ear.

I moan.

"Quiet," he breathes. "Don't make a sound."

Pulling my hair behind me, to my surprise, he starts braiding it in one large braid, his fingers fast and deft. He ties it with an unseen hair tie when he's finished and gives it a quick tug so I'm forced back against him.

"I like your hair braided in here," he whispers.

Hmm . . . why?

He releases my hair.

"Turn around," he orders.

I do as I'm bid, my breathing shallow, fear and longing mixed together. It's an intoxicating mix.

"When I tell you to come in here, this is how you will dress. Just in your panties. Do you understand?"

"Yes."

"Yes, what?" He glowers at me.

"Yes, Sir."

A trace of a smile lifts the corner of his mouth.

"Good girl." His eyes burn into mine. "When I tell you to come in here, I expect you to kneel over there." He points to a spot beside the door. "Do it now."

I blink, processing his words, then turn and rather clumsily kneel as directed.

"You can sit back on your heels."

I sit back.

"Place your hands and forearms flat on your thighs. Good. Now part your knees. Wider. Wider. Perfect. Look down at the floor."

He walks over to me, and I can see his feet and shins in my field of vision. Naked feet. I should be taking notes if he wants me to remember. He reaches down and grasps my braid again, then pulls my head back so I am looking up at him. It's only just not painful.

"Will you remember this position, Anastasia?"

"Yes, Sir."

"Good. Stay here, don't move." He leaves the room.

I'm on my knees, waiting. Where's he gone? What is he going to do to me? Time shifts. I have no idea how long he leaves me like this . . . a few minutes, five, ten? My breathing becomes shallower; the anticipation is devouring me from the inside out.

And suddenly he's back—and all at once I'm calmer and more excited in the same breath. *Could I be more excited?* I can see his feet. He's changed his jeans. These are older, ripped, soft, and over-washed. Holy cow. These jeans are hot. He shuts the door and hangs something on the back.

"Good girl, Anastasia. You look lovely like that. Well done. Stand up."

I stand, but I keep my face down.

"You may look at me."

I peek up at him, and he's staring at me intently, assessing, but his eyes soften. He's taken off his shirt. Oh my . . . I want to touch him. The top button of his jeans is undone.

"I'm going to chain you now, Anastasia. Give me your right hand."

I give him my hand. He turns it palm up, and before I know it, he swats the center with a riding crop I hadn't noticed is in his right hand. It happens so quickly that the surprise hardly registers. Even more astonishing—it doesn't hurt. Well, not much, just a slight ringing sting.

"How does that feel?" he asks.

I blink at him, confused.

"Answer me."

"Okay." I frown.

"Don't frown."

I blink and try for impassive. I succeed.

"Did that hurt?"

"No."

"This is not going to hurt. Do you understand?"

"Yes." My voice is uncertain. *Is it really not going to hurt?*

"I mean it," he says.

Jeez, my breathing is so shallow. Does he know what I'm thinking? He shows me the crop. It's brown plaited leather. My eyes jerk up to meet his, and they're alight with fire and a trace of amusement.

"We aim to please, Miss Steele," he murmurs. "Come." He takes my elbow and moves me to beneath the grid. He reaches up and takes down some shackles with black leather cuffs.

"This grid is designed so the shackles move across the grid."

I glance up. *Holy shit*—it's like a subway map.

"We're going to start here, but I want to fuck you standing up. So we'll end up by the wall over there." He points with the riding crop to where the large wooden X is on the wall.

"Put your hands above your head."

I oblige immediately, feeling like I'm exiting my body—a casual observer of events as they unfold around me. This is beyond fascinating, beyond erotic. It's singularly the most exciting and scary thing I've ever done. I'm entrusting myself to a beautiful man who, by his own admission, is fifty shades of fucked up. I suppress the brief thrill of fear. Kate and Elliot, they know I'm here.

He stands very close as he fastens the cuffs. I'm staring at his chest. His proximity is heavenly. He smells of body wash and Christian, an inebriating mix, and that drags me back into the now. I want to run my nose and tongue through that smattering of chest hair. I could just lean forward . . .

He steps back and gazes at me, his expression hooded, salacious, carnal, and I am helpless, my hands tied, but just looking at his lovely face, reading his need and longing for me, I can feel the dampness between my legs. He walks slowly around me.

"You look mighty fine trussed up like this, Miss Steele. And your smart mouth quiet for now. I like that."

Standing in front of me again, he hooks his fingers into my panties and, at a most unhurried pace, peels them down my legs, stripping me agonizingly slowly, so that he ends up kneeling in front of me. Not taking his eyes off mine, he scrunches my panties in his hand, holds them up to his nose, and inhales deeply. *Holy fuck. Did he just do that?* He grins wickedly at me and tucks them into the pocket of his jeans.

Uncoiling from the floor, rising lazily, like a jungle cat, he points the end of the riding crop at my navel, leisurely circling it—tantalizing me. At the touch of the leather, I quiver and gasp. He walks around me again, trailing the crop around the middle of my body. On his second circuit, he suddenly flicks the crop, and it hits me underneath my behind . . . against my sex. I cry out in surprise as all my nerve endings stand to attention. I pull against the restraints. The shock runs through me, and it's the sweetest, strangest, hedonistic feeling.

"Quiet," he whispers as he walks around me again, the crop slightly higher around the middle of my body. This time when he flicks it against me in the same place, I'm anticipating it. My body convulses at the sweet, stinging bite.

As he makes his way around me, he flicks again, this time hitting my nipple, and I throw my head back as my nerve endings sing. He hits the other . . . a brief, swift, sweet chastisement. My nipples harden and elongate from the assault, and I moan loudly, pulling on my leather cuffs.

"Does that feel good?" he breathes.

"Yes."

He hits me again across the buttocks. The crop stings this time.

"Yes, what?"

"Yes, Sir," I whimper.

He comes to a stop . . . but I can no longer see him. My eyes are closed as I try to absorb the myriad sensations coursing through my body. Very slowly, he rains small, biting licks of the crop down my belly, heading south. I know where this is leading, and I try to psyche myself up for it—but when he hits my clitoris, I cry out loudly.

"Oh . . . please!" I groan.

"Quiet," he orders, and he hits me again on my behind.

I did not expect this to be like this . . . I am lost. Lost in a sea of sensation. And suddenly, he's dragging the crop against my sex, through my pubic hair, down to the entrance of my vagina.

"See how wet you are for this, Anastasia. Open your eyes and your mouth."

I do as I'm told, completely seduced. He pushes the tip of the crop into my mouth, like my dream. *Holy shit.*

"See how you taste. Suck. Suck hard, baby."

My mouth closes around the crop as my eyes lock on his. I can taste the rich leather and the saltiness of my arousal. His eyes are blazing. He's in his element.

He pulls the tip from my mouth, and he stands forward and grabs me and kisses me hard, his tongue invading my mouth. Wrapping his arms around me, he pulls me against him. His chest crushes mine, and I itch to touch, but I can't, my hands useless above me.

"Oh, Anastasia, you taste mighty fine," he breathes. "Shall I make you come?"

"Please," I beg.

The crop bites my buttock. *Ow!*

"Please, what?"

"Please, Sir," I whimper.

He smiles at me, triumphant.

"With this?" He holds the crop up so I can see it.

"Yes, Sir."

"Are you sure?" He looks sternly at me.

"Yes, please, Sir."

"Close your eyes."

I shut the room out, him out . . . the crop out. He starts small, biting licks of the crop against my belly once more. Moving down, soft small licks against my clitoris, once, twice, three times, again and again, until finally, that's it—I can take no more—and I come, gloriously, loudly, sagging weakly. His arms curl around me as my legs turn to jelly. I dissolve in his embrace, my head against his chest, and I'm mewling and whimpering as the aftershocks of my orgasm consume me. He lifts me, and suddenly we're moving, my arms still tethered above my head, and I can feel the cool wood of the polished cross at my back, and he's popping the buttons on his jeans. He puts me down against the cross briefly while he slides on a condom, and then his hands wrap around my thighs as he lifts me again.

"Lift your legs, baby, wrap them around me."

I feel so weak, but I do as he asks as he wraps my legs around his hips and positions himself beneath me. With one thrust, he's inside me, and I cry out again, listening to his muffled moan at my ear. My arms are resting on his shoulders as he thrusts into me. Jeez, it's deep this way. He thrusts again and again, his face at my neck, his harsh breathing at my throat. I feel the build up again. Jeez, no . . . not again . . . I don't think my body will withstand another Earth-shattering moment. But I have no choice . . . and with an inevitability that's becoming familiar, I let go and come again, and it's sweet and agonizing and intense. I lose all sense of self. Christian follows, shouting his release through clenched teeth and holding me hard and close as he does.

He pulls out of me swiftly and sets me down against the cross, his body supporting mine. Unbuckling the cuffs, he frees my hands, and we both sink to the floor. He pulls me into his lap, cradling me, and I lean my head against his chest. If I had the strength, I'd touch him, but I don't. Belatedly, I realize he's still wearing his jeans.

"Well done, baby," he murmurs. "Did that hurt?"

"No," I breathe. I can barely keep my eyes open. *Why am I so tired?*

"Did you expect it to?" he whispers as he holds me close, his fingers pushing some escaped tendrils of hair off my face.

"Yes."

"You see, most of your fear is in your head, Anastasia." He pauses. "Would you do it again?"

I think for a moment as fatigue clouds my brain . . . *Again?*

"Yes." My voice is so soft.

He hugs me tightly.

"Good. So would I," he murmurs, then leans down and softly kisses the top of my head.

"And I haven't finished with you yet."

Not finished with me yet. Holy Moses. There's no way I can do any more. I am utterly spent and fighting an overwhelming desire to sleep. I'm leaning against his chest, my eyes are closed, and he's wrapped around me—arms and legs—and I feel . . . safe, and oh so comfortable. Will he let me sleep, perchance to dream? My mouth quirks up at the silly thought, and turning my face into Christian's chest, I inhale his unique scent and nuzzle him, but immediately he tenses . . . oh crap. I open my eyes and glance up at him. He's staring down at me.

"Don't," he breathes in warning.

I flush and look back at his chest in longing. I want to run my tongue through the hair, kiss him, and for the first time, I notice he has a few random and faint small, round scars dotted around his chest. *Chicken pox? Measles?* I think absently.

"Kneel by the door," he orders as he sits back, putting his hands on his knees, effectively releasing me. No longer warm, the temperature of his voice has dropped several degrees.

I stumble clumsily up into a standing position and scoot over to the door and kneel as instructed. I'm shaky and very, very tired, monumentally confused. Who would have thought I could have found such gratification in this room. Who could have thought it would be so *exhausting*? My limbs are deliciously heavy, sated. My inner goddess has a DO NOT DISTURB sign on the outside of her room.

Christian is moving about in the periphery of my vision. My eyes start to droop.

"Boring you, am I, Miss Steele?"

I jump awake, and Christian is standing in front of me, his arms crossed, glaring down at me. Oh, shit, caught napping—this is not going to be good. His eyes soften as I gaze up at him.

"Stand up," he orders.

I climb warily to my feet. He stares at me and his mouth quirks up.

"You're shattered, aren't you?"

I nod shyly, flushing.

"Stamina, Miss Steele." He narrows his eyes at me. "I haven't had my fill of you yet. Hold out your hands in front as if you're praying."

I blink at him. *Praying! Praying for you to go easy on me.* I do as I'm told. He takes a cable tie and fastens it around my wrists, tightening the plastic. Holy hell. My eyes fly to his.

"Look familiar?" he asks, unable to conceal his smile.

Jeez . . . the plastic cable ties. *Restocking* at Clayton's! It all becomes clear. I gape up at him as adrenaline spikes though my body anew. Okay—that's got my attention—I'm awake now.

"I have scissors here." He holds them up for me to see. "I can cut you out of this in a moment."

I try to pull my wrists apart, testing my bonds, and as I do, the plastic bites into my flesh. It's sore, but if I relax my wrists they're fine—the tie is not cutting into my skin.

"Come." He takes my hands and leads me over to the four-poster bed. I notice now that it has dark red sheets on it and a shackle at each corner.

He leans down and whispers in my ear, "I want more—much, much more."

And my heartbeat starts pounding again. *Oh boy.*

"But I'll make this quick. You're tired. Hold on to the post," he says.

I frown. *Not on the bed then?* I find I can part my hands as I grasp the ornately carved wooden post.

"Lower," he orders. "Good. Don't let go. If you do, I'll spank you. Understand?"

"Yes, Sir."

"Good."

He stands behind me and grasps my hips, and then quickly lifts me backward so I'm bending forward, holding the post.

"Don't let go, Anastasia," he warns. "I'm going to fuck you hard from behind. Hold the post to support your weight. Understand?"

"Yes."

He smacks me across my behind with his hand. *Ow . . .* It stings.

"Yes, Sir," I mutter quickly.

"Part your legs." He puts his leg between mine, and holding my hips, he pushes my right leg to the side.

"That's better. After this, I'll let you sleep."

Sleep? I'm panting. I'm not thinking of sleep now. He reaches up and gently strokes my back.

"You have such beautiful skin, Anastasia," he breathes as he bends down and kisses me along my spine, gentle featherlight kisses. At the same time, his hands move around to my front, palming my breasts, and as he does this he traps my nipples between his fingers and tugs them gently.

I stifle my moan as I feel my whole body respond, coming alive once more for him.

He gently bites and sucks me at my waist, tugging my nipples, and my hands tighten on the exquisitely carved post. His hands drop away, and I hear the now familiar tear of foil, and he kicks off his jeans.

"You have such a captivating, sexy ass, Anastasia Steele. What I'd like to do to it." His hands smooth and shape each of my buttocks, then his fingers glide down, and he slips two fingers inside me.

"So wet. You never disappoint, Miss Steele," he whispers, and I hear the wonder in his voice. "Hold tight . . . this is going to be quick, baby."

He grabs my hips and positions himself, and I brace myself for his assault. But he reaches over me and grabs my braid near the end and winds it around his wrist to my nape, holding my head in place. Very slowly he eases into me, pulling my hair at the same time . . . *Oh, the fullness.* He eases out of me slowly, and his other hand grabs my hip, holding tight, and then he slams into me, jolting me forward.

"Hold on, Anastasia!" he shouts through clenched teeth.

I grip the post harder and push back against him as he continues his merciless onslaught, again and again, his fingers digging into my hip. My arms are aching, my legs feel uncertain, my scalp is getting sore from his tugging my hair . . . and I can feel a gathering deep inside me. Oh no . . . and for the first time, I fear my orgasm . . . if I come . . . I'll collapse. Christian continues to move roughly against me, in me, his breathing harsh, moaning, groaning. My body is responding . . . *how?* I feel a quickening. But suddenly, Christian stills, slamming really deep.

"Come on, Ana, give it to me," he groans, and my name on his lips sends me over the edge as I become all body and spiraling sensation and sweet, sweet release, and then completely and utterly mindless.

When sense returns, I'm lying on him. He's on the floor, and I'm lying on top of him, my back to his front, and I'm staring at the ceiling, all postcoital, glowing, shattered. *Oh . . . the carabiners,* I think absently—I'd forgotten about those. Christian nuzzles my ear.

"Hold up your hands," he says softly.

My arms feel like they're made of lead, but I hold them up. He wields the scissors and passes one blade under the plastic.

"I declare this Ana open," he breathes, and cuts the plastic.

I giggle and rub my wrists as they're freed. I feel his grin.

"That is such a lovely sound," he says wistfully. He sits suddenly, taking me with him so that I'm once more sitting in his lap.

"That's my fault," he says, and shifts me so that he can rub my shoulders and arms. Gently he massages some life back into my limbs.

What?

I glance up at him behind me, trying to understand what he means.

"That you don't giggle more often."

"I'm not a great giggler," I mumble sleepily.

"Oh, but when it happens, Miss Steele, 'tis a wonder and joy to behold."

"Very flowery, Mr. Grey," I mutter, trying to keep my eyes open.

His eyes soften, and he smiles.

"I'd say you're thoroughly fucked and in need of sleep."

"That wasn't flowery at all," I grumble playfully.

He grins and gently lifts me off him and stands, gloriously naked. I wish momentarily that I were more awake to really appreciate him. Picking up his jeans, he slides them back on, commando.

"Don't want to frighten Taylor, or Mrs. Jones for that matter," he mutters.

Hmm . . . they must know what a kinky bastard he is. The thought preoccupies me.

He stoops to help me to my feet and leads me to the door, on the back of which hangs a gray waffle robe. He patiently dresses me as if I'm a small child. I don't have the strength to lift my arms. When I'm covered and respectable, he leans down and kisses me gently, his mouth quirks up in a smile.

"Bed," he says.

Oh . . . no . . .

"For sleep," he adds reassuringly when he sees my expression.

Suddenly, he scoops me up and carries me curled against his chest to the room down the corridor where earlier today Dr. Greene examined me. My head drops against his chest. I am exhausted. I don't remember ever being this tired. Pulling back the duvet, he lays me down and, even more surprisingly, climbs in beside me and holds me close.

"Sleep now, gorgeous girl," he whispers, and he kisses my hair.

And before I can make a facetious comment, I'm asleep.

CHAPTER NINETEEN

Soft lips brush across my temple, leaving sweet tender kisses in their wake, and part of me wants to turn and respond, but mostly I want to stay asleep. I moan and burrow into my pillow.

"Anastasia, wake up." Christian's voice is soft, cajoling.

"No," I moan.

"We have to leave in half an hour for dinner at my parents'." He's amused.

I open my eyes reluctantly. It's dusk outside. Christian is leaning over, gazing at me intently.

"Come on, sleepyhead. Get up." He stoops down and kisses me again.

"I've brought you a drink. I'll be downstairs. Don't go back to sleep, or you'll be in trouble," he threatens, but his tone is mild. He kisses me briefly and exits, leaving me blinking sleep from my eyes in the cool, stark room.

I'm refreshed but suddenly nervous. Holy cow, I am meeting his folks! He's just worked me over with a riding crop and trussed me up using a cable tie which I sold him, for heaven's sake—and I'm going to meet his parents. It will be Kate's first time meeting them, too—at least she'll be there for support. I roll my shoulders. They're stiff. His demands for a personal trainer don't seem so outlandish now. In fact, it's mandatory if I am to have any hope of keeping up with him.

I climb slowly out of bed and note that my dress is hanging outside the wardrobe and my bra is on the chair. Where are my panties? I check beneath the chair. Nothing. Then I remember—he squirreled them away in the pocket of his jeans. I flush at the memory, after he . . . I can't even bring myself to think about it, he was so—barbarous. I frown. *Why hasn't he given me back my panties?*

I steal into the bathroom, bewildered by my lack of underwear. While drying myself after my enjoyable but far too brief shower, I realize he's done this on purpose. He wants me to be embarrassed and ask for my panties back, and he'll either say yes or no. My inner goddess grins at me. *Hell . . . two can play that particular game.* Resolving there and then not to ask him for them and not give him that satisfaction, I shall go meet his parents sans culottes. *Anastasia Steele!* my subconscious chides me, but I don't want to listen to her—I almost hug myself with glee because I know this will drive him crazy.

Back in the bedroom, I put on my bra, slip into my dress, and climb into my shoes. I remove the braid and hastily brush out my hair, then glance down at the drink he's left. It's pale pink. What's this? Cranberry and sparkling water. Hmm . . . it tastes delicious and quenches my thirst.

Dashing back into the bathroom, I check myself in the mirror: eyes bright, cheeks slightly flushed, slightly smug look because of my panty plan, and I head downstairs. Fifteen minutes. Not bad, Ana.

Christian is standing by the panoramic window, wearing the grey flannel pants that I love, the ones that hang in that unbelievably sexy way off his hips, and, of course, a white linen shirt. Doesn't he have any other colors? Frank Sinatra sings softly over the surround-sound speakers.

Christian turns and smiles as I enter. He looks at me expectantly.

"Hi," I say softly, and my sphinxlike smile meets his.

"Hi," he says. "How are you feeling?" His eyes are alight with amusement.

"Good, thanks. You?"

"I feel mighty fine, Miss Steele."

He is so waiting for me to say something.

"Frank. I never figured you for a Sinatra fan."

He raises his eyebrows at me, his look speculative.

"Eclectic taste, Miss Steele," he murmurs, and he paces toward me like a panther until he's standing in front of me. His gaze so intense it takes my breath away.

Frank starts crooning . . . an old song, one of Ray's favorites, "*Witchcraft*." Christian leisurely traces his fingertips down my cheek, and I feel it all the way down *there*.

"Dance with me," he murmurs, his voice husky.

Taking the remote out of his pocket, he turns up the volume and holds his hand out to me, his gray gaze full of promise and longing and humor. He is totally beguiling, and I'm bewitched. I place my hand in his. He grins lazily down at me and pulls me into his embrace, his arm curling around my waist.

I put my free hand on his shoulder and grin up at him, caught in his infectious, playful mood. He sways once, then we're off. Boy, can he dance. We cover the floor, from the window to the kitchen and back again, whirling and turning in time to the music. And he makes it so effortless for me to follow.

We glide around the dining table, over to the piano, and backward and forward in front of the glass wall, Seattle twinkling outside, a dark and magical mural to our dance. I can't help my carefree laugh. He grins down at me as the song comes to a close.

"There's no nicer witch than you," he murmurs, then kisses me sweetly. "Well, that's brought some color to your cheeks, Miss Steele. Thank you for the dance. Shall we go and meet my parents?"

"You're welcome, and yes, I can't wait to meet them," I answer breathlessly.

"Do you have everything you need?"

"Oh yes," I respond sweetly.

"Are you sure?"

I nod as nonchalantly as I can manage under his intense, amused scrutiny. His face splits into a huge grin, and he shakes his head.

"Okay. If that's the way you want to play it, Miss Steele."

He grabs my hand, collects his jacket, which is hanging on

one of the barstools, and leads me through the foyer to the elevator. Oh, the many faces of Christian Grey. *Will I ever be able to understand this mercurial man?*

I peek up at him in the elevator. He's enjoying a private joke, a trace of a smile flirting with his lovely mouth. I fear that it may be at my expense. *What was I thinking?* I'm going to see his parents, and I'm not wearing any underwear. My subconscious gives me an unhelpful I-told-you-so expression. In the relative safety of his apartment, it seemed like a fun, teasing idea. Now, I'm almost outside with *no panties*! He peers down at me, and it's there, the charge building between us. The amused look disappears from his face and his expression clouds, his eyes dark . . . *oh my.*

The elevator doors open on the ground floor. Christian shakes his head as if to clear his thoughts and gestures for me to exit before him in a most gentlemanly manner. *Who's he kidding?* He's no gentleman. He has my panties.

Taylor pulls up in the large Audi. Christian opens the rear door for me, and I climb inside as elegantly as I can, considering my state of wanton undress. I'm grateful that Kate's plum dress is so clingy and hangs to the top of my knees.

We speed up Interstate 5, both of us quiet, no doubt inhibited by Taylor's steady presence in the front. Christian's mood is almost tangible and seems to shift, the humor dissipating slowly as we head north. He's brooding, staring out the window, and I know he's slipping away from me. What is he thinking? I can't ask him. What can I say in front of Taylor?

"Where did you learn to dance?" I ask tentatively. He turns to gaze at me, his eyes unreadable beneath the intermittent light of the passing street lamps.

"Do you really want to know?" he replies softly.

My heart sinks, and now I don't because I can guess.

"Yes," I murmur reluctantly.

"Mrs. Robinson was fond of dancing."

Oh, my worst suspicions confirmed. She has taught him well,

and the thought depresses me—there's nothing I can teach him. I have no special skills. "She must have been a good teacher."

"She was."

My scalp prickles. Did she have the best of him? Before he became so closed? Or did she bring him out of himself? He has such a fun, playful side. I smile involuntarily as I recall being in his arms as he spun me around his living room, so unexpected, and he has my panties somewhere.

And then there's the Red Room of Pain. I rub my wrists reflexively—thin strips of plastic will do that to a girl. She taught him all that, too, or ruined him, depending on one's point of view. Or perhaps he would have found his way there anyway in spite of Mrs. R. I realize, in that moment, that I hate her. I hope that I never meet her because I will not be responsible for my actions if I do. I can't remember ever feeling this passionately about anyone, especially someone I've never met. Gazing unseeing out the window, I nurse my irrational anger and jealousy.

My mind drifts back to the afternoon. Given what I understand of his preferences, I think he's been easy on me. *Would I do it again?* I can't even pretend to put up an argument against that. Of course I would, if he asked me—as long as he didn't hurt me and if it's the only way to be with him.

That's the bottom line. I want to be with him. My inner goddess sighs with relief. I reach the conclusion that she rarely uses her brain to think but another vital part of her anatomy, and at the moment, it's a rather exposed part.

"Don't," he murmurs.

I frown and turn to look at him.

"Don't what?" I haven't touched him.

"Overthink things, Anastasia." Reaching out, he grasps my hand, draws it up to his lips, and kisses my knuckles gently. "I had a wonderful afternoon. Thank you."

And he's back with me again. I blink up at him and smile shyly. He's so confusing. I ask a question that's been bugging me.

"Why did you use a cable tie?"

He grins at me.

"It's quick, it's easy, and it's something different for you to feel and experience. I know they're quite brutal, and I do like that in a restraining device." He smiles at me mildly. "Very effective at keeping you in your place."

I flush and glance nervously at Taylor, who remains impassive, eyes on the road. *What am I supposed to say to that?* Christian shrugs innocently.

"All part of my world, Anastasia." He squeezes my hand and lets go, staring out the window again.

His world, indeed, and I want to belong in it, but on his terms? I just don't know. He hasn't mentioned that damned contract. My inner musings do nothing to cheer me. I stare out the window and the landscape has changed. We're crossing one of the bridges, surrounded by inky darkness. The somber night reflects my introspective mood, closing in, suffocating.

I glance briefly at Christian, and he's staring at me.

"Penny for your thoughts?" he asks.

I sigh and frown.

"That bad, huh?" he says.

"I wish I knew what you were thinking."

He smirks. "Ditto, baby," he says as Taylor whisks us into the night toward Bellevue.

IT IS JUST BEFORE eight when the Audi turns into the driveway of a colonial-style mansion. It's breathtaking, even down to the roses around the door. Picture-book perfect.

"Are you ready for this?" Christian asks as Taylor pulls up outside the impressive front door.

I nod, and he gives my hand another reassuring squeeze.

"First for me, too," he whispers, then smiles wickedly. "Bet you wish you were wearing your underwear right now," he teases.

I flush. I'd forgotten my missing panties. Fortunately, Taylor has climbed out of the car and is opening my door so he can't hear our exchange. I scowl at Christian, who grins broadly as I turn and climb out of the car.

Dr. Grace Trevelyan-Grey is on the doorstep waiting for us. She looks elegantly sophisticated in a pale blue silk dress. Behind her stands Mr. Grey, I presume, tall, blond, and as handsome in his own way as Christian.

"Anastasia, you've met my mother, Grace. This is my dad, Carrick."

"Mr. Grey, what a pleasure to meet you." I smile and shake his outstretched hand.

"The pleasure is all mine, Anastasia."

"Please, call me Ana."

His blue eyes are soft and gentle.

"Ana, how lovely to see you again." Grace wraps me in a warm hug. "Come in, my dear."

"Is she here?" I hear a screech from within the house. I glance nervously at Christian.

"That would be Mia, my little sister," he says almost irritably, but not quite.

There's an undercurrent of affection in his words, the way his voice grows softer and his eyes crinkle as he mentions her name. Christian obviously adores her. It's a revelation. And she comes barreling down the hall, raven haired, tall, and curvaceous. She's about my age.

"Anastasia! I've heard so much about you." She hugs me hard.

Holy cow. I can't help but smile at her boundless enthusiasm.

"Ana, please," I murmur as she drags me into the large vestibule. It's all dark wood floors and antique rugs with a sweeping staircase to the second floor.

"He's never brought a girl home before," says Mia, dark eyes bright with excitement.

I glimpse Christian rolling his eyes, and I raise an eyebrow at him. He narrows his eyes at me.

"Mia, calm down," Grace admonishes softly. "Hello, darling," she says as she kisses Christian on both cheeks. He smiles down at her warmly, and then shakes hands with his father.

We all turn and head into the living room. Mia has not let go of my hand. The room is spacious, tastefully furnished in creams, browns, and pale blues—comfortable, understated, and very stylish. Kate and Elliot are cuddled together on a couch, clutching champagne flutes. Kate bounces up to embrace me, and Mia finally releases my hand.

"Hi, Ana!" She beams. "Christian." She nods curtly to him.

"Kate." He is equally formal with her.

I frown at their exchange. Elliot grasps me in an all-embracing hug. What is this, Hug Ana Week? This dazzling display of affection—I'm just not used to it. Christian stands at my side, wrapping his arm around me. Placing his hand on my hip, he spreads out his fingers and pulls me close. Everyone is staring at us. It's unnerving.

"Drinks?" Mr. Grey seems to recover himself. "Prosecco?"

"Please," Christian and I speak in unison.

Oh . . . this is beyond weird. Mia claps her hands.

"You're even saying the same things. I'll get them." She scoots out of the room.

I flush scarlet, and seeing Kate sitting with Elliot, it occurs to me suddenly that the only reason Christian invited me was because Kate is here. Elliot probably freely and happily asked Kate to meet his parents. Christian was trapped—knowing that I would have found out via Kate. I frown at the thought. He's been forced into the invitation. The realization is bleak and depressing. My subconscious nods sagely, a you've-finally-worked-it-out-stupid look on her face.

"Dinner's almost ready," Grace says as she follows Mia out of the room.

Christian frowns as he gazes at me.

"Sit," he commands, pointing to the plush couch, and I do as I'm told, carefully crossing my legs. He sits down beside me but doesn't touch me.

"We were just talking about vacations, Ana," Mr. Grey says

kindly. "Elliot has decided to follow Kate and her family to Barbados for a week."

I glance at Kate, and she grins, her eyes bright and wide. She's delighted. Katherine Kavanagh, show some dignity!

"Are you taking a break now that you've finished your degree?" Mr. Grey asks.

"I'm thinking about going to Georgia for a few days," I reply.

Christian gapes at me, blinking a couple of times, his expression unreadable. *Oh, shit.* I haven't mentioned this to him.

"Georgia?" he murmurs.

"My mother lives there, and I haven't seen her for a while."

"When were you thinking of going?" His voice is low.

"Tomorrow, late evening."

Mia saunters back into the living room and hands us champagne flutes filled with pale pink prosecco.

"Your good health!" Mr. Grey raises his glass. An appropriate toast from a doctor's husband, it makes me smile.

"For how long?" Christian asks, his voice deceptively soft.

Holy crap . . . he's angry.

"I don't know yet. It will depend how my interviews go tomorrow."

His jaw clenches, and Kate gets that interfering look on her face. She smiles over-sweetly.

"Ana deserves a break," she says pointedly at Christian. Why is she so antagonistic toward him? What is her problem?

"You have interviews?" Mr. Grey asks.

"Yes, for internships at two publishers, tomorrow."

"I wish you the best of luck."

"Dinner is ready," Grace announces.

We all stand. Kate and Elliot follow Mr. Grey and Mia out of the room. I go to follow, but Christian clutches my elbow, bringing me to an abrupt halt.

"When were you going to tell me you were leaving?" he asks urgently. His tone is soft, but he's masking his anger.

"I'm not leaving, I'm going to see my mother, and I was only thinking about it."

"What about our arrangement?"

"We don't have an arrangement yet."

He narrows his eyes, and then seems to remember himself. Releasing my hand, he takes my elbow and leads me out of the room.

"This conversation is not over," he whispers threateningly as we enter the dining room.

Oh, crapola. Don't get your panties in such a twist . . . *and give me back mine*. I glare at him.

The dining room reminds me of our private dinner at the Heathman. A crystal chandelier hangs over the dark wood table and there's a massive, ornately carved mirror on the wall. The table, covered with a crisp white linen tablecloth, is set, with a bowl of pale pink peonies as the centerpiece. It's stunning.

We take our places. Mr. Grey is at the head of the table, while I sit at his right hand, and Christian is seated beside me. Mr. Grey reaches for the opened bottle of red wine and offers some to Kate. Mia takes her seat beside Christian and, grabbing his hand, squeezes it tightly. Christian smiles warmly at her.

"Where did you meet, Ana?" Mia asks him.

"She interviewed me for the WSU student newspaper."

"Which Kate edits," I add, hoping to steer the conversation away from me.

Mia beams at Kate, seated opposite next to Elliot, and they start talking about the student newspaper.

"Wine, Ana?" Mr. Grey asks.

"Please." I smile at him. Mr. Grey rises to fill the rest of the glasses.

I peek up at Christian, and he turns to look at me, his head cocked to one side.

"What?" he asks.

"Please don't be mad at me," I whisper.

"I'm not mad at you."

I stare at him. He sighs.

"Yes, I am mad at you." He closes his eyes briefly.

"Palm-twitchingly mad?" I ask nervously.

"What are you two whispering about?" Kate interjects.

I flush, and Christian glares at her in a butt-out-of-this-Kavanagh kind of way. Even Kate wilts under his stare.

"Just about my trip to Georgia," I say sweetly, hoping to diffuse their mutual hostility.

Kate smiles, a wicked gleam in her eye.

"How was José when you went to the bar with him on Friday?"

Holy fuck, Kate. I widen my eyes at her. What is she doing? She widens her eyes back at me, and I realize she's trying to make Christian jealous. *How little she knows.* I thought I'd got away with this.

"He was fine," I murmur.

Christian leans over.

"Palm-twitchingly mad," he whispers. "Especially now." His tone is quiet and deadly.

Oh no. I squirm.

Grace reappears carrying two plates, followed by a pretty young woman with blond pigtails, dressed smartly in pale blue, carrying a tray of plates. Her eyes immediately find Christian's in the room. She blushes and gazes at him from under her long mascara-covered lashes. *What?*

Somewhere in the house the phone starts ringing.

"Excuse me." Mr. Grey rises again and exits.

"Thank you, Gretchen," Grace says gently, frowning as Mr. Grey exits. "Just leave the tray on the console." Gretchen nods, and with another furtive glance at Christian, she leaves.

So the Greys have staff, and the staff are eyeing up *my* would-be Dominant. Can this evening get any worse? I scowl at my hands in my lap.

Mr. Grey returns.

"Call for you, darling. It's the hospital," he says to Grace.

"Please start, everyone." Grace smiles as she hands me a plate and leaves.

It smells delicious—chorizo and scallops with roasted red

peppers and shallots, sprinkled with flat-leaf parsley. And in spite of the fact that my stomach is churning from Christian's veiled threats, the surreptitious glances from pretty little Miss Pigtails, and the debacle of my missing underwear, I am starving. I flush as I realize it's the physical effort of this afternoon that's given me such an appetite.

Moments later Grace returns, her brow furrowed. Mr. Grey cocks his head to one side . . . like Christian.

"Everything okay?"

"Another measles case." Grace sighs.

"Oh no."

"Yes, a child. The fourth case this month. If only people would get their kids vaccinated." She shakes her head sadly, and then smiles. "I'm so glad our children never went through that. They never caught anything worse than chicken pox, thank goodness. Poor Elliot," she says as she sits down, smiling indulgently at her son. Elliot frowns mid-chew and squirms uncomfortably. "Christian and Mia were lucky. They got it so mildly, only a spot to share between them."

Mia giggles, and Christian rolls his eyes.

"So, did you catch the Mariners game, Dad?" Elliot's clearly keen to move the conversation on.

The hors d'oeuvres are delicious, and I concentrate on eating while Elliot, Mr. Grey, and Christian talk baseball. Christian seems relaxed and calm talking to his family. My mind is working furiously. Damn Kate, what game is she playing? *Will he punish me?* I quail at the thought. I haven't signed that contract yet. Perhaps I won't. Perhaps I'll stay in Georgia where he can't reach me.

"How are you settling into your new apartment, dear?" Grace asks politely.

I'm grateful for her question, distracting me from my discordant thoughts, and I tell her about our move.

As we finish our starters, Gretchen appears, and not for the first time, I wish I felt able to put my hands freely on Christian just to let her know—he may be fifty shades of fucked up, but he's mine. She proceeds to clear the table, brushing rather too closely to Christian for my liking. Fortunately, he seems oblivious to her, but my inner goddess is smoldering and not in a good way.

Kate and Mia are waxing lyrical about Paris.

"Have you been to Paris, Ana?" Mia asks innocently, distracting me from my jealous reverie.

"No, but I'd love to go." I know I'm the only one at the table who has never left the USA.

"We honeymooned in Paris." Grace smiles at Mr. Grey, who grins back at her.

It's almost embarrassing to witness. They obviously love each other deeply, and I wonder for a brief moment what it must be like to grow up with both one's parents in situ.

"It's a beautiful city," Mia agrees. "In spite of the Parisians. Christian, you should take Ana to Paris," Mia states firmly.

"I think Anastasia would prefer London," Christian says softly.

Oh . . . he remembered. He places his hand on my knee—his fingers traveling up my thigh. My whole body tightens in response. *No . . . not here, not now.* I flush and shift, trying to pull away from him. His hand clamps down on my thigh, stilling me. I reach for my wine in desperation.

Little Miss European Pigtails returns, all coy glances and swaying hips, with our entrées: beef Wellington, I think. Fortunately, she gives us our plates and then leaves, although she lingers handing Christian his. He looks quizzically at me as I watch her close the dining room door.

"So what was wrong with the Parisians?" Elliot asks his sister. "Didn't they take to your winsome ways?"

"Ugh, no they didn't. And Monsieur Floubert, the ogre I was working for, he was such a domineering tyrant."

I splutter into my wine.

"Anastasia, are you okay?" Christian asks solicitously, taking his hand off my thigh.

Humor has returned to his voice. *Oh, thank heavens.* When I nod, he pats my back gently and only removes his hand when he knows I've recovered.

The beef is delicious and served with roasted sweet potatoes, carrots, parsnips, and green beans. It is even more palatable since Christian manages to retain his good humor for the rest of the meal. I suspect that it's because I'm eating so heartily. The conversation flows freely among the Greys, warm and caring, gently teasing one another. Over our dessert of lemon syllabub, Mia regales us with her exploits in Paris, lapsing at one point into fluent French. We all stare at her, and she stares back puzzled, until Christian tells her in equally fluent French what she's done, whereupon she bursts into a fit of giggles. She has a very infectious laugh, and soon we're all in stitches.

Elliot holds forth about his latest building project, a new eco-friendly community to the north of Seattle. I glance up at Kate, and she's hanging on every word Elliot says, her eyes glowing with lust or love. I haven't quite worked out which yet. He grins down at her, and it's as if an unspoken promise passes between them. *Laters, baby,* he's saying, and it's hot, freaking hot. I flush just watching them.

I sigh and peek up at Fifty Shades. I could stare at him forever. He has light stubble over his chin, and my fingers itch to scratch it and feel it against my face, against my breasts . . . between my thighs. I blush at the direction of my thoughts. He peers down at me and raises his hand to pull at my chin.

"Don't bite your lip," he murmurs huskily. "I want to do that."

Grace and Mia clear our dessert glasses and head to the kitchen, while Mr. Grey, Kate, and Elliot discuss the merits of solar panels in Washington State. Christian, feigning interest in their conversation, puts his hand once more on my knee, and his fingers travel up my thigh. My breathing hitches and I press my thighs together in a bid to halt his progress. I can see him smirk.

"Shall I give you a tour of the grounds?" he asks me quite openly.

I know I'm meant to say yes, but I don't trust him. Before I can answer, however, he's on his feet and holding his hand out to me. I place my hand in his, and I feel all the muscles clench deep in my belly, responding to his dark, hungry gaze.

"Excuse me," I say to Mr. Grey, and follow Christian out of the dining room.

He leads me through the hallway and into the kitchen, where Mia and Grace are stacking the dishwasher. European Pigtails is nowhere to be seen.

"I'm going to show Anastasia the backyard," Christian says innocently to his mother. She waves us out with a smile as Mia heads back to the dining room.

We step out onto a gray flagstone patio area lit by recessed lights in the rock. There are shrubs in gray stone tubs and a chic metal table and chairs set up in one corner. Christian walks past those, up some steps, and onto a vast lawn that leads down to the bay . . . oh my—it's beautiful. Seattle twinkles on the horizon and the cool, bright May moon etches a sparkling silver path across the water toward a jetty where two boats are moored. Beside the jetty stands a boathouse. It is so picturesque, so peaceful. I stand and gape for a moment.

Christian pulls me behind him, and my heels sink into the soft grass.

"Stop, please." I am stumbling in his wake.

He stops and gazes at me, his expression unfathomable.

"My heels. I need to take my shoes off."

"Don't bother," he says, and he bends down and scoops me over his shoulder. I squeal loudly with shocked surprise, and he gives me a ringing slap on my behind.

"Keep your voice down," he growls.

Oh no . . . this is not good. My subconscious is quaking at the knees. He's mad about something—could be José, Georgia, no panties, biting my lip. Jeez, he's easy to rile.

"Where are we going?" I breathe.

"Boathouse," he snaps.

I hang on to his hips as I'm tipped upside down, and he strides purposefully in the moonlight across the lawn.

"Why?" I sound breathless, bouncing on this shoulder.

"I need to be alone with you."

"What for?"

"Because I'm going to spank and then fuck you."

"Why?" I whimper softly.

"You know why," he hisses.

"I thought you were an in-the-moment guy?" I plead breathlessly.

"Anastasia, I'm in the moment, trust me."

Holy fuck.

CHAPTER TWENTY

Christian bursts through the wooden door of the boathouse and pauses to flick on some switches. Fluorescents ping and buzz in sequence as harsh white light floods the large wooden building. From my upside-down view, I can see an impressive cruiser in the dock floating gently on the dark water, but I only get a brief look before he's carrying me up some wooden stairs to the room above.

He pauses at the doorway and flips another switch—halogens, this time, that are softer, on a dimmer—and we're in an attic room with sloping ceilings. It's decorated with a nautical New England theme: navy blues and creams with dashes of red. The furnishings are sparse, just a couple of couches are all I can see.

Christian sets me on my feet on the wooden floor. I don't have time to examine my surroundings—my eyes can't leave him. I am mesmerized . . . watching him like one would watch a rare and dangerous predator, waiting for him to strike. His breathing is harsh, but then he's just carried me across the lawn and up a flight of stairs. Gray eyes blaze with anger, need, and pure unadulterated lust.

Holy shit. I could spontaneously combust from his look alone.

"Please don't hit me," I whisper, pleading.

His brow furrows, his eyes widening. He blinks twice.

"I don't want you to spank me, not here, not now. Please don't."

His mouth drops open in surprise, and beyond brave, I tentatively reach up and run my fingers down his cheek, along the edge of his sideburn, to the stubble on his chin. It's a curious mixture of soft and prickly. Slowly closing his eyes, he leans his face into my touch, and his breath hitches in his throat. Reaching up with my other hand, I run my fingers into his hair. I love his hair. His soft moan is barely audible, and when he opens his eyes, his look is wary, like he doesn't understand what I'm doing.

Stepping forward so I am flush against him, I pull gently on his hair, bringing his mouth down to mine, and I kiss him, forcing my tongue between his lips and into his mouth. He groans, and his arms embrace me, pulling me to him. His hands find their way into my hair, and he kisses me back, hard and possessive. His tongue and my tongue twist and turn together, consuming each other. He tastes divine.

He pulls back suddenly, our collective breathing ragged and mingling. My hands drop to his arms, and he glares down at me.

"What are you doing to me?" he whispers, confused.

"Kissing you."

"You said no."

"What?" *No to what?*

"At the dinner table, with your legs."

Oh . . . that's what this is all about.

"But we were at your parents' dining table." I stare up at him, completely bewildered.

"No one's ever said no to me before. And it's so—hot."

His eyes widen, filled with wonder and lust. It's a heady mix. I swallow instinctively. His hand moves down to my behind. He pulls me sharply against him, against his erection.

Oh my . . .

"You're mad and turned on because I said no?" I breathe, astonished.

"I'm mad because you never mentioned Georgia to me. I'm mad because you went drinking with that guy who tried to seduce you when you were drunk and who left you when you were ill with an almost complete stranger. What kind of friend does that? And I'm mad and aroused because you closed your legs on me." His eyes glitter dangerously, and he's slowly inching up the hem of my dress.

"I want you, and I want you now. And if you're not going to let me spank you—which you deserve—I'm going to fuck you on the couch this minute, quickly, for my pleasure, not yours."

My dress is now barely covering my naked behind. He moves suddenly so that his hand is cupping my sex, and one of his fingers sinks slowly into me. His other arm holds me firmly in place around my waist. I suppress my moan.

"This is mine," he whispers aggressively. "All mine. Do you understand?" He eases his finger in and out as he gazes down at me, gauging my reaction, his eyes burning.

"Yes, yours," I breathe as my desire, hot and heavy, surges through my bloodstream, affecting . . . everything. My nerve endings, my breathing. My heart is pounding, trying to leave my chest, the blood thrumming in my ears.

Abruptly, he moves, doing several things at once: withdrawing his fingers, leaving me wanting, unzipping his fly, and pushing me down onto the couch so he's lying on top of me.

"Hands on your head," he commands through gritted teeth as he kneels, forcing my legs wider, and reaches into the inside pocket of his jacket. He takes out a foil packet, gazing down at me, his expression dark, before shrugging off his jacket so it falls to the floor. He rolls the condom down over his impressive length.

I place my hands on my head, and I know it's so I won't touch him. I'm so turned on. I feel my hips moving already up to meet him—wanting him inside me, like this—rough and hard. Oh . . . the anticipation.

"We don't have long. This will be quick, and it's for me, not you. Do you understand? Don't come, or I will spank you," he says through clenched teeth.

Holy crap . . . how do I stop?

With one swift thrust, he's fully inside me. I groan loudly, gutturally, and revel in the fullness of his possession. He puts his hands on mine on top of my head, his elbows hold my arms out and down, and his legs pinion me. I am trapped. He's everywhere, overwhelming me, almost suffocating. But it's heavenly, too; this is my power, this is what I do to him, and it's a hedonistic, triumphant feeling. He moves quickly and furiously inside me, his breathing harsh at my ear, and my body responds, melting around him. *I mustn't come.* No. But I'm meeting him thrust for thrust, a perfect counterpoint. Abruptly, and all too soon, he rams into me and stills as he finds his release, air hissing through his teeth. He relaxes momentarily, so I feel his entire, delicious weight on me. I'm not ready to let him go, my body craving relief, but he's so heavy, and in that moment, I can't push against him. All of a sudden, he withdraws, leaving me aching and hungry for more. He glares down at me.

"Don't touch yourself. I want you frustrated. That's what you do to me by not talking to me, by denying me what's mine." His eyes blaze anew, angry again.

I nod, panting. He stands and removes the condom, knotting it at the end, and puts it in his pants pocket. I gaze at him, my breathing still erratic, and involuntarily I squeeze my thighs together, trying to find some relief. Christian does up his fly and runs his hand through his hair as he reaches down to collect his jacket. He turns back to gaze down at me, his expression softer.

"We'd better get back to the house."

I sit up, a little unsteadily, dazed.

"Here. You may put these on."

From his inside pocket, he produces my panties. I don't grin as I take them from him, but inside I know—I've taken a punishment fuck but gained a small victory over the panties. My inner goddess nods in agreement, a satisfied grin over her face: *You didn't have to ask for them.*

"*Christian!*" Mia shouts from the floor below.

He turns and raises his eyebrows at me. "Just in time. Christ, she can be really irritating."

I scowl back at him, hastily restore my panties to their rightful place, and stand with as much dignity as I can muster in my just-fucked state. Quickly, I attempt to smooth my just-fucked hair.

"Up here, Mia," he calls down. "Well, Miss Steele, I feel better for that—but I still want to spank you," he says softly.

"I don't believe I deserve it, Mr. Grey, especially after tolerating your unprovoked attack."

"Unprovoked? You kissed me." He tries his best to look wounded.

I purse my lips. "It was attack as the best form of defense."

"Defense against what?"

"You and your twitchy palm."

He cocks his head to one side and smiles at me as Mia comes clattering up the stairs. "But it was tolerable?" he asks softly.

I flush. "Barely," I whisper, but I can't help my smirk.

"Oh, there you are." She beams at us.

"I was showing Anastasia around." Christian holds his hand out to me, his gray eyes intense.

I put my hand into his, and he gives it a soft squeeze.

"Kate and Elliot are about to leave. Can you believe those two? They can't keep their hands off each other." Mia feigns disgust and looks from Christian to me. "What have you been doing in here?"

Jeez, she's forward. I blush scarlet.

"Showing Anastasia my rowing trophies," Christian says without missing a beat, completely poker-faced. "Let's go say good-bye to Kate and Elliot."

Rowing trophies? He pulls me gently in front of him, and as Mia turns to go, he swats my behind. I gasp in surprise.

"I will do it again, Anastasia, and soon," he threatens quietly close to my ear, then he pulls me into an embrace, my back to his front, and kisses my hair.

BACK IN THE HOUSE, Kate and Elliot are making their farewells to Grace and Mr. Grey. Kate hugs me hard.

"I need to speak to you about antagonizing Christian," I hiss quietly in her ear as she embraces me.

"He needs antagonizing; then you can see what he's really like. Be careful, Ana—he's so controlling," she whispers. "See you later."

I KNOW WHAT HE'S REALLY LIKE—YOU DON'T! I scream at her in my head. I'm fully aware that her actions come from a good place, but sometimes she just oversteps boundaries, and right now she's so far over that she's in the neighboring state. I scowl at her, and she pokes her tongue out at me, making me smile unwillingly. Playful Kate is novel; must be Elliot's influence. We wave them off at the doorway, and Christian turns to me.

"We should go, too—you have interviews tomorrow."

Mia embraces me warmly as we say our good-byes.

"We never thought he'd find anyone!" she gushes.

I flush, and Christian rolls his eyes again. I purse my lips. Why can he do that when I can't? I want to roll my eyes back at him, but I do not dare, not after his threat in the boathouse.

"Take care of yourself, Ana dear," Grace says kindly.

Christian, embarrassed or frustrated by the lavish attention I'm receiving from the remaining Greys, grabs my hand and pulls me to his side.

"Let's not frighten her away or spoil her with too much affection," he grumbles.

"Christian, stop teasing," Grace scolds him indulgently, her eyes glowing with love and affection for him.

Somehow, I don't think he's teasing. I surreptitiously watch their interaction. It's obvious Grace adores him with a mother's unconditional love. He bends and kisses her stiffly.

"Mom," he says, and there's an undercurrent in his voice—reverence maybe?

"Mr. Grey—good-bye and thank you." I hold out my hand to him, and he hugs me, too!

"Please, call me Carrick. I do hope we see you again very soon, Ana."

Our farewells said, Christian leads me to the car, where Taylor is waiting. *Has he been waiting here the whole time?* Taylor opens my door, and I slide into the back of the Audi.

I feel some of the tension leaving my shoulders. Jeez, what a day. I am exhausted, physically and emotionally. After a brief conversation with Taylor, Christian clambers into the car beside me. He turns to face me.

"Well, it seems my family likes you, too," he murmurs.

Too? The depressing thought about how I came to be invited pops unbidden and very unwelcome into my head. Taylor starts the car and heads away from the circle of light in the driveway to the darkness of the road. I gaze at Christian, and he's staring at me.

"What?" he asks, his voice quiet.

I flounder momentarily. No—I'll tell him. He's always complaining that I don't talk to him.

"I think that you felt trapped into bringing me to meet your parents." My voice is soft and hesitant. "If Elliot hadn't asked Kate, you'd never have asked me." I can't see his face in the dark, but he tilts his head, gaping at me.

"Anastasia, I'm delighted that you've met my parents. Why are you so filled with self-doubt? It never ceases to amaze me. You're such a strong, self-contained young woman, but you have such negative thoughts about yourself. If I hadn't wanted you to meet them, you wouldn't be here. Is that how you were feeling the whole time you were there?"

Oh! He wanted me there—and it's a revelation. He doesn't seem uncomfortable answering me as he would if he were hiding the truth. He seems genuinely pleased that I'm here . . . a warm glow spreads slowly through my veins. He shakes his head and reaches for my hand. I glance nervously at Taylor.

"Don't worry about Taylor. Talk to me."

I shrug.

"Yes. I thought that. And another thing, I only mentioned Georgia because Kate was talking about Barbados. I haven't made up my mind."

"Do you want to go and see your mother?"

"Yes."

He looks oddly at me, like he's having some internal struggle.

"Can I come with you?" he asks eventually.

What!

"Erm . . . I don't think that's a good idea."

"Why not?"

"I was hoping for a break from all this . . . intensity to try to think things through."

He stares at me.

"I'm too intense?"

I burst out laughing. "That's putting it mildly!"

In the light of the passing street lamps, I see his lips quirk up.

"Are you laughing at me, Miss Steele?"

"I wouldn't dare, Mr. Grey," I reply with mock seriousness.

"I think you dare, and I think you do laugh at me, frequently."

"You are quite funny."

"Funny?"

"Oh yes."

"Funny peculiar or funny ha-ha?"

"Oh . . . a lot of one and some of the other."

"Which way more?"

"I'll leave you to figure that out."

"I'm not sure if I can figure anything out around you, Anastasia," he says sardonically, and then continues quietly, "What do you need to think about in Georgia?"

"Us," I whisper.

He stares at me, impassive.

"You said you'd try," he murmurs.

"I know."

"Are you having second thoughts?"

"Possibly."

He shifts as if uncomfortable.

"Why?"

Holy crap. How did this suddenly become such an intense and meaningful conversation? It's been sprung on me, like an exam that I'm not prepared for. What do I say? Because I think I love you, and you just see me as a toy. Because I can't touch you, because I'm too frightened to show you any affection in case you flinch or tell me off or worse—beat me? What can I say?

I stare momentarily out of the window. The car is heading back across the bridge. We are both shrouded in darkness, masking our thoughts and feelings, but we don't need the night for that.

"Why, Anastasia?" Christian presses me for an answer.

I shrug, trapped. I don't want to lose him. In spite of all his demands, his need to control, his scary vices, I have never felt as alive as I do now. It's a thrill to be sitting here beside him. He's so unpredictable, sexy, smart, and funny. But his moods . . . oh—and he wants to hurt me. He says he'll think about my reservations, but it still scares me. I close my eyes. What can I say? Deep down I would just like more, more affection, more playful Christian, more . . . love.

He squeezes my hand.

"Talk to me, Anastasia. I don't want to lose you. This last week . . ."

We're coming near to the end of the bridge, and the road is once more bathed in the neon light of the street lamps so his face is intermittently in the light and the dark. And it's such a fitting metaphor. This man, whom I once thought of as a romantic hero, a brave shining white knight—or the dark knight, as he said. He's not a hero; he's a man with serious, deep emotional flaws, and he's dragging me into the dark. Can I not guide him into the light?

"I still want more," I whisper.

"I know," he says. "I'll try."

I blink up at him, and he relinquishes my hand and pulls at my chin, releasing my trapped lip.

"For you, Anastasia, I will try." He's radiating sincerity.

And that's my cue. I unbuckle my seatbelt, reach across, and clamber into his lap, taking him completely by surprise. Wrapping my arms around his head, I kiss him, long and hard, and in a nanosecond, he's responding.

"Stay with me, tonight," he breathes. "If you go away, I won't see you all week. Please."

“Yes,” I acquiesce. “And I’ll try, too. I’ll sign your contract.” And it’s a spur-of-the-moment decision.

He gazes down at me.

“Sign after Georgia. Think about it. Think about it hard, baby.”

“I will.” And we sit in silence for a mile or two.

“You really should wear your seat belt,” Christian whispers disapprovingly into my hair, but he makes no move to shift me from his lap.

I nuzzle up against him, eyes closed, my nose at his throat, drinking in his sexy Christian-and-spiced-musky-bodywash fragrance, my head on his shoulder. I let my mind drift, and I allow myself to fantasize that he loves me. Oh, and it’s so real, tangible almost, and a small part of my nasty harpy subconscious acts completely out of character and *dares to hope*. I’m careful not to touch his chest but just snuggle in his arms as he holds me tightly.

All too soon, I’m torn from my impossible daydream.

“We’re home,” Christian murmurs, and it’s such a tantalizing sentence, full of so much potential.

Home, with Christian. Except his apartment is an art gallery, not a home.

Taylor opens the door for us, and I thank him shyly, aware that he’s been within earshot of our conversation, but his kind smile is reassuring and gives nothing away. Once out of the car, Christian assesses me critically. *Oh no . . . what have I done now?*

“Why don’t you have a jacket?” he frowns as he shrugs out of his and drapes it over my shoulders.

Relief washes through me.

“It’s in my new car,” I reply sleepily, yawning.

He smirks at me.

“Tired, Miss Steele?”

“Yes, Mr. Grey.” I feel bashful under his teasing scrutiny. Nevertheless I feel an explanation is in order. “I’ve been prevailed upon in ways I never thought possible today.”

“Well, if you’re really unlucky, I may prevail upon you some more," he promises as he takes my hand and leads me into the building. *Holy shit . . . Again!*

I gaze up at him in the elevator. I have assumed he'd like me to sleep with him, and then I remember that he doesn't sleep with anyone, although he has with me a few times. I frown, and abruptly his gaze darkens. He reaches up and grasps my chin, freeing my lip from teeth.

"One day I will fuck you in this elevator, Anastasia, but right now you're tired—so I think we should stick to a bed."

Bending down, he clamps his teeth around my lower lip and pulls gently. I melt against him, and my breathing stops as my insides unfurl with longing. I reciprocate, fastening my teeth over his top lip, teasing him, and he groans. When the elevator doors open, he grabs my hand and tugs me into the foyer, through the double doors, and into the hallway.

"Do you need a drink or anything?"

"No."

"Good. Let's go to bed."

I raise my eyebrows. "You're going to settle for plain old vanilla?"

He cocks his head to one side. "Nothing plain or old about vanilla—it's a very intriguing flavor," he breathes.

"Since when?"

"Since last Saturday. Why? Were you hoping for something more exotic?"

My inner goddess pops her head above the parapet.

"Oh no. I've had enough exotic for one day." My inner goddess pouts at me, failing miserably to hide her disappointment.

"Sure? We cater for all tastes here—at least thirty-one flavors." He grins at me lasciviously.

"I've noticed," I reply dryly.

He shakes his head. "Come on, Miss Steele, you have a big day tomorrow. Sooner you're in bed, sooner you'll be fucked, and sooner you can sleep."

"Mr. Grey, you are a born romantic."

"Miss Steele, you have a smart mouth. I may have to subdue it some way. Come." He leads me down the hallway into his bedroom and kicks the door closed.

"Hands in the air," he commands.

I oblige, and in one breathtakingly swift move he removes my dress like a magician, grasping it at the hem and pulling it smoothly and fleetly over my head.

"Ta-da!" he says playfully.

I giggle and applaud politely. He bows gracefully, grinning. *How can I resist him when he's like this?* He places my dress on the lone chair beside his chest of drawers.

"And for your next trick?" I prompt, teasing.

"Oh, my dear Miss Steele. Get into my bed," he growls, "and I'll show you."

"Do you think that for once I should play hard to get?" I ask coquettishly.

His eyes widen with surprise, and I see a glimmer of excitement. "Well . . . the door's closed. Not sure how you're going to avoid me," he says sardonically. "I think it's a done deal."

"But I'm a good negotiator."

"So am I." He stares down at me, but as he does, his expression changes, confusion washes over him and the atmosphere in the room shifts abruptly, tensing. "Don't you want to fuck?" he asks.

"No," I breathe.

"Oh." He frowns.

Okay, here goes . . . deep breath.

"I want you to make love to me."

He stills and stares at me blankly. His expression darkens. Oh, shit, this doesn't look good. *Give him a minute!* My subconscious snaps.

"Ana, I . . ." He runs his hands through his hair. Two hands. Jeez, he's really bewildered. "I thought we did?" he says eventually.

"I want to touch you."

He takes an involuntary step back from me, his expression for a moment fearful, and then he reins it in.

"Please," I whisper.

He recovers himself. "Oh no, Miss Steele, you've had enough concessions from me this evening. And I'm saying no."

"No?"

"No."

Oh . . . I can't argue with that . . . can I?

"Look, you're tired, I'm tired. Let's just go to bed," he says, watching me carefully.

"So touching is a hard limit for you?"

"Yes. This is old news."

"Please tell me why."

"Oh, Anastasia, please. Just drop it for now," he mutters exasperated.

"It's important to me."

Again he runs both hands through his hair, and he utters an oath beneath his breath. Turning on his heel, he heads for the chest of drawers, pulls out a T-shirt, and throws it at me. I catch it, bemused.

"Put that on and get into bed," he snaps, irritated.

I frown but decide to humor him. Turning my back, I quickly remove my bra, pulling the T-shirt on as hastily as I can to cover my nakedness. I leave my panties on; I haven't worn them for most of the evening.

"I need the bathroom." My voice is a whisper.

He frowns, bemused.

"Now you're asking permission?"

"Er . . . no."

"Anastasia, you know where the bathroom is. Today, at this point in our strange arrangement, you don't need my permission to use it." He cannot hide his irritation. He shrugs out of his shirt, and I scoot into the bathroom.

I stare at myself in the over-large mirror, shocked that I still look the same. After all that I've done today, it's still the same ordinary girl gaping back at me. *What did you expect—that you'd grow horns and a little pointy tail?* my subconscious snaps at me. *And what the hell are you doing? Touching is his hard limit. Too soon, you idiot. He needs to walk before he can run.* My subconscious is furious, Medusa-like in her anger, hair flying, her hands clenched around her face like in Edvard Munch's *The Scream.* I ignore her, but she won't climb back into her box. *You are making him mad—think about all that's he's said, all he's conceded.* I scowl at my reflection. I need to be able to show him affection—then perhaps he can reciprocate.

I shake my head, resigned, and grasp Christian's toothbrush. My subconscious is right, of course. I'm rushing him. He's not ready and neither am I. We are balanced on the delicate seesaw that is our strange arrangement—at different ends, vacillating, and it tips and sways between us. We both need to edge closer to the middle. I just hope neither of us falls off in our attempt to do so. This is all so quick. Maybe I need some distance. Georgia seems more appealing than ever. As I begin brushing my teeth, he knocks.

"Come in," I splutter through a mouthful of toothpaste.

Christian stands in the doorway, his PJs hanging off his hips in that way that makes every little cell in my body stand up and take notice. He's bare-chested, and I drink him in like I'm crazed with thirst and he's clear, cool mountain spring water. He gazes at me impassively, then smirks and comes to stand beside me. Our eyes lock in the mirror, gray to blue. I finish with his toothbrush, rinse it off, and hand it to him, my look never leaving his. Wordlessly, he takes the toothbrush from me and puts it in his mouth. I smirk back at him, and his eyes are suddenly dancing with humor.

"Do feel free to borrow my toothbrush." His tone is gently mocking.

"Thank you, Sir," I smile sweetly, and I leave, heading back to bed.

A few minutes later he joins me.

"You know this is not how I saw tonight panning out," he mutters petulantly.

"Imagine if I said to you that you couldn't touch me."

He clambers onto the bed and sits cross-legged.

"Anastasia, I've told you. Fifty shades. I had a rough start in life—you don't want that shit in your head. Why would you?"

"Because I want to know you better."

"You know me well enough."

"How can you say that?" I struggle up onto my knees, facing him.

He rolls his eyes at me, frustrated.

"You're rolling your eyes. Last time I did that, I ended up over your knee."

"Oh, I'd like to put you there again."

Inspiration hits me.

"Tell me and you can."

"What?"

"You heard me."

"You're bargaining with me?" His voice resonates with astonished disbelief.

I nod. *Yes . . . this is the way.*

"Negotiating."

"It doesn't work that way, Anastasia."

"Okay. Tell me, and I'll roll my eyes at you."

He laughs, and I get a rare glimpse of carefree Christian. I've not seen him for a while. He sobers.

"Always so keen and eager for information." He gazes at me speculatively. After a moment, he gracefully climbs off the bed. "Don't go away," he says and exits the room.

Trepidation lances through me, and I hug myself. What's he doing? Does he have some evil plan? *Crap.* Suppose he returns with a cane, or some weird kinky implement? *Holy shit, what will I do then?* When he does return, he's holding something small in his hands. I can't see what it is, and I'm burning with curiosity.

"When's your first interview tomorrow?" he asks softly.

"Two."

A slow, wicked grin spreads across his face.

"Good." And before my eyes, he subtly changes. He's harder, intractable . . . hot. This is Dominant Christian.

"Get off the bed. Stand over here." He points to beside the bed, and I scramble up and off in double time. He stares intently down at me, his eyes glittering with promise. "Trust me?" he asks.

I nod. He holds out his hand, and in his palm are two shiny silver balls linked with a thick black thread.

"These are new," he says emphatically.

I look questioningly up at him.

"I am going to put these inside you, and then I'm going to spank you, not for punishment, but for your pleasure and mine." He pauses, gauging my wide-eyed reaction.

Inside me! I gasp, and all the muscles deep in my belly clench. My inner goddess is doing the dance of the seven veils.

"Then we'll fuck, and if you're still awake, I'll impart some information about my formative years. Agreed?"

He's asking my permission! Breathlessly, I nod. I'm incapable of speech.

"Good girl. Open your mouth."

Mouth?

"Wider."

Very gently, he puts the balls in my mouth.

"They need lubrication. Suck," he orders, his voice soft.

The balls are cold, smooth, surprisingly heavy, and metallic tasting. My dry mouth pools with saliva as my tongue explores the unfamiliar objects. Christian's gaze does not leave mine. Holy hell, this is turning me on. I squirm.

"Keep still, Anastasia," he warns.

"Stop." He tugs them from my mouth. Moving toward the bed, he throws the duvet aside and sits down on the edge.

"Come here."

I stand in front of him.

"Now turn around, bend down, and grab your ankles."

I blink at him, and his expression darkens.

"Don't hesitate," he admonishes me softly, an undercurrent in his voice, and he pops the balls in his mouth.

Fuck, this is sexier than the toothbrush. I follow his orders immediately. Jeez, can I touch my ankles? I find I can, with ease. The T-shirt slides up my back, exposing my behind. Thank heavens I have retained my panties, but I suspect I won't for long.

He places his hand reverently on my backside and very softly caresses it with his whole hand. With my eyes open, I can see his legs through mine, nothing else. I close my eyes tightly as he gently moves my panties to the side and slowly runs his finger up and down my sex. My body braces itself in a heady mix of wild anticipation and arousal. He slides one finger inside me, and he circles it deliciously slowly. Oh, it feels good. I moan.

His breathing halts and I hear him gasp as he repeats the motion. He withdraws his finger and very slowly inserts the objects, one slow, delicious ball at a time. *Oh my.* They're body temperature, warmed by our collective mouths. It's a curious feeling. Once they're inside me, I can't really feel them—but then again I know they're *there.*

He straightens my panties and leans forward, and his lips softly kiss my behind.

"Stand up," he orders, and shakily I get to my feet.

Oh! Now I can feel them . . . sort of. He grasps my hips to steady me while I reestablish my equilibrium.

"You okay?" he asks, his voice stern.

"Yes."

"Turn around." I turn and face him.

The balls pull downward and involuntarily I clench around them. The feeling startles me but not in a bad way.

"How does that feel?" he asks.

"Strange."

"Strange good or strange bad?"

"Strange good," I confess, blushing.

"Good." There's a trace of humor lurking in his eyes.

"I want a glass of water. Go and fetch one for me please."

Oh.

"And when you come back, I shall put you across my knee. Think about that, Anastasia."

Water? He wants water—now—why?

As I leave the bedroom, it becomes abundantly clear why he wants me to walk around—as I do, the balls weigh down inside me, massaging me internally. It's such a weird feeling and not entirely unpleasant. In fact, my breathing accelerates as I stretch up for a glass from the kitchen cabinet, and I gasp. *Oh my . . .* I may have to keep these. They make me needy, needy for sex.

He's watching me carefully when I return.

"Thank you," he says as he takes the glass from me.

Slowly, he takes a sip, then places the glass on his bedside table. There's a foil packet, ready and waiting, like me. And I know he's doing this to build the anticipation. My heart has picked up a beat. He turns his bright gray gaze to mine.

"Come. Stand beside me. Like last time."

I sidle up to him, my blood thrumming through my body, and this time . . . I'm excited. Aroused.

"Ask me," he says softly.

I frown. Ask him what?

"Ask me," his voice is slightly harder.

What? How was your water? What does he want?

"Ask me, Anastasia. I won't say it again." And there's such a threat implicit in his words, and it dawns on me. He wants me to ask him to spank me.

Holy shit. He's looking at me expectantly, his eyes growing colder. *Shit.*

"Spank me, please . . . Sir," I whisper.

He closes his eyes momentarily, savoring my words. Reaching up, he grasps my left hand and he tugs me over his knees. I fall instantly, and he steadies me as I land in his lap. My heart is in my mouth as his hand gently strokes my behind. I'm angled across his lap again so that my torso rests on the bed beside him. This time he doesn't throw his leg over mine but smoothes my hair out of my face and tucks it behind my ear. Once he's done, he clasps my hair at the nape to hold me in place. He tugs gently and my head shifts back.

"I want to see your face while I spank you, Anastasia," he murmurs, all the while softly rubbing my backside.

His hand moves down between the cheeks of my behind, and he pushes against my sex, and the full feeling is . . . I moan. Oh, the sensation is exquisite.

"This is for pleasure, Anastasia, mine and yours," he whispers.

He lifts his hand and brings it down in a resounding slap against the junction of my thighs, my behind, and my sex. The balls are forced forward inside me, and I'm lost in a quagmire of sensation. The stinging across my behind, the fullness of the balls inside me, and the fact that he's holding me down. I screw my face up as my faculties attempt to absorb all these foreign feelings. I note somewhere in my brain that he's not smacked me as hard as last time. He caresses my backside again, trailing his palm across my skin and over my underwear.

Why's he not removed my panties? Then his palm disappears, and he brings it down again. I groan as the sensation spreads. He starts a pattern: left to right and then down. The down ones are the best. Everything moving forward, inside me . . . and in between each smack he caresses me, kneads me—so I am massaged inside and out. It's such a stimulating, erotic feeling, and for some reason, because this is on my terms, I don't mind the pain. It's not painful as such—well, it is, but not unbearable. It's somehow manageable and, yes, pleasurable . . . even. I groan. *Yes, I can do this.*

He pauses as he slowly peels my panties down my legs. I writhe on his legs, not because I want to escape the blows, but I want more . . . release, something. His touch against my sensitized skin is all sensuous tingle. It's overwhelming, and he starts again. A few soft slaps, then building up, left to right and down. Oh, the downs. I groan.

"Good girl, Anastasia," he groans, and his breathing is ragged.

He spanks me twice more, and then he pulls at the small threads attached to the balls and jerks them out of me suddenly. I almost climax—the feeling is out of this world. Moving swiftly, he gently turns me over. I hear rather than see the rip of the foil packet, and then he's lying beside me. He seizes my hands, hoists them over my head, and eases himself onto me, into me, sliding slowly, filling me where the silver globes have been. I groan loudly.

"Oh, baby," he whispers as he moves back, forward, a slow sensual tempo, savoring me, feeling me.

It is the most gentle he has ever been, and it takes no time at all for me to fall over the edge, spiraling into a delicious, violent, exhausting orgasm. As I clench around him, it ignites his release, and he slides into me, stilling, gasping out my name in desperate wonder.

"*Ana!*"

He's silent and panting on top of me, his hands still entwined in mine above my head. Finally, he leans back and stares down at me.

"I enjoyed that," he whispers, and then kisses me sweetly.

He doesn't linger for more sweet kisses but rises, covers me with the duvet, and disappears into the bathroom. On his return, he's carrying a bottle of white lotion. He sits beside me on the bed.

"Roll over," he orders, and begrudgingly I move onto my front.

Honestly, all this fuss. I feel very sleepy.

"Your ass is a glorious color," he says approvingly, and he tenderly massages the cooling lotion into my pink behind.

"Spill the beans, Grey." I yawn.

"Miss Steele, you know how to ruin a moment."

"We had a deal."

"How do you feel?"

"Shortchanged."

He sighs, slides in beside me, and pulls me into his arms. Careful not to touch my stinging behind, we are spooning again. He kisses me very softly beside my ear.

"The woman who brought me into this world was a crack whore, Anastasia. Go to sleep."

Holy fuck . . . what does that mean?

"Was?"

"She's dead."

"How long?"

He sighs.

"She died when I was four. I don't really remember her. Carrick has given me some details. I only remember certain things. Please go to sleep."

"Good night, Christian."

"Good night, Ana."

And I slip into a dazed and exhausted sleep, dreaming of a four-year-old gray-eyed boy in a dark, scary, miserable place.

CHAPTER TWENTY-ONE

There is light everywhere. Bright, warm, piercing light, and I endeavor to keep it at bay for a few more precious minutes. I want to hide, just a few more minutes. But the glare is too strong, and I finally succumb to wakefulness. A glorious Seattle morning greets me—sunshine pouring through the full-height windows and flooding the room with too-bright light. Why didn't we close the blinds last night? I am in Christian Grey's vast bed minus one Christian Grey.

I lie back for a moment staring through the windows at the lofty vista of Seattle's skyline. Life in the clouds sure feels unreal. A fantasy—a castle in the air, adrift from the ground, safe from the realities of life—far away from neglect, hunger, and crack-whore mothers. I shudder to think what he went through as a small child, and I understand why he lives here, isolated, surrounded by beautiful, precious works of art—so far removed from where he started . . . mission statement indeed. I frown because it still doesn't explain why I can't touch him.

Ironically, I feel the same up here in his lofty tower. I'm adrift from reality. I'm in this fantasy apartment, having fantasy sex with my fantasy boyfriend, when the grim reality is he wants a special arrangement, though he's said he'll try more. What does that actually mean? This is what I need to clarify between us to see if we are still at opposite ends on the seesaw or if we are inching closer together.

I clamber out of bed feeling stiff and, for want of a better expression, well used. *Yes, that would be all the sex then.* My subconscious purses her lips in disapproval. I roll my eyes at her, grateful that a certain twitchy-palmed control freak is not in the room, and resolve to ask him about the personal trainer. That's if I sign. My inner goddess glares at me in desperation. *Of course you'll sign*. I ignore them both, and after a quick trip to the bathroom, I go in search of Christian.

He's not in the art gallery, but an elegant middle-aged woman is cleaning in the kitchen area. The sight of her stops me in my tracks. She has short blond hair and clear blue eyes; she wears a plain white tailored shirt and a navy-blue pencil skirt. She smiles broadly when she sees me.

"Good morning, Miss Steele. Would you like some breakfast?" Her tone is warm but businesslike, and I am stunned. Who is this attractive blonde in Christian's kitchen? I'm only wearing Christian's T-shirt. I feel self-conscious and embarrassed by my lack of clothing.

"I'm afraid you have me at a disadvantage." My voice is quiet, unable to hide the anxiety in my voice.

"Oh, I'm terribly sorry—I'm Mrs. Jones, Mr. Grey's housekeeper."

Oh.

"How do you do?" I manage.

"Would you like some breakfast, ma'am?"

Ma'am!

"Just some tea would be lovely, thank you. Do you know where Mr. Grey is?"

"In his study."

"Thank you."

I scuttle off toward the study, mortified. Why does Christian only have attractive blondes working for him? And a nasty thought comes involuntarily into my mind: *Are they all ex-subs?* I refuse to entertain that hideous idea. I poke my head shyly round the door. He's on the phone, facing the window, in black pants and a white shirt. His hair is still wet from the shower, and I'm completely distracted from my negative thoughts.

"Unless that company's P&L improves, I'm not interested, Ros. We're not carrying deadweight . . . I don't need any more lame excuses . . . Have Marco call me, it's shit or bust time . . . Yes, tell Barney that the prototype looks good, though I'm not sure about the interface . . . No, it's just missing something . . . I want to meet him this afternoon to discuss . . . In fact, him and his team, we can brainstorm. . . . Okay. Transfer me back to Andrea . . ." He waits, staring out the window, master of his universe, looking down at the little people below from this castle in the sky. "Andrea . . ."

Glancing up, he notices me at the door. A slow, sexy smile spreads across his lovely face, and I'm rendered speechless as my insides melt. He is without a doubt the most beautiful man on the planet, too beautiful for the little people below, too beautiful for me. *No*, my inner goddess scowls at me, not too beautiful for me. *He is sort of mine*, for now. The idea sends a thrill through my blood and dispels my irrational self-doubt.

He continues his conversation, his eyes never leaving mine.

"Clear my schedule this morning, but get Bill to call me. I'll be in at two. I need to talk to Marco this afternoon, that will need at least half an hour . . . Schedule Barney and his team in after Marco or maybe tomorrow, and find time for me to see Claude every day this week . . . Tell him to wait . . . Oh . . . No, I don't want publicity for Darfur . . . Tell Sam to deal with it . . . No . . . Which event? . . . That's next Saturday? . . . Hold on."

"When will you be back from Georgia?" he asks.

"Friday."

He resumes his phone conversation.

"I'll need an extra ticket because I have a date . . . Yes Andrea, that's what I said, a date, Miss Anastasia Steele will accompany me . . . That's all." He hangs up. "Good morning, Miss Steele."

"Mr. Grey." I smile shyly.

He walks around his desk with his usual grace and stands in front of me. He gently strokes my cheek with the back of his fingers.

"I didn't want to wake you, you looked so peaceful. Did you sleep well?"

"I am very well rested, thank you. I just came to say hi before I had a shower."

I gaze up at him, drinking him in. He leans down and gently kisses me, and I can't help myself. I throw my arms around his neck and my fingers twist in his still-damp hair. Pushing my body flush against his, I kiss him back. I want him. My attack takes him by surprise, but after a beat, he responds, a low groan in his throat. His hands slip into my hair and down my back to cup my naked behind, his tongue exploring my mouth. He pulls back, his eyes hooded.

"Well, sleep seems to agree with you," he murmurs. "I suggest you go and have your shower, or shall I lay you across my desk now?"

"I choose the desk," I whisper recklessly as desire sweeps like adrenaline through my system, waking everything in its path.

He stares bewildered down at me for a millisecond.

"You've really got a taste for this, haven't you, Miss Steele? You're becoming insatiable," he murmurs.

"I've only got a taste for you," I whisper.

His eyes widen and darken while his hands knead my naked backside.

"Damn right, only me," he growls, and suddenly, with one fluid movement, he clears all the plans and papers off his desk so that they scatter on the floor, sweeps me up in his arms, and lays me down across the short end of his desk so that my head is almost off the edge.

"You want it, you got it, baby," he mutters, producing a foil packet from his pants pocket while he unzips his pants. *Oh, Mr. Boy Scout.* He rolls the condom over his erection and gazes down at me. "I sure hope you're ready," he breathes, a salacious smile across his face. And in a moment, he's filling me, holding my wrists tightly by my side, and thrusting into me deeply.

I groan . . . *oh yes.*

"Christ, Ana. You're *so* ready," he whispers in veneration.

Wrapping my legs around his waist, I hold him the only way

I can as he stays standing, staring down at me, gray eyes glowing, passionate and possessive. He starts to move, really move. This is not making love, this is fucking—and I love it. I groan. It's so raw, so carnal, making me so wanton. I revel in his possession, his lust slaking mine. He moves with ease, luxuriating in me, enjoying me, his lips slightly parted as his breathing increases. He twists his hips from side to side, and the feeling is exquisite.

I close my eyes, feeling the build up—that delicious, slow, step-climbing build. Pushing me higher, higher to the castle in the air. Oh yes . . . his stroke increases fractionally. I moan loudly. I am all sensation . . . all him, enjoying every thrust, every push that fills me. And he picks up the pace, thrusting faster . . . harder . . . and my whole body is moving to his rhythm, and I can feel my legs stiffening, and my insides quivering and quickening.

"Come on, baby, give it up for me," he cajoles through gritted teeth, and the fervent need in his voice—the strain—sends me over the edge.

I cry out a wordless, passionate plea as I touch the sun and burn, falling around him, falling down, back to a breathless, bright summit on Earth. He slams into me and stops abruptly as he reaches his climax, pulling at my wrists and sinking gracefully and wordlessly onto me.

Wow . . . that was unexpected. I slowly materialize back on Earth.

"What the hell are you doing to me?" he breathes as he nuzzles my neck. "You completely beguile me, Ana. You weave some powerful magic."

He releases my wrists, and I run my fingers through his hair, coming down from my high. I tighten my legs around him.

"I'm the one beguiled," I whisper.

He gazes at me. His expression is disconcerted, alarmed even. Placing his hands on either side of my face, he holds my head in place.

"You. Are. Mine," he says, each word a staccato. "Do you understand?"

He's so earnest, so impassioned—a zealot. The force of his plea is so unexpected and disarming. I wonder why he's feeling like this. "Yes, yours," I whisper, derailed by his fervor.

"Are you sure you have to go to Georgia?"

I nod slowly. And in that brief moment, I watch his expression change and the shutters coming down. Abruptly he withdraws, making me wince.

"Are you sore?" he asks, leaning over me.

"A little," I confess.

"I like you sore." His eyes smolder. "Reminds you where I've been, and only me."

He grabs my chin and kisses me roughly, then stands and holds his hand out to help me up. I glance down at the foil packet beside me.

"Always prepared," I murmur.

He looks at me confused as he redoes his fly. I hold up the empty packet.

"A man can hope, Anastasia, dream even, and sometimes his dreams come true."

He sounds so odd, his eyes burning. I just don't understand. My postcoital glow is fading fast. *What is his problem?*

"So, on your desk, that's been a dream?" I ask dryly, trying humor to lighten the atmosphere between us.

He smiles an enigmatic smile that doesn't reach his eyes, and I know immediately this is not the first time he's had sex on his desk. The thought is unwelcome. I squirm uncomfortably as my postcoital glow evaporates.

"I'd better go and have a shower." I stand and start to move past him.

He frowns and runs a hand through his hair.

"I've got a couple more calls to make. I'll join you for breakfast once you're out of the shower. I think Mrs. Jones has laundered your clothes from yesterday. They're in the closet."

What? When the hell did she do that? Jeez, could she hear us? I flush.

"Thank you," I mutter.

"You're most welcome," he replies automatically, but there's an edge to his voice.

I'm not saying thank you for fucking me. Although, it was very . . .

"What?" he asks, and I realize I'm frowning.

"What's wrong?" I ask softly.

"What do you mean?"

"Well . . . you're being more weird than usual."

"You find me weird?" He tries to stifle a smile.

"Sometimes."

He regards me for a moment, his eyes speculative. "As ever, I'm surprised by you, Miss Steele."

"Surprised how?"

"Let's just say that was an unexpected treat."

"We aim to please, Mr. Grey." I cock my head to one side like he often does to me and give his words back to him.

"And please me you do," he says, but he looks uneasy. "I thought you were going to have a shower."

Oh, he's dismissing me.

"Yes . . . um, I'll see you in a moment." I scurry out of his office completely dumbfounded.

He seemed confused. *Why?* I have to say as physical experiences go, that was very satisfying. But emotionally—well, I'm rattled by his reaction, and that was about as emotionally enriching as cotton candy is nutritious.

Mrs. Jones is still in the kitchen. "Would you like your tea now, Miss Steele?"

"I'll have a shower first, thank you," I mutter and take my blazing face quickly out of the room.

In the shower, I try to figure out what's up with Christian. He is the most complicated person I know, and I cannot understand his ever-changing moods. He seemed fine when I went into his study. We had sex . . . and then he wasn't. No, I don't get it. I look to my subconscious. She's whistling with her hands behind her back and looking anywhere but at me. She hasn't got a clue, and my inner goddess is still basking in a remnant of postcoital glow. No—we're all clueless.

I towel-dry my hair, comb it through with Christian's one and only hair implement, and put my hair up in a bun. Kate's plum dress hangs laundered and ironed in the closet along with my clean bra and panties. Mrs. Jones is a marvel. Slipping on Kate's shoes, I straighten my dress, take a deep breath, and head back out to the great room.

Christian is still nowhere to be seen, and Mrs. Jones is checking the contents of the pantry.

"Tea now, Miss Steele?" she asks.

"Please." I smile at her. I feel slightly more confident now that I'm dressed.

"Would you like something to eat?"

"No, thank you."

"Of course you'll have something to eat," Christian snaps, glowering. "She likes pancakes, bacon, and eggs, Mrs. Jones."

"Yes, Mr. Grey. What would you like, sir?"

"Omelet, please, and some fruit." He doesn't take his eyes off me, his expression unfathomable. "Sit," he orders, pointing to one of the barstools.

I oblige, and he sits beside me while Mrs. Jones busies herself with breakfast. Gosh, it's unnerving having someone else listen to our conversation.

"Have you bought your air ticket?"

"No, I'll buy it when I get home—over the Internet."

He leans on his elbow, rubbing his chin.

"Do you have the money?"

Oh no.

"Yes," I say with mock patience as if I'm talking to a small child.

He raises a censorious eyebrow at me. *Crap.*

"Yes, I do, thank you," I amend rapidly.

"I have a jet. It's not scheduled to be used for three days; it's at your disposal."

I gape at him. Of course he has a jet, and I have to resist my body's natural inclination to roll my eyes at him. I want to laugh. But I don't, as I can't read his mood.

"We've already made serious misuse of your company's aviation fleet. I wouldn't want to do it again."

"It's my company, it's my jet." He sounds almost wounded. *Oh, boys and their toys!*

"Thank you for the offer. But I'd be happier taking a scheduled flight."

He looks like he wants to argue further but decides against it.

"As you wish." He sighs. "Do you have much preparation to do for your interview?"

"No."

"Good. You're still not going to tell me which publishing houses?"

"No."

His lips curl up in a reluctant smile. "I am a man of means, Miss Steele."

"I am fully aware of that, Mr. Grey. Are you going to track my phone?" I ask innocently.

"Actually, I'll be quite busy this afternoon, so I'll have to get someone else to do it." He smirks.

Is he joking?

"If you can spare someone to do that, you're obviously overstaffed."

"I'll send an e-mail to the head of human resources and have her look into our head count." His lips twitch to hide his smile.

Oh, thank the Lord, he's recovered his sense of humor.

Mrs. Jones serves us breakfast and we eat quietly for a few moments. After clearing the pans, tactfully, she heads out of the living area. I peek up at him.

"What is it, Anastasia?"

"You know, you never did tell me why you don't like to be touched."

He blanches, and his reaction makes me feel guilty for asking.

"I've told you more than I've ever told anybody." His voice is quiet as he gazes at me impassively.

And it's clear to me that he's never confided in anyone. Doesn't he have any close friends? Perhaps he told Mrs. Robinson? I want to ask him, but I can't—I can't pry that invasively. I shake my head at the realization. He really is an island.

"Will you think about our arrangement while you're away?" he asks.

"Yes."

"Will you miss me?"

I gaze at him, surprised by his question.

"Yes," I answer honestly.

How could he mean so much to me in such a short time? He's got right under my skin . . . literally. He smiles and his eyes light up.

"I'll miss you, too. More than you know," he breathes.

My heart warms at his words. He really is trying hard. He gently strokes my cheek, bends down, and kisses me softly.

It is late afternoon, and I sit nervous and fidgeting in the lobby waiting for Mr. J. Hyde of Seattle Independent Publishing. This is my second interview today, and the one I'm most anxious about. My first interview went well, but it was for a larger conglomerate with offices based throughout the United States, and I would be one of many editorial assistants there. I can imagine being swallowed up and spat out pretty quickly in such a corporate machine. SIP is where I want to be. It's small and unconventional, championing local authors, and has an interesting and quirky roster of clients.

My surroundings are sparse, but I think it's a design statement rather than frugality. I am seated on one of two dark green chesterfield couches made of leather—not unlike the couch that Christian has in his playroom. I stroke the leather appreciatively and wonder idly what Christian does on that couch. My mind wanders as I think of the possibilities . . . no—I must not go there now. I flush at my wayward and inappropriate thoughts.

The receptionist is a young African-American woman with large silver earrings and long straightened hair. She has a bohemian look about her, the sort of woman I could be friendly with. The thought is comforting. Every few moments she glances up at me, away from her computer, and smiles reassuringly. I tentatively return her smile.

My flight is booked, my mother is in seventh heaven that I am visiting, I am packed, and Kate has agreed to drive me to the airport. Christian has ordered me to take my BlackBerry and the Mac. I roll my eyes at the memory of his overbearing bossiness, but I realize now that's just the way he is. He likes control over everything, including me. Yet he's so unpredictably and disarmingly agreeable, too. He can be tender, good-humored, even sweet. And when he is, it's so left field and unexpected. He insisted on accompanying me all the way down to my car in the garage. Jeez, I'm only going for a few days; he's acting like I'm going for weeks. He always keeps me off balance.

"Ana Steele?" A woman with long, black, pre-Raphaelite hair standing by the reception desk distracts me from my introspection. She has the same bohemian, floaty look as the receptionist. She could be in her late thirties, maybe in her forties. It's so difficult to tell with older women.

"Yes," I reply, standing awkwardly.

She gives me a polite smile, her cool hazel eyes assessing me. I am wearing one of Kate's dresses, a black pinafore over a white blouse, and my black pumps. Very interview, I think. My hair is restrained in a tight bun, and for once the tendrils are behaving themselves. She holds her hand out to me.

"Hello, Ana, my name's Elizabeth Morgan. I'm head of human resources here at SIP."

"How do you do?" I shake her hand. She looks very casual to be the head of HR.

"Please follow me."

We go through the double doors behind the reception area into a large brightly decorated open-plan office, and from there head into a small meeting room. The walls are pale green, lined with pictures of book covers. At the head of the maple conference table sits a young man with red hair tied in a ponytail. Small silver hooped earrings glint in both his ears. He wears a pale blue shirt, no tie, and stone chinos. As I approach him, he stands and gazes at me with fathomless dark blue eyes.

"Ana Steele, I'm Jack Hyde, the acquisitions editor here at SIP, and I'm very pleased to meet you."

We shake hands, and his dark expression is unreadable, though friendly enough, I think.

"Have you traveled far?" he asks pleasantly.

"No, I've recently moved to the Pike Street Market area."

"Oh, not far at all then. Please, take a seat."

I sit, and Elizabeth takes a seat beside him.

"So why would you like to intern for us at SIP, Ana?" he asks.

He says my name softly and cocks his head to one side, like someone I know—it's unnerving. Doing my best to ignore the irrational wariness he inspires, I launch into my carefully prepared speech, conscious that a rosy flush is spreading across my cheeks. I look at both of them, remembering the Katherine Kavanagh Successful Interviewing Technique lecture: *Maintain eye contact, Ana!* Boy, that woman can be bossy, too, sometimes. Jack and Elizabeth both listen attentively.

"You have a very impressive GPA. What extracurricular activities did you indulge in at WSU?"

Indulge? I blink at him. What an odd choice of word. I launch into details of my librarianship at the campus central library and my one experience of interviewing an obscenely rich despot for the student newspaper. I gloss over the fact that I didn't actually write the article. I mention the two literary societies that I belonged to and conclude with working at Clayton's and all the useless knowledge I now possess about hardware and DIY. They both laugh, which is the response I'd hoped for. Slowly, I relax and begin to enjoy myself.

Jack Hyde asks sharp, intelligent questions, but I'm not

thrown—I keep up, and when we discuss my reading preferences and my favorite books, I think I hold my own. Jack, on the other hand, appears to only favor American literature written after 1950. Nothing else. No classics—not even Henry James or Upton Sinclair or F. Scott Fitzgerald. Elizabeth says nothing, just nods occasionally and takes notes. Jack, though argumentative, is charming in his way, and my initial wariness dissipates the longer we talk.

"And where do you see yourself in five years' time?" he asks.

With Christian Grey, the thought comes involuntarily into my head. My errant mind makes me frown.

"Copyediting, perhaps? Maybe a literary agent, I'm not sure. I am open to opportunities."

He grins. "Very good, Ana. I don't have any further questions. Do you?" he directs his question at me.

"When would you like someone to start?" I ask.

"As soon as possible," Elizabeth pipes up. "When could you start?"

"I'm available from next week."

"That's good to know," Jack says.

"If that's all everyone has to say"—Elizabeth glances at the two of us—"I think that concludes the interview." She smiles kindly.

"It's been a pleasure to meet you, Ana," Jack says softly as he takes my hand. He squeezes it gently, so that I blink up at him as I say good-bye.

I feel unsettled as I make my way to my car, though I'm not sure why. I think the interview went well, but it's so hard to say. Interviews seem such artificial situations; everyone on their best behavior trying desperately to hide behind a professional façade. Did my face fit? I shall have to wait and see.

I climb into my Audi A3 and head back to the apartment, though I take my time. I'm on the red-eye with a stopover in Atlanta, but my flight doesn't leave until 10:25 this evening, so I have plenty of time.

Kate is unpacking boxes in the kitchen when I return.

"How did they go?" she asks, excited. Only Kate can look gorgeous in an oversized shirt, tattered jeans, and a dark blue bandana.

"Good, thanks, Kate. Not sure this outfit was cool enough for the second interview."

"Oh?"

"Boho chic might have done it."

Kate raises an eyebrow.

"You and boho chic." She cocks her head to one side—gah! Why is everyone reminding me of my favorite Fifty Shades? "Actually, Ana, you're one of the few people who could really pull that look off."

I grin. "I really liked the second place. I think I could fit in there. The guy who interviewed me was unnerving, though . . ." I trail off—shit, I'm talking to Megaphone Kavanagh here. *Shut up, Ana!*

"Oh?" The Katherine Kavanagh radar for an interesting tidbit of information swoops into action—a tidbit that will only resurface at some inopportune and embarrassing moment, which reminds me.

"Incidentally, will you please stop winding Christian up? Your comment about José at dinner yesterday was out of line. He's a jealous guy. It doesn't do any good, you know."

"Look, if he wasn't Elliot's brother I'd have said a lot worse. He's a real control freak. I don't know how you stand it. I was trying to make him jealous—give him a little help with his commitment issues." She holds her hands up defensively. "But if you don't want me to interfere, I won't," she says hastily at my scowl.

"Good. Life with Christian is complicated enough, trust me."

Jeez, I sound like him.

"Ana." She pauses, staring at me. "You're okay, aren't you? You're not running to your mother's to escape?"

I flush. "No, Kate. It was you who said I needed a break."

She closes the distance between us and takes my hands—a most un-Kate thing to do. *Oh no . . .* tears threaten.

"You're just, I don't know . . . different. I hope you're okay, and whatever issues you're having with Mr. Moneybags, you can talk to me. And I will try not to wind him up, though frankly it's like shooting fish in a barrel with him. Look, Ana, if something's wrong, tell me, I won't judge. I'll try to understand."

I blink back tears. "Oh, Kate." I hug her. "I think I've really fallen for him."

"Ana, anyone can see that. And he's fallen for you. He's mad about you. Won't take his eyes off you."

I laugh uncertainly. "Do you think so?"

"Hasn't he told you?"

"Not in so many words."

"Have you told him?"

"Not in so many words." I shrug apologetically.

"Ana! Someone has to make the first move, otherwise you'll never get anywhere."

What . . . tell him how I feel?

"I'm just afraid I'll frighten him away."

"And how do you know he's not feeling the same?"

"Christian, afraid? I can't imagine him being frightened of anything." But as I say the words, I imagine him as a small child. Maybe fear was all he knew then. Sorrow grips and squeezes my heart at the thought.

Kate gazes at me with pursed lips and narrowed eyes, rather like my subconscious—all she needs are the half-moon specs.

"You two need to sit down and talk to each other."

"We haven't been doing much talking lately." I blush. Other stuff. Nonverbal communication and that's okay. Well, much more than okay.

She grins. "That'll be the sexing! If that's going well, then that's half the battle, Ana. I'll grab some Chinese takeout. Are you ready to go?"

"I will be. We don't have to leave for a couple of hours or so."

"No—I'll see you in twenty." She grabs her jacket and leaves, forgetting to close the door. I shut it behind her and head off to my bedroom, mulling over her words.

Is Christian afraid of his feelings for me? Does he even have feelings for me? He seems very keen, says I'm his—but that's just part of his I-must-own-and-have-everything-now control freak Dominant self, surely. I realize that while I'm away, I will have to run through all our conversations again and see if I can pick out telltale signs.

I'll miss you, too . . . more than you know . . .

You've completely beguiled me . . .

I shake my head. I don't want to think about it now. I am charging the BlackBerry, so I haven't had it with me all afternoon. I approach it with caution, and I'm disappointed that there are no messages. I switch on the mean machine, and there are no messages there, either. *Same e-mail address, Ana*—my subconscious rolls her eyes at me, and for the first time I understand why Christian wants to spank me when I do that.

Okay. Well, I'll write him an e-mail.

From: Anastasia Steele
Subject: Interviews
Date: May 30 2011 18:49
To: Christian Grey

Dear Sir,
My interviews went well today.

Thought you might be interested.

How was your day?

Ana

I sit and glare at the screen. Christian's responses are usually instantaneous. I wait . . . and wait, and finally I hear the welcome ping from my inbox.

From: Christian Grey
Subject: My Day
Date: May 30 2011 19:03
To: Anastasia Steele

Dear Miss Steele,
Everything you do interests me. You are the most fascinating woman I know.

I'm glad your interviews went well.

My morning was beyond all expectations.

My afternoon was very dull in comparison.

Christian Grey
CEO, Grey Enterprises Holdings, Inc.

From: Anastasia Steele
Subject: Fine Morning
Date: May 30 2011 19:05
To: Christian Grey

Dear Sir,
The morning was exemplary for me, too, in spite of you weirding out on me after the impeccable desk sex. Don't think I didn't notice.

Thank you for breakfast. Or thank Mrs. Jones.

I'd like to ask you questions about her—without you weirding out on me again.

Ana

My finger hovers over the "send" button, and I am reassured that I'll be on the other side of the continent this time tomorrow.

From: Christian Grey
Subject: Publishing and You?
Date: May 30 2011 19:10
To: Anastasia Steele

Anastasia,
"Weirding" is not a verb and should not be used by anyone who wants to go into publishing. Impeccable? Compared to what, pray tell? And what do you need to ask about Mrs. Jones? I'm intrigued.

Christian Grey
CEO, Grey Enterprises Holdings, Inc.

From: Anastasia Steele
Subject: You and Mrs. Jones
Date: May 30 2011 19:17
To: Christian Grey

Dear Sir,
Language evolves and moves on. It is an organic thing. It is not stuck in an ivory tower, hung with expensive works of art and overlooking most of Seattle with a helipad stuck on its roof.

Impeccable—compared to the other times we have . . . what's your word . . . oh yes . . . fucked. Actually the fucking has been pretty impeccable, period, in my humble opinion—but then, as you know, I have very limited experience.

Is Mrs. Jones an ex-sub of yours?

Ana

My finger hovers once more over the "send" button, and I press it.

From: Christian Grey
Subject: Language. Watch Your Mouth!
Date: May 30 2011 19:22
To: Anastasia Steele

Anastasia,
Mrs. Jones is a valued employee. I have never had any relationship with her beyond our professional one. I do not employ anyone I've had any sexual relations with. I am shocked that you would think so. The only person I would make an exception to this rule is you—because you are a bright young woman with remarkable negotiating skills. Though, if you continue to use such language, I may have to reconsider taking you on here. I am glad you have limited experience. Your experience will continue to be limited—just to me. I shall take impeccable as a compliment—though with you, I'm never sure if that's what you mean or if your sense of irony is getting the better of you—as usual.

Christian Grey
CEO, Grey Enterprises Holdings, Inc., from His Ivory Tower

From: Anastasia Steele
Subject: Not for All the Tea in China

Date: May 30 2011 19:27
To: Christian Grey

Dear Mr. Grey,
I think I have already expressed my reservations about working for your company. My views on this have not changed, are not changing, and will not change, ever. I must leave you now, as Kate has returned with food. My sense of irony and I bid you good night.

I will contact you once I'm in Georgia.

Ana

From: Christian Grey
Subject: Even Twinings English Breakfast Tea?
Date: May 30 2011 19:29
To: Anastasia Steele

Good night, Anastasia.
I hope you and your sense of irony have a safe flight.

Christian Grey
CEO, Grey Enterprises Holdings, Inc.

Kate and I pull up outside the drop-off area at Sea-Tac Airport departure terminal. Leaning across, she hugs me.

"Enjoy Barbados, Kate. Have a wonderful vacation."

"I'll see you when I get back. Don't let old moneybags grind you down."

"I won't."

We hug again—and then I'm on my own. I head over to

check-in and stand in line, waiting with my carry-on luggage. I haven't bothered with a suitcase, just a smart rucksack that Ray gave me for my last birthday.

"Ticket, please?" The bored young man behind the desk holds up his hand without looking at me.

Mirroring his boredom, I hand over my ticket and my driver's license as ID. I am hoping for a window seat if at all possible.

"Okay, Miss Steele. You've been upgraded to first class."

"What?"

"Ma'am, if you'd like to go through to the first class lounge and wait for your flight there . . ." He seems to have woken up and is beaming at me like I'm Santa Claus and the Easter Bunny rolled into one.

"Surely there's some mistake."

"No, no." He checks his computer screen again. "Anastasia Steele—upgrade." He simpers.

Ugh. I narrow my eyes. He hands me my boarding pass, and I head toward the first class lounge muttering under my breath. Damn Christian Grey, interfering control freak—he just can't leave well enough alone.

CHAPTER TWENTY-TWO

I am manicured, massaged, and I've had two glasses of champagne. The first class lounge has many redeeming features. With each sip of Moet, I feel slightly more inclined to forgive Christian and his intervention. I open up my MacBook, hoping to test the theory that it works anywhere on the planet.

From: Anastasia Steele
Subject: Over-Extravagant Gestures
Date: May 30 2011 21:53
To: Christian Grey

Dear Mr. Grey,
What really alarms me is how you knew which flight I was on.

Your stalking knows no bounds. Let's hope that Dr. Flynn is back from vacation.

I have had a manicure, a back massage, and two glasses of champagne—a very nice start to my vacation.

Thank you.

Ana

From: Christian Grey
Subject: You're Most Welcome
Date: May 30 2011 21:59
To: Anastasia Steele

Dear Miss Steele,

Dr. Flynn is back, and I have an appointment this week.

Who was massaging your back?

Christian Grey
CEO with friends in the right places,
Grey Enterprises Holdings, Inc.

Aha! Payback time. Our flight has been called, so I shall e-mail him from the plane. It will be safer. I almost hug myself with mischievous glee.

THERE IS SO MUCH room in first class. Champagne cocktail in hand, I settle myself into the sumptuous leather window seat as the cabin slowly fills. I call Ray to tell him where I am—a mercifully brief call, as it's so late for him.

"Love you, Dad," I murmur.

"You, too, Annie. Say hi to your mom. Good night."

"Good night." I hang up.

Ray is in good form. I stare at my Mac, and with the same childish glee building, I open my laptop and open up my e-mail.

From: Anastasia Steele
Subject: Strong Able Hands
Date: May 30 2011 22:22
To: Christian Grey

Dear Sir,

A very pleasant young man massaged my back. Yes. Very pleasant indeed. I wouldn't have encountered Jean-Paul in the ordinary departure lounge—so thank you again for that treat. I'm not sure if I'll be allowed to e-mail once we take off, and I need my beauty sleep since I've not been sleeping so well recently.

Pleasant dreams, Mr. Grey . . . thinking of you.

Ana

Oh, he's going to flip out—and I shall be airborne and out of reach. Serves him right. If I'd been in the ordinary departure lounge, then Jean-Paul wouldn't have gotten his hands on me. He was a very nice young man, in a blond, perma-tanned way—honestly, who has a tan in Seattle? It's just so wrong. I think he was gay—but I'll just keep that detail to myself. I stare at my e-mail. Kate is right. It is like shooting fish in a barrel with him. My subconscious stares at me with an ugly twist to her mouth; *Do you really want to wind him up?* What he's done is sweet, you know! He cares about you and wants you to travel in style. Yes, but he could have asked me or told me. Not made me look like a complete klutz at check-in. I press "send" and wait, feeling like a very naughty girl.

"Miss Steele, you'll need to stow your laptop for takeoff," the over-made-up flight attendant says politely. She makes me jump. My guilty conscience is at work.

"Oh, sorry."

Crap. Now I'll have to wait to know if he's replied. She hands me a soft blanket and pillow, showing her perfect teeth. I drape the blanket over my knees. It's nice to feel pampered sometimes.

First class has filled up, except for the seat beside me, which is still unoccupied. *Oh no* . . . a disturbing thought crosses my mind. *Perhaps the seat is Christian's.* Oh, shit . . . no . . . he wouldn't do that. Would he? I told him I didn't want him to come with me. I glance anxiously at my watch, and then the disembodied voice from the flight deck announces, "Cabin crew, doors to automatic and cross check."

What does that mean? Are they closing the doors? My scalp prickles as I sit in palpitating anticipation. The seat next to me is the only unoccupied one in the sixteen-seat cabin. The plane jolts as it pulls away from the gate, and I breathe a sigh of relief but feel a faint tingle of disappointment too . . . no Christian for four days. I take a sneak peek at my BlackBerry.

From: Christian Grey
Subject: Enjoy It While You Can
Date: May 30 2011 22:25
To: Anastasia Steele

Dear Miss Steele,
I know what you're trying to do—and trust me, you've succeeded. Next time you'll be in the cargo hold, bound and gagged in a crate. Believe me when I say that attending to you in that state will give me so much more pleasure than merely upgrading your ticket.

I look forward to your return.

Christian Grey
Palm-Twitching CEO,
Grey Enterprises Holdings, Inc.

Holy crap. That's the problem with Christian's humor—I can never be sure if he's joking or if he's seriously angry. I suspect on this occasion he's seriously angry. Surreptitiously, so the flight attendant can't see, I type a reply under the blanket.

From: Anastasia Steele
Subject: Joking?

Date: May 30 2011 22:30
To: Christian Grey

You see—I have no idea if you're joking—and if you're not, then I think I'll stay in Georgia. Crates are a hard limit for me. Sorry I made you mad. Tell me you forgive me.

A

From: Christian Grey
Subject: Joking
Date: May 30 2011 22:31
To: Anastasia Steele

How can you be e-mailing? Are you risking the life of everyone on board, including yourself, by using your BlackBerry? I think that contravenes one of the rules.

Christian Grey
Two Palms Twitching CEO,
Grey Enterprises Holdings, Inc.

Two palms! I put my BlackBerry away, sit back while the plane taxis to the runway, and pull out my tattered copy of *Tess*—some light reading for the journey. Once we're airborne, I tip my seat back, and soon I'm drifting off to sleep.

The flight attendant wakes me as we start our descent into Atlanta. Local time is 5:45 a.m., but I've only had four hours' sleep or so . . . I feel groggy but grateful for the glass of orange juice she hands me. I glance nervously at my BlackBerry. There are no further e-mails from Christian. Well, it's nearly three in the morning in Seattle, and he probably wants to discourage me from screwing up the avionics system or whatever prevents planes from flying if mobile phones are switched on.

. . .

THE WAIT IN ATLANTA is only an hour. And again I'm luxuriating in the confines of the first class lounge. I am tempted to curl up and go to sleep on one of the plush, inviting couches that sink softly under my weight. But it will just not be long enough. To keep myself awake, I start a long stream-of-consciousness e-mail to Christian on my laptop.

From: Anastasia Steele
Subject: Do you like to scare me?
Date: May 31 2011 06:52 EST
To: Christian Grey

You know how much I dislike you spending money on me. Yes, you're very rich, but still it makes me uncomfortable, like you're paying me for sex. However, I like traveling first class, it's so much more civilized than coach. So thank you. I mean it—and I did enjoy the massage from Jean Paul. He was very gay. I omitted that bit in my e-mail to you to wind you up, because I was annoyed with you, and I'm sorry about that.

But as usual you overreact. You can't write things like that to me—bound and gagged in a crate. (Were you serious or was it a joke?) That scares me . . . you scare me . . . I am completely caught up in your spell, considering a lifestyle with you that I didn't even know existed until last week, and then you write something like that and I want to run screaming into the hills. I won't, of course, because I'd miss you. Really miss you. I want us to work, but I am terrified of the depth of feeling I have for you and the dark path you're leading me down. What you are offering is erotic and sexy, and I'm curious, but I'm also scared you'll hurt me—physically and emotionally. After three months you could say good-bye, and where will that leave me if you do? But then I suppose that risk is there in any relationship. This just isn't the sort of relationship I ever envisaged having, especially as my first. It's a huge leap of faith for me.

You were right when you said I didn't have a submissive bone in my body . . . and I agree with you now. Having said that, I want to be with you, and if that's what I have to do, I would like to try, but I think I'll suck at it and end up black and blue—and I don't relish that idea at all.

I am so happy that you have said that you will try more. I just need to think about what "more" means to me, and that's one of the reasons why I wanted some distance. You dazzle me so much I find it very difficult to think clearly when we're together.

They are calling my flight. I have to go.

More later.

Your Ana

I press "send" and make my way sleepily to the departure gate to board a different plane. This one has only six seats in first class, and once we are in the air, I curl up under my soft blanket and fall asleep.

All too soon, I'm woken by the flight attendant offering me more orange juice as we begin our approach to Savannah International. I sip slowly, beyond fatigued, and I allow myself to feel a modicum of excitement. I'm going to see my mother for the first time in six months. Sneaking another covert look at my BlackBerry, I remember vaguely that I sent a long, rambling e-mail to Christian—but there's nothing in response. It's five in the morning in Seattle; hopefully he's still asleep and not up playing mournful laments on his piano.

. . .

THE BEAUTY OF CARRY-ON rucksacks is that one can breeze out of the airport and not wait endlessly for baggage at the carousels. The beauty of traveling first class is that they let you off the plane first.

My mom is waiting with Bob, and it is so good to see them. I don't know if it's because of exhaustion, the long journey, or the whole Christian situation, but as soon as I'm in my mother's arms, I burst into tears.

"Oh, Ana, honey. You must be so tired." She glances anxiously at Bob.

"No, Mom, it's just—I'm so pleased to see you." I hug her tightly.

She feels so good and welcoming, like home. Reluctantly, I relinquish her, and Bob gives me an awkward one-armed hug. He seems unsteady on his feet, and I remember that he's hurt his leg.

"Welcome back, Ana. Why you cryin'?" he asks.

"Aw, Bob, I'm just pleased to see you, too." I stare up into his handsome square-jawed face and his twinkling blue eyes that gaze at me fondly. I like this husband, Mom. You can keep him. He takes my backpack.

"Jeez, Ana, what have you got in here?"

That would be the Mac, and they both put their arms around me as we head for the parking lot.

I always forget how unbearably hot it is in Savannah. Leaving the cool air-conditioned confines of the arrival terminal, we step into the Georgia heat like we're wearing it. *Whoa!* It saps everything. I have to struggle out of Mom and Bob's embrace so I can remove my hoodie. I am so glad I packed shorts. I miss the dry heat of Las Vegas sometimes, where I lived with Mom and Bob when I was seventeen, but this wet heat, even at 8:30 in the morning, takes some getting used to. By the time I'm in the back of Bob's wonderfully air-conditioned Tahoe SUV, I feel limp, and my hair has started a frizzy protest at the heat. In the back of the SUV, I quickly text Ray, Kate, and Christian:

Arrived safely in Savannah. A :)

My thoughts stray briefly to José as I press "send," and through the fog of my fatigue, I remember that his show is next week. Should I invite Christian, knowing how he feels about José? Will Christian still want to see me after that e-mail? I shudder at the thought, and then put it out of my mind. I'll deal with that later. Right now I am going to enjoy my mom's company.

"Honey, you must be tired. Would you like to sleep when we get home?"

"No, Mom. I'd like to go to the beach."

I AM IN MY blue halter-neck tankini, sipping a Diet Coke, on a sun bed facing the Atlantic Ocean, and to think that only yesterday I was staring out at the Sound toward the Pacific. My mother lounges beside me in a ridiculously large floppy sun hat and Jackie O shades, sipping a Coke of her own. We are on Tybee Island Beach, just three blocks from home. She holds my hand. My fatigue has waned, and as I soak up the sun, I feel comfortable, safe, and warm. For the first time in forever, I start to relax.

"So, Ana . . . tell me about this man who has you in such a spin."

Spin! How can she tell? What to say? I can't talk about Christian in any great detail because of the NDA, but even then, would I choose to talk to my mother about it? I blanch at the thought.

"Well?" she prompts, and squeezes my hand.

"His name's Christian. He's beyond handsome. He's wealthy . . . too wealthy. He's very complicated and mercurial."

Yes—I feel inordinately pleased with my concise, accurate summary. I turn on my side to face her, just as she makes the same move. She gazes at me with her crystal-clear blue eyes.

"Complicated and mercurial are the two pieces of information I want to concentrate on, Ana."

Oh no . . .

"Oh, Mom, his mood swings make me dizzy. He's had a grim upbringing, so he's very closed, difficult to gauge."

"Do you like him?"

"I more than like him."

"Really?" She gapes at me.

"Yes, Mom."

"Men aren't really complicated, Ana, honey. They are very simple, literal creatures. They usually mean what they say. And we spend hours trying to analyze what they've said, when really it's obvious. If I were you, I'd take him literally. That might help."

I gape at her. This sounds like good advice. Take Christian literally. Immediately some of the things he's said spring into my mind.

I don't want to lose you . . .

You've bewitched me . . .

You've completely beguiled me . . .

I'll miss you, too . . . more than you know . . .

I gaze at my mom. She *is* on her fourth marriage. Maybe she does know something about men after all.

"Most men are moody, darling, some more than others. Take your father, for instance . . ." Her eyes soften and sadden whenever she thinks of my dad. My real dad, this mythical man I never knew, snatched so cruelly from us in a combat training accident when he was a marine. Part of me thinks my mom has been looking for someone like my dad all this time . . . maybe she's finally found what she's looking for in Bob. Pity she couldn't find it with Ray.

"I used to think your father was moody. But now when I look back, I just think he was too caught up in his job and trying to make a life for us." She sighs. "He was so young, we both were. Maybe that was the issue."

Hmm . . . Christian is not exactly old. I smile fondly at her. She can become very soulful thinking about my father, but I'm sure he had nothing on Christian's moods.

"Bob wants to take us out tonight for dinner. To his golf club."

"Oh no! Bob's started playing golf?" I scoff in disbelief.

"Tell me about it," groans my mother, rolling her eyes.

. . .

AFTER A LIGHT LUNCH back at the house, I start to unpack. I am going to treat myself to a siesta. My mother has disappeared to mold some candles or whatever she does with them, and Bob is at work, so I have time to catch up on some sleep. I open the Mac and fire it up. It's two in the afternoon in Georgia, eleven in the morning in Seattle. I wonder if I have a reply from Christian. Nervously, I open up my e-mail.

From: Christian Grey
Subject: Finally!
Date: May 31 2011 07:30
To: Anastasia Steele

Anastasia,
I am annoyed that as soon as you put some distance between us, you communicate openly and honestly with me. Why can't you do that when we're together?

Yes, I'm rich. Get used to it. Why shouldn't I spend money on you? We've told your father I'm your boyfriend, for heaven's sake. Isn't that what boyfriends do? As your Dom, I would expect you to accept whatever I spend on you with no argument. Incidentally, tell your mother, too.

I don't know how to answer your comment about feeling like a whore. I know that's not what you've written, but it's what you imply. I don't know what I can say or do to eradicate these feelings. I'd like you to have the best of everything. I work exceptionally hard so I can spend my money as I see fit. I could buy you your heart's desire, Anastasia, and I want to. Call it redistribution of wealth, if you will. Or simply know that I would not, could not *ever* think of you in the way you described, and I'm angry that's how you perceive yourself. For such a bright, witty, beautiful young woman, you have some real self-esteem issues, and I have half a mind to make an appointment for you with Dr. Flynn.

I apologize for frightening you. I find the thought of instilling fear in you abhorrent. Do you really think I'd let you travel in the hold? I offered you my private jet, for heaven's sake. Yes, it was a joke, a poor one obviously. However, the fact is the thought of you bound and gagged turns me on (this is not a joke—it's true). I can lose the crate—crates do nothing for me. I know you have issues with gagging—we've talked about that—and if/when I do gag you, we'll discuss it. What I think you fail to realize is that in Dom/sub relationships it is the sub who has all the power. That's you. I'll repeat this—you are the one with all the power. Not I. In the boathouse you said no. I can't touch you if you say no—that's why we have an agreement—what you will and won't do. If we try things and you don't like them, we can revise the agreement. It's up to you—not me. And if you don't want to be bound and gagged in a crate, then it won't happen.

I want to share my lifestyle with you. I have never wanted anything so much. Frankly, I'm in awe of you, that one so innocent would be willing to try. That says more to me than you could ever know. You fail to see I am caught in your spell, too, even though I have told you this countless times. I don't want to lose you. I am nervous that you've flown three thousand miles to get away from me for a few days, because you can't think clearly around me. It's the same for me, Anastasia. My reason vanishes when we're together—that's the depth of my feeling for you.

I understand your trepidation. I did try to stay away from you; I knew you were inexperienced, though I would never have pursued you if I had known exactly how innocent you were—and yet you still manage to disarm me completely in a way that nobody has before. Your e-mail for example: I have read and reread it countless times trying to understand your point of view. Three months is an arbitrary amount of time. We could make it six months, a year? How long do you want it to be? What would make you comfortable? Tell me.

I understand that this is a huge leap of faith for you. I have to earn your trust, but by the same token, you have to communicate with me when I am failing to do this. You seem so strong and self-contained, and then I read what you've written here, and I see another side to you. We have to guide each other, Anastasia, and I can only take my cues from you. You have to be honest with me, and we have to both find a way to make this arrangement work.

You worry about not being submissive. Well, maybe that's true. Having said that, the only time you do assume the correct demeanor for a sub is in the playroom. It seems that's the one place where you let me exercise proper control over you and the only place you do as you're told. "Exemplary" is the term that comes to mind. And I'd never beat you black and blue. I aim for pink. Outside the playroom, I like that you challenge me. It's a very novel and refreshing experience, and I wouldn't want to change that. So yes, tell me what you want in terms of more. I will endeavor to keep an open mind, and I shall try to give you the space you need and stay away from you while you are in Georgia. I look forward to your next e-mail.

In the meantime, enjoy yourself. But not too much.

Christian Grey
CEO, Grey Enterprises Holdings, Inc.

Holy crap. He's written an essay like we're back at school—*and most of it's good.* My heart is in my mouth as I reread his epistle, and I huddle on the spare bed practically hugging my Mac. Make our agreement a year? I have the power! Jeez, I'm going to have to think about that. *Take him literally*, that's what my mother says. He doesn't want to lose me. He's said that twice! He wants to make this work, too. *Oh, Christian, so do I!* He's going to try to stay away! Does this mean he might fail to stay away? Suddenly, I hope so. I want to see him. We've been apart less than twenty-four hours, and knowing that I can't see him for four days, I realize how much I miss him. How much I love him.

"Ana, honey." The voice is soft and warm, full of love and sweet memories of times gone by.

A gentle hand brushes my face. My mom wakes me, and I'm wrapped around my laptop, hugging it to me.

"Ana, sweetheart," she continues in her soft, singsong voice while I surface from sleep, blinking in the pale pink light of dusk.

"Hi, Mom." I stretch out and smile.

"We're going out for dinner in thirty minutes. You still want to come?" she asks kindly.

"Oh yes, Mom, of course." I try very hard but fail to stifle my yawn.

"Now that's an impressive piece of technology." She points to my laptop.

Oh, crap.

"Oh . . . this?" I strive for casual, surprised nonchalance.

Will Mom notice? She seems to have grown more astute since I acquired a "boyfriend."

"Christian lent it to me. I think I could pilot the space shuttle with it, but I just use it for e-mails and Internet access."

Really, it's nothing. Eyeing me suspiciously, she sits down on the bed and tucks a stray lock of hair behind my ear.

"Has he e-mailed you?"

Oh, double crap.

"Yeah." My nonchalance is wearing thin, and I flush.

"Perhaps he's missing you, huh?"

"I hope so, Mom."

"What does he say?"

Oh, triple crap. I frantically try to think of something acceptable from that e-mail I can tell my mother. I'm sure she doesn't want to hear about Doms and bondage and gagging, but then I can't tell her because there's the NDA.

"He's told me to enjoy myself but not too much."

"Sounds reasonable. I'll leave you to get ready, honey." Leaning over, she kisses my forehead. "I'm so glad you're here, Ana. It's wonderful to see you." And with that loving statement, she leaves.

Hmm, Christian and reasonable . . . two concepts that I thought were mutually exclusive, but after his e-mail, maybe all things are possible. I shake my head. I will need time to digest his words. Probably after dinner—and I can reply to him then. I climb out of bed and quickly slip out of my T-shirt and shorts and head to the shower.

I have brought Kate's gray halter-neck dress that I wore for my graduation. It's the only dressy item I have. One good thing about the heat is that the creases have dropped out, so I think it will do for the golf club. As I dress, I open up the laptop. There is nothing new from Christian, and I feel a stab of disappointment. Very quickly, I type him an e-mail.

From: Anastasia Steele
Subject: Verbose?
Date: May 31 2011 19:08 EST
To: Christian Grey

Sir, you are quite the loquacious writer. I have to go to dinner at Bob's golf club, and just so you know, I am rolling my eyes at the thought. But you and your twitchy palm are a long way from me so my behind is safe, for now. I loved your e-mail. Will respond when I can. I miss you already. Enjoy your afternoon.

Your Ana

From: Christian Grey
Subject: Your Behind
Date: May 31 2011 16:10
To: Anastasia Steele

Dear Miss Steele,
I am distracted by the title of this e-mail. Needless to say it *is* safe—for now.

Enjoy your dinner, and I miss you, too, especially your behind and your smart mouth.

My afternoon will be dull, brightened only by thoughts of you and your eye rolling. I think it was you who so judiciously pointed out to me that I, too, suffer from that nasty habit.

Christian Grey
CEO & Eye Roller,
Grey Enterprises Holdings, Inc.

From: Anastasia Steele
Subject: Eye Rolling
Date: May 31 2011 19:14 EST
To: Christian Grey

Dear Mr. Grey,
Stop e-mailing me. I am trying to get ready for dinner. You are

very distracting, even when you are on the other side of the continent. And yes—who spanks you when you roll your eyes?

Your Ana

I press "send," and immediately the image of that evil witch Mrs. Robinson comes into my mind. I just can't picture it. Christian being beaten by someone as old as my mother, it's just so wrong. Again I wonder what damage she's wrought. My mouth sets in a hard, grim line. I need a doll to stick pins in, maybe that way I can vent some of the anger I feel at this stranger.

From: Christian Grey
Subject: Your Behind
Date: May 31 2011 16:18
To: Anastasia Steele

Dear Miss Steele,
I still prefer my title to yours, in so many different ways. It is lucky that I am master of my own destiny and no one castigates me. Except my mother, occasionally, and Dr. Flynn, of course. And you.

Christian Grey
CEO, Grey Enterprises Holdings, Inc.

From: Anastasia Steele
Subject: Chastising . . . Me?
Date: May 31 2011 19:22 EST
To: Christian Grey

Dear Sir,
When have I ever plucked up the nerve to chastise you, Mr. Grey? I think you are mixing me up with someone else . . . which is very worrying. I really do have to get ready.

Your Ana

From: Christian Grey
Subject: Your Behind
Date: May 31 2011 16:25
To: Anastasia Steele

Dear Miss Steele,

You do it all the time in print. Can I zip up your dress?

Christian Grey
CEO, Grey Enterprises Holdings, Inc.

For some unknown reason, his words leap off the screen and make me gasp. Oh . . . he wants to play games.

From: Anastasia Steele
Subject: NC-17
Date: May 31 2011 19:28 EST
To: Christian Grey

I would rather you unzipped it.

From: Christian Grey
Subject: Careful what you wish for . . .

Date: May 31 2011 16:31
To: Anastasia Steele

SO WOULD I.

Christian Grey
CEO, Grey Enterprises Holdings, Inc.

From: Anastasia Steele
Subject: Panting
Date: May 31 2011 19:33 EST
To: Christian Grey

Slowly . . .

From: Christian Grey
Subject: Groaning
Date: May 31 2011 16:35
To: Anastasia Steele

Wish I were there.

Christian Grey
CEO, Grey Enterprises Holdings, Inc.

From: Anastasia Steele
Subject: Moaning
Date: May 31 2011 19:37 EST
To: Christian Grey

SO DO I.

"Ana!" My mother calls me, making me jump. *Shit.* Why do I feel so guilty?

"Just coming, Mom."

From: Anastasia Steele
Subject: Moaning
Date: May 31 2011 19:39 EST
To: Christian Grey

Gotta go.

Laters, baby.

I dash into the hall, where Bob and my mother are waiting. My mother frowns.

"Darling—are you feeling okay? You look a bit flushed."

"Mom, I'm fine."

"You look lovely, dear."

"Oh, this is Kate's dress. You like it?"

Her frown deepens.

"Why are you wearing Kate's dress?"

Oh . . . no.

"Well, I like this one and she doesn't," I improvise quickly.

She regards me shrewdly while Bob oozes impatience with his hangdog, hungry look.

"I'll take you shopping tomorrow," she says.

"Oh, Mom, you don't need to do that. I have plenty of clothes."

"Can't I do something for my own daughter? Come on, Bob's starving."

"Too right," moans Bob, rubbing his stomach and assuming a fake pained expression.

I giggle as he rolls his eyes, and we head out the door.

Later when I'm in the shower, cooling under the lukewarm water, I reflect on how much my mother has changed. Seeing her at dinner, she was in her element: funny and flirty and among many friends at the golf club. Bob was warm and attentive . . . they seem so good for each other. I'm really pleased for her. It means I can stop worrying about her and second-guessing her decisions and put the dark days of Husband Number Three behind us both. Bob is a keeper. And she's giving me good advice. *When did that start happening?* Since I met Christian. *Why is that?*

When I'm done, I dry myself quickly, keen to get back to Christian. There's an e-mail waiting for me, sent just after I left for dinner a few hours ago.

From: Christian Grey
Subject: Plagiarism
Date: May 31 2011 16:41
To: Anastasia Steele

You stole my line.
And left me hanging.

Enjoy your dinner.

Christian Grey
CEO, Grey Enterprises Holdings, Inc.

From: Anastasia Steele
Subject: Who are you to cry thief?
Date: May 31 2011 22:18 EST
To: Christian Grey

Sir, I think you'll find it was Elliot's line originally.

Hanging how?

Your Ana

From: Christian Grey
Subject: Unfinished Business
Date: May 31 2011 19:22
To: Anastasia Steele

Miss Steele,
You're back. You left so suddenly—just when things were getting interesting.

Elliot's not very original. He must have stolen that line from someone.

How was dinner?

Christian Grey
CEO, Grey Enterprises Holdings, Inc.

From: Anastasia Steele
Subject: Unfinished Business?
Date: May 31 2011 22:26 EST
To: Christian Grey

Dinner was filling—you'll be very pleased to hear I ate far too much.

Getting interesting? How?

From: Christian Grey
Subject: Unfinished Business—Definitely

Date: May 31 2011 19:30
To: Anastasia Steele

Are you being deliberately obtuse? I think you'd just asked me to unzip your dress.

And I was looking forward to doing just that. I am also glad to hear you are eating.

Christian Grey
CEO, Grey Enterprises Holdings, Inc.

From: Anastasia Steele
Subject: Well . . . There's Always the Weekend
Date: May 31 2011 22:36 EST
To: Christian Grey

Of course I eat . . . It's only the uncertainty I feel around you that puts me off my food.

And I would never be unwittingly obtuse, Mr. Grey.

Surely you've worked that out by now. ;)

From: Christian Grey
Subject: Can't Wait
Date: May 31 2011 19:40
To: Anastasia Steele

I shall remember that, Miss Steele, and no doubt use the knowledge to my advantage.

I'm sorry to hear that I put you off your food. I thought I had a more concupiscent effect on you. That has been my experience, and most pleasurable it has been, too.

I very much look forward to the next time.

Christian Grey
CEO, Grey Enterprises Holdings Inc.

From: Anastasia Steele
Subject: Gymnastic Linguistics
Date: May 31 2011 22:36 EST
To: Christian Grey

Have you been playing with the thesaurus again?

From: Christian Grey
Subject: Rumbled
Date: May 31 2011 19:40
To: Anastasia Steele

You know me so well, Miss Steele.

I am having dinner with an old friend now so I will be driving.

Laters, baby©.

Christian Grey
CEO, Grey Enterprises Holdings, Inc.

Which old friend? I didn't think Christian had any old friends, except . . . her. I frown at the screen. Why does he have to still see her? Searing, green, bilious jealousy courses through me unexpectedly. I want to hit something, preferably Mrs. Robinson. Switching the laptop off in a temper, I clamber into bed.

I should really respond to his long e-mail from this morning, but I'm suddenly too angry. Why can't he see her for what she is—a child molester? I switch off the light, seething, staring into the darkness. How dare she? How dare she pick on a vulnerable adolescent? Is she still doing it? Why did they stop? Various scenarios filter through my mind: If he had had enough, then why is he still friends with her? Ditto her—is she married? Divorced? Jeez—does she have children of her own? *Does she have Christian's children?* My subconscious rears her ugly head, leering, and I'm shocked and nauseated at the thought. Does Dr. Flynn know about her?

I struggle out of bed and fire the mean machine up again. I am on a mission. I drum my fingers impatiently waiting for the blue screen to appear. I hit Google images and enter "Christian Grey" into the search engine. The screen is suddenly littered with images of Christian: in black tie, be-suited, jeez—José's pictures from the Heathman, in his white shirt and flannel trousers. How did they get on the Internet? Boy, he looks good.

I move quickly on: some with business associates, then picture after glorious picture of the most photogenic man I know intimately. *Intimately? Do I know Christian intimately?* I know him sexually, and I figure there's a lot more to discover there. I know he's moody, difficult, funny, cold, warm . . . jeez, the man is a walking mass of contradictions. I click to the next page. He's still on his own in all these photographs, and I remember Kate mentioning that she couldn't find any photographs of him with a date, prompting her gay question. Then, on the third page, there's a picture of me, with him, at my graduation. His only picture with a woman, and it's me.

Holy cow! I'm on Google! I stare at us together. I look surprised by the camera, nervous, off balance. This was just before I agreed to try. For his part, Christian looks impossibly handsome, calm and collected, and he's wearing *that tie.* I gaze at him, such a beautiful face, a beautiful face that could be staring at Mrs. Damned Robinson right now. I save the picture in my favorites and click through all eighteen pages of search results . . . nothing. I won't find Mrs. Robinson on Google. But I have to know if he's with her. I type a quick e-mail to Christian.

From: Anastasia Steele
Subject: Suitable Dinner Companions
Date: May 31 2011 23:58 EST
To: Christian Grey

I hope you and your friend had a very pleasant dinner.

Ana

P.S. Was it Mrs. Robinson?

I press "send" and climb despondently back into bed, resolving to ask Christian about his relationship with that woman. Part of me is desperate to know more, and another part wants to forget he ever told me. And my period has started, so I must remember to take my pill in the morning. I quickly program an alarm into the calendar on my BlackBerry. Setting it aside on the bedside table, I lie down and eventually drift into an uneasy sleep, wishing that we were in the same city, not twenty-five hundred miles apart.

After a morning of shopping and an afternoon back at the beach, my mother has decreed we should spend the evening in a bar. Abandoning Bob to the TV, we find ourselves in the upscale bar of Savannah's most exclusive hotel. I am on my second Cosmopolitan. My mother is on her third. She is offering more insights into the fragile male ego. It's very disconcerting.

"You see, Ana, men think that anything that comes out of a woman's mouth is a problem to be solved. Not some vague idea that we'd like to kick around and talk about for a while and then forget. Men prefer action."

"Mom, why are telling me this?" I ask, failing to hide my exasperation. She's been like this all day.

"Darling, you sound so lost. You've never brought a boy home. You never even had a boyfriend when we were in Vegas. I thought something might develop with that guy you met in college, José."

"Mom, José's just a friend."

"I know, sweetheart. But something's up, and I don't think you're telling me everything." She gazes at me, her face etched with motherly concern.

"I just needed some distance from Christian to get my thoughts straight . . . that's all. He tends to overwhelm me."

"Overwhelm?"

"Yeah. I miss him, though." I frown.

I have not heard from Christian all day. No e-mails, nothing. I am tempted to call him to see if he's okay. My worst fear is that he's been in a car accident; my second worst fear is that Mrs. Robinson has gotten her evil claws into him again. I know it's irrational, but where she's concerned, I seem to have lost all sense of perspective.

"Darling, I have to visit the restroom."

My mother's brief absence allows me another chance to check my BlackBerry. I have been trying surreptitiously to check my e-mail all day. Finally—a response from Christian!

From: Christian Grey
Subject: Dinner Companions
Date: June 1 2011 21:40 EST
To: Anastasia Steele

Yes, I had dinner with Mrs. Robinson. She is just an old friend, Anastasia.

Looking forward to seeing you again. I miss you.

Christian Grey
CEO, Grey Enterprises Holdings, Inc.

He *was* having dinner with her. My scalp prickles as adrenaline and fury lance through my body, all my worst fears realized. *How could he?* I am away for two days, and he runs off to that evil bitch.

From: Anastasia Steele
Subject: OLD Dinner Companions
Date: June 1 2011 21:42 EST
To: Christian Grey

She's not just an old friend.

Has she found another adolescent boy to sink her teeth into?

Did you get too old for her?

Is that the reason your relationship finished?

I press "send" as my mother returns.

"Ana, you're so pale. What's happened?"

I shake my head.

"Nothing. Let's have another drink," I mutter mulishly.

Her brow furrows, but she glances up and attracts the attention of one of the waiters, pointing to our glasses. He nods. He understands the universal language of "another round, please." As she does, I quickly glance at my BlackBerry.

From: Christian Grey
Subject: Careful . . .
Date: June 1 2011 21:45 EST
To: Anastasia Steele

This is not something I wish to discuss via e-mail.

How many Cosmopolitans are you going to drink?

Christian Grey
CEO, Grey Enterprises Holdings, Inc.

Holy fuck, he's here.

CHAPTER TWENTY-THREE

I glance nervously around the bar but cannot see him.

"Ana, what is it? You look like you've seen a ghost."

"It's Christian, he's here."

"What? Really?" She glances around the bar, too.

I have neglected to mention Christian's stalker tendencies to my mom.

I see him. My heart leaps, beginning a jittery thumping beat as he makes his way toward us. *He's really here—for me.* My inner goddess leaps up cheering from her chaise longue. Moving smoothly through the crowd, his hair glints burnished copper and red under the recessed halogens. His bright gray eyes are shining with—anger? Tension? His mouth is set in a grim line, jaw tense. *Oh, holy shit . . . no.* I am so mad at him right now, and here he is. How can I be angry with him in front of my mother?

He arrives at our table, gazing at me warily. He's dressed in his customary white linen shirt and jeans.

"Hi," I squeak, unable to hide my shock and awe at seeing him here in the flesh.

"Hi," he replies, and leaning down, he kisses my cheek, taking me by surprise.

"Christian, this is my mother, Carla." My ingrained manners take over.

He turns to greet my mom. "Mrs. Adams, I am delighted to meet you."

How does he know her name? He gives her the heart-stopping, Christian Grey–patented, full-blown, no-prisoners smile. She doesn't have a hope. My mother's lower jaw practically hits the table. *Jeez, get a grip, Mom.* She takes his proffered hand, and they shake. My mother hasn't replied. Oh, complete dumbfounded speechlessness is genetic—I had no idea.

"Christian," she manages finally, breathlessly.

He smiles knowingly at her, his gray eyes twinkling. I narrow my eyes at them both.

"What are you doing here?" My question sounds more brittle than I mean, and his smile disappears, his expression now guarded. I am thrilled to see him but completely thrown off balance, my anger about Mrs. Robinson simmering through my veins. I don't know if I want to shout at him or throw myself into his arms—but I don't think he'd like either—and I want to know how long he has been watching us. I'm also a little anxious about the e-mail I just sent him.

"I came to see you, of course." He gazes down at me impassively. *Oh, what is he thinking?* "I'm staying in this hotel."

"You're staying here?" I sound like a sophomore on amphetamines, too high pitched even for my own ears.

"Well, yesterday you said you wished I was here." He pauses, trying to gauge my reaction. "We aim to please, Miss Steele." His voice is quiet with no trace of humor.

Crap—is he mad? Maybe the Mrs. Robinson comments? Or the fact that I am on my third, soon to be fourth, Cosmo? My mother is glancing anxiously at the two of us.

"Won't you join us for a drink, Christian?" She waves to the waiter, who is at her side in a nanosecond.

"I'll have a gin and tonic," Christian says. "Hendricks if you have it, or Bombay Sapphire. Cucumber with the Hendricks, lime with the Bombay."

Holy hell . . . only Christian could make a meal out of ordering a drink.

"And two more Cosmos, please," I add, looking anxiously at Christian. I am drinking with my mother—no way can he be angry about that.

"Please pull up a chair, Christian."

"Thank you, Mrs. Adams."

Christian pulls a nearby chair over and sits gracefully down beside me.

"So you just happen to be staying in the hotel where we're drinking?" I ask, trying hard to keep my tone light.

"Or you just happen to be drinking in the hotel where I'm staying," Christian replies. "I just finished dinner, came in here, and saw you. I was distracted, thinking about your most recent e-mail, and I glance up and there you are. Quite a coincidence, eh?" He cocks his head to one side, and I see a trace of a smile. *Thank heavens*—we may be able to save the evening after all.

"My mother and I were shopping this morning and on the beach this afternoon. We decided on a few cocktails this evening," I mutter, feeling that I owe him some sort of explanation.

"Did you buy that top?" He nods at my brand-new green silk camisole. "The color suits you. And you've caught some sun. You look lovely."

I flush, speechless at his compliment.

"Well, I was going to pay you a visit tomorrow. But here you are."

He reaches over, takes my hand, and squeezes it gently, running his thumb across my knuckles to and fro . . . and I feel the familiar pull. The electric charge zapping beneath my skin under the gentle pressure from his thumb, firing into my bloodstream and pulsing around my body, heating everything in its path. It's been more than two days since I saw him. *Oh my* . . . I want him. My breath hitches. I blink at him, smiling shyly, and see a smile play on his lips.

"I thought I'd surprise you. But as ever, Anastasia, you surprise me by being here."

I glance quickly at Mom, who is staring at Christian . . . yes staring! *Stop it, Mom.* As if he's some exotic creature, never seen before. I mean, I know I've never had a boyfriend, and Christian only qualifies as such for ease of reference—but is it so unbelievable that I could attract a man? *This man? Yes, frankly—look at him!* my subconscious snaps. Oh, shut up! Who invited you to the party? I scowl at my mom—but she doesn't seem to notice.

"I don't want to interrupt the time you have with your mother. I'll have a quick drink and then retire. I have work to do," he states earnestly.

"Christian, it's lovely to meet you finally," Mom interjects, finally finding her voice. "Ana has spoken very fondly of you."

He smiles at her. "Really?" He raises an eyebrow at me, an amused expression on his face, and I flush again.

The waiter arrives with our drinks.

"Hendricks, sir," he says with a triumphant flourish.

"Thank you," Christian murmurs in acknowledgment.

I sip my latest Cosmo nervously.

"How long are you in Georgia, Christian?" Mom asks.

"Until Friday, Mrs. Adams."

"Will you have dinner with us tomorrow evening? And please, call me Carla."

"I'd be delighted to, Carla."

"Excellent. If you two will excuse me, I need to visit the restroom."

Mom . . . you've just been. I look at her desperately as she stands and walks off, leaving us alone together.

"So, you're mad at me for having dinner with an old friend." Christian turns his burning, wary gaze to me, lifting my hand to his lips and kissing each knuckle gently.

Jeez, he wants to do this now?

"Yes," I murmur as my heated blood courses through me.

"Our sexual relationship was over long ago, Anastasia," he whispers. "I don't want anyone but you. Haven't you worked that out yet?"

I blink at him. "I think of her as a child molester, Christian." I hold my breath waiting for his reaction.

Christian blanches. "That's very judgmental. It wasn't like that," he whispers, shocked. He releases my hand.

Judgmental?

"Oh, how was it then?" I ask. The Cosmos are making me brave.

He frowns at me, bewildered. I continue. "She took advantage of a vulnerable fifteen-year-old boy. If you had been a fifteen-year-old girl and Mrs. Robinson was a Mr. Robinson, tempting you into a BDSM lifestyle, that would have been okay? If it was Mia, say?"

He gasps and scowls at me. "Ana, it wasn't like that."

I glare at him.

"Okay, it didn't feel like that to me," he continues quietly. "She was a force for good. What I needed."

"I don't understand." It's my turn to look bewildered.

"Anastasia, your mother will be back shortly. I'm not comfortable talking about this now. Later, maybe. If you don't want me here, I have a plane on standby at Hilton Head. I can go."

He's angry with me . . . no.

"No—don't go. Please. I'm thrilled you're here. I'm just trying to make you understand. I'm angry that as soon as I left, you had dinner with her. Think about how you are when I get anywhere near José. José is a good friend. I have never had a sexual relationship with him. Whereas you and her . . ." I trail off, unwilling to take that thought further.

"You're jealous?" He stares at me, dumbfounded, and his eyes soften slightly, warming.

"Yes, and angry about what she did to you."

"Anastasia, she helped me. That's all I'll say about that. And as for your jealousy, put yourself in my shoes. I haven't had to justify my actions to anyone in the last seven years. Not one person. I do as I wish, Anastasia. I like my autonomy. I didn't go and see Mrs. Robinson to upset you. I went because every now and then we have dinner. She's a friend and a business partner."

Business partner? Holy crap. This is news.

He gazes at me, assessing my expression. "Yes, we're business partners. The sex is over between us. It has been for years."

"Why did your relationship end?"

His mouth narrows and his eyes gleam. "Her husband found out."

Holy shit!

"Can we talk about this some other time—somewhere more private?" he growls.

"I don't think you'll ever convince me that she's not some kind of pedophile."

"I don't think of her that way. I never have. Now that's enough!" he snaps.

"Did you love her?"

"How are you two getting on?" My mother has returned, unseen by either of us.

I plaster a fake smile on my face as both Christian and I lean back hastily . . . guiltily. She gazes at me.

"Fine, Mom."

Christian sips his drink, watching me closely, his expression guarded. What is he thinking? Did he love her? I think if he did, I will lose it, big time.

"Well, ladies, I shall leave you to your evening."

No . . . no . . . he can't leave me hanging like this.

"Please, put these drinks on my tab, room number 612. I'll call you in the morning, Anastasia. Until tomorrow, Carla."

"Oh, it's so nice to hear someone use your full name."

"Beautiful name for a beautiful girl," Christian murmurs, shaking her outstretched hand, and she actually simpers.

Oh, Mom—et tu, Brute? I stand, gazing up at him, imploring him to answer my question, and he kisses my cheek chastely.

"Laters, baby," he whispers in my ear. Then he's gone.

Damned control freak bastard. My anger returns in full force. I slump into my chair and turn to face my mother.

"Well, strike me down with a feather, Ana. He's a catch. I don't know what's going on between you two though. I think you need to talk to each other. Phew—the UST in here, it's unbearable." She fans herself theatrically.

"MOM!"

"Go talk to him."

"I can't. I came here to see you."

"Ana, you came here because you're confused about that boy.

It's obvious you two are crazy about each other. You need to talk to him. He's just flown three-thousand-odd miles to see you, for heaven's sake. And you know how awful it is to fly."

I flush. I haven't told her about his private plane.

"What?" she snaps.

"He has his own plane," I mumble, embarrassed, "and it's only two and a half thousand miles, Mom."

Why am I embarrassed? Her eyebrows shoot up.

"Wow," she mutters. "Ana, there's something going on between you two. I've been trying to fathom it since you arrived here. But the only way you are going to sort the problem, whatever it is, is to talk it through with him. You can do all the thinking you like—but until you actually talk, you're not going to get anywhere."

I frown at my mother.

"Ana, honey, you've always had a tendency to overanalyze everything. Go with your gut. What does that tell you, sweetheart?"

I stare at my fingers.

"I think I'm in love with him," I mutter.

"I know darling. And he with you."

"No!"

"Yes, Ana. Hell—what do you need? A neon sign flashing on his forehead?"

I gape at her and tears prick the corner of my eyes.

"Ana, darling. Don't cry."

"I don't think he loves me."

"I don't care how rich you are, you don't drop everything and get in your private plane to cross a whole continent just for afternoon tea. Go to him! This is a beautiful location, very romantic. It's also neutral territory."

I squirm under her gaze. I want to go and I don't.

"Darling, don't feel you have to come back with me. I want you happy—and right now I think the key to your happiness is upstairs in room 612. If you need to come home later, the key is under the yucca plant on the front porch. If you stay—well . . . you're a big girl now. Just be safe."

I flush Stars and Stripes red. *Jeez, Mom.*

"Let's finish our Cosmos first."

"That's my girl, Ana." She grins.

I KNOCK TIMIDLY ON room 612 and wait. Christian opens the door. He's on his cell. He blinks at me in complete surprise, then holds the door open wide and beckons me into his room.

"All the redundancy packages concluded? . . . And the cost? . . ." Christian whistles between his teeth. "Sheesh . . . that was one expensive mistake . . . And Lucas? . . ."

I glance around the room. He's in a suite, like the one at the Heathman. The furnishings here are ultramodern, very now. All muted dark purples and golds with bronze starbursts on the walls. Christian walks over to a dark wood unit and pulls open a door to reveal a minibar. He indicates that I should help myself, then wanders into the bedroom. I assume it's so I can no longer hear his conversation. I shrug. He didn't stop his call when I entered his study that time. I hear water running . . . he's filling a bath. I help myself to an orange juice. He ambles back into the room.

"Have Andrea send me the schematics. Barney said he'd cracked the problem . . ." Christian laughs. "No, Friday . . . There's a plot of land here that I'm interested in . . . Yeah, get Bill to call . . . No, tomorrow . . . I want to see what Georgia will offer if we move in." Christian doesn't take his eyes off me. Handing me a glass, he points to an ice bucket.

"If their incentives are attractive enough . . . I think we should consider it, though I'm not sure about the damned heat here . . . I agree, Detroit has its advantages, too, and it's cooler . . ." His face darkens momentarily. *Why?* "Get Bill to call. Tomorrow . . . Not too early." He hangs up and stares at me, his face unreadable, and the silence stretches between us.

Okay . . . my turn to talk.

"You didn't answer my question," I murmur.

"No. I didn't," he says quietly, his gray eyes wide and cautious.

"No, you didn't answer my question, or no, you didn't love her?"

He folds his arms and leans against the wall, and a small smile plays upon his lips.

"What are you doing here, Anastasia?"

"I've just told you."

He takes a deep breath.

"No. I didn't love her." He frowns at me, amused yet puzzled.

I can't believe I'm holding my breath. I sag like an old cloth sack as I release it. *Well, thank heavens for that.* How would I feel if he actually loved the witch?

"You're quite the green-eyed goddess, Anastasia. Who would have thought?"

"Are you making fun of me, Mr. Grey?"

"I wouldn't dare." He shakes his head solemnly, but he has a wicked gleam in his eye.

"Oh, I think you would, and I think you do—often."

He smirks as I give him back the words he's said to me before. His eyes darken.

"Please stop biting your lip. You're in my room, I haven't set eyes on you for nearly three days, and I've flown a long way to see you." His tone has changed to soft, sensual.

His BlackBerry buzzes, distracting us both, and he switches it off without glancing to see who it is. My breath hitches. I know where this is going . . . *but we're supposed to talk.* He takes a step toward me wearing his sexy predatory look.

"I want you, Anastasia. Now. And you want me. That's why you're here."

"I really did want to know," I whisper as a defense.

"Well, now that you do, are you coming or going?"

I flush as he comes to a halt in front of me.

"Coming," I murmur, staring anxiously up at him.

"Oh, I hope so." He gazes down at me. "You were so mad at me," he breathes.

"Yes."

"I don't remember anyone but my family ever being mad at me. I like it."

He runs the tips of fingers down my cheek. *Oh my,* his proximity, his delicious Christian smell. We're supposed to be talking, but my heart is pounding, my blood singing as it courses through my body, desire pooling, unfurling . . . everywhere. Christian bends and runs his nose along my shoulder and up to the base of my ear, his fingers slipping into my hair.

"We should talk," I whisper.

"Later."

"There's so much I want to say."

"Me, too."

He plants a soft kiss under my earlobe while his fingers tighten in my hair. Pulling my head back, he exposes my throat to his lips. His teeth skim my chin, and he kisses my throat.

"I want you," he breathes.

I moan and reach up and grasp his arms.

"Are you bleeding?" He continues to kiss me.

Holy fuck. Does nothing slip by him?

"Yes," I whisper, embarrassed.

"Do you have cramps?"

"No." I flush. *Jeez . . .*

He stops and looks down at me.

"Did you take your pill?"

"Yes." How mortifying is this?

"Let's go have a bath."

Oh?

He takes my hand and leads me into the bedroom. It's dominated by a super-king-sized bed with elaborate drapes. But we don't stop there. He takes me into the bathroom, which is two rooms, all aquamarines and white limestone. It's huge. In the second room a sunken bath, big enough for four people with stone steps that lead into it, is slowly filling with water. Steam rises gently above the foam, and I notice a stone bench that runs all the way around the bath. Candles flicker to the side. Wow . . . he's done all this while on the phone.

"Do you have a hair tie?"

I blink at him, fish into my jeans pocket, and pull out a hair elastic.

"Put your hair up," he orders softly. I do as he asks.

It's warm and sultry beside the bath, and my camisole starts to stick. He leans over and shuts off the faucet. Leading me back into the first part of the bathroom, he stands behind me as we face the wall-sized mirror above the two glass sinks.

"Take your sandals off," he murmurs and I oblige quickly dropping them to the sandstone floor.

"Lift up your arms," he breathes. I do as I'm told, and he lifts my camisole over my head so that I'm topless standing in front of him. Not taking his eyes off mine, he reaches around and undoes the top button on my jeans and the zipper.

"I'm going to have you in the bathroom, Anastasia."

Leaning down, he kisses my neck. I move my head to one side to give him easier access. Hooking his thumbs into my jeans, he slowly slides them down my legs, sinking down behind me as he pulls them and my panties to the floor.

"Step out of your jeans."

Grasping the edge of the sink, I do just that. I am now naked, staring at myself, and he's kneeling behind me. He kisses and then softly bites my behind, making me gasp. He stands and stares at me once more in the mirror. I try hard to stay still, ignoring my natural inclination to cover myself. He splays his hand across my belly, the span of his hand almost reaching from hip to hip.

"Look at you. You are so beautiful," he murmurs. "See how you feel." He clasps both my hands in his, his palms against the backs of my hands, his fingers in between mine so that my fingers are splayed. He places my hands on my belly. "Feel how soft your skin is." His voice is soft and low. He moves my hands in a slow circle, then upward toward my breasts. "Feel how full your breasts are." He holds my hands so that they cup my breasts. He gently strokes my nipples with his thumbs over and over.

I moan between parted lips and arch my back so my breasts fill my palms. He squeezes my nipples between our thumbs, pulling gently so that they elongate further. I watch in fascination at the wanton creature writhing in front of me. *Oh, this feels good.* I groan and close my eyes, no longer wanting to see that libidinous woman in the mirror falling apart under her own hands . . . his hands . . . feeling my skin as he would, experiencing how arousing it is—just his touch and his calm, soft commands.

"That's right, baby," he murmurs.

He guides my hands down the sides of my body, past my waist to my hips, and across to my pubic hair. He slides his leg in between mine, pushing my feet farther apart, widening my stance, and runs my hands over my sex, one hand at a time in turn, setting up a rhythm. It is so erotic. Truly I am a marionette and he is the master puppeteer.

"Look at you glow, Anastasia," he whispers as he trails kisses and soft bites along my shoulder. I groan. Suddenly he lets go.

"Carry on," he orders, and stands back watching me.

I rub myself. *No.* I want him to do it. It doesn't feel the same. I'm lost without him. He pulls his shirt over his head and quickly takes off his jeans.

"You'd rather I do this?" His gray gaze scorches mine in the mirror.

"Oh yes . . . please," I breathe.

He wraps his arms around me again and takes my hands once more, continuing the sensual caress across my sex, over my clitoris. His chest hair scrapes against me, his erection presses against me. *Oh, soon . . . please.* He bites the nape of my neck, and I close my eyes, enjoying the myriad sensations: my neck, my groin . . . the feel of him behind me. He stops abruptly and spins me around, circling my wrists with one hand, imprisoning my hands behind me, and pulling at my ponytail with the other. I am flush against him, and he kisses me wildly, ravaging my mouth with his. Holding me in place.

His breathing is ragged, matching mine.

"When did you start your period, Anastasia?" he asks out of the blue, gazing down at me.

"Er . . . yesterday," I mumble in my highly aroused state.

"Good." He releases me and turns me around.

"Hold on to the sink," he orders, and drags my hips back again, like he did in the playroom, so I'm bending down.

He reaches between my legs and pulls on the blue string—*what?!*—and gently takes my tampon out and tosses it into the nearby toilet. *Holy fuck.* Sweet mother of all . . . Jeez. And then he's inside me . . . ah! Skin against skin . . . moving slowly at first . . . easily, testing me, pushing me . . . *oh my.* I grip on to the sink, panting, forcing myself back on him, feeling him inside me. Oh, the sweet agony . . . his hands clasp my hips. He sets a punishing rhythm—in, out, and he reaches around and finds my clitoris, massaging me . . . oh jeez. I can feel myself quicken.

"That's right, baby," he rasps as he grinds into me, angling his hips, and it's enough to send me flying, flying high.

Whoa . . . and I come, loudly, gripping for dear life onto the sink as I spiral down through my orgasm, everything spinning and clenching at once. He follows, clasping me tightly, his front on my back as he climaxes and calls my name like it's a litany or a prayer.

"Oh, Ana!" His breathing is ragged in my ear, in perfect synergy with mine. "Oh, baby, will I ever get enough of you?" he whispers.

We sink slowly to the floor, and he wraps his arms around me, imprisoning me. Will it always be like this? So overwhelming, so all-consuming, so bewildering and beguiling. I wanted to talk, but now I'm spent and dazed from his lovemaking and wondering if *I* will ever get enough of *him*?

I am curled on his lap, my head against his chest, as we both calm. Very subtly, I inhale his sweet, intoxicating Christian scent. *I must not nuzzle. I must not nuzzle.* I repeat the mantra in my head—though I am so tempted to do so. I want to lift my hand and draw patterns in his chest hair with my fingertips . . . but I resist, knowing that he'll hate it if I do. We are both quiet, lost in our thoughts. I am lost in him . . . lost to him.

I remember that I have my period.

"I'm bleeding," I murmur.

"Doesn't bother me," he breathes.

"I noticed." I can't keep the dryness out of my voice.

He tenses. "Does it bother you?" he asks softly.

Does it bother me? Maybe it should . . . should it? No, it doesn't. I lean back and look up at him, and he gazes down at me, his eyes a soft cloudy gray.

"No, not at all."

He smirks. "Good. Let's have a bath."

He uncurls from around me, placing me on the floor as he makes to stand. As he does, I notice again the small, round white scars on his chest. They are not chicken pox, I muse absentmindedly. Grace said he was hardly affected. *Holy shit* . . . they must be burns. Burns from what? I blanch at the realization, shock and revulsion coursing through me. From cigarettes? Mrs. Robinson, his birth mother, who? Who did this to him? Maybe there's a reasonable explanation, and I'm overreacting—wild hope blossoms in my chest, hope that I am wrong.

"What is it?" Christian's face is wide-eyed with alarm.

"Your scars," I whisper. "They're not from chicken pox."

I watch as in a split second he closes down, his stance changing from relaxed, calm, and at ease to defensive—angry even. He frowns, his face darkening, and his mouth presses into a thin, hard line.

"No, they're not," he snaps, but he does not elaborate further. He stands, holds his hand out for me, and hauls me to my feet.

"Don't look at me like that." His voice is colder and scolding as he lets go of my hand.

I flush, chastened, and stare down at my fingers, and I know, I know that someone stubbed cigarettes out on Christian. I feel sick.

"Did she do that?" I whisper before I can stop myself.

He says nothing, so I'm forced to look at him. He's glaring at me.

"She? Mrs. Robinson? She's not an animal, Anastasia. Of

course she didn't. I don't understand why you feel you have to demonize her."

He's standing there, naked, gloriously naked, with my blood on him . . . and we're finally having this conversation. And I'm naked, too—neither of us has anywhere to hide, except perhaps the bath. I take a deep breath, move past him, and step down into the water. It is deliciously warm, soothing, and deep. I melt into the fragrant foam and stare up at him, hiding among the bubbles.

"I just wonder what you would be like if you hadn't met her. If she hadn't introduced you to your . . . um, lifestyle."

He sighs and steps down into the bath opposite me, his jaw clenched with tension, his eyes frosty. As he gracefully submerges his body beneath the water, he's careful not to touch me. *Jeez—have I made him that mad?*

He stares impassively at me, his face unreadable, saying nothing. Again the silence stretches between us, but I hold my counsel. It's your turn, Grey—I am not caving this time. My subconscious is nervous, anxiously biting her nails—this could go either way. Christian and I stare at each other, but I am not backing down. Eventually, after what seems like a millennium, he shakes his head, and he smirks.

"I would probably have gone the way of my birth mother, had it not been for Mrs. Robinson."

Oh! I blink at him. Crack addict or whore? Possibly both?

"She loved me in a way I found . . . acceptable," he adds with a shrug.

What the hell does that mean?

"Acceptable?" I whisper.

"Yes." He stares intently at me. "She distracted me from the destructive path I found myself following. It's very hard to grow up in a perfect family when you're not perfect."

Oh no. My mouth dries as I digest his words. He gazes at me, his expression unfathomable. He's not going to tell me any more. How frustrating. Inside, I'm reeling—he sounds so full of self-loathing. And Mrs. Robinson loved him. *Holy shit* . . . does she still? I feel like I've been kicked in the stomach.

"Does she still love you?"

"I don't think so, not like that." He frowns as if he hasn't thought about the idea. "I keep telling you it was a long time ago. It's in the past. I couldn't change it even if I wanted to, which I don't. She saved me from myself." He's exasperated and runs a wet hand through his hair. "I've never discussed this with anyone." He pauses. "Except Dr. Flynn, of course. And the only reason I'm talking about this now, to you, is because I want you to trust me."

"I do trust you, but I do want to know you better, and whenever I try to talk to you, you distract me. There's so much I want to know."

"Oh, for pity's sake, Anastasia. What do you want to know? What do I have to do?" His eyes blaze, and though he doesn't raise his voice, I know he's trying to rein in his temper.

I glance down at my hands, clear beneath the water as the bubbles have started to disperse.

"I'm just trying to understand; you're such an enigma. Unlike anyone I've met before. I'm glad you're telling me what I want to know."

Jeez—maybe it's the Cosmopolitans making me brave, but suddenly I cannot bear the distance between us. I move through the water to his side and lean against him so we're touching, skin to skin. He tenses and eyes me warily, as if I might bite. *Well, that's a turnaround.* My inner goddess gazes at him in quiet, surprised speculation.

"Please don't be angry with me," I whisper.

"I am not angry with you, Anastasia. I'm just not used to this kind of talking—this probing. I only have this with Dr. Flynn and with—" He stops and frowns.

"With her. Mrs. Robinson. You talk to her?" I prompt, trying to rein in my own temper.

"Yes, I do."

"What about?"

He shifts in the bath so that he's facing me, causing the water to lap over the sides onto the floor. He places his arm around my shoulders, resting on the ledge of the bath.

"Persistent aren't you?" he murmurs, a trace of irritation in his voice. "Life, the universe—business. Anastasia, Mrs. R and I go way back. We can discuss anything."

"Me?" I whisper.

"Yes." Gray eyes watch me carefully.

I bite my bottom lip, trying to curb the sudden rush of anger that surfaces.

"Why do you talk about me?" I endeavor not to sound whiney and petulant, but I don't succeed. I know I should stop. I am pushing him too hard. My subconscious has her Munch's *Scream* face on again.

"I've never met anyone like you, Anastasia."

"What does that mean? Anyone who just didn't automatically sign your paperwork, no questions asked?"

He shakes his head. "I need advice."

"And you take advice from Mrs. Pedo?" I snap. The hold on my temper is more tentative than I thought.

"Anastasia—enough," he snaps back sternly, his eyes narrowing.

I'm skating on thin ice, and I'm heading into danger. "Or I'll put you across my knee. I have no sexual or romantic interest in her whatsoever. She's a dear, valued friend and a business partner. That's all. We have a past, a shared history, which was monumentally beneficial for me, though it fucked up her marriage—but that side of our relationship is over."

Jeez—another part I just can't understand. She was married as well. How did they get away with it for so long?

"And your parents never found out?"

"No," he growls. "I've told you this."

And I know that's it. I cannot ask him any further questions about her because he will lose it with me.

"Are you done?" he snaps.

"For now."

He takes a deep breath and visibly relaxes in front of me, like a great weight has been lifted from his shoulders or something.

"Right—my turn," he mutters, and his glare turns steely, speculative. "You haven't responded to my e-mail."

I flush. Oh, I hate the spotlight on me, and it seems he's going to get angry every time we have a discussion. I shake my head. Perhaps that's how he feels about my questions; he's not used to being challenged. The thought is revelatory, distracting, and unnerving.

"I was going to respond. But now you're here."

"You'd rather I wasn't?" he breathes, his expression impassive again.

"No, I'm pleased," I murmur.

"Good." He gives me a genuine, relieved smile. "I'm pleased I'm here, too—in spite of your interrogation. So, while it's acceptable to grill me, you think you can claim some kind of diplomatic immunity just because I've flown all this way to see you? I'm not buying it, Miss Steele. I want to know how you feel."

Oh no . . .

"I told you. I am pleased you're here. Thank you for coming all this way," I say feebly.

"It's my pleasure." His eyes shine as he leans down and kisses me gently. I feel myself responding automatically. The water is still warm, the bathroom still steamy. He stops and pulls back, gazing down at me.

"No. I think I want some answers first before we do any more."

More? There's that word again. And he wants answers . . . answers to what? I don't have a secret past—I don't have a harrowing childhood. What could he possibly want to know about me that he doesn't already know?

I sigh, resigned. "What do you want to know?"

"Well, how you feel about our would-be arrangement, for starters."

I blink at him. Truth or dare time—my subconscious and inner goddess glance nervously at each other. *Hell, let's go for truth.*

"I don't think I can do it for an extended period of time. A whole weekend being someone I'm not." I flush and stare at my hands.

He tips my chin up, and he's smirking at me, amused.

"No, I don't think you could, either."

And part of me feels slightly affronted and challenged. "Are you laughing at me?"

"Yes, but in a good way," he says with a small smile.

He leans down and kisses me softly, briefly.

"You're not a great submissive," he breathes as he holds my chin, his eyes dancing with humor.

I stare at him, shocked, then I burst out laughing—and he joins me.

"Maybe I don't have a good teacher."

He snorts. "Maybe. Perhaps I should be stricter with you." He cocks his head to one side and gives me an artful smile.

I swallow. Jeez, no. But at the same time, my muscles clench deliciously deep inside. It is his way of showing that he cares. Perhaps the only way he can show he cares—I realize that. He's staring at me, gauging my reaction.

"Was it that bad when I spanked you the first time?"

I gaze back at him, blinking. *Was it that bad?* I remember feeling confused by my reaction. It hurt, but not that much in retrospect. He's said over and over again it's more in my head. And the second time . . . Well, that was good . . . hot.

"No, not really," I whisper.

"It's more the idea of it?" he prompts.

"I suppose. Feeling pleasure, when one isn't supposed to."

"I remember feeling the same. Takes a while to get your head around it."

Holy hell. This was when he was a kid.

"You can always use the safeword, Anastasia. Don't forget that. And, as long as you follow the rules, which fulfill a deep need in me for control and to keep you safe, then perhaps we can find a way forward."

"Why do you need to control me?"

"Because it satisfies a need in me that wasn't met in my formative years."

"So it's a form of therapy?"

"I've not thought of it like that, but yes, I suppose it is."

This I can understand. This will help.

"But, here's the thing—one moment you say 'don't defy me,' the next you say you like to be challenged. That's a very fine line to tread successfully."

He gazes at me for a moment, then frowns.

"I can see that. But you seem to be doing fine so far."

"But at what personal cost? I'm tied up in knots here."

"I like you tied up in knots." He smirks.

"That's not what I meant!" I splash him in exasperation.

He gazes down at me, arching an eyebrow.

"Did you just splash me?"

"Yes." *Holy shit . . . that look.*

"Oh, Miss Steele." He grabs me and pulls me onto his lap, sloshing water all over the floor. "I think we've done enough talking for now."

He clasps his hands on either side of my head and kisses me. Deeply. Possessing my mouth. Angling my head . . . controlling me. I moan against his lips. This is what he likes. This is what he's so good at. Everything ignites inside me and my fingers are in his hair, holding him to me, and I'm kissing him back and saying I want you, too, the only way I know how. He groans, shifting me so I'm astride him, kneeling over him, his erection beneath me. He pulls back and looks at me, his eyes hooded, glowing and lustful. I drop my hands to grab on to the edge of the bath, but he grips both my wrists and pulls my hands behind my back, holding them together in one hand.

"I'm going to have you now," he whispers, and lifts me so that I'm hovering over him. "Ready?" he breathes.

"Yes," I whisper, and he eases me on to him, slowly, exquisitely slowly . . . filling me . . . watching me as he takes me.

I groan, closing my eyes, and I revel in the sensation, the stretching fullness. He flexes his hips, and I gasp, leaning forward, resting my forehead against his.

"Please, let my hands go," I whisper.

"Don't touch me," he pleads, and releasing my wrists, he grabs my hips.

Clasping the bath ledge, I move up and then down slowly, opening my eyes to gaze at him. He's watching me, his mouth open, his breathing halted, stilted—his tongue between his teeth. He looks so . . . hot. We're wet and slippery and moving against each other. I lean down and kiss him. He closes his eyes. Tentatively, I bring my hands up to his head and run my fingers through his hair, not taking my lips from his mouth. This is allowed. He likes this. I like this. And we move together. I tug his hair, tipping his head back and deepening the kiss, riding him—faster, picking up the rhythm. I moan against his mouth. He starts to lift me faster, faster . . . holding my hips. Kissing me back. We are wet mouths and tongues, tangled hair, and moving hips. All sensation . . . all consuming again. I am close . . . I am starting to recognize this delicious tightening . . . quickening. And the water . . . it's swirling around us, our own whirlpool, a stirring vortex as our movements become more frantic . . . sloshing everywhere, mirroring what's happening inside me . . . and I just don't care.

I love this man. I love his passion, the effect I have on him. I love that he's flown so far to see me. I love that he cares about me . . . he cares. It's so unexpected, so fulfilling. He is mine, and I am his.

"That's right, baby," he breathes.

And I come, my orgasm ripping through me, a turbulent, passionate apogee that devours me whole. And suddenly Christian crushes me to him . . . his arms wrapped around my back as he finds his release.

"Ana, baby!" he cries, and it's a wild invocation, stirring and touching the depths of my soul.

. . .

WE LIE STARING AT each other, gray eyes into blue, face-to-face, in the super king bed, both hugging our pillows on our fronts. Naked. Not touching. Just looking and admiring, covered by the sheet.

"Do you want to sleep?" Christian asks, his voice soft and full of concern.

"No. I'm not tired." I feel strangely energized. It's been so good to talk—I don't want to stop.

"What do you want to do?" he asks.

"Talk."

He smiles. "About what?"

"Stuff."

"What stuff?"

"You."

"What about me?"

"What's your favorite film?"

He grins. "Today, it's *The Piano*."

His grin is infectious.

"Of course. Silly me. Such a sad, exciting score, which no doubt you can play? So many accomplishments, Mr. Grey."

"And the greatest one is you, Miss Steele."

"So I am number seventeen."

He frowns at me not comprehending.

"Seventeen?"

"Number of women you've, um . . . had sex with."

His lips quirk up, his eyes shining with incredulity.

"Not exactly."

"You said fifteen." My confusion is obvious.

"I was referring to the number of women in my playroom. I thought that's what you meant. You didn't ask me how many women I'd had sex with."

"Oh." *Holy shit . . . there's more . . . How many?* I gape at him. "Vanilla?"

"No. You are my one vanilla conquest." He shakes his head, still grinning at me.

Why does he find this funny? And why am I grinning back at him like an idiot?

"I can't give you a number. I didn't put notches in the bedpost or anything."

"What are we talking—tens, hundreds . . . thousands?" My eyes grow wilder as the numbers get larger.

"Tens. We're in the tens, for pity's sake."

"All submissives?"

"Yes."

"Stop grinning at me," I scold him mildly, trying and failing to keep a straight face.

"I can't. You're funny."

"Funny peculiar or funny ha-ha?"

"A bit of both I think." His words mirror mine.

"That's damned cheeky, coming from you."

He leans across and kisses the tip of my nose. "This will shock you, Anastasia. Ready?"

I nod, wide-eyed, still with the stupid grin on my face.

"All submissives in training, when I was training. There are places in and around Seattle that one can go and practice. Learn to do what I do," he says.

What?

"Oh." I blink at him.

"Yep, I've paid for sex, Anastasia."

"That's nothing to be proud of," I mutter haughtily. "And you're right . . . I am deeply shocked. And cross that I can't shock you."

"You wore my underwear."

"Did that shock you?"

"Yes."

My inner goddess pole-vaults over the fifteen-foot bar.

"You didn't wear your panties to meet my parents."

"Did that shock you?"

"Yes."

Jeez, the bar's moved to sixteen feet.

"It seems I can only shock you in the underwear department."

"You told me you were a virgin. That's the biggest shock I've ever had."

"Yes, your face was a picture, a Kodak moment." I giggle.

"You let me work you over with a riding crop."

"Did that shock you?"

"Yep."

I grin. "Well, I may let you do it again."

"Oh, I do hope so, Miss Steele. This weekend?"

"Okay," I agree shyly.

"Okay?"

"Yes. I'll go to the Red Room of Pain again."

"You say my name."

"That shocks you?"

"The fact that I like it shocks me."

"Christian."

He grins. "I want to do something tomorrow." His eyes glow with excitement.

"What?"

"A surprise. For you." His voice is low and soft.

I raise an eyebrow and stifle a yawn at the same time.

"Am I boring you, Miss Steele?" His tone is sardonic.

"Never."

He leans across and kisses me gently on my lips.

"Sleep," he commands, then switches off the light.

And in this quiet moment as I close my eyes, spent and sated, I think I'm in the eye of the storm. And in spite of all he's said, and what he hasn't said, I don't think I have ever been so happy.

CHAPTER TWENTY-FOUR

Christian stands in a steel-barred cage. Wearing his soft, ripped jeans, his chest and feet are mouthwateringly naked, and he's staring at me. His private-joke smile is etched on his beautiful face and his eyes a molten gray. In his hands he holds a bowl of strawberries. He ambles with athletic grace to the front of the cage, gazing intently at me. Holding up a plump ripe strawberry, he extends his hand through the bars.

"Eat," he says, his tongue caressing the front of his palate as he enunciates the *t*.

I try to move toward him, but I'm tethered, held back by some unseen force around my wrist, holding me. *Let me go*.

"Come, eat," he says, smiling his delicious crooked smile.

I pull and pull . . . *let me go!* I want to scream and shout, but no sound emerges. I am mute. He stretches a little farther, and the strawberry is at my lips.

"Eat, Anastasia." His mouth forms my name, lingering sensually on each syllable.

I open my mouth and bite, the cage disappears, and my hands are free. I reach up to touch him, graze my fingers through his chest hair.

"Anastasia."

No. I moan.

"Come on, baby."

No. I want to touch you.

"Wake up."

No. Please. My eyes flicker unwillingly open for a split second. I'm in bed and someone is nuzzling my ear.

"Wake up, baby," he whispers, and the effect of his sweet voice spreads like warm melted caramel through my veins.

It's Christian. Jeez, it's still dark, and the images of him from my dream persist, disconcerting and tantalizing in my head.

"Oh . . . no," I groan. I want back at his chest, back to my dream. Why is he waking me? It's the middle of the night, or so it feels. *Holy shit.* Does he want sex—now?

"Time to get up, baby. I'm going to switch on the sidelight." His voice is quiet.

"No," I groan.

"I want to chase the dawn with you," he says, kissing my face, my eyelids, the tip of my nose, my mouth, and I open my eyes. The sidelight is on. "Good morning, beautiful," he murmurs.

I groan, and he smiles. "You are not a morning person," he murmurs.

Through the haze of light, I squint and see Christian leaning over me, smiling. Amused. Amused at me. Dressed! In black.

"I thought you wanted sex," I grumble.

"Anastasia, I always want sex with you. It's heartwarming to know that you feel the same," he says dryly.

I gaze at him as my eyes adjust to the light, but he still looks amused . . . thank heavens.

"Of course I do, just not when it's so late."

"It's not late, it's early. Come on—up you go. We're going out. I'll take a rain check on the sex."

"I was having such a nice dream," I whine.

"Dream about what?" he asks patiently.

"You." I blush.

"What was I doing this time?"

"Trying to feed me strawberries."

His lips twitch with a trace of a smile. "Dr. Flynn could have a field day with that. Up—get dressed. Don't bother to shower, we can do that later."

We!

I sit up, and the sheet pools at my waist, revealing my body. He stands to give me room, his eyes dark.

"What time is it?"

"Five thirty in the morning."

"Feels like three a.m."

"We don't have much time. I let you sleep as long as possible. Come."

"Can't I have a shower?"

He sighs.

"If you have a shower, I'll want one with you, and you and I know what will happen then—the day will just go. Come."

He's excited. Like a small boy, he's iridescent with anticipation and excitement. It makes me smile.

"What are we doing?'

"It's a surprise. I told you."

I can't help but grin up at him. "Okay." I clamber off the bed and search for my clothes. Of course they are neatly folded on the chair beside my bed. He's laid out a pair of his jersey boxer briefs, too—Ralph Lauren, no less. I slip them on, and he grins at me. Hmm, another piece of Christian Grey's underwear—a trophy to add to my collection—along with the car, the BlackBerry, the Mac, his black jacket, and a set of valuable old first editions. I shake my head at his largesse, and I frown as a scene from *Tess* crosses my mind: the strawberry scene. It evokes my dream. To hell with Dr. Flynn—Freud would have a field day—and then he'd probably die trying to deal with Fifty Shades.

"I'll give you some room now that you're up." Christian exits toward the living area, and I wander into the bathroom. I have needs to attend to, and I want a quick wash. Seven minutes later, I am in the living area, scrubbed, brushed, and dressed in jeans, my camisole, and Christian Grey's underwear. Christian glances up from the small dining table where he's eating breakfast. Breakfast! Jeez, at this time.

"Eat," he says.

Holy crap . . . my dream. I gape at him, thinking about his tongue on his palate. *Hmm, his expert tongue.*

"Anastasia," he says sternly, pulling me out of my reverie.

It really is too early for me. How to handle this?

"I'll have some tea. Can I take a croissant for later?"

He eyes me suspiciously, and I smile very sweetly.

"Don't rain on my parade, Anastasia," he warns softly.

"I will eat later when my stomach's woken up. About seven thirty a.m. . . . okay?"

"Okay." He peers down at me.

Honestly. I have to concentrate hard on not making a face at him.

"I want to roll my eyes at you."

"By all means, do, and you will make my day," he says sternly.

I gaze up at the ceiling.

"Well, a spanking would wake me up, I suppose." I purse my lips in quiet contemplation.

Christian's mouth drops open.

"On the other hand, I don't want you to be all hot and bothered; the climate here is warm enough." I shrug nonchalantly.

Christian closes his mouth and tries very hard to look displeased, but fails hopelessly. I can see the humor lurking in the back of his eyes.

"You are, as ever, challenging, Miss Steele. Drink your tea."

I notice the Twinings label, and inside, my heart sings. *See, he does care*, my subconscious mouths at me. I sit and face him, drinking in his beauty. Will I ever get enough of this man?

AS WE LEAVE THE room, Christian throws a sweatshirt at me.

"You'll need this."

I look at him, puzzled.

"Trust me." He grins, leans over, and kisses me quickly on the lips, then grabs my hand and we head out.

Outside, in the relative cool of the half light of predawn, the valet hands Christian a set of keys to a flashy sports car with a soft top. I raise an eyebrow at Christian, who smirks back at me.

"You know, sometimes it's great being me," he says with a conspiratorial but smug grin that I simply can't help emulating. He's so lovable when he's playful and carefree. He opens my car door with an exaggerated bow, and in I climb. He is in such a good mood.

"Where are we going?"

"You'll see." He grins as he slips the car into drive, and we head out on Savannah Parkway. He programs the GPS and presses a switch on the steering wheel, and a classical orchestral piece fills the car.

"What's this?" I ask as the sweet, sweet sound of a hundred violin strings assails us.

"It's from *La Traviata*. An opera by Verdi."

Oh, my . . . it's lovely.

"*La Traviata*? I've heard of that. I can't think where. What does it mean?"

Christian glances at me and smirks.

"Well, literally, 'the woman led astray.' It's based on Alexandre Dumas's book, *La Dame aux Camélias*."

"Ah. I've read it."

"I thought you might've."

"The doomed courtesan." I squirm uncomfortably in the plush leather seat. *Is he trying to tell me something?* "Hmm, it's a depressing story," I mutter.

"Too depressing? Do you want to choose some music? This is on my iPod." Christian has that secret smile again.

I can't see his iPod anywhere. He taps the screen on the console between us, and behold—there is a playlist.

"You choose." His lips twitch up into a smile, and I know it's a challenge.

Christian Grey's iPod, this should be interesting. I scroll through the touch screen and find the perfect song. I press "play." I wouldn't have figured him for a Britney fan. The club-mix, techno beat assaults us both, and Christian turns the volume down. Maybe it's too early for this: Britney's at her most sultry.

"'*Toxic*,' eh?" Christian grins.

"I don't know what you mean." I feign innocence.

He turns the music down a little more, and inside I am hugging myself. My inner goddess is standing on the podium awaiting her gold medal. He turned the music down. Victory!

"I didn't put that song on my iPod," he says casually, and puts his foot down so that I am thrown back into my seat as the car accelerates along the freeway.

What? He knows what he's doing, the bastard. *Who did?* And I have to listen to Britney going on and on. *Who . . . who?*

The song ends and the iPod shuffles to Damien Rice being mournful. *Who? Who?* I stare out the window, my stomach churning. Who?

"It was Leila," he answers my unspoken thoughts. *How does he do that?*

"Leila?"

"An ex, who put the song on my iPod."

Damien warbles away in the background as I sit stunned. An ex . . . ex-submissive? An ex—

"One of the fifteen?" I ask.

"Yes."

"What happened to her?"

"We finished."

"Why?"

Oh jeez. It's too early for this kind of conversation. But he looks relaxed, happy even, and, what's more, talkative.

"She wanted more." His voice is low, introspective even, and he leaves the sentence hanging between us, ending it with that powerful little word again.

"And you didn't?" I ask before I can employ my brain-to-mouth filter. Shit, do I want to know?

He shakes his head. "I've never wanted more, until I met you."

I gasp, reeling. Isn't this what I want? He wants more. *He wants it, too!* My inner goddess has backflipped off the podium and is doing cartwheels around the stadium. It's not just me.

"What happened to the other fourteen?" I ask.

Jeez, he's talking—take advantage.

"You want a list? Divorced, beheaded, died?"

"You're not Henry VIII."

"Okay. In no particular order, I've only had long-term relationships with four women, apart from Elena."

"Elena?"

"Mrs. Robinson to you." He half smiles his secret-private-joke smile.

Elena! Holy fuck. The evil one has a name and it's all foreign sounding. A vision of a glorious, pale-skinned vamp with raven hair and ruby-red lips comes to mind, and I know that she's beautiful. *I must not dwell. I must not dwell.*

"What happened to the four?" I ask to distract myself.

"So inquisitive, so eager for information, Miss Steele," he scolds playfully.

"Oh, Mr. When Is Your Period Due?"

"Anastasia—a man needs to know these things."

"Does he?"

"I do."

"Why?"

"Because I don't want you to get pregnant."

"Neither do I! Well, not for a few years yet."

Christian blinks, startled, then visibly relaxes. Okay. Christian doesn't want children. Now or never? I am reeling from his sudden, unprecedented attack of candor. Perhaps it's the early morning? Something in the Georgia water? The Georgia air? What else do I want to know? Carpe diem.

"So the other four, what happened?" I ask.

"One met someone else. The other three wanted—more. I wasn't in the market for more then."

"And the others?" I press.

He glances at me briefly and just shakes his head.

"Just didn't work out."

Whoa, a bucketload of information to process. I glance in the side mirror of the car, and I notice the soft swell of pink and aquamarine in the sky behind the car. Dawn is following us.

"Where are we headed?" I ask, perplexed, gazing out at Interstate 95. We're heading south, that's all I know.

"An airfield."

"We're not going back to Seattle, are we?" I gasp, alarmed. I haven't said good-bye to my mom. Jeez, she's expecting us for dinner.

He laughs. "No, Anastasia, we're going to indulge in my second favorite pastime."

"Second?" I frown at him.

"Yep. I told you my favorite this morning."

I glance at his glorious profile, frowning, racking my brain.

"Indulging in you, Miss Steele. That's got to be top of my list. Any way I can get you."

Oh.

"Well, that's quite high up on my list of diverting, kinky priorities, too," I mutter, blushing.

"I'm pleased to hear it," he mutters dryly.

"So, airfield?"

He grins at me. "Soaring."

The term rings a vague bell. He's mentioned it before.

"We're going to chase the dawn, Anastasia." He turns and grins at me as the GPS urges him to turn right into what looks like an industrial complex. He pulls up outside a large white building with a sign reading BRUNSWICK SOARING ASSOCIATION.

Gliding! We're going gliding?

He switches off the engine.

"You up for this?" he asks.

"You're flying?"

"Yes."

"Yes, please!" I don't hesitate. He grins and leans forward and kisses me.

"Another first, Miss Steele," he says as he climbs out of the car.

First? What sort of first? First time flying a glider . . . shit! No—he said that he's done it before. I relax. He walks around and opens my door. The sky has turned to a subtle opal, shimmering and glowing softly behind the sporadic childlike clouds. Dawn is upon us.

Taking my hand, Christian leads me around the building to a large stretch of tarmac where several planes are parked. Waiting beside them is a man with a shaved head and a wild look in his eye, accompanied by Taylor.

Taylor! Does Christian go anywhere without that man? I beam at him, and he smiles kindly back at me.

"Mr. Grey, this is your tow pilot, Mr. Mark Benson," says Taylor. Christian and Benson shake hands and strike up a conversation that sounds very technical about wind speed, directions, and the like.

"Hello, Taylor," I murmur shyly.

"Miss Steele." He nods a greeting at me, and I frown. "Ana," he corrects himself. "He's been hell on wheels the last few days. Glad we're here," he says conspiratorially.

Oh, this is news. Why? Surely not because of me! Revelation Thursday! Must be something in the Savannah water that makes these men loosen up a bit.

"Anastasia," Christian summons me. "Come." He holds out his hand.

"See you later." I smile at Taylor, and giving me a quick salute, he heads back to the parking lot.

"Mr. Benson, this is my girlfriend, Anastasia Steele."

"Pleased to meet you," I murmur as we shake hands.

Benson gives me a dazzling smile.

"Likewise," he says, and I can tell from his accent that he's British.

As I take Christian's hand, there's a mounting excitement in my belly. *Wow . . . gliding!* We follow Mark Benson out across the tarmac toward the runway. He and Christian keep up a running conversation. I catch the gist. We will be in a Blanik L-23, which is apparently better than the L-13, although this is open to debate. Benson will be flying a Piper Pawnee. He's been flying tail draggers for about five years now. It all means nothing to me, but glancing up at Christian, he is so animated, so in his element, it's a pleasure to watch him.

The plane itself is long, sleek, and white with orange stripes. It has a small cockpit with two seats, one in front of the other. It's attached by a long white cable to a small, conventional single-propeller plane. Benson opens the large, clear Perspex dome that frames the cockpit, allowing us to climb in.

"First we need to strap on your parachute."

Parachute!

"I'll do that," Christian interrupts him and takes the harness from Benson, who smiles amenably at him.

"I'll fetch some ballast," Benson says, and heads toward the plane.

"You like strapping me into things," I observe dryly.

"Miss Steele, you have no idea. Here, step into the straps."

I do as I'm told, placing my arm on his shoulder. Christian stiffens slightly but doesn't move. Once my feet are in the loops, he pulls the parachute up, and I place my arms through the shoulder straps. Deftly he fastens the harness and tightens all the straps.

"There, you'll do," he says mildly, but his eyes are gleaming. "Do you have your hair tie from yesterday?"

I nod.

"You want me to put my hair up?"

"Yes."

I quickly do as I'm asked.

"In you go," Christian commands. He's still so bossy. I go to climb into the back.

"No, front. The pilot sits in the back."

"But won't you be able to see?"

"I'll see plenty." He grins.

I don't think I have ever seen him so happy—bossy, but happy. I clamber in, settling down into the leather seat. It is surprisingly comfortable. Christian leans over, pulls the harness over my shoulders, reaches between my legs for the lower belt, and slots it into the fastener that rests against my belly. He tightens all the restraining straps.

"Hmm, twice in one morning, I am a lucky man," he whispers, and kisses me quickly. "This won't take long—twenty, thirty minutes at most. Thermals aren't great this time of the morning, but it's so breathtaking up there at this hour. I hope you're not nervous."

"Excited." I beam.

Where did this ridiculous grin come from? Actually, part of me is terrified. My inner goddess—she's under a blanket behind the sofa.

"Good." He grins back, stroking my face, then disappears from view.

I hear and feel his movements as he climbs in behind me. Of course he's strapped me in so tightly I can't move around to see him . . . typical! We are very low on the ground. In front of me is a panel of dials and levers and a big stick thing. I leave everything alone.

Mark Benson appears with a cheerful grin as he checks my straps and leans in and checks the cockpit floor. I think it's the ballast.

"Yep, that's secure. First time?" he asks me.

"Yes."

"You'll love it."

"Thanks, Mr. Benson."

"Call me Mark." He turns to Christian. "Okay?"

"Yep. Let's go."

I am so glad I haven't eaten anything. I am beyond excited, and I don't think my stomach would be game for food, excitement, and leaving the ground. Once again, I am putting myself into this beautiful man's skilled hands. Mark shuts the cockpit lid, strolls over to the plane in front, and climbs in.

The Piper's single propeller starts, and my nervous stomach relocates itself to my throat. *Jeez . . . I'm really doing this.* Mark taxis slowly down the runway, and as the cable takes the strain, we suddenly jolt forward. We're off. I hear chatter over the radio set behind me. I think it's Mark talking to the tower—but I can't make out what he's saying. As the Piper picks up speed, so do we. It's very bumpy, and in front of us the single prop plane is still on the ground. Jeez, will we ever get up? And suddenly, my stomach disappears from my throat and free-falls through my body to the ground—we're airborne.

"Here we go, baby!" Christian shouts from behind me. And

we are in our own bubble, just us two. All I hear is the sound of the wind ripping past and the distant hum of the Piper's engine.

I'm gripping the edge of my seat with both hands, so tightly my knuckles are white. We head west, inland, away from the rising sun, gaining height, crossing over fields and woods and homes and Interstate 95.

Oh my. This is amazing, above us only sky. The light is extraordinary, diffuse and warm in hue, and I remember José rambling on about "magic hour," a time of day that photographers adore—this is it . . . just after dawn, and I'm in it, with Christian.

Abruptly, I'm reminded of José's show. Hmm. I need to tell Christian. I wonder briefly how he'll react. But I won't worry about that, not now—I'm enjoying the ride. My ears pop as we gain height, and the ground slips farther and farther away. It is so peaceful. I completely get why he likes to be up here. Away from his BlackBerry and all the pressures of his job.

The radio crackles into life, and Mark mentions three thousand feet. Jeez, that sounds high. I check the ground, and I can no longer clearly distinguish anything down there.

"Release," Christian says into the radio, and suddenly the Piper disappears and the pulling sensation provided by the small plane ceases. We're floating, floating over Georgia.

Holy fuck—it's exciting. The plane banks and turns as the wing dips, and we spiral toward the sun. *Icarus. This is it.* I am flying close to the sun, but he's with me, leading me. I gasp at the realization. We spiral and spiral, and the view in this morning light is spectacular.

"Hold on tight!" he shouts, and we dip again—only this time he doesn't stop. Suddenly, I am upside down, looking at the ground through the top of the cockpit canopy.

I squeal loudly, my arms automatically lashing out, my hands splayed on the Perspex to stop me from falling. I can hear him laughing. *Bastard!* But his joy is infectious, and I am laughing, too, as he rights the plane.

"I'm glad I didn't have breakfast!" I shout at him.

"Yes, in hindsight, it's good you didn't, because I'm going to do that again."

He dips the plane once more until we are upside down. This time, because I'm prepared, I hang on to the harness, but it makes me grin and giggle like a fool. He levels the plane once more.

"Beautiful, isn't it?" he calls.

"Yes."

We fly, swooping majestically through the air, listening to the wind and the silence, in the early morning light. Who could ask for more?

"See the joystick in front of you?" he shouts again.

I look at the stick that is jerking between my legs. *Oh no*, where's he going with this?

"Grab hold."

Oh, shit. He's going to make me fly the plane. *No!*

"Go on, Anastasia. Grab it," he urges more vehemently.

Tentatively, I grasp it and feel the pitch and yaw of what I assume are rudders and paddles or whatever keeps this thing in the air.

"Hold tight . . . keep it steady. See the middle dial in front? Keep the needle dead center."

My heart is in my mouth. *Holy shit.* I am flying a glider . . . I'm soaring.

"Good girl." Christian sounds delighted.

"I am amazed you let me take control," I shout.

"You'd be amazed what I'd let you do, Miss Steele. Back to me now."

I feel the joystick move suddenly, and I let go as we spiral down several feet, my ears starting to pop again. The ground is getting closer, and it feels like we could be hitting it shortly. Jeez, that's scary.

"BMA, this is BG N Papa Three Alpha, entering left downwind runway seven to the grass, BMA." Christian sounds his usual authoritative self. The tower squawks back at him over the radio, but I don't understand what they say. We sail around again in a wide circle, sinking slowly to the ground. I can see the airport, the landing strips, and we're flying back over Interstate 95.

"Hang on, baby. This can get bumpy."

After another circle we dip, and suddenly we are on the ground with a brief thump, racing along the grass—*holy shit.* My teeth chatter as we bump at an alarming speed along the ground, until we finally come to a stop. The plane sways then dips to the right. I take a deep lungful of air while Christian leans over and opens the cockpit lid, clambering out and stretching.

"How was that?" he asks, and his eyes are a shining, dazzling silver gray. He leans down to unbuckle me.

"That was extraordinary. Thank you," I whisper.

"Was it more?" he asks, his voice tinged with hope.

"Much more," I breathe, and he grins.

"Come." He holds out his hand for me, and I clamber out of the cockpit.

As soon as I'm out, he grabs me and holds me flush against his body. Suddenly his hand is in my hair, tugging it so my head tips back, and his other hand travels down to the base of my spine. He kisses me, long, hard, and passionately, his tongue in my mouth. His breathing is mounting, his ardor . . . *Holy cow*—his erection . . . we're in a field. But I don't care. My hands twist in his hair, anchoring him to me. I want him, here, now, on the ground. He breaks away and gazes down at me, his eyes now dark and luminous in the early morning light, full of raw, arrogant sensuality. Wow. He takes my breath away.

"Breakfast," he whispers, making it sound deliciously erotic.

How can he make bacon and eggs sound like forbidden fruit? It's an extraordinary skill. He turns, clasping my hand, and we head back toward the car.

"What about the glider?"

"Someone will take care of that," he says dismissively. "We'll eat now." His tone is unequivocal.

Food! He's talking food, when really all I want is him.

"Come." He smiles.

I have never seen him like this, and it's a joy to behold. I find myself walking beside him, hand in hand, with a stupid, goofy grin plastered on my face. It reminds me of when I was ten and spent the day at Disneyland with Ray. It was a perfect day, and this is sure shaping out to be the same.

BACK IN THE CAR, as we head back along Interstate 95 toward Savannah, my phone alarm goes off. Oh yes . . . my pill.

"What's that?" Christian asks, curious, glancing at me.

I fumble in my purse for the packet.

"Alarm for my pill," I mutter as my cheeks flush.

His lips quirk up.

"Good, well done. I hate condoms."

I flush some more. He's as patronizing as ever.

"I like that you introduced me to Mark as your girlfriend," I murmur.

"Isn't that what you are?" He raises an eyebrow.

"Am I? I thought you wanted a submissive."

"So did I, Anastasia, and I do. But I've told you, I want more, too."

Oh my. He's coming around, and hope surges through me, leaving me breathless.

"I'm very happy that you want more," I whisper.

"We aim to please, Miss Steele." He smirks as we pull into the International House of Pancakes.

"IHOP." I grin back at him. I don't believe it. Who would have thought . . . ? Christian Grey at IHOP.

IT'S 8:30 A.M. BUT quiet in the restaurant. It smells of sweet batter, fried food, and disinfectant. *Hmm . . . not such an enticing aroma.* Christian leads me to a booth.

"I would never have pictured you here," I say as we slide into a booth.

"My dad used to bring us to one of these whenever my mom went away to a medical conference. It was our secret." He smiles at me, eyes dancing, then picks up a menu, running a hand through his wayward hair.

Oh, I want to run my hands through that hair. I pick up a menu and examine it. I realize I'm starving.

"I know what I want," he breathes, his voice low and husky.

I glance up at him, and he's staring at me in that way that tightens all the muscles in my belly and takes my breath away, his eyes dark and smoldering. *Holy shit.* I gaze at him, my blood singing in my veins, answering his call.

"I want what you want," I whisper.

He inhales sharply.

"Here?" he asks suggestively, raising an eyebrow at me, smiling wickedly, his teeth trapping the tip of his tongue.

Oh my . . . sex in IHOP. His expression changes, growing darker.

"Don't bite your lip," he orders. "Not here, not now." His eyes harden momentarily, and for a moment, he looks so deliciously dangerous. "If I can't have you here, don't tempt me."

"Hi, my name's Leandra. What can I get for you . . . er . . . folks . . . er . . . today, this mornin' . . . ?" Her voice trails off, stumbling over her words as she gets an eyeful of Mr. Beautiful opposite me. She flushes scarlet, and a small ounce of sympathy for her bubbles unwelcome into my consciousness because he still does that to me. Her presence allows me to escape briefly from his sensual glare.

"Anastasia?" he prompts me, ignoring her, and I don't think anyone could squeeze as much carnality into my name as he does at that moment.

I swallow, praying that I don't turn the same color as poor Leandra.

"I told you, I want what you want." I keep my voice soft, low, and he looks at me hungrily. *Jeez,* my inner goddess swoons. *Am I up to this game?*

Leandra looks from me to him and back again. She's practically the same color as her shiny red hair.

"Shall I give you folks another minute to decide?"

"No. We know what we want." Christian's mouth twitches with a small, sexy smile.

"We'll have two portions of the original buttermilk pancakes with maple syrup and bacon on the side, two glasses of orange juice, one black coffee with skim milk, and one English breakfast tea, if you have it," says Christian, not taking his eyes off me.

"Thank you, sir. Will that be all?" Leandra whispers, looking anywhere but at the two of us. We both turn to stare at her, and she flushes crimson again and scuttles away.

"You know, it's really not fair." I glance down at the Formica tabletop, tracing a pattern on it with my index finger, trying to sound nonchalant.

"What's not fair?"

"How you disarm people. Women. Me."

"Do I disarm you?"

I snort. "All the time."

"It's just looks, Anastasia," he says mildly.

"No, Christian, it's much more than that."

His brow creases. "You disarm me totally, Miss Steele. Your innocence. It cuts through all the crap."

"Is that why you've changed your mind?"

"Changed my mind?"

"Yes—about . . . er . . . us?"

He strokes his chin thoughtfully with his long, skilled fingers. "I don't think I've changed my mind per se. We just need to redefine our parameters, redraw our battle lines, if you will. We can make this work, I'm sure. I want you submissive in my playroom. I will punish you if you digress from the rules. Other than that . . . well, I think it's all up for discussion. Those are my requirements, Miss Steele. What say you to that?"

"So I get to sleep with you? In your bed?"

"Is that what you want?"

"Yes."

"I agree then. Besides, I sleep very well when you're in my bed. I had no idea." His brow creases as his voice fades.

"I was frightened you'd leave me if I didn't agree to all of it," I whisper.

"I'm not going anywhere, Anastasia. Besides . . ." He trails off, and after some thought, he adds, "We're following your advice, your definition: compromise. You e-mailed it to me. And so far, it's working for me."

"I love that you want more," I murmur shyly.

"I know."

"How do you know?"

"Trust me. I just do." He smirks at me. He's hiding something. *What?*

At that moment, Leandra arrives with breakfast and our conversation ceases. My stomach rumbles, reminding me how ravenous I am. Christian watches with annoying approval as I devour everything on my plate.

"Can I treat you?" I ask Christian.

"Treat me how?"

"Pay for this meal."

Christian snorts.

"I don't think so," he scoffs.

"Please. I want to."

He frowns at me.

"Are you trying to completely emasculate me?"

"This is probably the only place that I'll be able to afford to pay."

"Anastasia, I appreciate the thought. I do. But no."

I purse my lips.

"Don't scowl," he threatens, his eyes glinting ominously.

OF COURSE HE DOESN'T ask me for my mother's address. He knows it already, stalker that he is. When he pulls up outside the house, I don't comment. What's the point?

"Do you want to come in?" I ask shyly.

"I need to work, Anastasia, but I'll be back this evening. What time?"

I ignore the unwelcome stab of disappointment. Why do I

want to spend every single minute with this controlling sex god? Oh yes, I've fallen in love with him, and he can fly.

"Thank you . . . for the more."

"My pleasure, Anastasia." He kisses me, and I inhale his sexy Christian smell.

"I'll see you later."

"Try to stop me," he whispers.

I wave good-bye as he drives off into the Georgia sunshine. I'm still wearing his sweatshirt and his underwear, and I'm too warm.

In the kitchen, my mom is in a complete flap. It's not every day she has to entertain a multi-zillionaire, and it's stressing her out.

"How are you, darling?" she asks, and I flush because she must know what I was doing last night.

"I'm good. Christian took me gliding this morning." I hope the new information will distract her.

"Gliding? As in a small plane with no engine? That sort of gliding?"

I nod.

"Wow."

She's speechless—a novel concept for my mother. She gapes at me, but eventually recovers herself and resumes her original line of questioning.

"How was last night? Did you talk?"

Jeez. I flush bright scarlet.

"We talked—last night and today. It's getting better."

"Good." She turns her attention back to the four cookbooks she has open on the kitchen table.

"Mom . . . if you like, I'll cook this evening."

"Oh, honey, that's kind of you, but I want to do it."

"Okay." I grimace, knowing full well that my mother's cooking is pretty hit or miss. Perhaps she's improved since she moved to Savannah with Bob. There was a time I wouldn't subject anyone to her cooking . . . even—who do I hate? Oh yes—Mrs. Robinson—Elena. Well, maybe her. *Will I ever meet this damned woman?*

I decide to send a quick thank-you to Christian.

From: Anastasia Steele
Subject: Soaring as Opposed to Sore-ing
Date: June 2 2011 10:20 EST
To: Christian Grey

Sometimes, you really know how to show a girl a good time.

Thank you

Ana x

From: Christian Grey
Subject: Soaring vs Sore-ing
Date: June 2 2011 10:24 EST
To: Anastasia Steele

I'll take either of those over your snoring. I had a good time, too.

But I always do when I'm with you.

Christian Grey
CEO, Grey Enterprises Holdings, Inc.

From: Anastasia Steele
Subject: SNORING
Date: June 2 2011 10:26 EST
To: Christian Grey

I DO NOT SNORE. And if I do, it's very ungallant of you to point it out.

You are no gentleman, Mr. Grey! And you are in the Deep South, too!

Ana

From: Christian Grey
Subject: Somniloquy
Date: June 2 2011 10:28 EST
To: Anastasia Steele

I have never claimed to be a gentleman, Anastasia, and I think I have demonstrated that point to you on numerous occasions. I am not intimidated by your SHOUTY capitals. But I will confess to a small white lie: no—you don't snore, but you do talk. And it's fascinating.

What happened to my kiss?

Christian Grey
Cad & CEO, Grey Enterprises Holdings, Inc.

Holy shit. I know I talk in my sleep. Kate has told me enough times. What the hell have I said? *Oh no.*

From: Anastasia Steele
Subject: Spill the Beans
Date: June 2 2011 10:32 EST
To: Christian Grey

You are a cad and a scoundrel—definitely no gentleman.

So, what did I say? No kisses for you until you talk!

From: Christian Grey
Subject: Sleeping Talking Beauty
Date: June 2 2011 10:35 EST
To: Anastasia Steele

It would be most ungallant of me to say, and I have already been chastised for that.

But if you behave yourself, I may tell you this evening. I do have to go into a meeting now.

Laters, baby.

Christian Grey
CEO, Cad & Scoundrel, Grey Enterprises Holdings, Inc.

Right! I shall maintain radio silence until this evening. I fume. *Jeez.* Suppose I've said I hate him, or worse still, that I love him, in my sleep. Oh, I hope not. I am not ready to tell him that, and I'm sure he's not ready to hear it, if he ever wants to hear it. I scowl at my computer and decide that whatever Mom cooks, I will make bread to vent my frustrations while kneading the dough.

MY MOM HAS DECIDED on gazpacho soup and a barbecue with steaks marinated in olive oil, garlic, and lemon. Christian likes meat, and it's simple to do. Bob has volunteered to man the BBQ grill. *What is it about men and fire?* I ponder as I trail after my mother through the supermarket with the shopping cart.

As we browse the raw meat cabinet, my phone rings. I scramble for it, thinking it may be Christian. I don't recognize the number.

"Hello?" I answer breathlessly.

"Anastasia Steele?"

"Yes."

"It's Elizabeth Morgan from SIP."

"Oh—hi."

"I'm calling to offer you the job of assistant to Mr. Jack Hyde. We'd like you to start on Monday."

"Wow. That's great. Thank you!"

"You know the salary details?"

"Yes. Yes . . . that's—I mean, I accept your offer. I'd love to come and work for you."

"Excellent. We'll see you Monday at 8:30 a.m.?"

"See you then. Good-bye. And thank you."

I beam at my mom.

"You have a job?"

I nod gleefully, and she squeals and hugs me in the middle of Publix supermarket.

"Congratulations, darling! We have to buy some champagne!" She's clapping her hands and jumping up and down. *Is she forty-two or twelve?*

I glance down at my phone and frown; there's a missed call from Christian. He never phones me. I call him straight back.

"Anastasia," he answers immediately.

"Hi," I murmur shyly.

"I have to return to Seattle. Something's come up. I am on my way to Hilton Head now. Please apologize to your mother—I can't make dinner." He sounds very businesslike.

"Nothing serious, I hope?"

"I have a situation that I have to deal with. I'll see you tomorrow. I'll send Taylor to collect you from the airport if I can't come myself." He sounds cold. Angry even. But for the first time, I don't immediately think it's me.

"Okay. I hope you sort out your situation. Have a safe flight."

"You too, baby," he breathes, and with those words, my Christian is back. Then he hangs up.

Oh no. The last "situation" he had was my virginity. *Jeez, I hope it's nothing like that*. I gaze at my mom. Her earlier jubilation has metamorphosed into concern.

"It's Christian. He's had to go back to Seattle. He apologizes."

"Oh! That's a shame, darling. We can still have our barbecue, and now we have something to celebrate—your new job! You have to tell me all about it."

IT'S LATE AFTERNOON, AND Mom and I are lying beside the pool. My mother has relaxed to the point where she is literally horizontal now that Mr. Megabucks is not coming to dinner. As I lie in the sun, endeavoring to lose the pale, I think about yesterday evening and breakfast today. I think about Christian, and my ridiculous grin refuses to subside. It keeps creeping across my face, unbidden and disconcerting, as I recall our various conversations and what we did . . . what he did.

There seems to be a tidal shift in Christian's attitude. He denies it, but he admits he's trying for more. What could have changed? What has altered since he sent his long e-mail and when I saw him yesterday? What has he done? I sit up suddenly, almost spilling my soda. He had dinner with . . . her. Elena.

Holy fuck!

My scalp prickles at the realization. Did she say something to him? Oh . . . to have been a fly on the wall during their dinner. I could have landed in her soup or on her wine glass and choked her.

"What is it, Ana, honey?" Mom asks, startled from her torpor.

"I'm just having a moment, Mom. What time is it?"

"About six thirty p.m., darling."

Hmm . . . he wouldn't have landed yet. Can I ask him? Should I ask him? Or perhaps she has nothing to do with it. I fervently hope so. What did I say in my sleep? *Crap* . . . some unguarded remark while dreaming about him, I bet. Whatever it is, or was, I hope the sea change is coming from within him and not because of *her.*

I am sweltering in this damned heat. I need another dip in the pool.

AS I GET READY for bed, I switch on my computer. I have heard nothing from Christian. Not even a word that he's arrived safely.

From: Anastasia Steele
Subject: Safe Arrival?
Date: June 2 2011 22:32 EST
To: Christian Grey

Dear Sir,
Please let me know that you have arrived safely. I am starting to worry. Thinking of you.

Your Ana x

Three minutes later, I hear the ping from my e-mail inbox.

From: Christian Grey
Subject: Sorry
Date: June 2 2011 19:36
To: Anastasia Steele

Dear Miss Steele,
I have arrived safely, and please accept my apologies for not letting you know. I don't want to cause you any worry. It's heartwarming to know that you care for me. I am thinking of you, too, and as ever looking forward to seeing you tomorrow.

Christian Grey
CEO, Grey Enterprises Holdings, Inc.

I sigh. Christian is back to formality.

From: Anastasia Steele
Subject: The Situation
Date: June 2 2011 22:40 EST
To: Christian Grey

Dear Mr. Grey,
I think it is very evident that I care for you deeply. How could you doubt that?

I hope your "situation" is under control.

Your Ana x

P.S.: Are you going to tell me what I said in my sleep?

From: Christian Grey
Subject: Pleading the Fifth
Date: June 2 2011 19:45
To: Anastasia Steele

Dear Miss Steele,
I like very much that you care for me. The "situation" here is not yet resolved.

With regard to your P.S., the answer is no.

Christian Grey
CEO, Grey Enterprises Holdings, Inc.

From: Anastasia Steele
Subject: Pleading Insanity
Date: June 2 2011 22:48 EST
To: Christian Grey

I hope it was amusing. But you should know I cannot accept any responsibility for what comes out of my mouth when I am unconscious. In fact—you probably misheard me.

A man of your advanced years is surely a little deaf.

From: Christian Grey
Subject: Pleading Guilty
Date: June 2 2011 19:52
To: Anastasia Steele

Dear Miss Steele,
Sorry, could you speak up? I can't hear you.

Christian Grey
CEO, Grey Enterprises Holdings, Inc.

From: Anastasia Steele
Subject: Pleading Insanity Again
Date: June 2 2011 22:54 EST
To: Christian Grey

You are driving me crazy.

From: Christian Grey
Subject: I Hope So . . .
Date: June 2 2011 19:59
To: Anastasia Steele

Dear Miss Steele,

I intend to do exactly that on Friday evening. Looking forward to it.

;)

Christian Grey
CEO, Grey Enterprises Holdings, Inc.

From: Anastasia Steele
Subject: Grrrrrr
Date: June 2 2011 23:02 EST
To: Christian Grey

I am officially pissed at you.

Good night.

Miss A. R. Steele

From: Christian Grey
Subject: Wild Cat
Date: June 2 2011 20:05
To: Anastasia Steele

Are you growling at me, Miss Steele?

I possess a cat of my own for growlers.

Christian Grey
CEO, Grey Enterprises Holdings, Inc.

Cat of his own? I've never seen a cat in his apartment. No, I am not going to answer him. Oh, he can be so exasperating sometimes. Fifty shades of exasperating. I clamber into bed and lie glaring at the ceiling as my eyes adjust to the dark. I hear another ping from my computer. I am not going to look. No, definitely not. No, I am not going to look. Gah! Like the fool I am, I cannot resist the lure of Christian Grey's words.

From: Christian Grey
Subject: What You Said in Your Sleep

Date: June 2 2011 20:20
To: Anastasia Steele

Anastasia,

I'd rather hear you say the words that you uttered in your sleep when you're conscious, that's why I won't tell you. Go to sleep. You'll need to be rested with what I have in mind for you tomorrow.

Christian Grey
CEO, Grey Enterprises Holdings, Inc.

Oh no . . . What have I said? It's as bad as I think, I'm sure.

CHAPTER TWENTY-FIVE

My mother hugs me tightly.

"Follow your heart, darling, and please, please—try not to overthink things. Relax and enjoy yourself. You are so young, sweetheart. You have so much of life to experience yet, just let it happen. You deserve the best of everything." She whispers in my ear, her heartfelt words comforting. She kisses my hair.

"Oh, Mom." Hot, unwelcome tears prick my eyes as I cling to her.

"Darling, you know what they say. You have to kiss a lot of frogs before you find your prince."

I give her a lopsided, bittersweet smile.

"I think I've kissed a prince, Mom. I hope he doesn't turn into a frog."

She gives me her most endearing, motherly, absolute-unconditional-love smile, and I marvel at the love I feel for this woman as we hug again.

"Ana—they're calling your flight," Bob's voice is anxious.

"Will you visit, Mom?"

"Of course, darling—soon. Love you."

"Me, too."

Her eyes are red with unshed tears as she releases me. I hate leaving her. I hug Bob and, turning, head to the gate—I do not have time for the first class lounge today. I will myself not to glance back. But I do . . . and Bob is holding my mom, and tears are streaming down her face. I can no longer hold mine back. I put my head down and proceed to the gate, keeping my eyes on the shiny white floor, blurred through my watery tears.

Once on board, in the luxury of first class, I curl up in my seat and try to compose myself. It is always painful to wrench myself away from Mom . . . she is scatty, disorganized, but newly insightful, and she loves me. Unconditional love—what every child deserves from its parents. I frown at my wayward thoughts and, pulling out my BlackBerry, stare at it despondently.

What does Christian know of love? Seems he didn't get the unconditional love he was entitled to during his very early years. My heart twists, and my mother's words waft like a zephyr through my mind: *Yes, Ana. Hell, what do you need? A neon sign flashing on his forehead?* She thinks Christian loves me, but then she's my mother, of course she'd think that. She thinks I deserve the best of everything. I frown. It's true, and in a moment of startling clarity, I see it. It's very simple: I want his love. I *need* Christian Grey to love me. This is why I am so reticent about our relationship—because on some basic, fundamental level, I recognize within me a deep-seated compulsion to be loved and cherished.

And because of his fifty shades, I am holding myself back. The BDSM is a distraction from the real issue. The sex is amazing, he's wealthy, he's beautiful, but this is all meaningless without his love, and the real heart-fail is that I don't know if he's capable of love. He doesn't even love himself. I recall his self-loathing, *her* love being the only form he found *acceptable.* Punished—whipped, beaten, whatever their relationship entailed—he feels undeserving of love. Why does he feel like that? How can he feel like that? His words haunt me: *It's very hard to grow up in a perfect family when you're not perfect.*

I close my eyes, imagining his pain, and I can't begin to comprehend it. I shudder as I remember that I may have divulged too much. What have I confessed to Christian in my sleep? What secrets have I revealed?

I stare at the BlackBerry in the vague hope that it will give me some answers. Rather unsurprisingly, it is not very forthcoming. As we haven't taken off yet, I decide to e-mail my Fifty Shades.

From: Anastasia Steele
Subject: Homeward Bound
Date: June 3 2011 12:53 EST
To: Christian Grey

Dear Mr. Grey,
I am once again ensconced in first class, for which I thank you. I am counting the minutes until I see you this evening and perhaps torturing the truth out of you about my nocturnal admissions.

Your Ana x

From: Christian Grey
Subject: Homeward Bound
Date: June 3 2011 09:58
To: Anastasia Steele

Anastasia, I look forward to seeing you.

Christian Grey
CEO, Grey Enterprises Holdings, Inc.

His response makes me frown. It sounds clipped and formal, not his usual witty, pithy style.

From: Anastasia Steele
Subject: Homeward Bound
Date: June 3 2011 13:01 EST
To: Christian Grey

Dearest Mr. Grey,
I hope everything is okay re "the situation." The tone of your e-mail is worrying.

Ana x

From: Christian Grey
Subject: Homeward Bound
Date: June 3 2011 10:04
To: Anastasia Steele

Anastasia,

The situation could be better. Have you taken off yet? If so you should not be e-mailing. You are putting yourself at risk, in direct contravention of the rule regarding your personal safety. I meant what I said about punishments.

Christian Grey
CEO, Grey Enterprises Holdings, Inc.

Crap. Okay. Jeez. What is eating him? Perhaps "the situation"? Maybe Taylor's gone AWOL, maybe he's dropped a few million on the stock market—whatever the reason.

From: Anastasia Steele
Subject: Overreaction
Date: June 3 2011 13:06 EST
To: Christian Grey

Dear Mr. Grumpy,
The aircraft doors are still open. We are delayed but only by ten minutes. My welfare and that of the passengers around me is vouchsafed. You may stow your twitchy palm for now.

Miss Steele

From: Christian Grey
Subject: Apologies—Twitchy Palm Stowed
Date: June 3 2011 10:08
To: Anastasia Steele

I miss you and your smart mouth, Miss Steele.

I want you safely home.

Christian Grey
CEO, Grey Enterprises Holdings, Inc.

From: Anastasia Steele
Subject: Apology Accepted
Date: June 3 2011 13:10 EST
To: Christian Grey

They are shutting the doors. You won't hear another peep from me, especially given your deafness.

Laters.

Ana x

I switch off the BlackBerry, unable to shake my anxiety. Something is up with Christian. Perhaps "the situation" is out of hand. I sit back, glancing up at the overhead bin where my bags are stowed. I managed this morning, with my mother's help, to buy Christian a small gift to say thank you for first class and for the gliding. I smile at the memory of the soaring—that was something else. I don't know yet if I'll give my silly gift to him. He might think it's childish—and if he's in a strange mood, maybe not. I am both eager to return and apprehensive of what awaits me at my journey's end. As I mentally flick through all the scenarios that could be "the situation," I become aware that once again the only empty seat is beside me. I shake my head as the thought crosses my mind that Christian might have purchased the adjacent seat so that I couldn't talk to anyone. I dismiss the idea as ridiculous—no one could be that controlling, that jealous, surely. I close my eyes as the plane taxis toward the runway.

I EMERGE INTO THE Sea-Tac arrivals terminal eight hours later to find Taylor waiting and holding up a sign that reads MISS A. STEELE. *Honestly!* But it's good to see him.

"Hello, Taylor."

"Miss Steele," he greets me formally, but I see a hint of a smile in his sharp brown eyes. He looks his usual immaculate self—smart charcoal suit, white shirt, and charcoal tie.

"I do know what you look like, Taylor, you don't need a sign, and I do wish you'd call me Ana."

"Ana. Can I take your bags, please?"

"No, I can manage. Thank you."

His lips tighten perceptibly.

"B-but, if you'd be more comfortable taking them," I stammer.

"Thank you." He grabs my backpack and my newly acquired wheelie case for the clothes my mother has bought me. "This way, ma'am."

I sigh. He's so polite. I remember, though I would like to erase it from my memory, that this man has bought me underwear. In fact—and the thought unsettles me—he's the only man who's ever bought me underwear. Even Ray's never had to endure that hardship. We walk in silence to the black Audi SUV outside in the airport parking lot, and he holds the door open for me. I clamber in, wondering if wearing such a short skirt for the return to Seattle was a good idea. It was cool and welcome in Georgia. Here I feel exposed. Once Taylor has stowed my bags in the trunk, we set off for Escala.

The journey is slow, caught up in rush-hour traffic. Taylor keeps his eyes on the road ahead. Taciturn does not begin to describe him.

I can bear the silence no longer.

"How's Christian, Taylor?"

"Mr. Grey is preoccupied, Miss Steele."

Oh, this must be "the situation." I am mining a seam of gold. "Preoccupied?"

"Yes, ma'am."

I frown at Taylor, and he glances at me in the rearview mirror, our eyes meeting. He's saying no more. Jeez, he can be as tight lipped as the control freak himself.

"Is he okay?"

"I believe so, ma'am."

"Are you more comfortable calling me Miss Steele?"

"Yes, ma'am."

"Oh, okay."

Well, that curtails our conversation, and we continue in silence. I begin to think that Taylor's recent slip, when he told me that Christian had been hell on wheels, was an anomaly. Perhaps he's embarrassed about it, worried that he's been disloyal. The silence is suffocating.

"Could you put some music on, please?"

"Certainly, ma'am. What would you like to hear?"

"Something soothing."

I see a smile play on Taylor's lips as our eyes meet briefly again in the mirror.

"Yes, ma'am."

He pushes a few buttons on the steering wheel, and the gentle strains of Pachelbel's Canon fills the space between us. *Oh yes . . .* this is what I need.

"Thank you." I sit back as we drive slowly but steadily along Interstate 5 into Seattle.

TWENTY-FIVE MINUTES LATER HE drops me outside the impressive façade that is the entrance to Escala.

"In you go, ma'am," he says, holding the door open for me. "I'll bring up your luggage." His expression is soft, warm, avuncular even.

Jeez . . . Uncle Taylor, what a thought.

"Thank you for meeting me."

"It's a pleasure, Miss Steele." He smiles, and I head into the building. The doorman nods and waves.

As I ride up to the thirtieth floor, a thousand butterflies stretch their wings and flutter erratically in my stomach. *Why am I so nervous?* And I know it's because I have no idea what kind of mood Christian's going to be in when I arrive. My inner goddess is hopeful for one type of mood; my subconscious, like me, is fraught with nerves.

The elevator doors open, and I'm in the foyer. It is so strange not to be met by Taylor. Of course, he's parking the car. In the great room, Christian is on his BlackBerry, talking quietly as he stares through the glass doors at the early evening Seattle skyline. He's wearing a gray suit with the jacket undone, and he's running his hand through his hair. He's agitated, tense even. *Oh no—what's wrong?* Agitated or not, he's still a fine sight. How can he look so . . . arresting?

"No trace . . . Okay . . . Yes." He turns and sees me, and his whole demeanor changes. From tension to relief to something else: a look that calls directly to my inner goddess, a look of sensual carnality, his eyes scorching.

My mouth goes dry and desire blooms in my body . . . *whoa.*

"Keep me informed," he snaps, and shuts off his phone as he strides purposefully toward me. I stand paralyzed as he closes the distance between us, devouring me with his eyes. *Holy shit* . . . something's amiss—the strain in his jaw, the anxiety around his eyes. He shrugs out of his jacket, undoes his dark tie, and slings them both onto the couch en route to me. Then his arms are wrapped around me, and he's pulling me to him, hard, fast, gripping my ponytail to tilt my head up, kissing me like his life depends on it. *What the hell?* He drags the hair tie painfully out of my hair, but I don't care. There's a desperate, primal quality to his kiss. He needs me, for whatever reason, at this point in time, and I have never felt so desired and coveted. It's dark and sensual and alarming all at the same time. I kiss him back with equal fervor, my fingers twisting and fisting in his hair. Our tongues entwine, our passion and ardor erupting between us. He tastes divine, hot, sexy, and his scent—all body wash and Christian—is arousing. He drags his mouth away from mine, and he's staring down at me, gripped by some unnamed emotion.

"What's wrong?" I breathe.

"I'm so glad you're back. Shower with me—now."

I can't decide if it's a request or a command.

"Yes," I whisper, and he grabs my hand, leading me out of the big room into his bedroom to his bathroom.

Once there, he releases me and turns the water on in the far-too-spacious shower. Spinning around slowly, he gazes at me, eyes hooded.

"I like your skirt. It's very short," he says, his voice low. "You have great legs."

He steps out of his shoes and reaches down to take off each of his socks, never taking his eyes off me. I am rendered speechless by the look of hunger in his eyes. *Wow* . . . to be this wanted by this Greek god. I mirror his actions and step out of my black flats. Suddenly, he reaches for me, backing me up against the wall. Kissing me, my face, my throat, my lips . . . running his hands through my hair. I feel the cool, smooth tiled wall at my back as he pushes himself against me, so that I'm flattened between his heat and the chill of the ceramic. Tentatively, I place my arms on his upper arms, and he groans as I squeeze tightly.

"I want you now. Here . . . fast, hard," he breathes, and his hands are on my thighs, pushing up my skirt. "Are you still bleeding?"

"No." I flush.

"Good."

His thumbs hook over my white cotton panties, and abruptly he drops to his knees as he tugs them off. My skirt is now rucked up so that I'm naked from the waist down and panting, wanting. He grabs my hips, pushing me against the wall again, and kisses me at the apex of my thighs. Grabbing my upper thighs, he forces my legs apart. I groan loudly, feeling his tongue circling my clitoris. *Oh my.* Tipping my head back involuntarily, I moan as my fingers find their way into his hair.

His tongue is relentless, strong and insistent, washing over me—swirling around and around, again and again—nonstop. It's exquisite, the intensity of feeling—it's almost painful. My body starts to quicken, and he releases me. *What? No!* My breathing is ragged as I pant, gazing at him with delicious anticipation. He grabs my face with both hands, holding me firmly, and he kisses me hard, thrusting his tongue into my mouth so I can taste my arousal. Unzipping his fly, he frees himself, grabs the backs of my thighs, and lifts me.

"Wrap your legs around me, baby," he commands, his voice urgent, strained.

I do as I'm told and wrap my arms around his neck, and he moves quickly and sharply, filling me. *Ah!* He gasps, and I groan. Holding my behind, his fingers digging into my soft flesh, he begins to move, slowly at first—a steady even tempo . . . but as his control unravels, he speeds up . . . faster and faster. *Ahhh!* I tip my head back and concentrate on the invading, punishing, heavenly sensation . . . pushing me, pushing me . . . onward, higher, up . . . and when I can take no more, I explode around him, spiraling into an intense, all-consuming orgasm. He lets go with a deep growl, and he buries his head in my neck as he buries himself inside me, groaning loudly and incoherently as he finds his release.

His breathing is erratic, but he kisses me tenderly, not moving, still inside me, and I blink, unseeing, into his eyes. As he comes into focus, he gently pulls out of me, holding me steady while I place my feet on the floor. The bathroom is now cloudy with steam . . . and hot. I feel overdressed.

"You seem pleased to see me," I murmur with a shy smile.

His lips quirk up. "Yes, Miss Steele, I think my pleasure is pretty self-evident. Come—let me get you in the shower."

He undoes the next three buttons of his shirt, removes the cuff links, tugs it over his head, and discards it on the floor. Taking off his suit pants and boxer briefs, he kicks them to one side. He begins to undo the buttons on my blouse while I watch him, yearning to reach out and stroke his chest, but I contain myself.

"How was your journey?" he asks mildly. He seems so much calmer now, his apprehension gone, dissolved by sexual congress.

"Fine, thank you," I murmur, still breathless. "Thanks once again for first class. It really is a much nicer way to travel." I smile shyly at him. "I have some news," I add nervously.

"Oh?" He looks down at me as he undoes the last button, slips my blouse down my arms, and throws it on top of his discarded clothes.

"I have a job."

He stills, then smiles at me, his eyes warm and soft.

"Congratulations, Miss Steele. Now will you tell me where?" he teases.

"You don't know?"

He shakes his head, frowning. "Why would I know?"

"With your stalking capabilities, I thought you might have . . ." I trail off as his face falls.

"Anastasia, I wouldn't dream of interfering in your career, unless you ask me to, of course." He looks wounded.

"So you have no idea which company?"

"No. I know there are four publishing companies in Seattle—so I am assuming it's one of them."

"SIP."

"Oh, the small one, good. Well done." He leans forward and kisses my forehead. "Clever girl. When do you start?"

"Monday."

"That soon, eh? I'd better take advantage of you while I still can. Turn around."

I am thrown by his casual command but do as I'm bid, and he undoes my bra and unzips my skirt. He pushes my skirt down, cupping my behind as he does and kissing my shoulder. He leans against me and his nose nuzzles my hair, inhaling deeply. He squeezes my buttocks.

"You intoxicate me, Miss Steele, and you calm me. Such a heady combination." He kisses my hair. Grabbing my hand, he tugs me into the shower.

"Ow," I squeal. The water is practically scalding. Christian grins down at me as the water cascades over him.

"It's only a little hot water."

And actually he's right. It feels heavenly, washing off the sticky Georgia morning and the stickiness from our lovemaking.

"Turn around," he orders, and I comply, turning to face the wall. "I want to wash you," he murmurs, and reaches for the body wash. He squirts a little into his hand.

"I have something else to tell you," I murmur as his hands start on my shoulders.

"Oh yes?" he asks mildly.

I steel myself with a deep breath. "My friend José's photography show is opening Thursday in Portland."

He stills, his hands hovering over my breasts. I have emphasized the word "friend."

"Yes, what about it?" he asks sternly.

"I said I would go. Do you want to come with me?"

After what feels like a monumental amount of time, he slowly starts washing me again.

"What time?"

"The opening is at seven thirty p.m."

He kisses my ear.

"Okay."

Inside my subconscious relaxes and then collapses, slumped into an old battered armchair.

"Were you nervous about asking me?"

"Yes. How can you tell?"

"Anastasia, your whole body's just relaxed," he says dryly.

"Well, you just seem to be, um . . . on the jealous side."

"Yes, I am," he says darkly. "And you'd do well to remember that. But thank you for asking. We'll take *Charlie Tango*."

Oh, the helicopter of course, silly me. More flying . . . cool! I grin.

"Can I wash you?" I ask.

"I don't think so," he murmurs, and he kisses me gently on my neck to take the sting out of his refusal. I pout at the wall as he caresses my back with soap.

"Will you ever let me touch you?" I ask boldly.

He stills again, his hand on my behind.

"Put your hands on the wall, Anastasia. I'm going to take you again," he murmurs in my ear as he grabs my hips, and I know that the discussion is over.

LATER, WE ARE SEATED at the breakfast bar, dressed in bathrobes, having consumed Mrs. Jones's rather excellent pasta alle vongole.

"More wine?" Christian asks, gray eyes glowing.

"A small glass, please." The Sancerre is crisp and delicious. Christian pours one for me and one for himself.

"How's the, um . . . situation that brought you to Seattle?" I ask tentatively.

He frowns. "Out of hand," he murmurs bitterly. "But nothing for you to worry about, Anastasia. I have plans for you this evening."

"Oh?"

"Yes. I want you ready and waiting in my playroom in fifteen minutes." He stands and gazes down at me.

"You can get ready in your room. Incidentally, the walk-in closet is now full of clothes for you. I don't want any arguments about them." He narrows his eyes, daring me to say something. When I don't, he stalks off to his study.

Me! Argue? With you, Fifty Shades? It's more than my backside's worth. I sit on the barstool, momentarily stupefied, trying to assimilate this morsel of information. He's bought me clothes. I roll my eyes in an exaggerated fashion, knowing full well he can't see me. Car, phone, computer . . . clothes, it'll be a damn condo next, and then I really will be his mistress.

Ho! My subconscious has her snarky face on. I ignore her and make my way upstairs toward *my* room. So, it is still mine . . . why? I thought he'd agreed to let me sleep with him. I suppose he's not used to sharing his personal space, but then, neither am I. I console myself with the thought that at least I have somewhere to escape from him.

Examining the door, I find that it has a lock but no key. I wonder briefly if Mrs. Jones has a spare. I'll ask her. I open the closet door and close it again quickly. *Holy crap—he's spent a fortune.* It resembles Kate's—so many clothes hanging neatly on the rail. Deep down, I know that they'll all fit. But I have no time to think about that—I have to get kneeling in the Red Room of . . . Pain . . . or Pleasure, hopefully—this evening.

KNEELING BY THE DOOR, I am naked except for my panties. My heart is in my mouth. Jeez, I thought after the bathroom he would have had enough. The man is insatiable, or maybe all men are like him. I have no idea, no one to compare him to. Closing my eyes, I try to calm myself down, to connect with my inner sub. She's there somewhere, hiding behind my inner goddess.

Anticipation runs bubbling like soda through my veins. What will he do? I take a deep, steadying breath, but I cannot deny it, I'm excited, aroused, wet already. This is so . . . I want to think *wrong*, but somehow it's not. It's right for Christian. It's what he wants—and after the last few days . . . after all he's done, I have to man up and take whatever he decides he wants, whatever he thinks he needs.

The memory of his look when I came in this evening, the longing in his face, his determined stride toward me like I was an oasis in the desert. I'd do almost anything to see that look again. I press my thighs together at the delicious memory, and it reminds me that I need to spread my knees. I shuffle them apart. How long will he make me wait? The wait is crippling me, crippling me with a dark and tantalizing desire. I glance quickly around the subtly lit room: the cross, the table, the couch, the bench . . .

that bed. It looms so large, and it's made up with red satin sheets. Which piece of apparatus will he use?

The door opens and Christian breezes in, ignoring me completely. I glance down quickly, staring at my hands, positioned with care on my spread thighs. Placing something on the large chest beside the door, he strolls casually toward the bed. I indulge myself in a quick glimpse at him, and my heart almost lurches to a stop. He's naked except for those soft ripped jeans, top button casually undone. *Jeez, he looks so freaking hot.* My subconscious is frantically fanning herself, and my inner goddess is swaying and writhing to some primal carnal rhythm. She's so ready. I lick my lips instinctively. My blood pounds through my body, thick and heavy with salacious hunger. *What is he going to do to me?*

Turning, he nonchalantly walks back to the chest of drawers. Opening one, he begins to remove items and place them on the top. My curiosity burns, blazes even, but I resist the overwhelming temptation to sneak a quick peek. When he finishes what he's doing, he comes to stand in front of me. I can see his naked feet, and I want to kiss every inch of them . . . run my tongue over his instep, suck each of his toes. *Holy shit.*

"You look lovely," he breathes.

I keep my head down, conscious that he's staring at me while I am practically naked. I feel the flush as it slowly spreads over my face. He bends down and cups my chin, forcing my face up to meet his gaze.

"You are one beautiful woman, Anastasia. And you're all mine," he murmurs. "Stand up." His command is soft, full of sensual promise.

Shakily, I get to my feet.

"Look at me," he breathes, and I stare up into his smoldering gaze. It is his Dom gaze—cold, hard, and sexy as hell, seven shades of sin in one enticing look. My mouth dries, and I know I will do anything he asks. An almost cruel smile plays across his lips.

"We don't have a signed contract, Anastasia. But we've discussed limits. And I want to reiterate we have safewords, okay?"

Holy fuck . . . what has he got planned that I need safewords?

"What are they?" he asks authoritatively.

I frown slightly at his question, and his face hardens perceptibly.

"What are the safewords, Anastasia?" he says slowly and deliberately.

"'Yellow,'" I mumble.

"And?" he prompts, his mouth setting in a hard line.

"'Red,'" I breathe.

"Remember those."

And I can't help it . . . I raise my eyebrow at him and am about to remind him of my GPA, but the sudden frosty glint in his icy gray eyes stops me in my tracks.

"Don't start with your smart mouth in here, Miss Steele. Or I will fuck it with you on your knees. Do you understand?"

I swallow instinctively. *Okay.* I blink rapidly, chastened. Actually, it's his tone of voice, rather than the threat, that intimidates me.

"Well?"

"Yes, Sir," I mumble hastily.

"Good girl," he pauses as he stares at me. "My intention is not that you should use the safeword because you're in pain. What I intend to do to you will be intense. Very intense, and you have to guide me. Do you understand?"

Not really. Intense? Wow.

"This is about touch, Anastasia. You will not be able to see me or hear me. But you'll be able to feel me."

I frown—*not hear him?* How is that going to work? He turns, and I hadn't noticed that above the chest is a sleek, flat, matte black box. As he waves his hand in front, the box splits in half: two doors slide open revealing a CD player and a host of buttons. Christian presses several of these buttons in sequence. Nothing happens, but he seems satisfied. I am mystified. When he turns to face me again, he wears his small I-have-a-secret smile.

"I am going to tie you to that bed, Anastasia. But I'm going to blindfold you first and," he reveals his iPod in his hand, "you will not be able to hear me. All you will hear is the music I am going to play for you."

Okay. A musical interlude. Not what I was expecting. Does he ever do what I expect? *Jeez, I hope it's not rap.*

"Come." Taking my hand, he leads me over to the antique four-poster bed. There are shackles attached at each corner, fine metal chains with leather cuffs, glinting against the red satin.

Oh boy, I think my heart is going to jump out of my chest, and I'm melting from the inside out, desire coursing through me. Could I be any more excited?

"Stand here."

I am facing the bed. He leans down and whispers in my ear.

"Wait here. Keep your eyes on the bed. Picture yourself lying here bound and totally at my mercy."

Oh my.

He moves away for a moment, and I can hear him near the door fetching something. All my senses are hyperalert, my hearing more acute. He's picked up something from the rack of whips and paddles by the door. *Holy cow. What is he going to do?*

I feel him behind me. He takes my hair, pulls it into a ponytail behind me, and starts to braid it.

"While I like your pigtails, Anastasia, I am impatient to have you right now. So one will have to do." His voice is low, soft.

His deft fingers skim my back occasionally as they work down my hair, and each casual touch is like a sweet, electric shock against my skin. He fastens the end with a hair tie, then gently tugs the braid so that I'm forced to step back flush against him. He pulls again to the side so that I angle my head, giving him easier access to my neck. Leaning down, he nuzzles my neck, tracing his teeth and tongue from the base of my ear to my shoulder. He hums softly as he does, and the sound resonates through me. Right down . . . right down *there,* inside me. Unbidden, I groan quietly.

"Hush now," he breathes against my skin. He holds up his

hands in front of me, his arms touching mine. In his right hand is a flogger. I remember the name from my first introduction to this room.

"Touch it," he whispers, and he sounds like the devil himself. My body flames in response. Tentatively, I reach out and brush the long strands. It has many long fronds, all soft suede with small beads at the end.

"I will use this. It will not hurt, but it will bring your blood to the surface of your skin and make you very sensitive."

Oh, he says it won't hurt.

"What are the safewords, Anastasia?"

"Um . . . 'yellow' and 'red,' Sir," I whisper.

"Good girl. Remember, most of your fear is in your mind."

He drops the flogger on the bed, and his hands move to my waist.

"You won't be needing these," he murmurs, and hooks his fingers into my panties and sweeps them down my legs. I step unsteadily out of them, supporting myself on the ornate post of the bed.

"Stand still," he orders, and he kisses my behind and then gently nips me twice, making me tense. "Now lie down. Face up," he adds as he smacks me hard on the behind, making me jump.

Hastily, I crawl onto the bed's hard, unyielding mattress and lie down, looking up at him. The satin of the sheet beneath me is soft and cool against my skin. His face is impassive, except for his eyes, which glow with a barely leashed excitement.

"Hands above your head," he orders, and I do as I'm bid.

Jeez, my body hungers for him. I want him already.

He turns, and out of the corner of my eyes, I watch him saunter back over to the chest of drawers, returning with the iPod and what looks like an eye mask, similar to the one I used on my flight to Atlanta. The thought makes me want to smile, but I can't quite make my lips cooperate. I am too consumed with anticipation. I just know my face is completely immobile, my eyes huge, as I gaze at him.

Sitting down on the edge of the bed, he shows me the iPod. It has a strange antenna device as well as headphones. How odd. I frown as I try to figure this out.

"This transmits what's playing on the iPod to the system in the room," Christian answers my unspoken query as he taps the small antenna. "I can hear what you're hearing, and I have a remote control unit for it." He smirks his private-joke smile and holds up a small, flat device that looks like a very hip calculator. He leans across me, inserting the earbuds gently into my ears, and puts the iPod down somewhere on the bed above my head.

"Lift your head," he commands, and I do so immediately.

Slowly, he slides the mask on, pulling the elastic over the back of my head, and I'm blind. The elastic on the mask holds the earbuds in place. I can still hear him, though the sound is muffled as he rises from the bed. I'm deafened by my own breathing—it's shallow and erratic, reflecting my excitement. Christian takes my left arm, stretches it gently to the left-hand corner, and attaches the leather cuff around my wrist. His long fingers stroke the length of my arm once he's finished. *Oh!* His touch elicits a delicious, tickly shiver. I hear him move slowly around to the other side, where he takes my right arm and cuffs it. Again, his long fingers linger along my arm. *Oh my . . .* I am fit to burst already. Why is this so erotic?

He moves to the bottom of the bed and grabs both of my ankles.

"Lift your head again," he orders.

I comply, and he drags me down the bed so that my arms are stretched out and almost straining at the cuffs. Holy cow, I cannot move my arms. A frisson of trepidation mixed with tantalizing exhilaration sweeps through my body, making me wetter. I groan. Parting my legs, he cuffs first my right ankle and then my left so I am staked out, spread-eagled, and totally vulnerable to him. It's so unnerving that I can't see him. I listen hard . . . what's he doing? And I hear nothing, just my breathing and the pounding thud of my heart as blood pulses furiously against my eardrums.

Abruptly, the soft silent hiss and pop of the iPod springs into life. From inside my head, a lone angelic voice sings unaccompanied a long sweet note, and it's joined almost immediately by another voice, and then more voices—holy cow, a celestial choir—singing a capella in my head, an ancient, ancient hymnal. *What in heaven's name is this?* I have never heard anything like it. Something almost unbearably soft brushes against my neck, running languidly down my throat, slowly across my chest, over my breasts, caressing me . . . pulling at my nipples, it's so soft, skimming underneath. It's so *unexpected. It's fur! A fur glove?*

Christian trails his hand, unhurried and deliberate, down to my belly, circling my navel, then carefully from hip to hip, and I'm trying to anticipate where he's going next . . . but the music . . . it's in my head . . . transporting me . . . the fur across the line of my pubic hair . . . between my legs, along my thighs, down one leg . . . up the other . . . it almost tickles . . . but not quite . . . more voices join . . . the heavenly choir all singing different parts, their voices blending blissfully and sweetly together in a melodic harmony that is beyond anything I've ever heard. I catch one word—"*deus*"—and I realize they are singing in Latin. And still, the fur is moving down my arms and around my waist . . . back up across my breasts. My nipples harden beneath the soft touch . . . and I'm panting . . . wondering where his hand will go next. Suddenly, the fur is gone, and I can feel the fronds of the flogger flowing over my skin, following the same path as the fur, and it's so hard to concentrate with the music in my head—it sounds like a hundred voices singing, weaving an ethereal tapestry of fine, silken gold and silver through my head, mixed with the feel of the soft suede against my skin . . . trailing over me . . . *oh my* . . . abruptly, it disappears. Then suddenly, sharply, it bites down on my belly.

"Aagghh!" I cry out. It takes me by surprise, but it doesn't exactly hurt and tingles all over, and he hits me again. Harder.

"Aaah!"

I want to move, to writhe . . . to escape, or to welcome, each blow . . . I don't know—it's so overwhelming . . . I can't pull my arms . . . my legs are stuck . . . I am held very firmly in place . . . and again he strikes across my breasts—I cry out. And it's a sweet agony—bearable, just . . . pleasant—no, not immediately, but as my skin sings with each blow in perfect counterpoint to the music in my head, I am dragged into a dark, dark part of my psyche that surrenders to this most erotic sensation. *Yes—I get this.* He hits me across my hip, then moves in swift blows over my pubic hair, on my thighs, and down my inner thighs . . . and back up my body . . . across my hips. He keeps going as the music reaches a climax, and then suddenly the music stops. And so does he. Then the singing starts again . . . building and building, and he rains down blows on me . . . and I groan and writhe. Once again, it ceases and all is quiet . . . except my wild breathing . . . and wild yearning. For . . . oh . . . what's happening? What's he going to do now? The excitement is almost unbearable. I've entered a very dark, carnal place.

The bed moves and shifts as I feel him clamber over me, and the song starts again. He's got it on repeat . . . this time it's his nose and lips that take the place of the fur . . . running down my neck and throat, kissing, sucking . . . trailing down to my breasts . . . Ah! Taunting each of my nipples in turn . . . his tongue swirling around one while his fingers relentlessly tease the other . . . I groan, loudly I think, though I can't hear. I am lost. Lost in him . . . lost in the astral, seraphic voices . . . lost to all the sensations I cannot escape . . . I am completely at the mercy of his expert touch.

He moves down to my belly—his tongue circling my navel—following the path of the flogger and the fur . . . I moan. He's kissing and sucking and nibbling . . . moving south . . . and then his tongue is *there.* At the junction of my thighs. I throw my head back and cry out as I almost detonate into orgasm . . . I'm on the brink, and he stops.

No! The bed shifts, and he kneels between my legs. He leans toward the bedpost, and the cuff on my ankle is suddenly gone. I pull my leg to the middle of the bed . . . resting it against him.

He leans over to the opposite post and frees my other leg. His hands travel quickly down both my legs, squeezing and kneading, bringing life back into them. Then, grasping my hips, he lifts me so that my back is no longer on the bed. I am arched, resting on my shoulders. *What?* He's kneeling up between my legs . . . and in one swift, slamming move he's inside me . . . *oh, fuck* . . . and I cry out again. The quiver of my impending orgasm begins, and he stills. The quiver dies . . . *oh no* . . . he's going to torture me further.

"Please!" I wail.

He grips me harder . . . in warning? I don't know, his fingers digging into the flesh of my behind as I lay panting . . . so I purposefully still. Very slowly, he starts to move again . . . out and then in . . . agonizingly slowly. *Holy fuck—please!* I'm screaming inside . . . And as the number of voices in the choral piece increases, so does his pace, infinitesimally, he's so controlled . . . so in time with the music. And I can no longer bear it.

"Please," I beg, and in one swift move, he lowers me back onto the bed, and he's lying on top of me, his hands on the bed beside my breasts as he supports his weight, and he thrusts into me. As the music reaches its climax, I fall . . . free-fall . . . into the most intense, agonizing orgasm I have ever had, and Christian follows me . . . thrusting hard into me three more times . . . finally stilling, then collapsing on top of me.

As my consciousness returns from wherever it's been, Christian pulls out of me. The music has stopped, and I can feel him stretch across my body as he undoes the cuff on my right wrist. I groan as my hand is freed. He quickly frees my other hand, gently pulls the mask from my eyes, and removes the earbuds. I blink in the dim soft light and stare up into his intense gray gaze.

"Hi," he murmurs.

"Hi, yourself," I breathe shyly back at him. His lips quirk up into a smile, and he leans down and kisses me softly.

"Well done, you," he whispers. "Turn over."

Holy fuck—what's he going to do now? His eyes soften.

"I'm just going to rub your shoulders."

"Oh . . . okay."

I roll stiffly onto my front. I am so tired. Christian sits astride me and starts to massage my shoulders. I groan loudly—he has such strong, knowing fingers. Leaning down, he kisses my head.

"What was that music?" I mumble almost inarticulately.

"It's called *Spem in Alium*, a forty-part motet by Thomas Tallis."

"It was . . . overwhelming."

"I've always wanted to fuck to it."

"Not another first, Mr. Grey?"

"Indeed, Miss Steele."

I groan again as his fingers work their magic on my shoulders.

"Well, it's the first time I've fucked to it, too," I murmur sleepily.

"Hmm . . . you and I, we're giving each other many firsts." His voice is matter-of-fact.

"What did I say to you in my sleep, Chris—er, Sir?"

His hands pause their ministrations for a moment.

"You said lots of things, Anastasia. You talked about cages and strawberries . . . that you wanted more . . . and that you missed me."

Oh, thank heavens for that.

"Is that all?" The relief in my voice is evident.

Christian stops his heavenly massage and shifts so that he's lying beside me, his head propped up on his elbow. He's frowning.

"What did you think you'd said?"

Oh crap.

"That I thought you were ugly, conceited, and that you were hopeless in bed."

The crease on his brow deepens.

"Well, naturally I am all those things, and now you've got me really intrigued. What are you hiding from me, Miss Steele?"

I blink at him innocently. "I'm not hiding anything."

"Anastasia, you are a hopeless liar."

"I thought you were going to make me giggle after sex; this isn't doing it for me."

His lips quirk up. "I can't tell jokes."

"Mr. Grey! Something you can't do?" I grin at him, and he grins back.

"No, hopeless joke teller." He looks so proud of himself that I start to giggle.

"I'm a hopeless joke teller, too."

"That is such a lovely sound," he murmurs, and he leans forward and kisses me.

"And you are hiding something, Anastasia. I may have to torture it out of you."

CHAPTER TWENTY-SIX

I wake with a jolt. I think I've just fallen down some stairs in a dream, and I bolt upright, momentarily disoriented. It is dark, and I'm in Christian's bed alone. Something has woken me, some nagging thought. I glance over at the alarm clock on his bedside. It is five in the morning, but I feel rested. Why is that? Oh—it's the time difference—it would be eight a.m. in Georgia. *Holy crap . . . I need to take my pill.* I clamber out of bed, grateful for whatever it is that has woken me. I can hear faint notes from the piano. Christian is playing. This I must see. I love watching him play. Naked, I grab my bathrobe from the chair and wander quietly down the corridor, slipping on my robe and listening to the magical sound of the melodic lament that's coming from the great room.

Shrouded in darkness, Christian sits in a bubble of light as he plays, and his hair glints with burnished copper highlights. He looks naked, though I know he's wearing his PJ bottoms. He's concentrating, playing beautifully, lost in the melancholy of the music. I hesitate, watching from the shadows, not wanting to interrupt him. I want to hold him. He looks lost, sad even, and achingly lonely—or maybe it's just the music that's so full of poignant sorrow. He finishes the piece, pauses for a split second, then starts to play it again. I move cautiously toward him, drawn as the moth to the flame . . . the idea makes me smile. He glances up at me and frowns before his gaze returns to his hands.

Oh, crap, is he pissed off that I am disturbing him?

"You should be asleep," he scolds mildly.

I can tell he's preoccupied with something.

"So should you," I retort not quite as mildly.

He glances up again, his lips twitching with a trace of a smile. "Are you scolding me, Miss Steele?"

"Yes, Mr. Grey, I am."

"Well, I can't sleep." He frowns once more as a trace of irritation or anger flashes across his face. With me? Surely not.

I ignore his facial expression and very bravely sit down beside him on the piano stool, placing my head on his bare shoulder to watch his deft, agile fingers caress the keys. He pauses fractionally, and then continues to the end of the piece.

"What was that?" I ask softly.

"Chopin. Prelude opus twenty-eight, number four. In E minor, if you're interested," he murmurs.

"I'm always interested in what you do."

He turns and softly presses his lips against my hair.

"I didn't mean to wake you."

"You didn't. Play the other one."

"Other one?"

"The Bach piece that you played the first night I stayed."

"Oh, the Marcello."

He starts to play slowly and deliberately. I feel the movement of his hands in his shoulders as I lean against him and close my eyes. The sad, soulful notes swirl slowly and mournfully around us, echoing off the walls. It is a hauntingly beautiful piece, sadder even than the Chopin, and I lose myself to the beauty of the lament. To a certain extent, it reflects how I feel. The deep poignant longing I have to know this extraordinary man better, to try to understand *his* sadness. All too soon, the piece is at an end.

"Why do you only play such sad music?"

I sit upright and gaze up at him as he shrugs in answer to my question, his expression wary.

"So you were just six when you started to play?" I prompt.

He nods, his wary look intensifying. After a moment he volunteers. "I threw myself into learning the piano to please my new mother."

"To fit into the perfect family?"

"Yes, so to speak," he says evasively. "Why are you awake? Don't you need to recover from yesterday's exertions?"

"It's eight in the morning for me. And I need to take my pill."

He raises his eyebrows in surprise. "Well remembered," he murmurs, and I can tell he's impressed. "Only you would start a course of time-specific birth control pills in a different time zone. Perhaps you should wait half an hour and then another half hour tomorrow morning. So eventually you can take them at a reasonable time."

"Good plan," I breathe. "So what shall we do for half an hour?" I blink innocently at him.

"I can think of a few things." He grins salaciously. I gaze back impassively as my insides clench and melt under his knowing look.

"On the other hand, we could talk," I suggest quietly.

His brow creases.

"I prefer what I have in mind." He scoops me onto his lap.

"You'd always rather have sex than talk." I laugh, steadying myself by holding on to his upper arms.

"True. Especially with you." He nuzzles my hair and starts a steady trail of kisses from below my ear to my throat. "Maybe on my piano," he whispers.

Oh my. My whole body tightens at the thought. *Piano. Wow.*

"I want to get something straight," I whisper as my pulse starts to accelerate, and my inner goddess closes her eyes, reveling in the feel of his lips on me.

He pauses momentarily before continuing his sensual assault. "Always so eager for information, Miss Steele. What needs straightening out?" he breathes against my skin at the base of my neck, continuing his soft gentle kisses.

"Us," I whisper as I close my eyes.

"Hmm. What about us?" He pauses his trail of kisses along my shoulder.

"The contract."

He lifts his head to gaze down at me, a hint of amusement in his eyes, and sighs. He strokes his fingertips down my cheek.

"Well, I think the contract is moot, don't you?" His voice is low and husky, his eyes soft.

"Moot?"

"Moot." He smiles. I gape at him quizzically.

"But you were so keen."

"Well, that was before. Anyway, the Rules aren't moot, they still stand." His expression hardens slightly.

"Before? Before what?"

"Before . . ." He pauses, and the wary expression is back. "More." He shrugs.

"Oh."

"Besides, we've been in the playroom twice now, and you haven't run screaming for the hills."

"Do you expect me to?"

"Nothing you do is expected, Anastasia," he says dryly.

"So, let me be clear. You just want me to follow the Rules element of the contract all the time but not the rest of the contract?"

"Except in the playroom. I want you to follow the spirit of the contract in the playroom, and yes, I want you to follow the Rules—all the time. Then I know you'll be safe, and I'll be able to have you anytime I wish."

"And if I break one of the Rules?"

"Then I'll punish you."

"But won't you need my permission?"

"Yes, I will."

"And if I say no?"

He gazes at me for a moment, with a confused expression.

"If you say no, you'll say no. I'll have to find a way to persuade you."

I pull away from him and stand. I need some distance. He frowns as I stare down at him. He looks puzzled and wary again.

"So the punishment aspect remains."

"Yes, but only if you break the Rules."

"I'll need to reread them," I say, trying to recall the detail.

"I'll fetch them for you." His tone is suddenly businesslike.

Whoa. This has gotten serious so quickly. He rises from the piano and walks lithely to his study. My scalp prickles. Jeez, I need some tea. The future of our so-called relationship is being discussed at 5:45 in the morning when he's preoccupied with something else—is this wise? I head into the kitchen, which is still shrouded in darkness. Where are the light switches? I find them, flick them on, and pour water into the kettle. *My pill!* I rummage in my purse, which I left on the breakfast bar, and find them quickly. One swallow and I'm done. By the time I finish, Christian is back, sitting on one of the barstools, watching me intently.

"Here you go." He pushes a typed piece of paper toward me, and I notice that he's crossed some things out.

RULES

Obedience:

The Submissive will obey any instructions given by the Dominant immediately without hesitation or reservation and in an expeditious manner. The Submissive will agree to any sexual activity deemed fit and pleasurable by the Dominant excepting those activities that are outlined in hard limits (Appendix 2). She will do so eagerly and without hesitation.

Sleep:

The Submissive will ensure she achieves a minimum of ~~eight~~ seven hours' sleep a night when she is not with the Dominant.

Food:

~~The Submissive will eat regularly to maintain her health and wellbeing from a prescribed list of foods (Appendix 4). The Submissive will not snack between meals, with the exception of fruit.~~

Clothes:

While with the Dominant, the Submissive will wear clothing only approved by the Dominant. The Dominant will provide a clothing budget for the Submissive, which the Submissive shall utilize. The Dominant shall accompany the Submissive to purchase clothing on an ad hoc basis.

Exercise:
The Dominant shall provide the Submissive with a personal trainer ~~four~~ three times a week in hour-long sessions at times to be mutually agreed upon by the personal trainer and the Submissive. The personal trainer will report to the Dominant on the Submissive's progress.
Personal Hygiene/Beauty:
The Submissive will keep herself clean and shaved and/or waxed at all times. The Submissive will visit a beauty salon of the Dominant's choosing at times to be decided by the Dominant and undergo whatever treatments the Dominant sees fit.
Personal Safety:
The Submissive will not drink to excess, smoke, take recreational drugs or put herself in any unnecessary danger.
Personal Qualities:
The Submissive will not enter into any sexual relations with anyone other than the Dominant. The Submissive will conduct herself in a respectful and modest manner at all times. She must recognize that her behavior is a direct reflection on the Dominant. She shall be held accountable for any misdeeds, wrongdoings and misbehavior committed when not in the presence of the Dominant.

Failure to comply with any of the above will result in immediate punishment, the nature of which shall be determined by the Dominant.

"So the obedience thing still stands?"

"Oh yes." He grins.

I shake my head amused, and before I realize it, I roll my eyes at him.

"Did you just roll your eyes at me, Anastasia?" he breathes.

Oh, fuck.

"Possibly, depends what your reaction is."

"Same as always," he says, shaking his head, his eyes alight with excitement.

I swallow instinctively and a frisson of exhilaration runs through me.

"So . . ." *Holy shit. What am I going to do?*

"Yes?" He licks his lower lip.

"You want to spank me now."

"Yes. And I will."

"Oh, really, Mr. Grey?" I challenge, grinning back at him. Two can play this game.

"Are you going to stop me?"

"You're going to have to catch me first."

His eyes widen a fraction, and he grins, slowly getting to his feet.

"Oh, really, Miss Steele?"

The breakfast bar is between us. I have never been more grateful for its existence than in this moment.

"And you're biting your lip," he breathes, moving slowly to his left as I move to mine.

"You wouldn't," I tease. "After all, you roll your eyes." I try reasoning with him. He continues to move toward his left, as do I.

"Yes, but you've just raised the bar on the excitement stakes with this game." His eyes blaze, and wild anticipation emanates from him.

"I'm quite fast, you know." I try for nonchalance.

"So am I."

He's stalking me in his own kitchen.

"Are you going to come quietly?" he asks.

"Do I ever?"

"Miss Steele, what do you mean?" He smirks. "It'll be worse for you if I have to come and get you."

"That's only if you catch me, Christian. And right now, I have no intention of letting you catch me."

"Anastasia, you may fall and hurt yourself. Which will put you in direct contravention of rule number seven, now six."

"I have been in danger since I met you, Mr. Grey, rules or no rules."

"Yes, you have." He pauses, and his brow furrows.

Suddenly, he lunges for me, making me squeal and run for the dining room table. I manage to escape, putting the table between us. My heart is pounding and adrenaline has spiked through my body . . . boy . . . this is thrilling. I'm a child again, though that's not right. I watch him carefully as he paces deliberately toward me. I inch away.

"You certainly know how to distract a man, Anastasia."

"We aim to please, Mr. Grey. Distract you from what?"

"Life. The universe." He waves one of his hands vaguely.

"You did seem very preoccupied as you were playing."

He stops and folds his arms, his expression amused.

"We can do this all day, baby, but I will get you, and it will just be worse for you when I do."

"No, you won't." I must not be overconfident. I repeat this as a mantra. My subconscious has found her Nikes, and she's on the starting blocks.

"Anyone would think you didn't want me to catch you."

"I don't. That's the point. I feel about punishment the way you feel about my touching you."

His entire demeanor changes in a nanosecond. Gone is playful Christian, and he stands staring at me as if I've slapped him. He's ashen.

"That's how you feel?" he whispers.

Those four words, and the way he utters them, speak volumes. *Oh no.* They tell me so much more about him and how he feels. They tell me about his fear and loathing. I frown. No, I don't feel *that* bad. No way. Do I?

"No. It doesn't affect me quite as much as that, but it gives you an idea," I murmur, staring anxiously at him.

"Oh," he says.

Crap. He looks completely and utterly lost, like I've pulled the rug from under his feet.

Taking a deep breath, I move around the table until I am standing in front of him, gazing into his apprehensive eyes.

"You hate it that much?" he breathes, his eyes filled with horror.

"Well . . . no," I reassure him. *Jeez—that's how he feels about people touching him?* "No. I feel ambivalent about it. I don't like it, but I don't hate it."

"But last night, in the playroom, you . . ."

"I do it for you, Christian, because you need it. I don't. You didn't hurt me last night. That was in a different context, and I can rationalize that internally, and I trust you. But when you want to punish me, I worry that you'll hurt me."

His eyes darken like a turbulent storm. Time moves and expands and slips away before he answers softly.

"I want to hurt you. But not beyond anything that you couldn't take."

Fuck!

"Why?"

He runs his hand through his hair, and he shrugs.

"I just need it." He pauses, gazing at me with anguish, and he closes his eyes and shakes his head. "I can't tell you," he whispers.

"Can't or won't?"

"Won't."

"So you know why."

"Yes."

"But you won't tell me."

"If I do, you will run screaming from this room, and you'll never want to return." He stares at me warily. "I can't risk that, Anastasia."

"You want me to stay."

"More than you know. I couldn't bear to lose you."

Oh my.

He gazes down at me, and suddenly, he pulls me into his arms and he's kissing me, kissing me passionately. It takes me completely by surprise, and I sense his panic and desperate need in his kiss.

"Don't leave me. You said you wouldn't leave me, and you begged me not to leave you, in your sleep," he murmurs against my lips.

Oh . . . my nocturnal confessions.

"I don't want to go." And my heart clenches, turning itself inside out.

This is a man in need. His fear is naked and obvious, but he's lost . . . somewhere in his darkness. His eyes are wide and bleak and tortured. I can soothe him, join him briefly in the darkness and bring him into the light.

"Show me," I whisper.

"Show you?"

"Show me how much it can hurt."

"What?"

"Punish me. I want to know how bad it can get."

Christian steps back away from me, completely confused.

"You would try?"

"Yes. I said I would." But I have an ulterior motive. If I do this for him, maybe he will let me touch him.

He blinks. "Ana, you're so confusing."

"I'm confused, too. I'm trying to work this out. And you and I will know, once and for all, if I can do this. If I can handle this, then maybe you—" My words fail me, and his eyes widen again. He knows I am referring to the touch thing. For a moment, he looks torn, but then a steely resolve settles on his features, and he narrows his eyes, gazing at me speculatively as if weighing up alternatives.

Abruptly, he clasps my arm in a firm grip and turns, leading me out of the great room, up the stairs, and to the playroom. Pleasure and pain, reward and punishment—his words from so long ago echo through my mind.

"I'll show you how bad it can be, and you can make your own mind up." He pauses by the door. "Are you ready for this?"

I nod, my mind made up, and I'm vaguely lightheaded, faint as all the blood leaves my face.

He opens the door and, still grasping my arm, grabs what looks like a belt from the rack beside the door, then leads me over to the red leather bench in the far corner of the room.

"Bend over the bench," he murmurs softly.

Okay. I can do this. I bend over the smooth soft leather. He's left my bathrobe on. In a quiet part of my brain, I'm vaguely surprised that he hasn't made me take it off. *Holy fuck, this is going to hurt . . . I know.*

"We're here because you said yes, Anastasia. And you ran from me. I am going to hit you six times, and you will count with me."

Why the hell doesn't he just get on with it? He always makes such a meal of punishing me. I roll my eyes, knowing full well he can't see me.

He lifts the hem of my bathrobe, and for some reason, this feels more intimate than being naked. He gently caresses my behind, running his warm hand all over both cheeks and down to the tops of my thighs.

"I am doing this so that you remember not to run from me, and as exciting as it is, I never want you to run from me," he whispers.

And the irony is not lost on me. I was running to avoid this. If he'd opened his arms, I'd run to him, not away from him.

"And you rolled your eyes at me. You know how I feel about that." Suddenly, it's gone—that nervous edgy fear in his voice. He's back from wherever he's been. I hear it in his tone, in the way he places his fingers on my back, holding me—and the atmosphere in the room changes.

I close my eyes, bracing myself for the blow. It comes hard, snapping across my backside, and the bite of the belt is everything I feared. I cry out involuntarily and take a huge gulp of air.

"Count, Anastasia!" he commands.

"One!" I shout at him, and it sounds like an expletive.

He hits me again, and the pain pulses and echoes along the line of the belt. *Holy shit . . . that smarts.*

"Two!" I scream. It feels so good to scream.

His breathing is ragged and harsh, whereas mine is almost nonexistent as I desperately scrabble around my psyche looking for some internal strength. The belt cuts into my flesh again.

"Three!" Tears spring unwelcome into my eyes. Jeez—this is harder than I thought—so much harder than the spanking. He's not holding anything back.

"Four!" I yell as the belt bites me again, and now the tears are streaming down my face. I don't want to cry. It angers me that I am crying. He hits me again.

"Five." My voice is more a choked, strangled sob, and in this moment I think I hate him. One more, I can do one more. My backside feels as if it's on fire.

"Six," I whisper as the blistering pain cuts across me again, and I hear him drop the belt behind me, and he's pulling me into his arms, all breathless and compassionate . . . and I want none of him.

"Let go . . . no . . ." And I find myself struggling out of his grasp, pushing him away. Fighting him.

"Don't touch me!" I hiss. I straighten and stare at him, and he's watching me as if I might bolt, eyes wide, bemused. I dash the tears angrily out of my eyes with the backs of my hands, glaring at him.

"This is what you really like? Me, like this?" I use the sleeve of the bathrobe to wipe my nose.

He gazes at me warily.

"Well, you are one fucked-up son of a bitch."

"Ana," he pleads, shocked.

"Don't you dare 'Ana' me! You need to sort your shit out, Grey!" And with that, I turn stiffly, and I walk out of the playroom, closing the door quietly behind me.

I clasp the door handle behind me and briefly lean back against the door. Where to go? Do I run? Do I stay? I am so mad, scalding tears spill down my cheeks, and I brush them furiously aside. I just want to curl up. Curl up and recuperate in some way. Heal my shattered faith. How could I have been so stupid? Of course it hurts.

Tentatively, I rub my backside. Aah! It's sore. Where to go? Not his room. My room, or the room that will be mine, no, *is* mine . . . *was* mine. This is why he wanted me to keep it. He knew I would need distance from him.

I launch myself stiffly in that direction, conscious that Christian may follow me. It is still dark in the bedroom, dawn only a whisper in the skyline. I climb awkwardly into bed, careful not to sit on my aching and tender backside. I keep the bathrobe on, wrapping it around me, and curl up and really let go—sobbing hard into my pillow.

What was I thinking? Why did I let him do that to me? I wanted the dark, to explore how bad it could be—but it's too dark for me. I cannot do this. Yet, this is what he does; this is how he gets his kicks.

What a monumental wake-up call. And to be fair to him, he warned me and warned me, time and again. He's not normal. He has needs that I cannot fulfill. I realize that now. I don't want him to hit me like that again, ever. I think of the couple of times he has hit me, and how easy he was on me by comparison. Is that enough for him? I sob harder into the pillow. I am going to lose him. He won't want to be with me if I can't give him this. Why, why, why have I fallen in love with Fifty Shades? Why? Why can't I love José, or Paul Clayton, or someone like me?

Oh, his distraught look as I left. I was so cruel, shocked by the savagery . . . will he forgive me . . . will I forgive him? My thoughts are all haywire and jumbled, echoing and bouncing off the inside of my skull. My subconscious is shaking her head sadly, and my inner goddess is nowhere to be seen. Oh, this is a dark morning of the soul for me. I'm so alone. I want my mom. I remember her parting words at the airport:

Follow your heart, darling, and please, please—try not to overthink things. Relax and enjoy. You are so young, sweetheart, you have so much to experience, just let it happen. You deserve the best of everything.

I did follow my heart, and I have a sore ass and an anguished, broken spirit to show for it. I have to go. That's it . . . I have to leave. He's no good for me, and I am no good for him. How can we possibly make this work? And the thought of not seeing him again practically chokes me . . . my Fifty Shades.

I hear the door click open. *Oh no—he's here.* He puts something down on the bedside table, and the bed shifts under his weight as he climbs in behind me.

"Hush," he breathes, and I want to pull away from him, move to the other side of the bed, but I'm paralyzed. I cannot move and lie stiffly, not yielding at all. "Don't fight me, Ana, please," he whispers. Gently, he pulls me into his arms, burying his nose in my hair, kissing my neck.

"Don't hate me," he breathes softly against my skin, his voice achingly sad. My heart clenches anew and releases a fresh wave of silent sobbing. He continues to kiss me softly, tenderly, but I remain aloof and wary.

We lie together like this, neither saying anything for ages. He just holds me, and very gradually, I relax and stop crying. Dawn comes and goes, and the soft light gets brighter as morning moves on, and still we lie quietly.

"I brought you some Advil and some arnica cream," he says after a long while.

I turn very slowly in his arms so I can face him. I am resting my head on his arm. His eyes are flinty gray and guarded.

I gaze at his beautiful face. He's giving nothing away, but he keeps his eyes on mine, hardly blinking. Oh, he is so breathtakingly good-looking. In such a short time, he's become so, so dear to me. Reaching up, I caress his cheek and run the tips of my fingers through his stubble. He closes his eyes and exhales.

"I'm sorry," I whisper.

He opens his eyes and looks at me puzzled.

"What for?"

"What I said."

"You didn't tell me anything I didn't know." And his eyes soften with relief. "I am sorry I hurt you."

I shrug. "I asked for it." And now I know. I swallow. Here

goes. I need to say my piece. "I don't think I can be everything you want me to be," I whisper. His eyes widen, and he blinks, his fearful expression returning.

"You are everything I want you to be."

What?

"I don't understand. I'm not obedient, and you can be as sure as hell I'm not going to let you do *that* to me again. And that's what you need, you said so."

He closes his eyes again, and I can see myriad emotions cross his face. When he reopens them, his expression is bleak. *Oh no.*

"You're right. I should let you go. I am no good for you."

My scalp prickles as every single hair follicle on my body stands to attention, and the world falls away from me, leaving a wide, yawning abyss for me to fall into. *Oh no.*

"I don't want to go," I whisper. Fuck—this is it. Pay or play. Tears swim in my eyes once more.

"I don't want you to go, either," he whispers, his voice raw. He reaches up and gently strokes my cheek and wipes away a falling tear with his thumb. "I've come alive since I met you." His thumb traces the contours of my lower lip.

"Me, too," I whisper. "I've fallen in love with you, Christian."

His eyes widen again, but this time with pure, undiluted fear.

"No," he breathes as if I've knocked the wind out of him.

Oh no.

"You can't love me, Ana. No . . . that's wrong." He's horrified.

"Wrong? Why's it wrong?"

"Well, look at you. I can't make you happy." His voice is anguished.

"But you do make me happy." I frown.

"Not at the moment, not doing what I want to do."

Holy fuck. This really is it. This is what it boils down to—incompatibility—and all those poor subs come to mind.

"We'll never get past that, will we?" I whisper, my scalp prickling in fear.

He shakes his head bleakly. I close my eyes. I cannot bear to look at him.

"Well . . . I'd better go, then," I murmur, wincing as I sit up.

"No, don't go." He sounds panicked.

"There's no point in me staying." Suddenly, I feel tired, really dog-tired, and I want to go now. I climb out of bed, and Christian follows.

"I'm going to get dressed. I'd like some privacy," I say, my voice flat and empty as I leave him standing in the bedroom.

Heading downstairs, I glance at the great room, thinking how only hours before I had rested my head on his shoulder as he played the piano. So much has happened since then. I have had my eyes opened and glimpsed the extent of his depravity, and I now know he's not capable of love—of giving or receiving love. My worst fears have been realized. And strangely, it's liberating.

The pain is such that I refuse to acknowledge it. I feel numb. I have somehow escaped from my body and am now a casual observer to this unfolding tragedy. I shower quickly and methodically, thinking only of each second in front of me. Now squeeze body wash bottle. Put body wash bottle back in rack. Rub cloth on face, on shoulders . . . on and on, all simple, mechanical actions, requiring simple, mechanical thoughts.

I finish my shower—and as I haven't washed my hair, I can dry myself quickly. I dress in the bathroom, taking my jeans and T-shirt out of my small suitcase. My jeans chafe against my backside, but quite frankly, it's a pain I welcome as it distracts my mind from what's happening to my splintering, shattered heart.

I stoop to shut my suitcase and the bag holding Christian's gift catches my eye, a model kit for a Blanik L23 glider, something for him to build. Tears threaten. *Oh no . . .* happier times, when there was hope of more. I take it out of the case, knowing that I need to give it to him. Quickly, I rip a small piece of paper from my notebook, hastily scribble a note for him, and leave it on top of the box.

This reminded me of a happy time.
Thank you.

Ana

I gaze at myself in the mirror. A pale and haunted ghost stares back at me. I scoop my hair into a bun and ignore how swollen my eyelids are from the crying. My subconscious nods with approval. Even she knows not to be snarky right now. I cannot believe that my world is crumbling around me into a sterile pile of ashes, all my hopes and dreams cruelly dashed. No, no, don't think about it. Not now, not yet. Taking a deep breath, I pick up my case, and after placing the glider kit and my note on his pillow, I head for the great room.

Christian is on the phone. He's dressed in black jeans and a T-shirt. His feet are bare.

"He said what?" he shouts, making me jump. "Well, he could have told us the fucking truth. What's his number? I need to call him . . . Welch, this is a real fuckup." He glances up and doesn't take his dark and brooding eyes off me. "Find her," he snaps and presses the off switch.

I walk over to the couch and collect my backpack, doing my best to ignore him. I take the Mac out of it and walk back toward the kitchen, placing it carefully on the breakfast bar, along with the BlackBerry and the car key. When I turn to face him, he's staring at me, stupefied with horror.

"I need the money that Taylor got for my Beetle." My voice is clear and calm, devoid of emotion . . . *extraordinary.*

"Ana, I don't want those things, they're yours," he says in disbelief. "Take them."

"No, Christian. I only accepted them under sufferance—and I don't want them anymore."

"Ana, be reasonable," he scolds me, even now.

"I don't want anything that will remind me of you. I just need the money that Taylor got for my car." My voice is quite monotone.

He gasps. "Are you really trying to wound me?"

"No." I frown, staring at him. Of course not . . . I love you. "I'm not. I'm trying to protect myself," I whisper. Because you don't want me the way I want you.

"Please, Ana, take that stuff."

"Christian, I don't want to fight—I just need the money."

He narrows his eyes, but I'm no longer intimidated by him. Well, only a little. I gaze impassively back, not blinking or backing down.

"Will you take a check?" he says acidly.

"Yes. I think you're good for it."

He doesn't smile; he just turns on his heel and stalks into his study. I take a last, lingering look around his apartment—at the art on the walls—all abstracts, serene, cool . . . cold, even. *Fitting,* I think absently. My eyes stray to the piano. Jeez—if I'd kept my mouth shut, we'd have made love on the piano. No, fucked, we would have fucked on the piano. Well, I would have made love. The thought lies heavy and sad in my mind and what's left of my heart. He has never made love to me, has he? It's always been fucking to him.

Christian returns and hands me an envelope.

"Taylor got a good price. It's a classic car. You can ask him. He'll take you home." He nods in the direction over my shoulder. I turn, and Taylor is standing in the doorway, wearing his suit, as impeccable as ever.

"That's fine. I can get myself home, thank you."

I turn to stare at Christian, and I see the barely contained fury in his eyes.

"Are you going to defy me at every turn?"

"Why change a habit of a lifetime?" I give him a small, apologetic shrug.

He closes his eyes in frustration and runs his hand through his hair.

"Please, Ana, let Taylor take you home."

"I'll get the car, Miss Steele," Taylor announces authoritatively. Christian nods at him, and when I glance around, Taylor has gone.

I turn back to face Christian. We are four feet apart. He steps forward, and instinctively I step back. He stops, and the anguish in his expression is palpable, his gray eyes burning.

"I don't want you to go," he murmurs, his voice full of longing.

"I can't stay. I know what I want and you can't give it to me, and I can't give you what you need."

He takes another step forward, and I hold up my hands.

"Don't, please." I recoil from him. There's no way I can tolerate his touch now, it will slay me. "I can't do this."

Grabbing my suitcase and my backpack, I head for the foyer. He follows me, keeping a careful distance. He presses the elevator button, and the doors open. I climb in.

"Good-bye, Christian," I murmur.

"Ana, good-bye," he says softly, and he looks utterly, utterly broken, a man in agonizing pain, reflecting how I feel inside. I tear my gaze away from him before I change my mind and try to comfort him.

The elevator doors close and it whisks me down to the bowels of the basement and to my own personal hell.

TAYLOR HOLDS THE DOOR open for me, and I climb into the back of the car. I avoid eye contact. Embarrassment and shame wash over me. I'm a complete failure. I had hoped to drag my Fifty Shades into the light, but it's proved a task beyond my meager abilities. Desperately, I try to keep my emotions banked and at bay. As we head out onto Fourth Avenue, I stare blankly out the window, and the enormity of what I've done slowly washes over me. *Shit—I've left him.* The only man I've ever loved. The only man I've ever slept with. I gasp, as crippling pain slices through me, and the levees burst. Tears course unbidden and unwelcome down my cheeks, and I wipe them away hurriedly with my fingers, scrambling in my bag for my sunglasses. As we pause at some traffic light, Taylor holds out a linen handkerchief for me. He says nothing and doesn't look in my direction, and I take it with gratitude.

"Thank you," I mutter, and this small discreet act of kindness is my undoing. I sit back in the luxurious leather seat and weep.

THE APARTMENT IS ACHINGLY empty and unfamiliar. I have not lived here long enough for it to feel like home. I head straight to my room, and there, hanging limply at the end of my bed, is a very sad, deflated helicopter balloon. Charlie Tango, looking and feeling exactly like me. I grab it angrily off my bedrail, snapping the tie, and hug it to me. *Oh—what have I done?*

I fall onto my bed, shoes and all, and howl. The pain is indescribable . . . physical, mental . . . metaphysical . . . it is everywhere, seeping into the marrow of my bones. Grief. This is grief—and I've brought it on myself. Deep down, a nasty, unbidden thought comes from my inner goddess, her lips contorted in a snarl . . . the physical pain from the bite of a belt is nothing, nothing compared to this devastation. I curl up, desperately clutching the flat foil balloon and Taylor's handkerchief, and surrender myself to my grief.